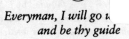

*Everyman, I will go ....
and be thy guide*

Elizabeth Gaskell

CRANFORD

with
MR HARRISON'S CONFESSIONS
and
THE CAGE AT CRANFORD

Edited by
GRAHAM HANDLEY

EVERYMAN
J. M. DENT · LONDON
CHARLES E. TUTTLE
VERMONT

Series Editor for the Everyman Elizabeth Gaskell
Graham Handley

Introduction and other critical material
© J. M. Dent 1995

Cranford first published by Everyman in 1906
Revised 1954
This edition 1995

J. M. Dent
Orion Publishing Group
Orion House
5 Upper St Martin's Lane
London WC2H 9EA
and
Charles E. Tuttle Co. Inc.
28 South Main Street
Rutland, Vermont 05701, USA

Typeset by CentraCet Limited, Cambridge
Printed in Great Britain by
The Guernsey Press Co. Ltd, Guernsey, C.I.

British Library Cataloguing-in-Publication Data
is available upon request.

ISBN 0 460 87553 1

CONTENTS

NOTE ON THE AUTHOR AND EDITOR

ELIZABETH GASKELL was born Elizabeth Cleghorn Stevenson in Chelsea, London, on 20 September 1810. Her father William Stevenson, who had been a Unitarian preacher, was a clerk and also a journalist at this time. After the death of her mother, when Elizabeth was a year old, she was sent to Knutsford in Cheshire (the town upon which Cranford is modelled) where she was brought up by her aunt, Hannah Lumb, and where she attended the Misses Byerleys' school in Warwickshire from 1821–6. In 1832 she married William Gaskell, a minister at Cross Street Unitarian Chapel, Manchester. The Gaskells had five children, the only son William dying before he was a year old in 1845. To alleviate her grief Mrs Gaskell began writing fiction: her first stories appeared in *Howitt's Journal* in 1847, and *Mary Barton*, her novel about industrial life in Manchester, in 1848. Despite these being published anonymously, her name became known. She contributed stories and then *Cranford* to Charles Dickens's magazine *Household Words* from 1850 onwards. *Ruth* (1853) boldly dealt with the controversial subject of the unmarried mother, while *North and South* was serialised in *Household Words* in 1854–5. Her next major undertaking, at the suggestion of Patrick Brontë, was *The Life of Charlotte Brontë* (1857). Mrs Gaskell was an untiring worker in support of her husband in Manchester, but she also found time for much travel in Europe. She produced a remarkable number of stories which reflect her talent. *Sylvia's Lovers* (1863) is a major historical novel, while her masterpiece, *Wives and Daughters* (1864–5) was unfinished at her death from a heart attack at Alton, Hampshire, on 12 November 1865.

GRAHAM HANDLEY has written widely on nineteenth-century literature, particularly on George Eliot and Trollope. His books include *George Eliot: The State of the Art* (1990), *George Eliot's Midlands: Passion in Exile* (1991) and *Trollope the Traveller* (1993).

CHRONOLOGY OF
ELIZABETH GASKELL'S LIFE

Year	Age	Life
1810		Born 29 September, second surviving child of William and Elizabeth Stevenson, in Chelsea, London. (An older brother, John)
1811	1	October. Her mother dies. In November Elizabeth is taken to Knutsford, Cheshire, where she will be brought up by her aunt, Hannah Lumb
1821	10	Goes to the Misses Byerleys' school at Barford, Warwickshire
1824	14	The school moves to 'Avonbank', Stratford-upon-Avon
1826	16	June. Leaves school

CHRONOLOGY OF
HER TIMES

_____

Year	Literary Context	Historical Events
1812	Birth of Charles Dickens Crabbe, *Tales* Byron, *Childe Harold's Pilgrimage*	
1813	Jane Austen, *Pride and Prejudice*	Wellington defeats French at Vittoria, Spain
1814	Scott, *Waverley* Wordsworth, *Excursion*	
1815		Battle of Waterloo, Napoleon banished to St Helena
1816	Birth of Charlotte Brontë	
1817	Death of Jane Austen Ricardo, *Principles of Political Economy and Taxation*	
1818	Mary Shelley, *Frankenstein* Scott, *Heart of Midlothian*	Frontier between USA and Canada agreed
1819	Birth of George Eliot (Mary Ann Evans) Byron, *Don Juan*	'Peterloo massacre': troops fire on workers in Manchester
1820		George III dies, succeeded by George IV
1821	Death of Keats	Napoleon dies on St Helena
1822	Shelley drowns at Lerici Beethoven, *Missa Solemnis*	
1823	Lamb, *Essays of Elia*	
1824	Death of Byron at Missolonghi	
1826	Fenimore Cooper, *Last of the Mohicans*	

Year	Age	Life
1827	17	Knutsford, holiday in Wales
1828	18	Her brother John disappears on a voyage to India. Elizabeth goes to Chelsea to live with her father and stepmother
1829	19	March. William Stevenson dies. Elizabeth goes to stay with Revd William Turner, Newcastle-upon-Tyne
1830	20	Spent in Knutsford and Newcastle
1831	21	Visits Edinburgh with Anne Turner. Summer in Liverpool then Knutsford. In Manchester meets Revd William Gaskell, junior minister at Cross Street Unitarian Chapel
1832	22	30 August. Marries William Gaskell, moves to Manchester
1833	23	Birth of a still-born daughter
1834	24	12 September. Her daughter, Marianne, is born
1837	27	January. 'Sketches among the Poor' (with William), in *Blackwood's Edinburgh Magazine* 5 February. Margaret Emily (Meta) born May. Aunt Lumb dies
1840	30	'Clopton Hall' included in William Howitt, *Visits to Remarkable Places*
1841	31	Visits Germany with William

Year	Literary Context	Historical Events
1827	Keble, *Christian Year* Manzoni, *I Promessi Sposi*	Treaty between Britain, Russia and France to assure independence of Greece (confirmed 1830)
1830	Tennyson, *Poems, chiefly Lyrical* Charles Lyell, *Principles of Geology*	George IV dies, succeeded by William IV Revolutionary uprisings in Germany, Poland, Belgium, France (abdication of Charles IX; election of Louis Philippe as King)
1831	Ebenezer Elliot, *Corn Law Rhymes*	Russell introduces first Reform Bill
1832	Deaths of Sir Walter Scott and Goethe	First Reform Act passed
1833	Carlyle, *Sartor Resartus*	Factory inspection introduced in England
1834		Slavery ended in British possessions
1836	Dickens, *Pickwick Papers*	
1837	Dickens, *Oliver Twist*	William IV dies, succeeded by Queen Victoria
1838		Anti-Corn-Law League founded in Manchester
1839	Carlyle, *Chartism*	Chartist petition presented to Parliament Opium war with China: Hong Kong taken New Zealand declared a British colony
1840	Browning, *Sordello*	Marriage of Queen Victoria to Prince Albert of Saxe-Coburg-Gotha
1841		Peel succeeds Melbourne as British Prime Minister

Year	Age	Life
1842	32	7 October. Florence Elizabeth (Flossy) born
1844	34	23 October. Birth of her son, William
1845	34	10 August. William dies, aged ten months, in North Wales
1846	36	3 September. Fourth daughter Julia Margaret Bradford born
1847–8	37	'Libbie Marsh's Three Eras', 'The Sexton's Hero', 'Christmas Storms and Sunshine', in *Howitt's Journal*
1848	38	November. *Mary Barton*
1849	39	Visits London: meets Dickens, Carlyle, Forster
1850	40–41	Begins to write for Dickens's *Household Words*: 'Lizzie Leigh', 'The Well of Pen Morfa', 'The Heart of John Middleton' The Gaskells move to 84 Plymouth Grove, Manchester August. First meeting with Charlotte Brontë December. *The Moorland Cottage*

Year	Literary Context	Historical Events
1842	Comte, *Cours de la philosophie positive* Macaulay, *Lays of Ancient Rome*	Hong Kong ceded to Britain Widespread Chartist riots
1843	Carlyle, *Past and Present* Ruskin, *Modern Painters, I*	
1844	Disraeli, *Coningsby*	
1845	Disraeli, *Sybil*	Texas made USA state, Mexico loses Arizona, California, New Mexico (join USA in 1847) Beginning of potato famine in Ireland
1846	Edward Lear, *Book of Nonsense*	Pius IX elected Pope Repeal of Corn Laws in Britain
1847	Tennyson, *The Princess* Charlotte Brontë, *Jane Eyre* Emily Brontë, *Wuthering Heights*	Poland made a Russian province
1848	Thackeray, *Vanity Fair* J. S. Mill, *Principles of Political Economy*	Revolutions in Sicily, Austria (Emperor Ferdinand abdicates in favour of nephew, Francis Joseph), and France (Republic proclaimed: Louis Napoleon elected President). Uprisings against Austria in Italy Lord Dalhousie appointed Governor-General of India First Women's Rights Convention, Seneca Falls, USA Pre-Raphaelite Brotherhood formed
1849	Charlotte Brontë, *Shirley*	Garibaldi enters Rome Britain annexes Punjab
1850	Dickens, *David Copperfield*: *Household Words* founded Tennyson, *In Memoriam* Death of Wordsworth; Tennyson becomes Poet Laureate	Australian Constitution Act

Year	Age	Life
1851	40–41	July. Visits Great Exhibition December (51)–May (53) *Cranford* episodes in *Household Words*
1852	42	'The Old Nurse's Story'
1853	42	January. *Ruth* May. Visit to Paris July. Holiday in Normandy 19–23 September. Visit to Haworth
1854	43–4	February. Visits Paris September–January 1855. *North and South* in *Household Words*
1855	44	February. Visits Paris 31 March. Death of Charlotte Brontë June. Patrick Brontë asks her to write Charlotte's *Life*
1856	45	'The Poor Clare'
1857	46	February. The *Life* completed: holiday in Italy. Meets Charles Eliot Norton March. *The Life of Charlotte Brontë*: libel cases and revisions
1858	48	June–September. *My Lady Ludlow* in *Household Words* September: holiday in Germany
1859	49	*Lois the Witch*

Year	Literary Context	Historical Events
1851	Ruskin, *The Stones of Venice* Melville, *Moby-Dick*	Great Exhibition in London Gold found in New South Wales and Victoria First women's suffrage petition presented to House of Commons
1852	Harriet Beecher Stowe, *Uncle Tom's Cabin*	South African Republic established at Sand River Convention
1853	Charlotte Brontë, *Villette* Dickens, *Bleak House*	France: Napoleon III proclaimed Emperor Russian army enters Turkey: Turkey declares war
1854	Thoreau, *Walden*	France and Britain declare war on Russia: armies land in Crimea
1855	Death of Charlotte Brontë Browning, *Men and Women*	Paris World Exhibition
1856		Paris Peace Congress ends Crimean War
1857	Dickens, *Little Dorrit* Trollope, *Barchester Towers* George Eliot, *Scenes of Clerical Life* Barrett Browning, *Aurora Leigh* Flaubert, *Madame Bovary* Baudelaire, *Les fleurs du mal*	'Indian Mutiny': Massacre of Cawnpore, loss of Delhi
1858	Tennyson, *Idylls of the King*	Ottawa declared capital of Canada
1859	Charles Darwin, *The Origin of Species* J. S. Mill, *On Liberty* George Eliot, *Adam Bede* Dickens, *A Tale of Two Cities*	Revolutions against Austrian rule in Parma, Modena and Tuscany USA: John Brown's raid on Harper's Ferry De Lesseps begins Suez Canal
1860	George Eliot, *The Mill on the Floss*	Plebiscites in favour of Italian unification, Garibaldi enters Naples Abraham Lincoln elected President of USA

Year	Age	Life
1861	51	*The Grey Woman*
1862	52	Spring. Visits France, planning the memoir of Mme de Sevigné
		Autumn. Intense relief work in the Manchester 'cotton famine' due to the American Civil War
1863	53	February. *Sylvia's Lovers*
		March–June. Trip to France and Italy
		September. Florence Gaskell marries
1864	53	*Cousin Phillis* concluded in *The Cornhill Magazine*
1865	54–5	August. *Wives and Daughters* begins in the *Cornhill* (Concluded January 1866)
		12 November. Elizabeth dies of a heart attack at her newly bought house, 'The Lawn', Holybourne, Hampshire

Year	Literary Context	Historical Events
1861	George Eliot, *Silas Marner* Dickens, *Great Expectations*	Confederation of Southern States proclaimed: American Civil War Victor Emanuel King of Italy Prince Consort dies
1862		Bismarck appointed Prussian Premier
1863	Death of Thackeray Tolstoy begins *War and Peace* (published 1868–9)	
1864	Browning, *Dramatis Personae* J. H. Newman, *Apologia Pro Vita Sua*	
1865	Lewis Carroll, *Alice in Wonderland* Dickens, *Our Mutual Friend*	Lincoln assassinated: Confederate army surrender Palmerston dies: Russell Prime Minister; Gladstone Leader of the House

To Jenny Uglow, with love

INTRODUCTION

Cranford is unquestionably the most loved of Mrs Gaskell's works: charming, kindly, ironically humorous and easy to read. It is technically a novel but, conveniently, a series of episodes or stories, too. In an age of massive novels – *Vanity Fair* (1848) and *David Copperfield* (1850) precede it and *Bleak House* (1853) follows it – *Cranford* is small and mini-plotted beside these multi-faceted giants. Yet it is an example of high art: its seemingly casual execution masking many subtleties and innuendoes. Mrs Gaskell's comment about it to Ruskin, more than a dozen years after she had completed it, has all the advantage of considered hindsight: 'The beginning of *Cranford* was one paper in *Household Words*, and I never meant to write more, so killed off Capt. Brown very much against my will' (Letter 562, p. 748, *The Letters of Mrs Gaskell*, ed., Chapple and Pollard). The skillful bonding, the integrated narrative standpoint which mediates between the reader and the community described, the consummate blend in which the humour is sometimes subdued by the pathos or runs naturally with it, all these and more bear witness to the aesthetic and artistic control exercised by Mrs Gaskell. Individual isolation and domestic ritual are set against community interaction and supportiveness. It is indeed the contemplation of 'the last generation in England', and it compels the reader, without pressure, to feel and think as well as smile. There is as much social and moral comment in *Cranford* as there is in *Mary Barton* (1848) and *Ruth* (1853), Gaskell's two novels of recognisably serious intent between which it stands. The difference is one of tone and perspective: if *Cranford* lacks their obvious theses, it more than compensates in its equivalence of humanitarian – Mrs Gaskell would say Christian – concern.

One is cautious of using the term 'novel' in view of Mrs Gaskell's explanation of how she came to write *Cranford*, but the caution is misplaced. Before she even began, she had written an episode, 'The Last Generation in England', which was printed in America in *Sartain's Union Magazine* in July 1849. Though the connection with *Cranford* is clear, the literary gap between the episode and the chapters of *Cranford* is remarkable. The development in maturity, the handling of both general and specific material, the psychological assurance and the depth of appraisal in *Cranford* are amazing. In 'The Last Generation' the incidents are *recorded* (for example, the placing of plates of food under the couch, and the cat swallowing the lace), whereas in *Cranford* incidents are fully integrated into the narrative and come, so to speak, with an endearing (and in the case of the cat, daring) comic whimsicality. We feel, through the personality of her narrator, Mrs Gaskell's own delight: there are times when *Cranford* bubbles with recollected truths, sheer inventiveness, or both. *Cranford* was published serially, though irregularly, from December 1851 to May 1853 in *Household Words*, and it celebrates the emergence of an assured literary artist.

The first striking thing about *Cranford* is the relaxed style in which it is written. The first few paragraphs immediately evoke the rhythmically slow way of life which is characteristic of the town. Here even the punctuation, the qualifying sequence of semi-colons, establishes that life through the leisurely unwinding of generalisations, emphatic, definitive, with the word 'Cranford' repeated half a dozen times. The life of the community is expressed with a light irony, its little idiosyncrasies conveyed in an intimate, confiding tone: anecdotes, conventions, closet gossip and the attendant pathos of 'elegant economy' constitute the medium of action. The narrative voice sets the pattern of consistency: it is that of the outsider who comes to be regarded as the trusted insider. Eventually Mary Smith has two distinct roles, that of establishing perspective with regard to the community, and of sympathetic identification with and care of its most loveable member, Miss Matty. In the latter's regard she is carefully, subtly, protective, indulging her nostalgia, and personal pain or sadness, helping her through financial crises with exquisite tact and understanding, cushioning her with supportive sympathy on the return of 'poor' Peter: for Miss Matty this is the ultimate consummation, the long wished-for reconciliation providing a happy close to her quiet life.

The theme of reconciliation runs throughout Mrs Gaskell's works. It is the emblem of her Christian idealism, though sometimes it is employed at the expense of her realism. Before the happy homecoming in *Cranford*, there is the strained death-bed amity of John Barton and Mr Carson in *Mary Barton*, and the nursing of her seducer, Donne, by the eponymous heroine in *Ruth*. Ruth, like Barton before her, dies, but as a result of an altruistic rather than criminal action. In *Cranford* Mrs Gaskell's compassionate irony – the term almost defines her sympathetic narrative mode throughout the book – embraces reconciliation and realism. Her analysis is simple, direct, true: Cranford is reconciled to Captain Brown before his death, but much more positively and humanely after it. Miss Deborah, obstinate and self-willed in her exchanges with the Captain, almost yields up Dr Johnson in this aftermath. And Mrs Gaskell, structurally aware and sharply focussed, has the Captain and his daughter reconciled, so to speak, in death, with the surviving daughter Jessie neatly reclaimed by her suitor Major Gordon in life. The outsiders have made their mark in Cranford.

The focus on the outsiders and their various impacts is prelude to the considered exposure of what appears to be unchanging – the community – and an extended series of further outsider influences right up to the finality of 'poor' Peter, the one-time insider who is received back and proceeds to live largely on his outside experiences, those tall tales with which his conversation is embellished. Mrs Gaskell, through her narrator Mary Smith, has an 'elegant economy' of expression which fits the subdued emotional temperature, the sympathetic immediacy, the quiet but insistent humour with which these quiet lives are revealed. Reconciliation, then, is linked to returning, though Frederick in *North and South* (1855) leaves after his mother's death, and the glamorous, sexual Kinraid in *Sylvia's Lovers* (1863) is not reconciled to Sylvia (who has reluctantly married her cousin) but instead makes a socially advantageous marriage. Peter's return in *Cranford* is not distinguished by Mrs Gaskell's other-wise sure sense of realism. Rather, it is part of her facility as a plot-maker and story-teller. Cunningly, she has Peter come home earlier when he is a Lieutenant ('he did not get to be Admiral', says Miss Matty, regretful of family ambition thwarted) before his extended wanderings in India. Cunningly because it prepares the way for his ultimate return. Peter is in fact the stereotypical drop-out grown old, and the assimilated Aga Jenkyns continues to fool and fantasise where he began. He re-enters the community, and it is that community which is central to any appraisal of *Cranford*.

Apart from the relaxed verbal confidence, the novel has structural cohesion, sophisticated and unobtrusive, which almost gives the lie to Mrs Gaskell's own testimony to Ruskin. Although the main period of action is the near past, Mrs Gaskell delves into the more distant past, too. The result is, particularly with Miss Matty, a thorough integration of character. But there is also an ongoing integration of situation where Mrs Gaskell's sense of form is certainly in evidence, as with the treatment of servants. Miss Matty does not know how to act first with Fanny and then with Martha over 'followers', her own inability to 'provide' for a gentleman being obliquely stressed. This prepares the way for her failure on a practical level to deal with the visit of Major Jenkyns and then, through the narrator's seemingly casual sleight of hand ('And *now* I come to the love affair'), her failure in the past to 'provide' for Mr Thomas Holbrook, who had 'offered' to her.

Miss Matty was pressurised as always by the snobbery of Deborah then, and Miss Pole, functional and fully realised in so many ways, is pivotal to the plot here as she is elsewhere in the novel. The graceful transition from one sequence to the next (Chapter 4, 'A Visit to an Old Bachelor') is achieved by an easy art which is stringent, disciplined, and satisfying to the reader. By the end of Chapter 3, the meeting in the shop, with its natural, truthful and reflexive dialogue ('God bless my soul! I should not have known you. How are you?') and the corollary of Miss Matty's reaction ('She went straight to her room, and never came back to our early tea-time, when I thought she looked as if she had been crying') ensures sympathetic reader involvement. The visit to Mr Holbrook clearly marks the passage of time as he and Miss Matty are brought into interaction again. Here Mrs Gaskell not only evaluates the 'soft plaintiveness' of loss, she also provides an ironic sub-text which suggests that what might have been – the marriage of Holbrook and Matty in the distant past – may not have worked out happily. In implying this she is ironically and certainly critically giving a dual emphasis to those snobbish standards which prevented the marriage in the first place. Holbrook, despite his rural table-manners, is Miss Matty's superior in culture, intelligence, width of interest and general knowledge of life. The

presentation of Miss Matty, though profoundly sympathetic, is
not literalised into symbol or romanticised into sentiment. She
is not very bright, and this is not just because of the oppressive
nurture of her father or the domination of Deborah in the past.
It is simply that it takes her time to think things through and,
having thought, she is still sometimes vague or inconclusive.
This is redolent of pathos, definitive of limitation. On the visit
to Holbrook with Mary, the natural dialogue reveals both: Miss
Matty falls asleep during Holbrook's recitation of 'Locksley
Hall', and wakes up to observe:

> 'What a pretty book!'
>
> 'Pretty! madam! it's beautiful! Pretty, indeed!'
>
> 'Oh yes! I meant beautiful!' said she, fluttered at his disapproval
> of her word. 'It is so like that beautiful poem of Dr Johnson's my
> sister used to read – I forget the name of it, what was it, my dear?'
> turning to me.
>
> 'What do you mean, ma'am? What was it about?'
>
> 'I don't remember what it was about, and I've quite forgotten
> what the name of it was; but it was written by Dr Johnson, and
> was very beautiful, and very like what Mr Holbrook has just been
> reading.' (Chapter 4)

For an illuminating moment one glimpses a marriage that might
have been, or perhaps ponders what might have been made of
Miss Matty all those years ago if she had had the temerity to
become Mrs Holbrook. The ironic silence behind the contained
narrator is not unkind: rather it is informed with a quiet realism,
already reflecting Mrs Gaskell's maturity of appraisal and
implication.

As Jenny Uglow[1] has put it in the sub-title of her fine critical
biography of Mrs Gaskell, she had 'A Habit of Stories'. This is
exemplified in *Cranford*, where the habit is structured and
sedulously channelled into an unforced and feeling flow. The
atmosphere, despite the intrusions of outsiders, is deliberately
low-key, and most of the crises are internally manufactured,
with the exception of the small-world-shattering news that the
Town and County Bank has stopped payment.

In Chapter 4 Mrs Gaskell extends her own sub-text through
sophisticated nuances. Elizabeth Porges Watson[2] has pointed
out that the lost love theme of 'Locksley Hall' relates to the
situation of Miss Matty and Mr Holbrook: I would go further

and suggest that the most remembered or quoted lines of the poem are evocative of a deeper poignancy:

> In the Spring a livelier iris changes on the burnished dove;
> In the Spring a young man's fancy lightly turns to thoughts of love.
>
> (ll. 19–20)

Mrs Gaskell's literary awareness, her premeditated setting up of associations, has often passed unnoticed. The lines quoted above are related to the natural beauty so appreciated by Mr Holbrook, and to the natural movement towards mating character- istic of youth. But soon Mr Holbrook is to die, and Miss Matty is to affect widowhood. She pretends to be thinking only of the 'style' of widows' caps, but the depth of her feelings, perhaps playing over that unconsummated past, is obvious to the com- passionate narrator: 'This effort at concealment was the begin- ning of the tremulous motion of head and hands which I have seen ever since in Miss Matty' (Chapter 4). In fact her tendency to live in the past, to prefer its security despite its tribulations, is one of Miss Matty's recurring states. The chapter on 'Old Letters' is a delving into the past beyond the past, the correspon- dence between her parents before their marriage and after: it is another interlude in the narrative of the present, another mode of integration, since so much is filtered through Miss Matty's own episodic narration.

Miss Matty is caressed by the lambent humour of the narra- tor, Mary Smith, so that her rituals of behaviour, the patterns of her reticence, the texture of her uncertainties, are all warmed into being. Take the 'elegant economy' with the candles, the burning of one at a time (perhaps symbols of the simple single lives never to be doubled) where the narrator observes:

> As we lived in constant preparation for a friend who might come in any evening (but who never did) it required some contrivance to keep out two candles of the same length, ready to be lighted, and to look as if we burnt two always. (Chapter 5)

Even with the reading of the letters only one candle is employed ('the pale, faded ink' reflects this pale, faded life). But while we appreciate the nostalgia of Miss Matty and her familial identifi- cation, we note Mrs Gaskell's convincing fictional re-creation of that distant material, her ability to give the letters the stamp and seal of authenticity. Mrs Gaskell lives in and with what she creates. Both her novels and her stories reflect this. *Sylvia's Lovers* is magisterial in its sense of location and historical time and, even more remarkable, a *novella* like *Lois the Witch* presents successfully a genuine evocation of Puritan persecution in New England in the seventeenth century. These examples serve to reinforce the claim that in *Cranford* Mrs Gaskell is already showing her particular strengths, her flair within her given form, her sense and sensibility of history, invigorating her readers with the fresh air of her distinctive irony.

Mrs Gaskell's historical sense is qualified and deepened by her accompanying literary range of reference. In *Mary Barton* and *North and South*, her two novels of industrial usage and abusage, she uses epigraphs (or mottoes) from other writers to point up situations in her own work. This practice, perhaps derived from the simplistic literary embroidery of Sir Walter Scott, is not employed in *Cranford*: instead Mrs Gaskell uses a speaking range of literary reference within the text. The most obvious example is Captain Brown's preference for the writings of Boz (Dickens) as against Miss Jenkyns's elevation of Dr Johnson. The Captain has the final word (his analogy the recent publication of *The Pickwick Papers* [1836–7] in monthly parts) when he asks 'How was the "Rambler" published, Ma'am?' (Chapter 1). This is a statement which Miss Jenkyns 'could not have heard', but where the innuendo is that she 'would not have heard' anyway. It has been correctly suggested that these references are the registers of more than literary change: they represent the cultural and social movements between the eighteenth and nineteenth centuries, but they also provide a living context for the characters of *Cranford*, and a living sub-text, too. While Miss Matty, still in the eighteenth century in terms of conditioning and nostalgia, reads those distant letters, Mrs Gaskell uses a literary device which anticipates the pertinent allusiveness of twentieth-century practice. Two friends of Dr Johnson, the moral letter-writer Hester Chapone and the scholar Mrs Carter (also an important letter-writer) as well as Maria Edgeworth through *Patronage* (1813), provide referential accompaniment to Miss Matty's readings. Mrs Gaskell's knowledge of literature and her use of analogy enhance her own literary representation. She moves easily into the period of *Cranford* and encompasses the period which informed it.

But the elements of change are always there, and Mary Smith, belonging to a different generation, signals their coming. Although she has a natural reflex spontaneity, as she shows in her parody 'I saw, I imitated, I survived!' (Chapter 4), her episodic visits to Cranford enable her to record the shifts and the degrees of movement: her perspectives are part of the time-scale used by Mrs Gaskell throughout. The story of 'poor' Peter, with its poignant, even tragic, results, is structurally so placed that the idea of his reappearance is subliminally present from then on in the reader's mind. The chapter in which Mrs Gaskell describes his major offence is inlaid with direct and subtle psychological understanding, intuitively Freudian, pre-Freud. Today it looks like a classic case of parent-child, generation-gap division, with the failure of the autocratic father and the indulgent mother, the ambitions, deviations and situations given immediate currency through Mrs Gaskell's graphic art. The flogging of Peter exemplifies this. His reaction to the stultifying pedantic grind – supposedly the only discipline which would ensure that you lived up to your family's expectations – is to dress up periodically as a woman: 'for Peter was a lady then', as Miss Matty innocently puts it. The uselessness of rote classical learning and copying – Tom Tulliver endures a like torment with different results in George Eliot's *The Mill on the Floss* (1860) – drives the joker to his actions, and these have their own resonances in the plot: 'And he went and walked up and down in the Filbert Walk – just half-hidden by the rails, and half-seen; and he cuddled his pillow, just like a baby; and talked to it all the nonsense people do' (Chapter 6). The Rector's retribution wrecks lives: Mrs Gaskell has suggested sexual aberration (Peter never marries, despite the late fear that Mrs Jamieson is angling for him) intuitively and tolerantly. In Peter's factual impersonation we have the type of Miss Matty's covert maternalism, the imaginary child she talks to out of loneliness, the reflex of a deprivation which she can't articulate. This is yet another example of the tautness of structure in *Cranford*. Miss Matty's timidity is conditioned by the Rector's autocracy and her own sibling status.

Cranford has long been staple fare for amateur dramatic societies, and there is little wonder: the dialogue alone contains the timeless truths of social exchange, for it is heard accurately, recorded, stored, steeped in insights. Mrs Gaskell is taking the first steps on the road to Hollingford (*Wives and Daughters*,

1864–6), in which the dry wit of Mr Gibson as he prescribes for the importunate Mr Coxe, or the pellucid egoism of Mrs Kirkpatrick as she prescribes for herself, are informed with a wise and natural humour. Perhaps these two characters from her final, incomplete masterpiece represent the summit of Mrs Gaskell's artistic achievement, but she scales the lower peaks of *Cranford* with an assured foothold which signals the intrepid assault to come.

In the Cranford community we are always aware of the exploration of appearance and reality. Lady Glenmire becomes Mrs Hoggins, ignoring the frills and flounces of Cranford's genteel posturing. Another variant on this theme is the arrival of 'Signor Brunoni' (or Samuel Brown, as we should prefer to call him), Miss Pole's encounter with him, and the atmosphere of credulity and excitement in the small-town community. The interaction between Miss Pole as informed audience, the 'Grand Turk' and the uninformed audience, is superbly conveyed. Mrs Gaskell's verbal camcorder sweeps that audience with its casual close-ups via Mary Smith: 'I saw the tall, thin, dry, dusty rector, sitting surrounded by National School boys, guarded by troops of his own sex from any approach of the many Cranford spinsters' (Chapter 9). Any break or disturbance in the communal routine is registered. Mrs Gaskell's sequence moves easily from conjuring and witchcraft to speculation, burglary and possible assault. Here the functional Miss Pole reflects the extremes of the emotional temperature: she is the pivot of mood. A gossip-raiser of feverish imagination, she provides a natural contrast with the narrator, Mary Smith, who represents the norm of reaction. The aftermath of 'Signor Brunoni's' performance provides Miss Pole (and Mrs Gaskell) with 'The Panic', where the power of rumour is searched and exposed, the comic stress being balanced in its turn by the pathos of the death of Carlo. The rumour-robbery of Mr Hoggins is suitably enlarged by Miss Pole, who has seen, she declares, an 'Irishman dressed up in woman's clothes, who came spying about my house, with the story about the starving children' (Chapter 10).

But we can pass on from this structural shade of 'poor' Peter to note another Gaskellian device – the use of a subsidiary narrator within the narrative who also has 'A Habit of Stories'. Her sensationalism contrasts with the low-key narratives of *Cranford*, and Mrs Gaskell, through Miss Pole, is parodying her own capacity for the melodramatic and sensational which was later to embrace the supernatural as well. In *Cranford* Mrs Gaskell is in part laughing at herself, at us, and at them. She delights in Miss Pole as well as castigating her self-indulgence. Having set neurotic speculation in train, Miss Pole puts down Mrs Forrester's introduction of ghosts – one suspects that this is a usurping of her province – and then reveals her own suscepti-bility by clutching Mary Smith's arm and bribing the chairmen when they are taken home. This use of narrator within the narrative is a favourite ploy of Mrs Gaskell's: Job Legh's moving account of going to London, finding his daughter dead and bringing her baby back with him in *Mary Barton*; the telling of Frederick's story in *North and South*; Kinraid's tales in *Sylvia's Lovers*. Essentially *Cranford* is a series of stories bonded into a novel by artistic integrity of a high order which embraces psychological consistency and locational reality.

The last third of the novel is adroitly managed. The illness of 'Signor Brunoni' leads to the revelation by the Signora (or Mrs Brown as she prefers to be called) about 'that good, kind Aga Jenkyns' (Chapter 11) which initiates the denouément. Narrative interest is consistently sustained, even manipulated. Miss Pole brings the news that Lady Glenmire is engaged to Mr Hoggins: Mary Smith colours this with delightful mock-romantic innu-endo when she observes (of Mr Hoggins's visits to treat one of Mrs Jamieson's servants) that 'the wolf had got into the fold, and now he was carrying off the shepherdess' (Chapter 12). While tension is aroused by the community waiting on Mrs Jamieson's reaction, the failure of the Bank takes economic and sympathetic precedence in the narrative. Miss Matty, after all, *is* the heroine of *Cranford*, an unlikely one, true, but the positive moral centre of the novel. Her kindness, her probity, her concern and sympathy, her practical and unconsidered generosity to Mr Dobson in the shop, these and other generous traits ensure her primacy in the reader's mind. From now on her own role enhances the reconciliatory theme. She moves towards approval of the Glenmire-Hoggins liaison ('She fell off into a soft reverie about Mr Holbrook', Chapter 13), is sad because she feels that her mother would have been grieved by her economic plight, and broods about Martha's loss of income on her own account. Martha, however, has always been aggressively attached to her, and stands as living evidence of Miss Matty's sympathetic appeal and inherent goodness. The exotic pudding of the lion *couchant* is her expression of reciprocal loyalty, with the production of Jem Hearn a kind of comic and economic back-up both to the pudding and to the Amazonian power of its maker, with her downstairs humanity of tears and temper.

The wider support is inevitably organised by Miss Pole, whose heart of gold betrays her overactive mouth and reduces Mary Smith to tears. The pathos of Miss Matty is supplemented by the particularised pathos of 'genteel poverty', for example in Mrs Forrester, while Peter's return signals the inevitable imposition of romance on reality. Mrs Gaskell, intent on laying out happiness after sadness, provides the conventional rounding off. The ironic perspectives fade into 'peace', the word heading her final chapter and definitive of her theme.

In *Cranford* Mrs Gaskell came of age. With striking originality she extended the range of her known voices, moving from the hard and harsh experiences of *Mary Barton* to the deceptively soft, supposedly cushioned insularity of her beloved Knutsford. Humanity and art merge, and *Cranford* is as searching and revealing in small compass as anything she wrote, subserving her claims to be considered a major writer. Brilliantly and skillfully constructed in the head, it comes from the heart.

Mr Harrison's Confessions, a sequence of incidents in the life of a newly-practising doctor in Duncombe (Knutsford), was published anonymously between February and April 1851 in *The Ladies' Companion*. It precedes the first number of *Cranford* by more than six months, but shares with the major work the device of a first-person narrator as well as location. The points of contrast outweigh the parallels, but the techniques and emphases make an interesting prelude to *Cranford*. *Mr Harrison's Confessions* lacks the exemplary structure of Mrs Gaskell's later serial, though it makes its own distinctive contribution to the developing Gaskell fictional milieu by virtue of its fun, an element of self-mockery, and its pathos. Again, it is an early step on the road to Hollingford. Harrison, first slackly 'Will' then 'Frank' in the text (it is unlikely that Mrs Gaskell ever revised this story) is a doctor doing the rounds, just like his successor Mr Gibson in *Wives and Daughters*. Harrison is vulnerable to female machinations, and at one stage a victim of Duncombe gossip: Mr Gibson, in his supposedly stable widowerhood, is

lured into matrimony by Mrs Kirkpatrick. Harrison is a good
young catch, Gibson a good older one, reduced by the pseudo-
refined wiles of a determined widow. But *Wives and Daughters*
is a study in depth whereas *Mr Harrison's Confessions*, though
written with great verve, often tips over from fun into farce.
This latter element is enhanced by the speed of the narrative, the
short, staccato chapters providing pace and excitement, with
incident succeeding incident. The misunderstandings and revelations move, as in *Cranford*, towards the reconciliation which is
at the heart of Mrs Gaskell's work.

The achievements of *Cranford* derive in part from this story.
Harrison, male narrator who falls in love with and ultimately
marries the Vicar's daughter Sophy, is naturally and easily
entered by Mrs Gaskell, who is laughing at him as well as feeling
with him (there is built-in criticism but no hint of unkindness).
His relationship with his fellow practitioner Mr Morgan and
with his landlady Mrs Rose is finely handled in areas of prejudice
and expectations: there is some wonderfully self-important
name-dropping, and the conventions and courtesies of the time
are given with a running ironic commentary. As in *Cranford*,
gossip rules. As in *Cranford*, the truth will out. What appears is
rarely what is: women and girls set their caps – or have their
caps set for them – at the male narrator, until a pattern of
coincidences is stamped with farce. The style, as in *Cranford*, is
relaxed, emanating from the fireside opening which sets a
comfortable scene for the story recollected in tranquillity. The
tale is a romantic comedy, the self-conceit of Harrison contrast-
ing with the set ways of the natives. Two outsiders, Harrison
and Jack Marshland, make an impact on the small community,
but a major part of the humour is in the author's underpinning
of her narrator's condescension. Interest is sustained, for there
is no let-up in the range of incidents which make the loose
adhesive of this story, from the graphically humorous picnic at
the Old Hall, to the pathos of the death of Sophy's little brother
Walter. Comic tension is achieved through the hostility of
predatory women and their relations as they feed on the rumours
of Harrison's matrimonial intentions. One of his strengths,
however, is his resilience, and this is allied to his skill as a doctor
(despite his inexperience). He saves John Brouncker's arm
(rumour says that he has killed him) and is instrumental in
bringing Sophy back from the edge of death. The first incident

is beautifully encapsulated in a passing comment which defines (as in *Cranford*) the nature and the focus of the community: 'That is a charm in a little town, everybody is so sympathetically full of the same events' (Chapter 14). This carries the overriding concern that Brouncker will not suffer amputation and the loss of his means of livelihood.

Despite the range of literary (and medical) references the slackness, both in the structure and in the writing, is evident. Yet the very lightness of the story is part of its appeal. Mrs Gaskell captures the *attitudes* of the narrator admirably, just as she does with Mary Smith: the episodes match the pace of the doctor's life; the interactions of outsider and set community have the touch of truth. At times the humour is refreshing, deft, direct: Jack Marshland's account of Harrison's arrest, as compared with the somewhat complacent account of it which Harrison gives, shows the familiar Gaskell sleight of hand. Jack is a practical joker: note his inducing Harrison to try and cure his grey hairs and his sending up of Harrison's 'docterly' behaviour. In some ways, the story itself is a running Gaskellian joke in which she is laughing covertly at her narrator. But, as A. W. Ward correctly observed of *Mr Harrison's Confessions*, its merits 'are such as to be perfectly self-supporting'.[3] If the comedy is broad, even facile, it emphasises Mrs Gaskell's range. The caricatures of the story are not stereotypes: they are anticipations of the fuller roundness to come, and their dialogue – one of Mrs Gaskell's great strengths – is redolent of a simple truth to life. *Mr Harrison's Confessions* is a delightful and entertaining romp, and much of its inherent vivacity is carried over into *Cranford*.

GRAHAM HANDLEY

References

1. Jenny Uglow, *Elizabeth Gaskell: A Habit of Stories*, Faber & Faber, 1993.
2. Elizabeth Porges Watson, ed., *Cranford*, Oxford University Press, World's Classics series, 1980, p. 183.
3. A. W. Ward, ed., *Works of Mrs Gaskell*, The Knutsford Edition (*My Lady Ludlow*, etc.), Vol. 5, Smith, Elder & Co., 1906, p. xxiii.

NOTE ON THE TEXT

Cranford was first published in Dickens's *Household Words* irregularly from December 1851 to May 1853. The text used here is that of the second edition of 1853, published by Chapman & Hall. The alterations made from the serial issue in *Household Words* are not given in the explanatory notes: for example, in the serial issue Dickens altered references to himself. Thus the first chapter ('Our Society') has 'Hood's Own' for 'The Pickwick Papers' of the second edition. Mrs Gaskell obviously restored her preferences for the second edition.

The text of *Mr Harrison's Confessions* has been taken from the Knutsford edition of Mrs Gaskell's works, edited by A. W. Ward (1906), and that of *The Cage at Cranford* from the original publication in *All The Year Round* in 1863.

For the convenience of today's readers the spelling has been modernised.

CRANFORD

Chapter 1

OUR SOCIETY

In the first place, Cranford is in possession of the Amazons;* all the holders of houses, above a certain rent, are women. If a married couple come to settle in the town, somehow the gentleman disappears; he is either fairly frightened to death by being the only man in the Cranford evening parties, or he is accounted for by being with his regiment, his ship, or closely engaged in business all the week in the great neighbouring commercial town of Drumble,* distant only twenty miles on a railroad. In short, whatever does become of the gentlemen, they are not at Cranford. What could they do if they were there? The surgeon has his round of thirty miles, and sleeps at Cranford; but every man cannot be a surgeon. For keeping the trim gardens full of choice flowers without a weed to speck them;* for frightening away little boys who look wistfully at the said flowers through the railings; for rushing out at the geese that occasionally venture into the gardens if the gates are left open; for deciding all questions of literature and politics without troubling themselves with unnecessary reasons and arguments; for obtaining clear and correct knowledge of everybody's affairs in the parish; for keeping their neat maid-servants in admirable order; for kindness (somewhat dictatorial) to the poor, and real tender good offices to each other whenever they are in distress, the ladies of Cranford are quite sufficient. 'A man,' as one of them observed to me once, 'is *so* in the way in the house!' Although the ladies of Cranford know all each other's proceedings, they are exceedingly indifferent to each other's opinions. Indeed, as each has her own individuality, not to say eccentricity, pretty strongly developed, nothing is so easy as verbal retaliation; but somehow good-will reigns among them to a considerable degree.

The Cranford ladies have only an occasional little quarrel, spurted out in a few peppery words and angry jerks of the head; just enough to prevent the even tenor of their lives* from becoming too flat. Their dress is very independent of fashion; as they observe, 'What does it signify how we dress here at Cranford, where everybody knows us?' And if they go from home, their reason is equally cogent: 'What does it signify how we dress here, where nobody knows us?' The materials of their clothes are, in general, good and plain, and most of them are nearly as scrupulous as Miss Tyler, of cleanly memory;* but I will answer for it, the last gigot, the last tight and scanty petticoat in wear in England, was seen in Cranford – and seen without a smile.

I can testify to a magnificent family red silk umbrella, under which a gentle little spinster, left alone of many brothers and sisters, used to patter to church on rainy days. Have you any red silk umbrellas in London? We had a tradition of the first that had ever been seen in Cranford; and the little boys mobbed it, and called it 'a stick in petticoats'. It might have been the very red silk one I have described, held by a strong father over a troop of little ones; the poor little lady – the survivor of all – could scarcely carry it.

Then there were rules and regulations for visiting and calls; and they were announced to any young people, who might be staying in the town with all the solemnity with which the old Manx laws were read once a year on the Tinwald Mount.

'Our friends have sent to inquire how you are after your journey tonight, my dear, (fifteen miles, in a gentleman's carriage); they will give you some rest tomorrow, but the next day, I have no doubt, they will call; so be at liberty after twelve; – from twelve to three are our calling-hours.'

Then, after they had called,

'It is the third day; I dare say your mamma has told you, my dear, never to let more than three days elapse between receiving a call and returning it; and also, that you are never to stay longer than a quarter of an hour.'

'But am I to look at my watch? How am I to find out when a quarter of an hour has passed?'

'You must keep thinking about the time, my dear, and not allow yourself to forget it in conversation.'

As everybody had this rule in their minds, whether they received or paid a call, of course no absorbing subject was ever spoken about. We kept ourselves to short sentences of small talk, and were punctual to our time.

I imagine that a few of the gentlefolks of Cranford were poor, and had some difficulty in making both ends meet; but they were like the Spartans, and concealed their smart under a smiling face. We none of us spoke of money, because that subject savoured of commerce and trade, and though some might be poor, we were all aristocratic. The Cranfordians had that kindly *esprit de corps* which made them overlook all deficiences in success when some among them tried to conceal their poverty. When Mrs Forrester, for instance, gave a party in her baby-house of a dwelling, and the little maiden disturbed the ladies on the sofa by a request that she might get the tea-tray out from underneath, everyone took this novel proceeding as the most natural thing in the world; and talked on about household forms and ceremonies, as if we all believed that our hostess had a regular servants' hall, second table, with housekeeper and steward; instead of the one little charity-school maiden, whose short ruddy arms could never have been strong enough to carry the tray upstairs, if she had not been assisted in private by her mistress, who now sat in state, pretending not to know what cakes were sent up; though she knew, and we knew, and she knew that we knew, and we knew that she knew that we knew, she had been busy all the morning making tea-bread and sponge-cakes.

There were one or two consequences arising from this general but unacknowledged poverty, and this very much acknowledged gentility, which were not amiss, and which might be introduced into many circles of society to their great improvement. For instance, the inhabitants of Cranford kept early hours, and clattered home in their pattens, under the guidance of a lantern-bearer, about nine o'clock at night; and the whole town was abed and asleep by half-past ten. Moreover, it was considered 'vulgar' (a tremendous word in Cranford) to give anything expensive, in the way of eatable or drinkable, at the evening entertainments. Wafer bread-and-butter and sponge-biscuits were all that the Honourable Mrs Jamieson gave; and she was sister-in-law to the late Earl of Glenmire, although she did practise such 'elegant economy'.

'Elegant economy'! How naturally one falls back into the phraseology of Cranford! There, economy was always 'elegant', and money-spending always 'vulgar and ostentatious'; a sort of sour-grapeism, which made us very peaceful and satisfied. I never shall forget the dismay felt when a certain Captain Brown

came to live at Cranford, and openly spoke about his being poor
– not in a whisper to an intimate friend, the doors and windows
being previously closed; but, in the public street! in a loud
military voice! alleging his poverty as a reason for not taking a
particular house. The ladies of Cranford were already rather
moaning over the invasion of their territories by a man and a
gentleman. He was a half-pay Captain, and had obtained some
situation on a neighbouring railroad, which had been vehemently petitioned against by the little town; and if, in addition
to his masculine gender, and his connection with the obnoxious
railroad, he was so brazen as to talk of being poor – why! then,
indeed, he must be sent to Coventry. Death was as true and as
common as poverty; yet people never spoke about that, loud
out in the streets. It was a word not to be mentioned to ears
polite. We had tacitly agreed to ignore that any with whom we
associated on terms of visiting equality could ever be prevented
by poverty from doing anything that they wished. If we walked
to or from a party, it was because the night was *so* fine, or the
air *so* refreshing; not because sedan-chairs were expensive. If we
wore prints, instead of summer silks, it was because we preferred
a washing material; and so on, till we blinded ourselves to the
vulgar fact, that we were, all of us, people of very moderate
means. Of course, then, we did not know what to make of a
man who could speak of poverty as if it was not a disgrace. Yet,
somehow Captain Brown made himself respected in Cranford,
and was called upon, in spite of all resolutions to the contrary. I
was surprised to hear his opinions quoted as authority, at a visit
which I paid to Cranford, about a year after he had settled in
the town. My own friends had been among the bitterest
opponents of any proposal to visit the Captain and his daughters, only twelve months before; and now he was even admitted
in the tabooed hours before twelve. True, it was to discover the
cause of a smoking chimney, before the fire was lighted; but still
Captain Brown walked upstairs, nothing daunted, spoke in a
voice too large for the room, and joked quite in the way of a
tame man, about the house. He had been blind to all the small
slights and omissions of trivial ceremonies with which he had
been received. He had been friendly, though the Cranford ladies
had been cool; he had answered small sarcastic compliments in
good faith; and with his manly frankness had overpowered all
the shrinking which met him as a man who was not ashamed to

be poor. And, at last, his excellent masculine common sense, and his facility in devising expedients to overcome domestic dilemmas, had gained him an extraordinary place as authority among the Cranford ladies. He, himself, went on in his course, as unaware of his popularity, as he had been of the reverse; and I am sure he was startled one day, when he found his advice so highly esteemed, as to make some counsel which he had given in jest, be taken in sober, serious earnest.

It was on this subject; – an old lady had an Alderney cow, which she looked upon as a daughter. You could not pay the short quarter-of-an-hour call, without being told of the wonderful milk or wonderful intelligence of this animal. The whole town knew and kindly regarded Miss Betty Barker's* Alderney; therefore great was the sympathy and regret when, in an unguarded moment, the poor cow tumbled into a lime-pit. She moaned so loudly that she was soon heard, and rescued; but meanwhile the poor beast had lost most of her hair, and came out looking naked, cold, and miserable, in a bare skin. Everybody pitied the animal, though a few could not restrain their smiles at her droll appearance. Miss Betty Barker absolutely cried with sorrow and dismay; and it was said she thought of trying a bath of oil. This remedy, perhaps, was recommended by someone of the number whose advice she asked; but the proposal, if ever it was made, was knocked on the head by Captain Brown's decided 'Get her a flannel waistcoat and flannel drawers, Ma'am, if you wish to keep her alive. But my advice is, kill the poor creature at once.'

Miss Betty Barker dried her eyes, and thanked the Captain heartily; she set to work, and by-and-by all the town turned out to see the Alderney meekly going to her pasture, clad in dark grey flannel. I have watched her myself many a time. Do you ever see cows dressed in grey flannel in London?

Captain Brown had taken a small house on the outskirts of the town, where he lived with his two daughters. He must have been upwards of sixty at the time of the first visit I paid to Cranford, after I had left it as a residence. But he had a wiry, well-trained, elastic figure; a stiff military throw-back of his head, and a springing step, which made him appear much younger than he was. His eldest daughter looked almost as old as himself, and betrayed the fact that his real, was more than his apparent, age. Miss Brown must have been forty; she had a

sickly, pained, careworn expression on her face, and looked as
if the gaiety of youth had long faded out of sight. Even when
young she must have been plain and hard-featured. Miss Jessie
Brown was ten years younger than her sister, and twenty shades
prettier. Her face was round and dimpled. Miss Jenkyns once
said, in a passion against Captain Brown (the cause of which I
will tell you presently), 'that she thought it was time for Miss
Jessie to leave off her dimples, and not always to be trying to
look like a child'. It was true there was something child-like in
her face; and there will be, I think, till she dies, though she
should live to be a hundred. Her eyes were large blue wondering
eyes, looking straight at you; her nose was unformed and snub,
and her lips were red and dewy; she wore her hair, too, in little
rows of curls, which heightened this appearance. I do not know
if she was pretty or not; but I liked her face, and so did everybody, and I do not think she could help her dimples. She had
something of her father's jauntiness of gait and manner; and any
female observer might detect a slight difference in the attire of
the two sisters – that of Miss Jessie being about two pounds per
annum more expensive than Miss Brown's. Two pounds was a
large sum in Captain Brown's annual disbursements.

Such was the impression made upon me by the Brown family,
when I first saw them altogether in Cranford church. The
Captain I had met before – on the occasion of the smoky
chimney, which he had cured by some simple alteration in the
flue. In church, he held his double eye-glass to his eyes during
the Morning Hymn, and then lifted up his head erect, and sang
out loud and joyfully. He made the responses louder than the
clerk – an old man with a piping feeble voice, who, I think, felt
aggrieved at the Captain's sonorous bass, and quavered higher
and higher in consequence.

On coming out of church, the brisk Captain paid the most
gallant attention to his two daughters. He nodded and smiled to
his acquaintances; but he shook hands with none until he had
helped Miss Brown to unfurl her umbrella, had relieved her of
her prayer-book, and had waited patiently till she, with trembling nervous hands, had taken up her gown to walk through
the wet roads.

I wondered what the Cranford ladies did with Captain Brown
at their parties. We had often rejoiced, in former days, that there
was no gentleman to be attended to, and to find conversation

for, at the card-parties. We had congratulated ourselves upon
the snugness of the evenings; and, in our love for gentility, and
distaste of mankind, we had almost persuaded ourselves that to
be a man was to be 'vulgar'; so that when I found my friend and
hostess, Miss Jenkyns, was going to have a party in my honour,
and that Captain and the Miss Browns were invited, I v ondered
much what would be the course of the evening. Card-tables,
with green-baize tops, were set out by daylight, just as usual; it
was the third week in November, so the evenings closed in about
four. Candles, and clean packs of cards were arranged on each
table. The fire was made up, the neat maid-servant had received
her last directions; and, there we stood dressed in our best, each
with a candle-lighter in our hands, ready to dart at the candles
as soon as the first knock came. Parties in Cranford were solemn
festivities, making the ladies feel gravely elated, as they sat
together in their best dresses. As soon as three had arrived, we
sat down to 'Preference',* I being the unlucky fourth. The next
four comers were put down immediately to another table; and
presently the tea-trays, which I had seen set out in the store-
room as I passed in the morning, were placed each on the middle
of a card-table. The china was delicate egg-shell; the old-
fashioned silver glittered with polishing; but the eatables were
of the slightest description. While the trays were yet on the
tables, Captain and the Miss Browns came in; and I could see,
that somehow or other the Captain was a favourite with all the
ladies present. Ruffled brows were smoothed, sharp voices
lowered at his approach. Miss Brown looked ill, and depressed
almost to gloom. Miss Jessie smiled as usual, and seemed nearly
as popular as her father. He immediately and quietly assumed
the man's place in the room; attended to everyone's wants,
lessened the pretty maid-servant's labour by waiting on empty
cups, and bread-and-butterless ladies; and yet did it all in so
easy and dignified a manner, and so much as if it were a matter
of course for the strong to attend to the weak, that he was a
true man throughout. He played for three-penny points with as
grave an interest as if they had been pounds; and yet, in all his
attention to strangers he had an eye on his suffering daughter;
for suffering I was sure she was, though to many eyes she might
only appear to be irritable. Miss Jessie could not play cards; but
she talked to the sitters-out, who, before her coming, had been

rather inclined to be cross. She sang, too, to an old cracked piano, which I think had been a spinnet in its youth. Miss Jessie sang 'Jock of Hazeldean'* a little out of tune; but we were none of us musical, though Miss Jenkyns beat time, out of time, by way of appearing to be so.

It was very good of Miss Jenkyns to do this; for I had seen that, a little before, she had been a good deal annoyed by Miss Jessie Brown's unguarded admission (*à propos* of Shetland wool) that she had an uncle, her mother's brother, who was a shopkeeper in Edinburgh. Miss Jenkyns tried to drown this confession by a terrible cough — for the Honourable Mrs Jamieson was sitting at the card-table nearest Miss Jessie, and what would she say or think, if she found out she was in the same room with a shopkeeper's niece! But Miss Jessie Brown (who had no tact, as we all agreed, the next morning) *would* repeat the information, and assure Miss Pole she could easily get her the identical Shetland wool required, 'through my uncle, who has the best assortment of Shetland goods of anyone in Edinbro''. It was to take the taste of this out of our mouths, and the sound of this out of our ears, that Miss Jenkyns proposed music; so I say again, it was very good of her to beat time to the song.

When the trays reappeared with biscuits and wine, punctually at a quarter to nine, there was conversation; comparing of cards, and talking over tricks; but, by-and-by, Captain Brown sported a bit of literature.

'Have you seen any numbers of "The Pickwick Papers"?'* said he. (They were then publishing in parts.) 'Capital thing!'

Now, Miss Jenkyns was daughter of a deceased rector of Cranford; and, on the strength of a number of manuscript sermons, and a pretty good library of divinity, considered herself literary, and looked upon any conversation about books as a challenge to her. So she answered and said, 'Yes, she had seen them; indeed, she might say she had read them.'

'And what do you think of them?' exclaimed Captain Brown. 'Aren't they famously good?'

So urged, Miss Jenkyns could not but speak.

'I must say I don't think they are by any means equal to Dr Johnson.* Still, perhaps, the author is young. Let him persevere, and who knows what he may become if he will take the great Doctor for his model.' This was evidently too much for Captain

Brown to take placidly; and I saw the words on the tip of his tongue before Miss Jenkyns had finished her sentence.

'It is quite a different sort of thing, my dear madam,' he began.

'I am quite aware of that,' returned she. 'And I make allowances, Captain Brown.'

'Just allow me to read you a scene out of this month's number,' pleaded he. 'I had it only this morning, and I don't think the company can have read it yet.'

'As you please,' said she, settling herself with an air of resignation. He read the account of the 'swarry' which Sam Weller gave at Bath.* Some of us laughed heartily. *I* did not dare, because I was staying in the house. Miss Jenkyns sat in patient gravity. When it was ended, she turned to me, and said with mild dignity,

'Fetch me "Rasselas",* my dear, out of the book-room.'

When I brought it to her, she turned to Captain Brown:

'Now allow *me* to read you a scene, and then the present company can judge between your favourite, Mr Boz* and Dr Johnson.'

She read one of the conversations between Rasselas and Imlac,* in a high-pitched majestic voice; and when she had ended, she said, 'I imagine I am now justified in my preference of Dr Johnson, as a writer of fiction.' The Captain screwed his lips up, and drummed on the table, but he did not speak. She thought she would give a finishing blow or two.

'I consider it vulgar, and below the dignity of literature, to publish in numbers.'

'How was the "Rambler"* published, Ma'am?' asked Captain Brown, in a low voice; which I think Miss Jenkyns could not have heard.

'Dr Johnson's style is a model for young beginners. My father recommended it to me when I began to write letters. – I have formed my own style upon it; I recommend it to your favourite.'

'I should be very sorry for him to exchange his style for any such pompous writing,' said Captain Brown.

Miss Jenkyns felt this as a personal affront, in a way of which the Captain had not dreamed. Epistolary writing, she and her friends considered as her *forte.** Many a copy of many a letter have I seen written and corrected on the slate, before she 'seized the half-hour just previous to post-time to assure' her friends of this or of that; and Dr Johnson was, as she said, her model in these compositions. She drew herself up with dignity, and only replied to Captain Brown's last remark by saying with marked emphasis on every syllable, 'I prefer Dr Johnson to Mr Boz.'

It is said – I won't vouch for the fact – that Captain Brown was heard to say, *sotto voce*,* 'D—n Dr Johnson!' If he did, he was penitent afterwards, as he showed by going to stand near Miss Jenkyns's armchair, and endeavouring to beguile her into conversation on some more pleasing subject. But she was inexorable. The next day, she made the remark I have mentioned, about Miss Jessie's dimples.

Chapter 2

THE CAPTAIN

It was impossible to live a month at Cranford, and not know the daily habits of each resident; and long before my visit was ended, I knew much concerning the whole Brown trio. There was nothing new to be discovered respecting their poverty; for they had spoken simply and openly about that from the very first. They made no mystery of the necessity for their being economical. All that remained to be discovered was the Captain's infinite kindness of heart, and the various modes in which, unconsciously to himself, he manifested it. Some little anecdotes were talked about for some time after they occurred. As we did not read much, and as all the ladies were pretty well suited with servants, there was a dearth of subjects for conversation. We therefore discussed the circumstance of the Captain taking a poor old woman's dinner out of her hands, one very slippery Sunday. He had met her returning from the bakehouse* as he came from church, and noticed her precarious footing; and, with the grave dignity with which he did everything, he relieved her of her burden, and steered along the street by her side, carrying her baked mutton and potatoes safely home. This was thought very eccentric; and it was rather expected that he would pay a round of calls, on the Monday morning, to explain and apologise to the Cranford sense of propriety: but he did no such thing; and then it was decided that he was ashamed, and was keeping out of sight. In a kindly pity for him, we began to say – 'After all, the Sunday morning's occurrence showed great goodness of heart'; and it was resolved that he should be comforted on his next appearance amongst us; but, lo! he came down upon us, untouched by any sense of shame, speaking loud and bass as ever, his head thrown back, his wig as jaunty and well-curled as usual, and we were obliged to conclude he had forgotten all about Sunday.

Miss Pole and Miss Jessie Brown had set up a kind of intimacy, on the strength of the Shetland wool and the new knitting stitches; so it happened that when I went to visit Miss

Pole, I saw more of the Browns than I had done while staying with Miss Jenkyns; who had never got over what she called Captain Brown's disparaging remarks upon Dr Johnson, as a writer of light and agreeable fiction. I found that Miss Brown was seriously ill of some lingering, incurable complaint, the pain occasioned by which gave the uneasy expression to her face that I had taken for unmitigated crossness. Cross, too, she was at times, when the nervous irritability occasioned by her disease became past endurance. Miss Jessie bore with her at these times even more patiently than she did with the bitter self-upbraidings by which they were invariably succeeded. Miss Brown used to accuse herself, not merely of hasty and irritable temper; but also of being the cause why her father and sister were obliged to pinch, in order to allow her the small luxuries which were necessaries in her condition. She would so fain* have made sacrifices for them and have lightened their cares, that the original generosity of her disposition added acerbity to her temper. All this was borne by Miss Jessie and her father with more than placidity – with absolute tenderness. I forgave Miss Jessie her singing out of tune, and her juvenility of dress, when I saw her at home. I came to perceive that Captain Brown's dark Brutus wig* and padded coat (alas! too often threadbare) were remnants of the military smartness of his youth, which he now wore unconsciously. He was a man of infinite resources, gained in his barrack experience. As he confessed, no one could black his boots to please him, except himself; but, indeed, he was not above saving the little maid-servant's labours in every way, – knowing, most likely, that his daughter's illness made the place a hard one.

He endeavoured to make peace with Miss Jenkyns soon after the memorable dispute I have named, by a present of a wooden fire-shovel (his own making), having heard her say how much the grating of an iron one annoyed her. She received the present with cool gratitude, and thanked him formally. When he was gone, she bade me put it away in the lumber-room; feeling, probably, that no present from a man who preferred Mr Boz to Dr Johnson could be less jarring than an iron fire-shovel.

Such was the state of things when I left Cranford and went to Drumble. I had, however, several correspondents who kept me *au fait** to the proceedings of the dear little town. There was Miss Pole, who was becoming as much absorbed in crochet as she had been once in knitting; and the burden of whose letter was something like, 'But don't you forget the white worsted at Flint's',* of the old song; for, at the end of every sentence of news, came a fresh direction as to some crochet commission which I was to execute for her. Miss Matilda Jenkyns (who did not mind being called Miss Matty, when Miss Jenkyns was not by) wrote nice, kind, rambling letters; now and then venturing into an opinion of her own; but suddenly pulling herself up, and either begging me not to name what she had said, as Deborah thought differently, and *she* knew; or else, putting in a postscript to the effect that, since writing the above, she had been talking over the subject with Deborah, and was quite convinced that, etc.; – (here, probably, followed a recantation of every opinion she had given in the letter). Then came Miss Jenkyns – Debōrah, as she liked Miss Matty to call her; her father having once said that the Hebrew name ought to be so pronounced. I secretly think she took the Hebrew prophetess* for a model in character; and, indeed, she was not unlike the stern prophetess in some ways; making allowance, of course, for modern customs and difference in dress. Miss Jenkyns wore a cravat, and a little bonnet like a jockey-cap, and altogether had the appearance of a strong-minded woman; although she would have despised the modern idea of women being equal to men. Equal, indeed! she knew they were superior. – But to return to her letters. Everything in them was stately and grand, like herself. I have been looking them over (dear Miss Jenkyns, how I honoured her!) and I will give an extract, more especially because it relates to our friend Captain Brown:—

'The Honourable Mrs Jamieson has only just quitted me; and, in the course of conversation, she communicated to me the intelligence, that she had yesterday received a call from her revered husband's quondam* friend, Lord Mauleverer. You will not easily conjecture what brought his lordship within the precincts of our little town. It was to see Captain Brown, with whom, it appears, his lordship was acquainted in the "plumed wars",* and who had the privilege of averting destruction from his lordship's head, when some great peril was impending over it, off the misnomered Cape of Good Hope. You know our friend the Honourable Mrs Jamieson's deficiency in the spirit of innocent curiosity; and you will therefore not be so much surprised when I tell you she was quite unable to disclose to me the exact nature of the peril in question. I was anxious, I confess, to ascertain in what manner Captain Brown, with his limited establishment, could receive so distinguished a guest; and I discovered that his lordship retired to rest, and, let us hope, to refreshing slumbers, at the Angel Hotel; but shared the Brunonian meals during the two days that he honoured Cranford with his august presence. Mrs Johnson, our civil butcher's wife, informs me that Miss Jessie purchased a leg of lamb; but, besides this, I can hear of no preparation whatever to give a suitable reception to so distinguished a visitor. Perhaps they entertained him with "the feast of reason and the flow of soul";* and to us, who are acquainted with Captain Brown's sad want of relish for "the pure wells of English undefiled",* it may be matter for congratulation, that he has had the opportunity of improving his taste by holding converse with an elegant and refined member of the British aristocracy. But from some mundane feelings who is free?'

Miss Pole and Miss Matty wrote to me by the same post. Such a piece of news as Lord Mauleverer's visit was not to be lost on the Cranford letter-writers: they made the most of it. Miss Matty humbly apologised for writing at the same time as her sister, who was so much more capable than she to describe the honour done to Cranford; but, in spite of a little bad spelling, Miss Matty's account gave me the best idea of the commotion occasioned by his lordship's visit, after it had occurred; for, except the people at the Angel, the Browns, Mrs Jamieson, and a little lad his lordship had sworn at for driving a dirty hoop against the aristocratic legs, I could not hear of anyone with whom his lordship had held conversation.

My next visit to Cranford was in the summer. There had been neither births, deaths, nor marriages since I was there last. Everybody lived in the same house, and wore pretty nearly the same well-preserved, old-fashioned clothes. The greatest event was, that Miss Jenkyns had purchased a new carpet for the drawing-room. Oh the busy work Miss Matty and I had in chasing the sunbeams, as they fell in an afternoon right down on this carpet through the blindless window! We spread newspapers over the places, and sat down to our book or our work; and, lo! in a quarter of an hour the sun had moved, and was blazing away on a fresh spot; and down again we went on our knees to alter the position of the newspapers. We were very busy, too, one whole morning before Miss Jenkyns gave her party, in following her directions, and in cutting out and stitching together pieces of newspaper, so as to form little paths to every chair, set for the expected visitors, lest their shoes might dirty or defile the purity of the carpet. Do you make paper paths for every guest to walk upon in London?

Captain Brown and Miss Jenkyns were not very cordial to each other. The literary dispute, of which I had seen the beginning, was a 'raw', the slightest touch on which made them wince. It was the only difference of opinion they had ever had; but that difference was enough. Miss Jenkyns could not refrain from talking *at* Captain Brown; and though he did not reply, he drummed with his fingers; which action she felt and resented as disparaging to Dr Johnson. He was rather ostentatious in his preference of the writings of Mr Boz; would walk through the street so absorbed in them, that he all but ran against Miss Jenkyns; and though his apologies were earnest and sincere, and though he did not, in fact, do more than startle her and himself, she owned to me she had rather he had knocked her down, if he had only been reading a higher style of literature. The poor, brave Captain! he looked older, and more worn, and his clothes were very threadbare. But he seemed as bright and cheerful as ever, unless he was asked about his daughter's health.

'She suffers a great deal, and she must suffer more; we do what we can to alleviate her pain — God's will be done!' He took off his hat at these last words. I found, from Miss Matty, that everything had been done, in fact. A medical man, of high repute in that country neighbourhood, had been sent for, and every injunction he had given was attended to, regardless of expense. Miss Matty was sure they denied themselves many things in order to make the invalid comfortable; but they never spoke about it; and as for Miss Jessie! 'I really think she's an angel,' said poor Miss Matty, quite overcome. 'To see her way of bearing with Miss Brown's crossness, and the bright face she puts on after she's been sitting up a whole night and scolded above half of it, is quite beautiful. Yet she looks as neat and as ready to welcome the Captain at breakfast-time, as if she had been asleep in the Queen's bed all night. My dear! you could never laugh at her prim little curls or her pink bows again, if you saw her as I have done.' I could only feel very penitent, and greet Miss Jessie with double respect when I met her next. She looked faded and pinched; and her lips began to quiver, as if she was very weak, when she spoke of her sister. But she brightened, and sent back the tears that were glittering in her pretty eyes, as she said: —

'But, to be sure, what a town Cranford is for kindness! I don't suppose anyone has a better dinner than usual cooked, but the best part of all comes in a little covered basin for my sister. The poor people will leave their earliest vegetables at our door for her. They speak short and gruff, as if they were ashamed of it; but I am sure it often goes to my heart to see their thoughtfulness.' The tears now came back and overflowed; but after a minute or two, she began to scold herself, and ended by going away, the same cheerful Miss Jessie as ever.

'But why does not this Lord Mauleverer do something for the man who saved his life?' said I.

'Why, you see, unless Captain Brown has some reason for it, he never speaks about being poor; and he walked along by his lordship, looking as happy and cheerful as a prince; and as they never called attention to their dinner by apologies, and as Miss Brown was better that day, and all seemed bright, I dare say his lordship never knew how much care there was in the background. He did send game in the winter pretty often, but now he is gone abroad.'

I had often occasion to notice the use that was made of fragments and small opportunities in Cranford; the rose-leaves that were gathered ere they fell, to make into a pot-pourri for someone who had no garden; the little bundles of lavender-flowers sent to strew the drawers of some town-dweller, or to burn in the chamber of some invalid. Things that many would despise, and actions which it seemed scarcely worth while to perform, were all attended to in Cranford. Miss Jenkyns stuck an apple full of cloves, to be heated and smell pleasantly in Miss Brown's room; and as she put in each clove, she uttered a Johnsonian sentence. Indeed, she never could think of the Browns without talking Johnson; and, as they were seldom absent from her thoughts just then, I heard many a rolling three-piled sentence.*

Captain Brown called one day to thank Miss Jenkyns for many little kindnesses, which I did not know until then that she had rendered. He had suddenly become like an old man; his deep bass voice had a quavering in it; his eyes looked dim, and the lines on his face were deep. He did not – could not – speak cheerfully of his daughter's state, but he talked with manly pious resignation, and not much. Twice over he said, 'What Jessie has been to us, God only knows!' and after the second time, he got up hastily, shook hands all round without speaking, and left the room.

That afternoon we perceived little groups in the street, all listening with faces aghast to some tale or other. Miss Jenkyns wondered what could be the matter, for some time before she took the undignified step of sending Jenny out to inquire.

Jenny came back with a white face of terror. 'Oh, Ma'am! oh, Miss Jenkyns, Ma'am! Captain Brown is killed by them nasty cruel railroads!' and she burst into tears. She, along with many others, had experienced the poor Captain's kindness.

'How? – where – where? Good God! Jenny, don't waste time in crying, but tell us something.' Miss Matty rushed out into the street at once, and collared the man who was telling the tale.

'Come in – come to my sister at once, – Miss Jenkyns, the rector's daughter. Oh, man, man! say it is not true,' – she cried, as she brought the affrighted carter, sleeking down his hair, into the drawing-room, where he stood with his wet boots on the new carpet, and no one regarded it.

'Please mum, it is true. I seed it myself,' and he shuddered at the recollection. 'The Captain was a-reading some new book as he was deep in, a-waiting for the down train; and there was a little lass as wanted to come to its mammy, and gave its sister the slip, and came toddling across the line. And he looked up sudden at the sound of the train coming, and seed the child, and he darted on the line and cotched it up,* and his foot slipped, and the train came over him in no time. Oh Lord, Lord! Mum, it's quite true – and they've come over to tell his daughters. The child's safe, though, with only a bang on its shoulder, as he threw it to its mammy. Poor Captain would be glad of that, mum, would not he? God bless him!' The great rough carter puckered up his manly face, and turned away to hide his tears. I turned to Miss Jenkyns. She looked very ill, as if she were going to faint, and signed to me to open the window.

'Matilda, bring me my bonnet. I must go to those girls. God pardon me if ever I have spoken contemptuously to the Captain!'

Miss Jenkyns arrayed herself to go out, telling Miss Matilda to give the man a glass of wine. While she was away, Miss

Matty and I huddled over the fire, talking in a low and awestruck voice. I know we cried quietly all the time.

Miss Jenkyns came home in a silent mood, and we durst not ask her many questions. She told us that Miss Jessie had fainted, and that she and Miss Pole had had some difficulty in bringing her round: but that, as soon as she recovered, she begged one of them to go and sit with her sister.

'Mr Hoggins says she cannot live many days, and she shall be spared this shock,' said Miss Jessie, shivering with feelings to which she dared not give way.

'But how can you manage, my dear?' asked Miss Jenkyns; 'you cannot bear up, she must see your tears.'

'God will help me – I will not give way – she was asleep when the news came; she may be asleep yet. She would be so utterly miserable, not merely at my father's death, but to think of what would become of me; she is so good to me.' She looked up earnestly in their faces with her soft true eyes, and Miss Pole told Miss Jenkyns afterwards she could hardly bear it, knowing, as she did, how Miss Brown treated her sister.

However, it was settled according to Miss Jessie's wish. Miss Brown was to be told her father had been summoned to take a short journey on railway business. They had managed it in some way – Miss Jenkyns could not exactly say how. Miss Pole was to stop with Miss Jessie. Mrs Jamieson had sent to inquire. And this was all we heard that night; and a sorrowful night it was. The next day a full account of the fatal accident was in the country paper, which Miss Jenkyns took in. Her eyes were very weak, she said, and she asked me to read it. When I came to the 'gallant gentleman was deeply engaged in the perusal of a number of "Pickwick", which he had just received', Miss Jenkyns shook her head long and solemnly, and then sighed out, 'Poor, dear, infatuated man!'

The corpse was to be taken from the station to the parish church, there to be interred. Miss Jessie had set her heart on following it to the grave; and no dissuasives* could alter her resolve. Her restraint upon herself made her almost obstinate; she resisted all Miss Pole's entreaties, and Miss Jenkyns's advice. At last Miss Jenkyns gave up the point; and after a silence, which I feared portended some deep displeasure against Miss Jessie, Miss Jenkyns said she should accompany the latter to the funeral.

'It is not fit for you to go alone. It would be against both propriety and humanity were I to allow it.'

Miss Jessie seemed as if she did not half like this arrangement; but her obstinacy, if she had any, had been exhausted in her determination to go to the internment. She longed, poor thing! I have no doubt, to cry alone over the grave of the dear father to whom she had been all in all; and to give way, for one little half-hour, uninterrupted by sympathy, and unobserved by friendship. But it was not to be. That afternoon Miss Jenkyns sent out for a yard of black crape, and employed herself busily in trimming the little black silk bonnet I have spoken about. When it was finished she put it on, and looked at us for approbation – admiration she despised. I was full of sorrow, but, by one of those whimsical thoughts which come unbidden into our heads, in times of deepest grief, I no sooner saw the bonnet than I was reminded of a helmet; and in that hybrid bonnet, half-helmet, half-jockey cap, did Miss Jenkyns attend Captain Brown's funeral; and I believe supported Miss Jessie with a tender indulgent firmness which was invaluable, allowing her to weep her passionate fill before they left.

Miss Pole, Miss Matty, and I, meanwhile, attended to Miss Brown: and hard work we found it to relieve her querulous and never-ending complaints. But if we were so weary and dispirited, what must Miss Jessie have been! Yet she came back almost calm, as if she had gained a new strength. She put off her mourning dress, and came in, looking pale and gentle; thanking us each with a soft long pressure of the hand. She could even smile – a faint, sweet, wintry smile, as if to reassure us of her power to endure; but her look made our eyes fill suddenly with tears, more than if she had cried outright.

It was settled that Miss Pole was to remain with her all the watching live-long night; and that Miss Matty and I were to return in the morning to relieve them, and give Miss Jessie the opportunity for a few hours of sleep. But when the morning came, Miss Jenkyns appeared at the breakfast table, equipped in her helmet bonnet, and ordered Miss Matty to stay at home, as she meant to go and help to nurse. She was evidently in a state of great friendly excitement, which she showed by eating her breakfast standing, and scolding the household all round.

No nursing – no energetic strong-minded woman could help Miss Brown now. There was that in the room as we entered, which was stronger than us all, and made us shrink into solemn awestruck helplessness. Miss Brown was dying. We hardly knew her voice, it was so devoid of the complaining tone we had always associated with it. Miss Jessie told me afterwards that it, and her face too, were just what they had been formerly, when her mother's death left her the young anxious head of the family, of whom only Miss Jessie survived.

She was conscious of her sister's presence, though not, I think, of ours. We stood a little behind the curtain: Miss Jessie knelt with her face near her sister's, in order to catch the last soft awful whispers.

'Oh, Jessie! Jessie! How selfish I have been! God forgive me for letting you sacrifice yourself for me as you did. I have so loved you – and yet I have thought only of myself. God forgive me!'

'Hush, love! hush!' said Miss Jessie, sobbing.

'And my father! my dear, dear father! I will not complain now, if God will give me strength to be patient. But, oh, Jessie! tell my father how I longed and yearned to see him at last, and to ask his forgiveness. He can never know now how I loved him – oh! if I might but tell him, before I die; what a life of sorrow his has been, and I have done so little to cheer him!'

A light came into Miss Jessie's face. 'Would it comfort you, dearest, to think that he does know – would it comfort you, love, to know that his cares, his sorrows—' Her voice quivered, but she steadied it into calmness, – 'Mary! he has gone before you to the place where the weary are at rest. He knows now how you loved him.'

A strange look, which was not distress, came over Miss Brown's face. She did not speak for some time, but then we saw her lips form the words, rather than heard the sound – 'Father, mother, Harry, Archy!' – then, as if it was a new idea throwing a filmy shadow over her darkening mind – 'But you will be alone – Jessie!'

Miss Jessie had been feeling this all during the silence, I think; for the tears rolled down her cheeks like rain, at these words; and she could not answer at first. Then she put her hands together tight, and lifted them up, and said, – but not to us—

'Though He slay me, yet will I trust in Him.'*

In a few moments more, Miss Brown lay calm and still; never to sorrow or murmur more.

After this second funeral, Miss Jenkyns insisted that Miss Jessie should come to stay with her, rather than go back to the desolate house; which, in fact, we learned from Miss Jessie, must now be given up, as she had not wherewithal to maintain it. She had something about twenty pounds a year, besides the interest of the money for which the furniture would sell; but she could not live upon that: and so we talked over her qualifications for earning money.

'I can sew neatly,' said she, 'and I like nursing. I think, too, I could manage a house, if anyone would try me as housekeeper; or I would go into a shop, as saleswoman, if they would have patience with me at first.'

Miss Jenkyns declared, in an angry voice, that she should do no such thing; and talked to herself about 'some people having no idea of their rank as a Captain's daughter', nearly an hour afterwards, when she brought Miss Jessie up a basin of delicately-made arrow-root, and stood over her like a dragoon until the last spoonful was finished: then she disappeared. Miss Jessie began to tell me some more of the plans which had suggested themselves to her, and insensibly fell into talking of the days that were past and gone, and interested me so much, I neither knew nor heeded how time passed. We were both startled when Miss Jenkyns reappeared, and caught us crying. I was afraid lest she would be displeased, as she often said that crying hindered digestion, and I knew she wanted Miss Jessie to get strong; but, instead, she looked queer and excited, and fidgeted round us without saying anything. At last she spoke. 'I have been so much startled – no, I've not been at all startled – don't mind me, my dear Miss Jessie – I've been very much surprised – in fact, I've had a caller, whom you knew once, my dear Miss Jessie—'

Miss Jessie went very white, then flushed scarlet, and looked eagerly at Miss Jenkyns –

'A gentleman, my dear, who wants to know if you would see him.'

'Is it? – it is not—' stammered out Miss Jessie – and got no farther.

'This is his card,' said Miss Jenkyns, giving it to Miss Jessie; and while her head was bent over it, Miss Jenkyns went through a series of winks and odd faces to me, and formed her lips into a long sentence, of which, of course, I could not understand a word.

'May he come up?' asked Miss Jenkyns at last.

'Oh, yes! certainly!' said Miss Jessie, as much as to say, this is your house, you may show any visitor where you like. She took up some knitting of Miss Matty's and began to be very busy, though I could see how she trembled all over.

Miss Jenkyns rang the bell, and told the servant who answered it to show Major Gordon upstairs; and, presently, in walked a tall, fine, frank-looking man of forty, or upwards. He shook hands with Miss Jessie; but he could not see her eyes, she kept them so fixed on the ground. Miss Jenkyns asked me if I would come and help her to tie up the preserves in the store-room; and, though Miss Jessie plucked at my gown, and even looked up at me with begging eye, I durst not refuse to go where Miss Jenkyns asked. Instead of tying up preserves in the store-room, however, we went to talk in the dining-room; and there Miss Jenkyns told me what Major Gordon had told her; – how he had served in the same regiment with Captain Brown, and had become acquainted with Miss Jessie, then a sweet-looking, blooming girl of eighteen; how the acquaintance had grown into love, on his part, though it had been some years before he had spoken; how, on becoming possessed, through the will of an uncle, of a good estate in Scotland, he had offered, and been refused, though with so much agitation, and evident distress, that he was sure she was not indifferent to him; and how he had discovered that the obstacle was the fell disease which was, even then, too surely threatening her sister. She had mentioned that the surgeons foretold intense suffering; and there was no one but herself to nurse her poor Mary, or cheer and comfort her father during the time of illness. They had had long discussions; and, on her refusal to pledge herself to him as his wife, when all should be over, he had grown angry, and broken off entirely, and gone abroad, believing that she was a cold-hearted person, whom he would do well to forget. He had been travelling in the East, and was on his return home when, at Rome, he saw the account of Captain Brown's death in 'Galignani'.*

Just then Miss Matty, who had been out all the morning, and had only lately returned to the house, burst in with a face of dismay and outraged propriety: –

'Oh, goodness me!' she said. 'Deborah, there's a gentleman sitting in the drawing-room, with his arm round Miss Jessie's waist!' Miss Matty's eyes looked large with terror.

Miss Jenkyns snubbed her down in an instant: —

'The most proper place in the world for his arm to be in. Go away, Matilda, and mind your own business.' This from her sister, who had hitherto been a model of feminine decorum, was a blow for poor Miss Matty, and with a double shock she left the room.

The last time I ever saw poor Miss Jenkyns was many years after this. Mrs Gordon had kept up a warm and affectionate intercourse with all at Cranford. Miss Jenkyns, Miss Matty, and Miss Pole had all been to visit her, and returned with wonderful accounts of her house, her husband, her dress, and her looks. For, with happiness, something of her early bloom returned; she had been a year or two younger than we had taken her for. Her eyes were always lovely, and, as Mrs Gordon, her dimples were not out of place. At the time to which I have referred, when I last saw Miss Jenkyns, that lady was old and feeble, and had lost something of her strong mind. Little Flora Gordon was staying with the Misses Jenkyns, and when I came in she was reading aloud to Miss Jenkyns, who lay feeble and changed on the sofa. Flora put down the 'Rambler' when I came in.

'Ah!' said Miss Jenkyns, 'you find me changed, my dear. I can't see as I used to do. If Flora were not here to read to me, I hardly know how I should get through the day. Did you ever read the "Rambler"? It's a wonderful book — wonderful! and the most improving reading for Flora' — (which I dare say it would have been, if she could have read half the words without spelling, and could have understood the meaning of a third) — 'better than that strange old book, with the queer name, poor Captain Brown was killed for reading — that book by Mr Boz, you know — "Old Poz"; when I was a girl, but that's a long time ago, — I acted Lucy in "Old Poz"'* — she babbled on long enough for Flora to get a good long spell at the 'Christmas Carol',* which Miss Matty had left on the table.

Chapter 3

A LOVE AFFAIR OF LONG AGO

I thought that probably my connection with Cranford would cease after Miss Jenkyns's death; at least, that it would have to be kept up by correspondence, which bears much the same relation to personal intercourse that the books of dried plants I sometimes see ('Hortus Siccus',* I think they call the thing), do to the living and fresh flowers in the lanes and meadows. I was pleasantly surprised, therefore, by receiving a letter from Miss Pole (who had always come in for a supplementary week after my annual visit to Miss Jenkyns) proposing that I should go and stay with her; and then, in a couple of days after my acceptance, came a note from Miss Matty, in which, in a rather circuitous and very humble manner, she told me how much pleasure I should confer, if I could spend a week or two with her, either before or after I had been at Miss Pole's; 'for,' she said, 'since my dear sister's death, I am well aware I have no attraction to offer; it is only to the kindness of my friends that I can owe their company.'

Of course, I promised to come to dear Miss Matty, as soon as I had ended my visit to Miss Pole; and the day after my arrival at Cranford, I went to see her, much wondering what the house would be like without Miss Jenkyns, and rather dreading the changed aspect of things. Miss Matty began to cry as soon as she saw me. She was evidently nervous from having anticipated my call. I comforted her as well as I could; and I found the best consolation I could give was the honest praise that came from my heart as I spoke of the deceased. Miss Matty slowly shook her head over each virtue as it was named and attributed to her sister; at last she could not restrain the tears which had long been silently flowing, but hid her face behind her handkerchief, and sobbed aloud.

'Dear Miss Matty!' said I, taking her hand – for indeed I did not know in what way to tell her how sorry I was for her, left deserted in the world. She put down her handkerchief, and said –

'My dear, I'd rather you did not call me Matty. *She* did not like it; but I did many a thing she did not like, I'm afraid – and now she's gone! If you please, my love, will you call me Matilda?'

I promised faithfully, and began to practise the new name with Miss Pole that very day; and, by degrees, Miss Matilda's feeling on the subject was known through Cranford, and we all tried to drop the more familiar name, but with so little success that by and by we gave up the attempt.

My visit to Miss Pole was very quiet. Miss Jenkyns had so long taken the lead in Cranford, that, now she was gone, they hardly knew how to give a party. The Honourable Mrs Jamieson, to whom Miss Jenkyns herself had always yielded the post of honour, was fat and inert, and very much at the mercy of her old servants. If they chose that she should give a party, they reminded her of the necessity for so doing; if not, she let it alone. There was all the more time for me to hear old-world stories from Miss Pole, while she sat knitting, and I making my father's shirts. I always took a quantity of plain sewing to Cranford; for, as we did not read much, or walk much, I found it a capital time to get through my work. One of Miss Pole's stories related to a shadow of a love affair that was dimly perceived or suspected long years before.

Presently, the time arrived when I was to remove to Miss Matilda's house. I found her timid and anxious about the arrangements for my comfort. Many a time, while I was unpacking, did she come backwards and forwards to stir the fire, which burned all the worse for being so frequently poked.

'Have you drawers enough, dear?' asked she. 'I don't know exactly how my sister used to arrange them. She had capital methods. I am sure she would have trained a servant in a week to make a better fire than this, and Fanny has been with me four months.'

This subject of servants was a standing grievance, and I could not wonder much at it; for if gentlemen were scarce, and almost unheard of in the 'genteel society' of Cranford, they or their counterparts – handsome young men – abounded in the lower classes. The pretty neat servant-maids had their choice of desirable 'followers';* and their mistresses, without having the sort of mysterious dread of men and matrimony that Miss Matilda had, might well feel a little anxious, lest the heads of their comely maids should be turned by the joiner, or the butcher, or the gardener; who were obliged, by their callings, to come to the house; and who, as ill-luck would have it, were generally handsome and unmarried. Fanny's lovers, if she had any – and Miss Matilda suspected her of so many flirtations, that, if she had not been very pretty, I should have doubted her having one – were a constant anxiety to her mistress. She was forbidden, by the articles of her engagement, to have 'followers'; and though she had answered innocently enough, doubling up the hem of her apron as she spoke, 'Please, ma'am, I never had more than one at a time', Miss Matty prohibited that one. But a vision of a man seemed to haunt the kitchen. Fanny assured me that it was all fancy; or else I should have said myself that I had seen a man's coat-tails whisk into the scullery once, when I went on an errand into the store-room at night; and another evening, when, our watches having stopped, I went to look at the clock, there was a very odd appearance, singularly like a young man squeezed up between the clock and the back of the open kitchen-door: and I thought Fanny snatched up the candle very hastily, so as to throw the shadow on the clock-face, while she very positively told me the time half-an-hour too early, as we found out afterwards by the church-clock. But I did not add to Miss Matty's anxieties by naming my suspicions, especially as Fanny said to me, the next day, that it was such a queer kitchen for having odd shadows about it, she really was almost afraid to stay; 'for you know Miss,' she added, 'I don't see a creature from six o'clock tea, till Missus rings the bell for prayers at ten.'

However, it so fell out that Fanny had to leave; and Miss Matilda begged me to stay and 'settle her'* with the new maid; to which I consented, after I had heard from my father that he did not want me at home. The new servant was a rough, honest-looking country-girl, who had only lived in a farm place before; but I liked her looks when she came to be hired; and I promised Miss Matilda to put her in the ways of the house. The said ways were religiously such as Miss Matilda thought her sister would approve. Many a domestic rule and regulation had been a subject of plaintive whispered murmur to me, during Miss Jenkyns's life; but now that she was gone, I do not think that even I, who was a favourite, durst have suggested an alteration. To give an instance: we constantly adhered to the forms which were observed, at meal times, in 'my father, the Rector's house'.

Accordingly, we had always wine and dessert; but the decanters were only filled when there was a party; and what remained was seldom touched, though we had two wine glasses apiece every day after dinner, until the next festive occasion arrived; when the state of the remainder wine was examined into, in a family council. The dregs were often given to the poor; but occasionally, when a good deal had been left at the last party (five months ago, it might be), it was added to some of a fresh bottle, brought up from the cellar. I fancy poor Captain Brown did not much like wine; for I noticed he never finished his first glass, and most military men take several. Then, as to our dessert, Miss Jenkyns used to gather currants and gooseberries for it herself, which I sometimes thought would have tasted better fresh from the trees; but then, as Miss Jenkyns observed, there would have been nothing for dessert in summer-time. As it was, we felt very genteel with our two glasses apiece, and a dish of gooseberries at the top, of currants and biscuits at the sides, and two decanters at the bottom. When oranges came in, a curious proceeding was gone through. Miss Jenkyns did not like to cut the fruit; for, as she observed, the juice all ran out nobody knew where; sucking (only I think she used some more recondite word) was in fact the only way of enjoying oranges; but then there was the unpleasant association with a ceremony frequently gone through by little babies; and so, after dessert, in orange season, Miss Jenkyns and Miss Matty used to rise up, possess themselves each of an orange in silence, and withdraw to the privacy of their own rooms, to indulge in sucking oranges.

I had once or twice tried, on such occasions, to prevail on Miss Matty to stay; and had succeeded in her sister's life-time. I held up a screen,* and did not look, and, as she said, she tried not to make the noise very offensive; but now that she was left alone, she seemed quite horrified when I begged her to remain with me in the warm dining-parlour, and enjoy her orange as she liked best. And so it was in everything. Miss Jenkyns's rules were made more stringent than ever, because the framer of them was gone where there could be no appeal. In all things else Miss Matilda was meek and undecided to a fault. I have heard Fanny turn her round twenty times in a morning about dinner, just as the little hussy chose; and I sometimes fancied she worked on Miss Matilda's weakness in order to bewilder her, and to make her feel more in the power of her clever servant. I determined

that I would not leave her till I had seen what sort of person
Martha was; and, if I found her trustworthy, I would tell her
not to trouble her mistress with every little decision.

Martha was blunt and plain-spoken to a fault; otherwise she
was a brisk, well-meaning, but very ignorant girl. She had not
been with us a week before Miss Matilda and I were astounded
one morning by the receipt of a letter from a cousin of hers,
who had been twenty or thirty years in India, and who had
lately, as we had seen by the 'Army List',* returned to England,
bringing with him an invalid wife, who had never been introduced to her English relations. Major Jenkyns wrote to propose
that he and his wife should spend a night at Cranford, on his
way to Scotland – at the inn, if it did not suit Miss Matilda to
receive them into her house; in which case, they should hope to
be with her as much as possible during the day. Of course, it
must suit her, as she said; for all Cranford knew that she had
her sister's bedroom at liberty; but I am sure she wished the
Major had stopped in India and forgotten his cousins out and
out.

'Oh! how must I manage?' asked she, helplessly. 'If Deborah
had been alive, she would have known what to do with a
gentleman-visitor. Must I put razors in his dressing-room? Dear!
dear! and I've got none. Deborah would have had them. And
slippers, and coat-brushes?' I suggested that probably he would
bring all these things with him. 'And after dinner, how am I to
know when to get up, and leave him to his wine? Deborah
would have done it so well; she would have been quite in her
element. Will he want coffee, do you think?' I undertook the
management of the coffee, and told her I would instruct Martha
in the art of waiting, in which it must be owned she was terribly
deficient; and that I had no doubt Major and Mrs Jenkyns
would understand the quiet mode in which a lady lived by
herself in a country town. But she was sadly fluttered. I made
her empty her decanters, and bring up two fresh bottles of wine.
I wished I could have prevented her from being present at my
instructions to Martha; for she frequently cut in with some fresh
direction, muddling the poor girl's mind, as she stood open-
mouthed, listening to us both.

'Hand the vegetables round,' said I (foolishly, I see now – for
it was aiming at more than we could accomplish with quietness
and simplicity): and then, seeing her look bewildered, I added,

'Take the vegetables round to people, and let them help themselves.'

'And mind you go first to the ladies,' put in Miss Matilda. 'Always go to the ladies before gentlemen, when you are waiting.'

'I'll do it as you tell me, ma'am,' said Martha; 'but I like the lads best.'

We felt very uncomfortable and shocked at this speech of Martha's; yet I don't think she meant any harm; and, on the whole, she attended very well to our directions, except that she 'nudged' the Major, when he did not help himself as soon as she expected, to the potatoes, while she was handing them round.

The Major and his wife were quiet, unpretending people enough when they did come; languid, as all East Indians are, I suppose. We were rather dismayed at their bringing two servants with them, a Hindoo body-servant for the Major, and a steady elderly maid for his wife; but they slept at the inn, and took off a good deal of the responsibility of attending carefully to their master's and mistress's comfort. Martha, to be sure, had never ended her staring at the East Indian's white turban, and brown complexion, and I saw that Miss Matilda shrunk away from him a little as he waited at dinner. Indeed, she asked me, when they were gone, if he did not remind me of Blue Beard?* On the whole, the visit was most satisfactory, and is a subject of conversation even now with Miss Matilda; at the time, it greatly excited Cranford, and even stirred up the apathetic and Honourable Mrs Jamieson to some expression of interest, when I went to call and thank her for the kind answers she had vouchsafed to Miss Matilda's inquiries as to the arrangement of a gentleman's dressing-room – answers which I must confess she had given in the wearied manner of the Scandinavian prophetess,—

Leave me, leave me to repose.*

And *now* I come to the love affair.

It seems that Miss Pole had a cousin, once or twice removed, who had offered to Miss Matty long ago. Now, this cousin lived four or five miles from Cranford on his own estate; but his property was not large enough to entitle him to rank higher than a yeoman; or rather, with something of the 'pride which apes humility',* he had refused to push himself on, as so many of his class had done, into the ranks of the squires. He would

not allow himself to be called Thomas Holbrook, *Esq*; he even
sent back letters with this address, telling the postmistress at
Cranford that his name was *Mr* Thomas Holbrook, yeoman. He
rejected all domestic innovations; he would have the house door
stand open in summer, and shut in winter, without knocker or
bell to summon a servant. The closed fist or the knob of the
stick did this office for him, if he found the door locked. He
despised every refinement which had not its root deep down in
humanity. If people were not ill, he saw no necessity for
moderating his voice. He spoke the dialect of the country in
perfection, and constantly used it in conversation; although
Miss Pole (who gave me these particulars) added, that he read
aloud more beautifully and with more feeling than anyone she
had ever heard, except the late Rector.

'And how came Miss Matilda not to marry him?' asked I.

'Oh, I don't know. She was willing enough, I think; but you
know Cousin Thomas would not have been enough of a
gentleman for the Rector, and Miss Jenkyns.'

'Well! but they were not to marry him,' said I, impatiently.

'No; but they did not like Miss Matty to marry below her
rank. You know she was the Rector's daughter, and somehow
they are related to Sir Peter Arley: Miss Jenkyns thought a deal
of that.'

'Poor Miss Matty!' said I.

'Nay, now, I don't know anything more than that he offered
and was refused. Miss Matty might not like him – and Miss
Jenkyns might never have said a word – it is only a guess of
mine.'

'Has she ever seen him since?' I inquired.

'No, I think not. You see, Woodley, Cousin Thomas's house,
lies half-way between Cranford and Misselton; and I know he
made Misselton his market-town very soon after he had offered
to Miss Matty; and I don't think he has been into Cranford
above once or twice since – once, when I was walking with Miss
Matty, in High Street; and suddenly she darted from me, and
went up Shire Lane. A few minutes after, I was startled by
meeting Cousin Thomas.'

'How old is he?' I asked, after a pause of castle-building.

'He must be about seventy, I think, my dear,' said Miss Pole,
blowing up my castle,* as if by gunpowder, into small
fragments.

Very soon after – at least during my long visit to Miss Matilda – I had the opportunity of seeing Mr Holbrook; seeing, too, his first encounter with his former love, after thirty or forty years' separation. I was helping to decide whether any of the new assortment of coloured silks which they had just received at the shop, would do to match a grey and black mousseline-de-laine* that wanted a new breadth, when a tall, thin, Don Quixote-looking* old man came into the shop for some woollen gloves. I had never seen the person (who was rather striking) before, and I watched him rather attentively, while Miss Matty listened to the shopman. The stranger wore a blue coat with brass buttons, drab breeches, and gaiters, and drummed with his fingers on the counter until he was attended to. When he answered the shopboy's question, 'What can I have the pleasure of showing you today, Sir?' I saw Miss Matilda start, and then suddenly sit down; and instantly I guessed who it was. She had made some inquiry which had to be carried round to the other shopman.

'Miss Jenkyns wants the black sarsenet* two-and-twopence the yard'; and Mr Holbrook had caught the name, and was across the shop in two strides.

'Matty – Miss Matilda – Miss Jenkyns! God bless my soul! I should not have known you. How are you? how are you?' He kept shaking her hand in a way which proved the warmth of his friendship; but he repeated so often, as if to himself, 'I should not have known you!' that any sentimental romance which I might be inclined to build, was quite done away with by his manner.

However, he kept talking to us all the time we were in the shop; and then waving the shopman with the unpurchased gloves on one side, with 'Another time, sir! another time!' he walked home with us. I am happy to say my client, Miss Matilda, also left the shop in an equally bewildered state, not having purchased either green or red silk. Mr Holbrook was evidently full with honest, loud-spoken joy at meeting his old love again; he touched on the changes that had taken place; he even spoke of Miss Jenkyns as 'Your poor sister! Well, well! we have all our faults'; and bade us good-bye with many a hope that he should soon see Miss Matty again. She went straight to her room; and never came back till our early tea-time, when I thought she looked as if she had been crying.

Chapter 4

A VISIT TO AN OLD BACHELOR

A few days after, a note came from Mr Holbrook, asking us –
impartially asking both of us – in a formal, old-fashioned style,
to spend a day at his house – a long June day – for it was June
now. He named that he had also invited his cousin, Miss Pole;
so that we might join in a fly,* which could be put up at his
house.

I expected Miss Matty to jump at this invitation; but, no!
Miss Pole and I had the greatest difficulty in persuading her to
go. She thought it was improper; and was even half annoyed
when we utterly ignored the idea of any impropriety in her going
with two other ladies to see her old lover. Then came a more
serious difficulty. She did not think Deborah would have liked
her to go. This took us half a day's good hard talking to get
over; but, at the first sentence of relenting, I seized the opportunity, and wrote and despatched an acceptance in her name –
fixing day and hour, that all might be decided and done with.

The next morning she asked me if I would go down to the
shop with her; and there, after much hesitation, we chose out
three caps to be sent home and tried on, that the most becoming
might be selected to take with us on Thursday.

She was in a state of silent agitation all the way to Woodley.*
She had evidently never been there before; and, although she
little dreamt I knew anything of her early story, I could perceive
she was in a tremor at the thought of seeing the place which
might have been her home, and round which it is probable that
many of her innocent girlish imaginations had clustered. It was
a long drive there, through paved jolting lanes. Miss Matilda sat
bolt upright, and looked wistfully out of the windows, as we
drew near the end of our journey. The aspect of the country was
quiet and pastoral. Woodley stood among fields; and there was
an old-fashioned garden, where roses and currant-bushes
touched each other, and where the feathery asparagus formed a
pretty background to the pinks and gilly-flowers; there was no

drive up to the door: we got out at a little gate, and walked up a straight box-edged path.

'My cousin might make a drive, I think,' said Miss Pole, who was afraid of ear-ache, and had only her cap on.

'I think it is very pretty,' said Miss Matty, with a soft plaintiveness in her voice, and almost in a whisper; for just then Mr Holbrook appeared at the door, rubbing his hands in very effervescence of hospitality. He looked more like my idea of Don Quixote than ever, and yet the likeness was only external. His respectable housekeeper stood modestly at the door to bid us welcome; and, while she led the elder ladies upstairs to a bed-room, I begged to look about the garden. My request evidently pleased the old gentleman; who took me all round the place, and showed me his six-and-twenty cows, named after the different letters of the alphabet. As we went along, he surprised me occasionally by repeating apt and beautiful quotations from the poets, ranging easily from Shakespeare and George Herbert* to those of our own day. He did this as naturally as if he were thinking aloud, that their true and beautiful words were the best expression he could find for what he was thinking or feeling. To be sure, he called Byron* 'my lord Bẙrron', and pronounced the name of Goethe strictly in accordance with the English sound of the letters – 'As Goëthe says, "Ye ever-verdant palaces",'* etc. Altogether, I never met with a man, before or since, who had spent so long a life in a secluded and not impressive country, with ever-increasing delight in the daily and yearly change of season and beauty.

When he and I went in, we found that dinner was nearly ready in the kitchen, – for so I suppose the room ought to be called, as there were oak dressers and cupboards all round, all over by the side of the fire-place, and only a small Turkey carpet in the middle of the flag-floor.* The room might have been easily made into a handsome dark-oak dining-parlour, by removing the oven, and a few other appurtenances of a kitchen, which were evidently never used; the real cooking place being at some distance. The room in which we were expected to sit was a stiffly furnished, ugly apartment; but that in which we did sit was what Mr Holbrook called the counting-house, when he paid his labourers their weekly wages, at a great desk near the door. The rest of the pretty sitting-room – looking into the orchard, and all covered over with dancing tree-shadows – was filled with books. They lay on the ground, they covered the walls, they strewed the table. He was evidently half ashamed and half proud of his extravagance in this respect. They were of all kinds, – poetry, and wild weird tales prevailing. He evidently chose his books in accordance with his own tastes, not because such and such were classical, or established favourites.

'Ah!' he said, 'we farmers ought not to have much time for reading; yet somewhow one can't help it.'

'What a pretty room!' said Miss Matty, *sotto voce.*

'What a pleasant place!' said I, aloud, almost simultaneously.

'Nay! if you like it,' – replied he; 'but can you sit on these great black leather three-cornered chairs? I like it better than the best parlour; but I thought ladies would take that for the smarter place.'

It was the smarter place; but, like most smart things, not at all pretty, or pleasant, or home-like; so, while we were at dinner, the servant-girl dusted and scrubbed the counting-house chairs, and we sat there all the rest of the day.

We had pudding before meat; and I thought Mr Holbrook was going to make some apology for his old-fashioned ways, for he began, –

'I don't know whether you like new-fangled ways.'

'Oh! not at all!' said Miss Matty.

'No more do I,' said he. 'My housekeeper *will* have these in her new fashion; or else I tell her, that when I was a young man, we used to keep strictly to my father's rule, "No broth, no ball; no ball, no beef"; and always began dinner with broth. Then we had suet puddings, boiled in the broth with the beef; and then the meat itself. If we did not sup our broth, we had no ball, which we liked a deal better; and the beef came last of all, and only those had it who had done justice to the broth and the ball. Now folks begin with sweet things, and turn their dinners topsy-turvy.'

When the ducks and green peas came, we looked at each other in dismay; we had only two-pronged, black-handled forks. It is true, the steel was as bright as silver; but what were we to do? Miss Matty picked up her peas, one by one, on the point of the prongs, much as Aminé ate her grains of rice after her previous feast with the Ghoul.* Miss Pole sighed over her delicate young peas as she left them on one side of her plate untasted; for they *would* drop between the prongs. I looked at my host: the peas were going wholesale into his capacious mouth, shovelled up by his large round-ended knife. I saw, I imitated, I survived!* My friends, in spite of my precedent, could not muster up courage enough to do an ungenteel thing; and, if Mr Holbrook had not been so heartily hungry, he would probably have seen that the good peas went away almost untouched.

After dinner, a clay pipe was brought in, and a spittoon; and, asking us to retire to another room, where he would soon join us if we disliked tobacco-smoke, he presented his pipe to Miss Matty, and requested her to fill the bowl. This was a compliment to a lady in his youth; but it was rather inappropriate to propose it as an honour to Miss Matty, who had been trained by her sister to hold smoking of every kind in utter abhorrence. But if it was a shock to her refinement, it was also a gratification to her feelings to be thus selected; so she daintily stuffed the strong tobacco into the pipe; and then we withdrew.

'It is very pleasant dining with a bachelor,' said Miss Matty, softly, as we settled ourselves in the counting-house. 'I only hope it is not improper; so many pleasant things are!'

'What a number of books he has!' said Miss Pole, looking round the room. 'And how dusty they are!'

'I think it must be like one of the great Dr Johnson's rooms,' said Miss Matty. 'What a superior man your cousin must be!'

'Yes!' said Miss Pole; 'he's a great reader; but I am afraid he has got into very uncouth habits with living alone.'

'Oh! uncouth is too hard a word. I should call him eccentric; very clever people always are!' replied Miss Matty.

When Mr Holbrook returned, he proposed a walk in the fields; but the two elder ladies were afraid of damp, and dirt; and had only very unbecoming calashes* to put over their caps; so they declined; and I was again his companion in a turn which he said he was obliged to take, to see after his men. He strode along, either wholly forgetting my existence, or soothed into silence by his pipe – and yet it was not silence exactly. He walked before me, with a stooping gait, his hands clasped behind him; and, as some tree or cloud, or glimpse of distant upland pastures, struck him, he quoted poetry to himself; saying it out loud in a grand sonorous voice, with just the emphasis that true feeling and appreciation give. We came upon an old cedar-tree, which stood at one end of the house;

The cedar spreads his dark-green layers of shade.*

'Capital term – "layers!" Wonderful man!' I did not know whether he was speaking to me or not; but I put in an assenting 'wonderful', although I knew nothing about it; just because I was tired of being forgotten, and of being consequently silent.

He turned sharp round. 'Aye! you may say "wonderful". Why, when I saw the review of his poems in "Blackwood",* I set off within an hour, and walked seven miles to Misselton (for the horses were not in the way) and ordered them. Now, what colour are ash-buds in March?'

Is the man going mad? thought I. He is very like Don Quixote.

'What colour are they, I say?' repeated he vehemently.

'I am sure I don't know, sir,' said I, with the meekness of ignorance.

'I knew you didn't. No more did I – an old fool that I am! till this young man comes and tells me. Black as ash-buds in March.* And I've lived all my life in the country; more shame for me not to know. Black: they are jet-black, madam.' And he went off again, swinging along to the music of some rhyme he had got hold of.

When we came back, nothing would serve him but he must read us the poems he had been speaking of; and Miss Pole encouraged him in his proposal, I thought, because she wished me to hear his beautiful reading, of which she had boasted; but she afterwards said it was because she had got to a difficult part of her crochet, and wanted to count her stitches without having to talk. Whatever he had proposed would have been right to Miss Matty; although she did fall sound asleep within five minutes after he had begun a long poem, called 'Locksley Hall',* and had a comfortable nap, unobserved, till he ended; when the cessation of his voice wakened her up, and she said, feeling that something was expected, and that Miss Pole was counting: –

'What a pretty book!'

'Pretty! madam! it's beautiful! Pretty, indeed!'

'Oh yes! I meant beautiful!' said she, fluttered at his disapproval of her word. 'It is so like that beautiful poem of Dr Johnson's* my sister used to read – I forget the name of it, what was it, my dear?' turning to me.

'Which do you mean, ma'am? What was it about?'

'I don't remember what it was about, and I've quite forgotten what the name of it was; but it was written by Dr Johnson, and was very beautiful, and very like what Mr Holbrook has just been reading.'

'I don't remember it,' said he, reflectively. 'But I don't know Dr Johnson's poems well. I must read them.'

As we were getting into the fly to return, I heard Mr Holbrook say he should call on the ladies soon, and inquire how they got home; and this evidently pleased and fluttered Miss Matty at the time he said it; but after we had lost sight of the old house among the trees, her sentiments towards the master of it were gradually absorbed into a distressing wonder as to whether Martha had broken her word, and seized on the opportunity of her mistress's absence to have a 'follower'. Martha looked good, and steady, and composed enough, as she came to help us out; she was always careful of Miss Matty, and tonight she made use of this unlucky speech: –

'Eh! dear ma'am, to think of your going out in an evening in such a thin shawl! It is no better than muslin. At your age, ma'am, you should be careful.'

'My age!' said Miss Matty, almost speaking crossly, for her; for she was usually gentle. 'My age! Why, how old do you think I am, that you talk about my age?'

'Well, ma'am! I should say you were not far short of sixty; but folks' looks is often against them – and I'm sure I meant no harm.'

'Martha, I'm not yet fifty-two!' said Miss Matty, with grave emphasis; for probably the remembrance of her youth had come very vividly before her this day, and she was annoyed at finding that golden time so far away in the past.

But she never spoke of any former and more intimate acquaintance with Mr Holbrook. She had probably met with so little sympathy in her early love, that she had shut it up close in her heart; and it was only by a sort of watching, which I could hardly avoid, since Miss Pole's confidence, that I saw how faithful her poor heart had been in its sorrow and its silence.

She gave me some good reason for wearing her best cap every day, and sat near the window, in spite of her rheumatism, in order to see, without being seen, down into the street.

He came. He put his open palms upon his knees, which were far apart, as he sat with his head bent down, whistling, after we had replied to his inquiries about our safe return. Suddenly, he jumped up.

'Well, madam! have you any commands for Paris? I am going there in a week or two.'

'To Paris!' we both exclaimed.

'Yes, madam! I've never been there, and always had a wish to go; and I think if I don't go soon, I mayn't go at all; so as soon as the hay is got in I shall go, before harvest-time.'

We were so much astonished, that we had no commissions.

Just as he was going out of the room, he turned back, with his favourite exclamation:

'God bless my soul, madam! but I nearly forgot half my errand. Here are the poems for you, you admired so much the other evening at my house.' He tugged away at a parcel in his coat-pocket. 'Good-bye, miss,' said he; 'good-bye, Matty! take care of yourself.' And he was gone. But he had given her a book, and he had called her Matty, just as he used to do thirty years ago.

'I wish he would not go to Paris,' said Miss Matilda, anxiously. 'I don't believe frogs will agree with him; he used to have to be very careful what he ate, which was curious in so strong-looking a young man.'

Soon after this I took my leave, giving many an injunction to Martha to look after her mistress, and to let me know if she thought that Miss Matilda was not so well; in which case I would volunteer a visit to my old friend, without noticing Martha's intelligence to her.*

Accordingly I received a line or two from Martha every now and then; and, about November, I had a note to say her mistress was 'very low and sadly off her food'; and the account made me so uneasy, that, although Martha did not decidedly summon me, I packed up my things and went.

I received a warm welcome, in spite of the little flurry produced by my impromptu visit, for I had only been able to give a day's notice. Miss Matilda looked miserably ill; and I prepared to comfort and cosset her.

I went down to have a private talk with Martha.

'How long has your mistress been so poorly?' I asked, as I stood by the kitchen fire.

'Well! I think it's better than a fortnight; it is, I know: it was one Tuesday, after Miss Pole had been, that she went into this moping way. I thought she was tired, and it would go off with a night's rest; but, no! she has gone on and on ever since, till I thought it my duty to write to you, ma'am.'

'You did quite right, Martha. It is a comfort to think she has so faithful a servant about her. And I hope you find your place comfortable?'

'Well, ma'am, missus is very kind, and there's plenty to eat and drink, and no more work but what I can do easily, – but' – Martha hesitated.

'But what, Martha?'

'Why, it seems so hard of missus not to let me have any followers; there's such lots of young fellows in the town; and many a one has as much as offered to keep company with me; and I may never be in such a likely place again, and it's like wasting an opportunity. Many a girl as I know would have 'em unbeknownst to missus; but I've given my word, and I'll stick to it; or else this is just the house for missus never to be the wiser if they did come: and it's such a capable kitchen* – there's such good dark corners in it – I'd be bound to hide anyone. I counted up last Sunday night – for I'll not deny I was crying because I had to shut the door in Jem Hearn's face; and he's a steady young man, fit for any girl; only I had given missus my word.' Martha was all but crying again; and I had little comfort to give her, for I knew, from old experience, of the horror with which both the Miss Jenkynses looked upon 'followers'; and in Miss Matty's present nervous state this dread was not likely to be lessened.

I went to see Miss Pole the next day, and took her completely by surprise; for she had not been to see Miss Matilda for two days.

'And now I must go back with you, my dear, for I promised to let her know how Thomas Holbrook went on; and I'm sorry to say his housekeeper has sent me word today that he hasn't long to live. Poor Thomas! That journey to Paris was quite too much for him. His housekeeper says he has hardly ever been round his fields since; but just sits with his hands on his knees in the counting-house, not reading or anything, but only saying, what a wonderful city Paris was! Paris has much to answer for, if it's killed my cousin Thomas, for a better man never lived.'

'Does Miss Matilda know of his illness?' asked I; – a new light as to the cause of her indisposition dawning upon me.

'Dear! to be sure, yes! Has not she told you? I let her know a fortnight ago, or more, when first I heard of it. How odd, she shouldn't have told you!'

Not at all, I thought; but I did not say anything. I felt almost guilty of having spied too curiously into that tender heart, and I was not going to speak of its secrets, – hidden, Miss Matty believed, from all the world. I ushered Miss Pole into Miss Matilda's little drawing-room; and then left them alone. But I was not surprised when Martha came to my bedroom door, to ask me to go down to dinner alone, for that missus had one of her bad headaches. She came into the drawing-room at tea-time; but it was evidently an effort to her; and, as if to make up for some reproachful feeling against her late sister, Miss Jenkyns, which had been troubling her all the afternoon, and for which she now felt penitent, she kept telling me how good and how clever Deborah was in her youth; how she used to settle what gowns they were to wear at all the parties (faint, ghostly ideas of grim parties far away in the distance, when Miss Matty and Miss Pole were young!); and how Deborah and her mother had started the benefit society for the poor, and taught girls cooking and plain sewing; and how Deborah had once danced with a lord; and how she used to visit at Sir Peter Arley's, and try to remodel the quiet rectory establishment on the plans of Arley Hall,* where they kept thirty servants; and how she had nursed Miss Matty through a long, long illness, of which I had never heard before, but which I now dated in my own mind as following the dismissal of the suit of Mr Holbrook. So we talked softly and quietly of old times, through the long November evening.

The next day Miss Pole brought us word that Mr Holbrook was dead. Miss Matty heard the news in silence; in fact, from the account of the previous day, it was only what we had to expect. Miss Pole kept calling upon us for some expression of regret, by asking if it was not sad that he was gone: and saying,

'To think of that pleasant day last June, when he seemed so well! And he might have lived this dozen years if he had not gone to that wicked Paris, where they are always having Revolutions.'*

She paused for some demonstration on our part. I saw Miss Matty could not speak, she was trembling so nervously; so I said what I really felt: and after a call of some duration – all the time of which I have no doubt Miss Pole thought Miss Matty received the news very calmly – our visitor took her leave. But the effort at self-control Miss Matty had made to conceal her feelings – a concealment she practised even with me, for she has never alluded to Mr Holbrook again, although the book he gave her lies with her Bible on the little table by her bedside; she did not think I heard her when she asked the little milliner of Cranford to make her caps something like the Honourable Mrs Jamieson's, or that I noticed the reply –

'But she wears widows' caps, ma'am?'

'Oh! I only meant something in that style; not widows', of course, but rather like Mrs Jamieson's.'

This effort at concealment was the beginning of the tremulous motion of head and hands which I have seen ever since in Miss Matty.

The evening of the day on which we heard of Mr Holbrook's death, Miss Matilda was very silent and thoughtful; after prayers she called Martha back, and then she stood uncertain what to say.

'Martha!' she said at last; 'you are young,' – and then she made so long a pause that Martha, to remind her of her half-finished sentence, dropped a courtesy, and said –

'Yes, please, ma'am; two-and-twenty last third of October, please, ma'am.'

'And perhaps, Martha, you may some time meet with a young man you like, and who likes you. I did say you were not to have followers; but if you meet with such a young man, and tell me, and I find he is respectable, I have no objection to his coming to see you once a week. God forbid!' said she, in a low voice, 'that I should grieve any young hearts.' She spoke as if she were providing for some distant contingency, and was rather startled when Martha made her ready eager answer: –

'Please, ma'am, there's Jim Hearn, and he's a joiner, making three-and-sixpence a-day, and six foot one in his stocking-feet, please, ma'am; and if you'll ask about him tomorrow morning, everyone will give him a character for steadiness; and he'll be glad enough to come tomorrow night, I'll be bound.'

Though Miss Matty was startled, she submitted to Fate and Love.

Chapter 5

OLD LETTERS

I have often noticed that almost every one has his own individual small economies — careful habits of saving fractions of pennies in some one peculiar direction — any disturbance of which annoys him more than spending shillings or pounds on some real extravagance. An old gentleman of my acquaintance, who took the intelligence of the failure of a Joint-Stock Bank, in which some of his money was invested, with stoical mildness, worried his family all through a long summer's day, because one of them had torn (instead of cutting) out the written leaves of his now useless bank-book; of course, the corresponding pages at the other end came out as well; and this little unnecessary waste of paper (his private economy) chafed him more than all the loss of his money. Envelopes fretted his soul terribly when they first came in; the only way in which he could reconcile himself to such waste of his cherished article was by patiently turning inside out all that were sent to him, and so making them serve again. Even now, though tamed by age, I see him casting wistful glances at his daughters when they send a whole instead of a half sheet of note-paper, with the three lines of acceptance to an invitation, written on only one of the sides. I am not above owning that I have this human weakness myself. String is my foible. My pockets get full of little hanks of it, picked up and twisted together, ready for uses that never come. I am seriously annoyed if anyone cuts the string of a parcel, instead of patiently and faithfully undoing it fold by fold. How people can bring themselves to use Indian-rubber rings, which are a sort of deification of string, as lightly as they do, I cannot imagine. To me an Indian-rubber ring is a precious treasure. I have one which is not new; one that I picked up off the floor, nearly six years ago. I have really tried to use it; but my heart failed me, and I could not commit the extravagance.

Small pieces of butter grieve others. They cannot attend to conversation, because of the annoyance occasioned by the habit which some people have of invariably taking more butter than they want. Have you not seen the anxious look (almost mesmeric) which such persons fix on the article? They would feel it a relief if they might bury it out of their sight, by popping it into their own mouths, and swallowing it down; and they are really made happy if the person on whose plate it lies unused, suddenly breaks off a piece of toast (which he does not want at all) and eats up his butter. They think that this is not waste.

Now Miss Matty Jenkyns was chary of candles. We had many devices to use as few as possible. In the winter afternoons she would sit knitting for two or three hours; she could do this in the dark, or by fire-light; and when I asked if I might not ring for candles to finish stitching my wristbands, she told me to 'keep blind man's holiday'.* They were usually brought in with tea; but we only burnt one at a time. As we lived in constant preparation for a friend who might come in, any evening (but who never did), it required some contrivance to keep our two candles of the same length, ready to be lighted, and to look as if we burnt two always. The candles took it in turns; and, whatever we might be talking about or doing, Miss Matty's eyes were habitually fixed upon the candle, ready to jump up and extinguish it, and to light the other before they had become too uneven in length to be restored to equality in the course of the evening.

One night, I remember that this candle economy particularly annoyed me. I had been very much tired of my compulsory 'blind-man's holiday', – especially as Miss Matty had fallen asleep, and I did not like to stir the fire, and run the risk of awakening her; so I could not even sit on the rug, and scorch myself with sewing by firelight, according to my usual custom. I fancied Miss Matty must be dreaming of her early life; for she spoke one or two words, in her uneasy sleep, bearing reference to persons who were dead long before. When Martha brought in the lighted candle and tea, Miss Matty started into wakefulness, with a strange bewildered look around, as if we were not the people she expected to see about her. There was a little sad expression that shadowed her face as she recognised me; but immediately afterwards she tried to give me her usual smile. All through tea-time, her talk ran upon the days of her childhood and youth. Perhaps this reminded her of the desirableness of looking over all the old family letters, and destroying such as ought not to be allowed to fall into the hands of strangers; for she had often spoken of the necessity of this task, but had always shrunk from it, with a timid dread of something painful. Tonight, however, she rose up after tea, and went for them – in the dark; for she piqued herself on the precise neatness of all her chamber arrangements, and used to look uneasily at me, when I lighted a bed-candle to go to another room for anything. When she returned, there was a faint pleasant smell of Tonquin beans* in the room. I had always noticed this scent about any of the things which had belonged to her mother; and many of the letters were addressed to her – yellow bundles of love-letters, sixty or seventy years old.

Miss Matty undid the packet with a sigh; but she stifled it directly, as if it were hardly right to regret the flight of time, or of life either. We agreed to look them over separately, each taking a different letter out of the same bundle, and describing its contents to the other, before destroying it. I never knew what sad work the reading of old letters was before that evening, though I could hardly tell why. The letters were as happy as letters could be – at least those early letters were. There was in them a vivid and intense sense of the present time, which seemed so strong and full, as if it could never pass away, and as if the warm, living hearts that so expressed themselves could never die, and be as nothing to the sunny earth. I should have felt less melancholy, I believe, if the letters had been more so. I saw the tears quietly stealing down the well-worn furrows of Miss Matty's cheeks, and her spectacles often wanted wiping. I trusted at last that she would light the other candle, for my own eyes were rather dim, and I wanted more light to see the pale, faded ink; but no – even through her tears, she saw and remembered her little economical ways.

The earliest set of letters were two bundles tied together, and ticketed (in Miss Jenkyns's handwriting), 'Letters interchanged between my ever-honoured father and my dearly-beloved mother, prior to their marriage, in July, 1774.' I should guess that the Rector of Cranford was about twenty-seven years of age when he wrote those letters; and Miss Matty told me that her mother was just eighteen at the time of her wedding. With my idea of the Rector, derived from a picture in the dining parlour, stiff and stately, in a huge full-bottomed wig,* with gown, cassock, and bands, and his hand upon a copy of the only sermon he ever published, – it was strange to read these letters.

They were full of eager, passionate ardour; short homely sentences, right fresh from the heart; (very different from the grand Latinised, Johnsonian style of the printed sermon, preached before some judge at assize time). His letters were a curious contrast to those of his girl-bride. She was evidently rather annoyed at his demands upon her for expressions of love, and could not quite understand what he meant by repeating the same thing over in so many different ways; but what she was quite clear about was her longing for a white 'Paduasoy',* – whatever that might be; and six or seven letters were principally occupied in asking her lover to use his influence with her parents (who evidently kept her in good order) to obtain this or that article of dress, more especially the white 'Paduasoy'. He cared nothing how she was dressed; she was always lovely enough for him, as he took pains to assure her, when she begged him to express in his answers a predilection for particular pieces of finery, in order that she might show what he said to her parents. But at length he seemed to find out that she would not be married till she had a 'trousseau' to her mind; and then he sent her a letter, which had evidently accompanied a whole box full of finery, and in which he requested that she might be dressed in everything her heart desired. This was the first letter, ticketed in a frail, delicate hand, 'From my dearest John.' Shortly afterwards they were married, – I suppose, from the intermission in their correspondence.

'We must burn them, I think,' said Miss Matty, looking doubtfully at me. 'No one will care for them when I am gone.' And one by one she dropped them into the middle of the fire; watching each blaze up, die out, and rise away, in faint, white, ghostly semblance, up the chimney, before she gave up another to the same fate. The room was light enough now; but I, like her, was fascinated into watching the destruction of those letters, into which the honest warmth of a manly heart had been poured forth.

The next letter, likewise docketed by Miss Jenkyns, was endorsed, 'Letter of pious congratulation and exhortation from my venerable grandfather to my mother, on occasion of my own birth. Also some practical remarks on the desirability of keeping warm the extremities of infants, from my excellent grandmother.'

The first part was, indeed, a severe and forcible picture of the responsibilities of mothers, and a warning against the evils that were in the world, and lying in ghastly wait for the little boy of two days old. His wife did not write, said the old gentleman, because he had forbidden it, she being indisposed with a sprained ankle, which (he said) quite incapacitated her from holding a pen. However, at the foot of the page was a small 'T.O.', and on turning it over, sure enough, there was a letter to 'my dear, dearest Molly', begging her, when she left her room, whatever she did, to go *up*stairs before going *down*: and telling her to wrap her baby's feet up in flannel, and keep it warm by the fire, although it was summer, for babies were so tender.

It was pretty to see from the letters, which were evidently exchanged with some frequency, between the young mother and the grandmother, how the girlish vanity was being weeded out of her heart by love for her baby. The white 'Paduasoy' figured again in the letters, with almost as much vigour as before. In one, it was being made into a christening cloak for the baby. It decked it when it went with its parents to spend a day or two at Arley Hall. It added to its charms when it was 'the prettiest little baby that ever was seen. Dear mother, I wish you could see her! Without any parshality, I do think she will grow up a regular bewty!' I thought of Miss Jenkyns, grey, withered, and wrinkled; and I wondered if her mother had known her in the courts of heaven; and then I knew that she had, and that they stood there in angelic guise.

There was a great gap before any of the Rector's letters appeared. And then his wife had changed her mode of endorsement. It was no longer from 'My dearest John'; it was from 'My honoured Husband'. The letters were written on occasion of the publication of the same Sermon which was represented in the picture. The preaching before 'My Lord Judge', and the 'publishing by request', was evidently the culminating point – the event of his life. It had been necessary for him to go up to London to superintend it through the press. Many friends had to be called upon, and consulted, before he could decide on any printer fit for so onerous a task; and at length it was arranged that J. and J. Rivingtons* were to have the honourable responsibility. The worthy Rector seemed to be strung up by the occasion to a high literary pitch, for he could hardly write a letter to his wife without cropping out into Latin. I remember the end of one of his letters ran thus: – 'I shall ever hold the virtuous qualities of my Molly in remembrance, *dum memor ipse mei, dum spiritus regit artus'*,* which, considering that the English of his correspondent was sometimes at fault in grammar, and often in spelling, might be taken as a proof of how much he 'idealised' his Molly; and, as Miss Jenkyns used to say, 'People talk a great deal about idealising now-a-days, whatever that may mean.' But this was nothing to a fit of writing classical poetry, which soon seized him; in which his Molly figured away* as 'Maria'. The letter containing the *carmen** was endorsed by her, 'Hebrew verses sent me by my honoured husband. I thowt to have had a letter about killing the pig, but must wait. Mem., to send the poetry to Sir Peter Arley, as my husband desires.' And in a postscriptum note in his handwriting, it was stated that the Ode had appeared in the 'Gentleman's Magazine',* December, 1782.

Her letters back to her husband (treasured as fondly by him as if they had been M. T. Ciceronis Epistolæ)* were more satisfactory to an absent husband and father, than his could ever have been to her. She told him how Deborah sewed her seam very neatly every day, and read to her in the books he had set her; how she was a very 'forrard',* good child, but *would* ask questions her mother could not answer; but how she did not let herself down by saying she did not know, but took to stirring the fire, or sending the 'forrard' child on an errand. Matty was now the mother's darling, and promised (like her sister at her age) to be a great beauty. I was reading this aloud to Miss Matty, who smiled and sighed a little at the hope, so fondly expressed, that 'little Matty might not be vain, even if she were a beauty'.

'I had very pretty hair, my dear,' said Miss Matilda; 'and not a bad mouth.' And I saw her soon afterwards adjust her cap and draw herself up.

But to return to Mrs Jenkyns's letters. She told her husband about the poor in the parish; what homely domestic medicines she had administered; what kitchen physic she had sent. She had evidently held his displeasure as a rod in pickle over the heads of all the n'er-do-wells. She asked for his directions about the cows and pigs; and did not always obtain them, as I have shown before.

The kind old grandmother was dead, when a little boy was born, soon after the publication of the Sermon; but there was another letter of exhortation from the grandfather, more stringent and admonitory than ever, now that there was a boy to be guarded from the snares of the world. He described all the various sins into which men might fall, until I wondered how any man ever came to a natural death. The gallows seemed as if it must have been the termination of the lives of most of the grandfather's friends and acquaintance; and I was not surprised at the way in which he spoke of this life being 'a vale of tears'.*

It seemed curious that I should never have heard of this brother before; but I concluded that he had died young; or else surely his name would have been alluded to by his sisters.

By-and-by we came to packets of Miss Jenkyns's letters. These, Miss Matty did regret to burn. She said all the others had been only interesting to those who loved the writers; and that it seemed as if it would have hurt her to allow them to fall into the hands of strangers, who had not known her dear mother, and how good she was, although she did not always spell quite in the modern fashion; but Deborah's letters were so very superior! Anyone might profit by reading them. It was a long time since she had read Mrs Chapone,* but she knew she used to think that Deborah could have said the same things quite as well; and as for Mrs Carter! people thought a deal of her letters, just because she had written Epictetus,* but she was quite sure Deborah would never have made use of such a common expression as 'I canna be fashed!'*

Miss Matty did grudge burning these letters, it was evident. She would not let them be carelessly passed over with any quiet reading, and skipping, to myself. She took them from me, and even lighted the second candle in order to read them aloud with a proper emphasis, and without stumbling over the big words. Oh dear! how I wanted facts instead of reflections, before those letters were concluded! They lasted us two nights; and I won't deny that I made use of the time to think of many other things, and yet I was always at my post at the end of each sentence.

The Rector's letters, and those of his wife and mother-in-law, had all been tolerably short and pithy, written in a straight hand, with the lines very close together. Sometimes the whole letter was contained on a mere scrap of paper. The paper was very yellow, and the ink very brown; some of the sheets were (as Miss Matty made me observe) the old original Post,* with the stamp in the corner, representing a post-boy riding for life and twanging his horn. The letters of Mrs Jenkyns and her mother were fastened with a great round, red wafer; for it was before Miss Edgeworth's 'Patronage' had banished wafers* from polite society. It was evident, from the tenor of what was said, that franks were in great request, and were even used as a means of paying debts by needy Members of Parliament. The Rector sealed his epistles with an immense coat of arms, and showed by the care with which he had performed this ceremony, that he expected they should be cut open, not broken by any thoughtless or impatient hand. Now, Miss Jenkyns's letters were of a later date in form and writing. She wrote on the square sheet, which we have learned to call old-fashioned. Her hand was admirably calculated, together with her use of many-syllabled words, to fill up a sheet, and then came the pride and delight of crossing. Poor Miss Matty got sadly puzzled with this, for the words gathered size like snowballs, and towards the end of her letter, Miss Jenkyns used to become quite sesquipedalian.* In one to her father, slightly theological and controversial in its tone, she had spoken of Herod, Tetrarch of Idumea.* Miss Matty read it 'Herod Petrarch of Etruria', and was just as well pleased as if she had been right.

I can't quite remember the date, but I think it was in 1805 that Miss Jenkyns wrote the longest series of letters; on occasion of her absence on a visit to some friends near Newcastle-upon-Tyne. These friends were intimate with the commandant of the garrison there, and heard from him of all the preparations that were being made to repel the invasion of Buonaparte,* which some people imagined might take place at the mouth of the Tyne. Miss Jenkyns was evidently very much alarmed; and the first part of her letters was often written in pretty intelligible English, conveying particulars of the preparations which were made in the family with whom she was residing against the dreaded event; the bundles of clothes that were packed up ready for a flight to Alston Moor (a wild hilly piece of ground between Northumberland and Cumberland); the signal that was to be given for this flight, and for the simultaneous turning out of the volunteers under arms; which said signal was to consist (if I remember rightly) in ringing the church bells in a particular and ominous manner. One day, when Miss Jenkyns and her hosts were at a dinner-party in Newcastle, this warning-summons was actually given (not a very wise proceeding, if there be any truth in the moral attached to the fable of the Boy and the Wolf;* but so it was), and Miss Jenkyns, hardly recovered from her fright, wrote the next day to describe the sound, the breathless shock, the hurry and alarm; and then, taking breath, she added, 'How trivial, my dear father, do all our apprehensions of the last evening appear, at the present moment, to calm and inquiring minds!' And here Miss Matty broke in with – 'But, indeed, my dear, they were not at all trivial or trifling at the time. I know I used to wake up in the night many a time, and think I heard the tramp of the French entering Cranford. Many people talked of hiding themselves in the salt-mines;* – and meat would have kept capitally down there, only perhaps we should have been thirsty. And my father preached a whole set of sermons on the occasion; one set in the mornings, all about David and Goliath,* to spirit up the people to fighting with spades or bricks, if need were; and the other set in the afternoons, proving that Napoleon (that was another name for Bony, as we used to call him) was all the same as an Apollyon and Abaddon.* I remember, my father rather thought he should be asked to print this last set; but the parish had, perhaps, had enough of them with hearing.'

Peter Marmaduke Arley Jenkyns, ('poor Peter!' as Miss Matty began to call him) was at school at Shrewsbury* by this time. The Rector took up his pen, and rubbed up his Latin, once more, to correspond with his boy. It was very clear that the lad's were what are called show-letters. They were of a highly mental description, giving an account of his studies, and his intellectual hopes of various kinds, with an occasional quotation from the classics; but, now and then, the animal nature broke out in such a little sentence as this, evidently written in a trembling hurry, after the letter had been inspected: 'Mother, dear, do send me a cake, and put plenty of citron in.' The 'mother, dear', probably answered her boy in the form of cakes and 'goody', for there were none of her letters among this set; but a whole collection of the Rector's, to whom the Latin in his boy's letters was like a trumpet to the old war-horse. I do not know much about Latin, certainly, and it is, perhaps, an ornamental language; but not very useful, I think – at least to judge from the bits I remember out of the Rector's letters. One was: 'You have not got that town in your map of Ireland; but *Bonus Bernardus non videt omnia,** as the Proverbia say.' Presently it became very evident that 'poor Peter' got himself into many scrapes. There were letters of stilted penitence to his father, for some wrong-doing;

and, among them all, was a badly written, badly-sealed, badly-directed, blotted note – 'My dear, dear, dear, dearest mother, I will be a better boy – I will, indeed; but don't, please, be ill for me; I am not worth it; but I will be good, darling mother.'

Miss Matty could not speak for crying, after she had read this note. She gave it to me in silence, and then got up and took it to her sacred recesses in her own room, for fear, by any chance, it might get burnt. 'Poor Peter!' she said; 'he was always in scrapes; he was too easy. They led him wrong, and then left him in the lurch. But he was too fond of mischief. He could never resist a joke. Poor Peter!'

Chapter 6

POOR PETER

Poor Peter's career lay before him rather pleasantly mapped out by kind friends, but *Bonus Bernardus non videt omnia*, in this map too. He was to win honours at Shrewsbury School, and carry them thick to Cambridge, and after that, a living awaited him, the gift of his godfather, Sir Peter Arley. Poor Peter! his lot in life was very different to what his friends had hoped and planned. Miss Matty told me all about it, and I think it was a relief to her when she had done so.

He was the darling of his mother, who seemed to dote on all her children, though she was, perhaps, a little afraid of Deborah's superior acquirements. Deborah was the favourite of her father, and when Peter disappointed him, she became his pride. The sole honour Peter brought away from Shrewsbury, was the reputation of being the best good fellow that ever was, and of being the captain of the school in the art of practical joking. His father was disappointed, but set about remedying the matter in a manly way. He could not afford to send Peter to read with any tutor, but he could read with him himself; and Miss Matty told me much of the awful preparations in the way of dictionaries and lexicons that were made in her father's study the morning Peter began.

'My poor mother!' said she. 'I remember how she used to stand in the hall, just near enough to the study-door to catch the tone of my father's voice. I could tell in a moment if all was going right, by her face. And it did go right for a long time.'

'What went wrong at last?' said I. 'That tiresome Latin, I dare say.'

'No! it was not the Latin. Peter was in high favour with my father, for he worked up well for him. But he seemed to think that the Cranford people might be joked about, and made fun of, and they did not like it; nobody does. He was always hoaxing them; "hoaxing" is not a pretty word, my dear, and I hope you won't tell your father I used it, for I should not like him to think that I was not choice in my language, after living with such a woman as Deborah. And be sure you never use it yourself. I don't know how it slipped out of my mouth, except it was that I was thinking of poor Peter, and it was always his expression. But he was a very gentlemanly boy in many things. He was like dear Captain Brown in always being ready to help any old person or a child. Still, he did like joking and making fun; and he seemed to think the old ladies in Cranford would believe anything. There were many old ladies living here then; we are principally ladies now, I know; but we are not so old as the ladies used to be when I was a girl. I could laugh to think of some of Peter's jokes. No! my dear, I won't tell you of them, because they might not shock you as they ought to do; and they were very shocking. He even took in my father once, by dressing himself up as a lady that was passing through the town and wished to see the Rector of Cranford, "who had published that admirable Assize Sermon". Peter said, he was awfully frightened himself when he saw how my father took it all in, and even offered to copy out all his Napoleon Buonaparte sermons for her – him, I mean – no, her, for Peter was a lady then. He told me he was more terrified than he ever was before, all the time my father was speaking. He did not think my father would have believed him; and yet if he had not, it would have been a sad thing for Peter. As it was, he was none so glad of it, for my father kept him hard at work copying out all those twelve Buonaparte sermons for the lady – that was for Peter himself, you know. He was the lady. And once when he wanted to go fishing, Peter said, "Confound the woman!" – very bad language, my dear; but Peter was not always so guarded as he should have been; my father was so angry with him, it nearly frightened me out of my wits: and yet I could hardly keep from laughing at the little curtsies Peter kept making, quite slyly, whenever my father spoke of the lady's excellent taste and sound discrimination.'

'Did Miss Jenkyns know of these tricks?' said I.

'Oh no! Deborah would have been too much shocked. No! no one knew but me. I wish I had always known of Peter's plans; but sometimes he did not tell me. He used to say, the old ladies in the town wanted something to talk about; but I don't think they did. They had the St James's Chronicle* three times a-week, just as we have now, and we have plenty to say; and I remember the clacking noise there always was when some of the ladies got together. But, probably, school-boys talk more than ladies. At last there was a terrible sad thing happened.' Miss Matty got up, went to the door, and opened it; no one was there. She rang the bell for Martha; and when Martha came, her mistress told her to go for eggs to a farm at the other end of the town.

'I will lock the door after you, Martha. You are not afraid to go, are you?'

'No, Ma'am, not at all; Jem Hearn will be only too proud to go with me.'

Miss Matty drew herself up, and, as soon as we were alone, she wished that Martha had more maidenly reserve.

'We'll put out the candle, my dear. We can talk just as well by fire-light, you know. There! well! you see, Deborah had gone from home for a fortnight or so; it was a very still, quiet day, I remember, overhead; and the lilacs were all in flower, so I suppose it was spring. My father had gone out to see some sick people in the parish; I recollect seeing him leave the house, with his wig and shovel-hat,* and cane. What possessed our poor Peter I don't know; he had the sweetest temper, and yet he always seemed to like to plague Deborah. She never laughed at his jokes, and thought him ungenteel, and not careful enough about improving his mind; and that vexed him.

'Well! he went to her room, it seems, and dressed himself in her old gown, and shawl, and bonnet; just the things she used to wear in Cranford, and was known by everywhere; and he made the pillow into a little – you are sure you locked the door, my dear, for I should not like anyone to hear – into – into – a little baby, with white long clothes. It was only, as he told me afterwards, to make something to talk about in the town: he never thought of it as affecting Deborah. And he went and walked up and down in the Filbert walk – just half hidden by the rails, and half seen; and he cuddled his pillow, just like a baby; and talked to it all the nonsense people do. Oh dear! and my father came stepping stately up the street, as he always did; and what should he see but a little black crowd of people – I dare say as many as twenty – all peeping through his garden rails. So he thought, at first, they were only looking at a new rhododendron that was in full bloom, and that he was very proud of; and he walked slower, that they might have more time to admire. And he wondered if he could make out a sermon

from the occasion, and thought, perhaps, there was some relation between the rhododendrons and the lilies of the field. My
poor father! When he came nearer, he began to wonder that
they did not see him; but their heads were all so close together,
peeping and peeping! My father was amongst them, meaning,
he said, to ask them to walk into the garden with him, and
admire the beautiful vegetable production, when – oh, my dear!
I tremble to think of it – he looked through the rails himself,
and saw – I don't know what he thought he saw, but old Clare
told me his face went quite grey-white with anger, and his eyes
blazed out under his frowning black brows; and he spoke out –
oh, so terribly! – and bade them all stop where they were – not
one of them to go, not one to stir a step; and, swift as light, he
was in at the garden door, and down the Filbert walk, and seized
hold of poor Peter, and tore his clothes off his back – bonnet,
shawl, gown, and all – and threw the pillow among the people
over the railings: and then he was very, very angry indeed; and
before all the people he lifted up his cane, and flogged Peter!

'My dear! that boy's trick, on that sunny day, when all seemed
going straight and well, broke my mother's heart, and changed
my father for life. It did, indeed. Old Clare said, Peter looked as
white as my father; and stood as still as a statue to be flogged;
and my father struck hard! When my father stopped to take
breath, Peter said, "Have you done enough, Sir?" quite hoarsely,
and still standing quite quiet. I don't know what my father said
– or if he said anything. But old Clare said, Peter turned to
where the people outside the railing were, and made them a low
bow, as grand and as grave as any gentleman; and then walked
slowly into the house. I was in the store-room helping my
mother to make cowslip-wine. I cannot abide the wine now, nor
the scent of the flowers; they turn me sick and faint, as they did
that day, when Peter came in, looking as haughty as any man –
indeed, looking like a man, not like a boy. "Mother!" he said,
"I am come to say, God bless you for ever." I saw his lips quiver
as he spoke; and I think he durst not say anything more loving,
for the purpose that was in his heart. She looked at him rather
frightened, and wondering, and asked him what was to do? He
did not smile or speak, but put his arms around her, and kissed
her as if he did not know how to leave off; and before she could
speak again, he was gone. We talked it over, and could not
understand it, and she bade me go and seek my father, and ask

what it was all about. I found him walking up and down,
looking very highly displeased.

'"Tell your mother I have flogged Peter, and that he richly
deserved it."

'I durst not ask any more questions. When I told my mother,
she sat down, quite faint, for a minute. I remember, a few days
after, I saw the poor, withered cowslip-flowers thrown out to
the leaf-heap, to decay and die there. There was no making of
cowslip-wine that year at the Rectory – nor, indeed, ever after.

'Presently, my mother went to my father. I know I thought of
Queen Esther and King Ahasuerus;* for my mother was very
pretty and delicate-looking, and my father looked as terrible as
King Ahasuerus. Some time after, they came out together; and
then my mother told me what had happened, and that she was
going up to Peter's room, at my father's desire – though she was
not to tell Peter this – to talk the matter over with him. But no
Peter was there. We looked over the house; no Peter was there!
Even my father, who had not liked to join in the search at first,
helped us before long. The Rectory was a very old house: steps
up into a room, steps down into a room, all through. At first,
my mother went calling low and soft – as if to reassure the poor
boy – "Peter! Peter, dear! it's only me"; but, by-and-by, as the
servants came back from the errands my father had sent them,
in different directions, to find where Peter was – as we found he
was not in the garden, nor the hayloft, nor anywhere about –
my mother's cry grew louder and wilder – "Peter! Peter, my
darling! where are you?" for then she felt and understood that
that long kiss meant some sad kind of "good-bye". The afternoon went on – my mother never resting, but seeking again and
again in every possible place that had been looked into twenty
times before; nay, that she had looked into over and over again
herself. My father sat with his head in his hands, not speaking,
except when his messengers came in, bringing no tidings; then
he lifted up his face so strong and sad, and told them to go again
in some new direction. My mother kept passing from room to
room, in and out of the house, moving noiselessly, but never
ceasing. Neither she nor my father durst leave the house, which
was the meeting-place for all the messengers. At last (and it was
nearly dark), my father rose up. He took hold of my mother's
arm, as she came with wild, sad pace, through one door, and

quickly towards another. She started at the touch of his hand, for she had forgotten all in the world but Peter.

'"Molly!" said he, "I did not think all this would happen." He looked into her face for comfort – her poor face, all wild and white; for neither she nor my father had dared to acknowledge – much less act upon – the terror that was in their hearts, lest Peter should have made away with himself. My father saw no conscious look in his wife's hot, dreary eyes, and he missed the sympathy that she had always been ready to give him – strong man as he was; and at the dumb despair in her face, his tears began to flow. But when she saw this, a gentle sorrow came over her countenance, and she said, "Dearest John! don't cry; come with me, and we'll find him", almost as cheerfully as if she knew where he was. And she took my father's great hand in her little soft one, and led him along, the tears dropping, as he walked on that same unceasing, weary walk, from room to room, through house and garden.

'Oh! how I wished for Deborah! I had no time for crying, for now all seemed to depend on me. I wrote for Deborah to come home. I sent a message privately to that same Mr Holbrook's house – poor Mr Holbrook! – you know who I mean. I don't mean I sent a message to him, but I sent one that I could trust, to know if Peter was at his house. For at one time Mr Holbrook was an occasional visitor at the Rectory – you know he was Miss Pole's cousin – and he had been very kind to Peter, and taught him to fish – he was very kind to everybody, and I thought Peter might have gone off there. But Mr Holbrook was from home, and Peter had never been seen. It was night now; but the doors were all wide open, and my father and mother walked on and on; it was more than an hour since he had joined her, and I don't believe they had ever spoken all that time. I was getting the parlour fire lighted, and one of the servants was preparing tea, for I wanted them to have something to eat and drink and warm them, when old Clare asked to speak to me.

'"I have borrowed the nets from the weir, Miss Matty. Shall we drag the ponds tonight, or wait for the morning?"

'I remember staring in his face to gather his meaning; and when I did, I laughed out loud. The horror of that new thought – our bright, darling Peter, cold, and stark, and dead! I remember the ring of my own laugh now.

'The next day Deborah was at home before I was myself

again. She would not have been so weak to give way as I had done; but my screams (my horrible laughter had ended in crying) had roused my sweet dear mother, whose poor wandering wits were called back and collected, as soon as a child needed her care. She and Deborah sat by my bedside; I knew by the looks of each that there had been no news of Peter – no awful, ghastly news, which was what I most had dreaded in my dull state between sleeping and waking.

'The same result of all the searching had brought something of the same relief to my mother, to whom I am sure, the thought that Peter might even then be hanging dead in some of the familiar home places, had caused that never-ending walk of yesterday. Her soft eyes never were the same again after that; they had always a restless craving look, as if seeking for what they could not find. Oh! it was an awful time; coming down like a thunderbolt on the still sunny day, when the lilacs were all in bloom.'

'Where was Mr Peter?' said I.

'He had made his way to Liverpool; and there was war then; and some of the king's ships lay off the mouth of the Mersey; and they were only too glad to have a fine likely boy such as him (five foot nine he was) come to offer himself. The captain wrote to my father, and Peter wrote to my mother. Stay! those letters will be somewhere here.'

We lighted the candle, and found the captain's letter, and Peter's too. And we also found a little simple begging letter from Mrs Jenkyns to Peter, addressed to him at the house of an old school-fellow, whither she fancied he might have gone. They had returned it unopened; and unopened it had remained ever since, having been inadvertently put by among the other letters of that time. This is it: –

My dearest Peter,

   You did not think we should be so sorry as we are, I know, or you would never have gone away. You are too good. Your father sits and sighs till my heart aches to hear him. He cannot hold up his head for grief; and yet he only did what he thought was right. Perhaps he has been too severe, and perhaps I have not been kind enough; but God knows how we love you, my dear only boy. Dor* looks so sorry you are gone. Come back, and make us happy, who love you so much. I *know* you will come back.

But Peter did not come back. That spring day was the last time he ever saw his mother's face. The writer of the letter – the last – the only person who had ever seen what was written in it, was dead long ago – and I, a stranger, not born at the time when this occurrence took place, was the one to open it.

The captain's letter summoned the father and mother to Liverpool instantly, if they wished to see their boy; and by some of the wild chances of life, the captain's letter had been detained somewhere, somehow.

Miss Matty went on: – 'And it was race-time, and all the post-horses at Cranford were gone to the races; but my father and mother set off in our own gig, – and, oh! my dear, they were too late – the ship was gone! And now, read Peter's letter to my mother!'

It was full of love, and sorrow, and pride in his new profession, and a sore sense of his disgrace in the eyes of the people at Cranford; but ending with a passionate entreaty that she would come and see him before he left the Mersey: – 'Mother! we may go into battle. I hope we shall, and lick those French; but I must see you again before that time.'

'And she was too late,' said Miss Matty; 'too late!'

We sat in silence, pondering on the full meaning of those sad, sad words. At length I asked Miss Matty to tell me how her mother bore it.

'Oh!' she said, 'she was patience itself. She had never been strong, and this weakened her terribly. My father used to sit looking at her: far more sad than she was. He seemed as if he could look at nothing else when she was by; and he was so humble, – so very gentle now. He would, perhaps, speak in his old way – laying down the law, as it were – and then, in a minute or two, he would come round and put his hand on our shoulders, and ask us in a low voice if he had said anything to hurt us? I did not wonder at his speaking so to Deborah, for she was so clever; but I could not bear to hear him talking so to me.

'But, you see, he saw what we did not – that it was killing my mother. Yes! killing her – (put out the candle, my dear; I can talk better in the dark) – for she was but a frail woman, and ill fitted to stand the fright and shock she had gone through; and she would smile at him and comfort him, not in words but in her looks and tones, which were always cheerful when he was there. And she would speak of how she thought Peter stood a good chance of being admiral very soon – he was so brave and clever; and how she thought of seeing him in his navy uniform, and what sort of hats admirals wore; and how much more fit he was to be a sailor than a clergyman; and all in that way, just to make my father think she was quite glad of what came of that unlucky morning's work, and the flogging which was always in his mind, as we all knew. But, oh, my dear! the bitter, bitter crying she had when she was alone; – and at last, as she grew weaker, she could not keep her tears in, when Deborah or me was by, and would give us message after message for Peter, – (his ship had gone to the Mediterranean, or somewhere down there, and then he was ordered off to India, and there was no overland route then); – but she still said that no one knew where their death lay in wait, and that we were not to think hers was near. We did not think it, but we knew it, as we saw her fading away.

'Well, my dear, it's very foolish of me, I know, when in all likelihood I am so near seeing her again.

'And only think, love! the very day after her death – for she did not live quite a twelvemonth after Peter went away – the very day after – came a parcel for her from India – from her poor boy. It was a large, soft, white India shawl, with just a little narrow border all round; just what my mother would have liked.

'We thought it might rouse my father, for he had sat with her hand in his all night long; so Deborah took it in to him, and Peter's letter to her, and all. At first, he took no notice; and we tried to make a kind of light careless talk about the shawl, opening it out and admiring it. Then, suddenly, he got up, and spoke: – "She shall be buried in it," he said; "Peter shall have that comfort; and she would have liked it."

'Well! perhaps it was not reasonable, but what could we do or say? One gives people in grief their own way. He took it up and felt it – "It is just such a shawl as she wished for when she was married, and her mother did not give it her. I did not know of it till after, or she should have had it – she should; but she shall have it now."

'My mother looked so lovely in her death! She was always pretty, and now she looked fair, and waxen, and young – younger than Deborah, as she stood trembling and shivering by her. We decked her in the long soft folds; she lay, smiling, as if pleased; and people came – all Cranford came – to beg to see her, for they had loved her dearly – as well they might; and the country-women brought posies; old Clare's wife brought some white violets, and begged they might lie on her breast.

'Deborah said to me, the day of my mother's funeral, that if she had a hundred offers, she never would marry and leave my father. It was not very likely she would have so many – I don't know that she had one; but it was not less to her credit to say so. She was such a daughter to my father, as I think there never was before, or since. His eyes failed him, and she read book after book, and wrote, and copied, and was always at his service in any parish business. She could do many more things than my poor mother could; she even once wrote a letter to the bishop for my father. But he missed my mother sorely; the whole parish noticed it. Not that he was less active; I think he was more so, and more patient in helping everyone. I did all I could to set Deborah at liberty to be with him; for I knew I was good for little, and that my best work in the world was to do odd jobs quietly, and set others at liberty. But my father was a changed man.'

'Did Mr Peter ever come home?'

'Yes, once. He came home a Lieutenant; he did not get to be Admiral. And he and my father were such friends! My father took him into every house in the parish, he was so proud of him. He never walked out without Peter's arm to lean upon. Deborah used to smile (I don't think we ever laughed again after my mother's death), and say she was quite put in a corner. Not but what my father always wanted her when there was letter-writing, or reading to be done, or anything to be settled.'

'And then?' said I, after a pause.

'Then Peter went to sea again; and, by-and-by, my father died, blessing us both, and thanking Deborah for all she had been to him; and, of course, our circumstances were changed; and, instead of living at the Rectory, and keeping three maids and a man, we had to come to this small house, and be content with a servant-of-all-work; but, as Deborah used to say, we have always lived genteelly, even if circumstances have compelled us to simplicity. – Poor Deborah!'

'And, Mr Peter?' asked I.

'Oh, there was some great war in India* – I forget what they call it – and we have never heard of Peter since then. I believe he is dead myself; and it sometimes fidgets me that we have never put on mourning for him. And then, again, when I sit by myself, and all the house is still, I think I hear his step coming up the street, and my heart begins to flutter and beat; but the sound always goes past – and Peter never comes.'

'That's Martha back? No! I'll go, my dear; I can always find my way in the dark, you know. And a blow of fresh air at the door will do my head good, and it's rather got a trick of aching.'

So she pattered off. I had lighted the candle, to give the room a cheerful appearance against her return.

'Was it Martha?' asked I.

'Yes. And I am rather uncomfortable, for I heard such a strange noise just as I was opening the door.'

'When?' I asked, for her eyes were round with affright.

'In the street – just outside – it sounded like – '

'Talking?' I put in, as she hesitated a little.

'No! kissing – '

Chapter 7

VISITING

One morning, as Miss Matty and I sat at our work – it was before twelve o'clock, and Miss Matty had not yet changed the cap with yellow ribbons, that had been Miss Jenkyns's best, and which Miss Matty was now wearing out in private, putting on the one made in imitation of Mrs Jamieson's at all times when she expected to be seen – Martha came up, and asked if Miss Betty Barker might speak to her mistress. Miss Matty assented, and quickly disappeared to change the yellow ribbons, while Miss Barker came upstairs; but, as she had forgotten her spectacles, and was rather flurried by the unusual time of the visit, I was not surprised to see her return with one cap on the top of the other. She was quite unconscious of it herself, and looked at us with bland satisfaction. Nor do I think Miss Barker perceived it; for, putting aside the little circumstance that she was not so young as she had been, she was very much absorbed in her errand; which she delivered herself of, with an oppressive modesty that found vent in endless apologies.

Miss Betty Barker was the daughter of the old clerk at Cranford, who had officiated in Mr Jenkyns's time. She and her sister had had pretty good situations as ladies' maids, and had saved up money enough to set up a milliner's shop, which had been patronised by the ladies in the neighbourhood. Lady Arley, for instance, would occasionally give Miss Barkers the pattern of an old cap of hers, which they immediately copied and circulated among the *élite* of Cranford. I say the *élite*, for Miss Barkers had caught the trick of the place, and piqued themselves upon their 'aristocratic connection'. They would not sell their caps and ribbons to anyone without a pedigree. Many a farmer's wife or daughter turned away huffed from Miss Barkers' select millinery, and went rather to the universal shop, where the profits of brown soap and moist sugar enabled the proprietor to go straight to (Paris, he said, until he found his customers too patriotic and John Bullish to wear what the Mounseers* wore) London; where, as he often told his customers, Queen Adelaide had appeared, only the very week before, in a cap exactly like the one he showed them, trimmed with yellow and blue ribbons, and had been complimented by King William* on the becoming nature of her head-dress.

Miss Barkers, who confined themselves to truth, and did not approve of miscellaneous customers, throve notwithstanding. They were self-denying, good people. Many a time have I seen the eldest of them (she that had been maid to Mrs Jamieson) carrying out some delicate mess* to a poor person. They only aped their betters in having 'nothing to do' with the class immediately below theirs. And when Miss Barker died, their profits and income were found to be such that Miss Betty was justified in shutting up shop, and retiring from business. She also (as I think I have before said) set up her cow; a mark of respectability in Cranford, almost as decided as setting up a gig is among some people. She dressed finer than any lady in Cranford; and we did not wonder at it; for it was understood that she was wearing out all the bonnets and caps, and outrageous ribbons, which had once formed her stock in trade. It was five or six years since they had given up shop: so in any other place than Cranford her dress might have been considered *passée*.*

And now, Miss Betty Barker had called to invite Miss Matty to tea at her house on the following Tuesday. She gave me also an impromptu invitation, as I happened to be a visitor; though I could see she had a little fear lest, since my father had gone to live in Drumble, he might have engaged in that 'horrid cotton trade', and so dragged his family down out of 'aristocratic society'. She prefaced this invitation with so many apologies, that she quite excited my curiosity. 'Her presumption' was to be excused. What had she been doing? She seemed so overpowered by it, I could only think that she had been writing to Queen Adelaide, to ask for a receipt for washing lace; but the act which she so characterised was only an invitation she had carried to her sister's former mistress, Mrs Jamieson. 'Her former occupation considered, could Miss Matty excuse the liberty?' Ah! thought I, she has found out that double cap, and is going to rectify Miss Matty's head-dress. No! it was simply to extend her invitation to Miss Matty and to me. Miss Matty bowed accept-ance; and I wondered that, in the graceful action, she did not feel the unusual weight and extraordinary height of her head-dress. But I do not think she did; for she recovered her balance, and went on talking to Miss Betty in a kind, condescending manner, very different from the fidgety way she would have had, if she had suspected how singular her appearance was.

'Mrs Jamieson is coming, I think you said?' asked Miss Matty.

'Yes. Mrs Jamieson most kindly and condescendingly said she would be happy to come. One little stipulation she made, that she should bring Carlo. I told her that if I had a weakness, it was for dogs.'

'And Miss Pole?' questioned Miss Matty, who was thinking of her pool at Preference,* in which Carlo would not be available as a partner.

'I am going to ask Miss Pole. Of course, I could not think of asking her until I had asked you, Madam – the rector's daughter, Madam. Believe me, I do not forget the situation my father held under yours.'

'And Mrs Forrester, of course?'

'And Mrs Forrester. I thought, in fact, of going to her before I went to Miss Pole. Although her circumstances are changed, Madam, she was born a Tyrrell, and we can never forget her alliance to the Bigges, of Bigelow Hall.'

Miss Matty cared much more for the little circumstance of her being a very good card-player.

'Mrs Fitz-Adam – I suppose' –

'No, Madam. I must draw a line somewhere. Mrs Jamieson would not, I think, like to meet Mrs Fitz-Adam. I have the greatest respect for Mrs Fitz-Adam – but I cannot think her fit society for such ladies as Mrs Jamieson and Miss Matilda Jenkyns.'

Miss Betty Barker bowed low to Miss Matty, and pursed up her mouth. She looked at me with sidelong dignity, as much as to say, although a retired milliner, she was no democrat, and understood the difference of ranks.

'May I beg you to come as near half-past six, to my little dwelling, as possible, Miss Matilda? Mrs Jamieson dines at five, but has kindly promised not to delay her visit beyond that time – half-past six.' And with a swimming curtsey Miss Betty Barker took her leave.

My prophetic soul foretold a visit that afternoon from Miss Pole, who usually came to call on Miss Matilda after any event – or indeed in sight of any event – to talk it over with her.

'Miss Betty told me it was to be a choice and select few,' said Miss Pole, as she and Miss Matty compared notes.

'Yes, so she said. Not even Mrs Fitz-Adam.'

Now Mrs Fitz-Adam was the widowed sister of the Cranford surgeon, whom I have named before. Their parents were respectable farmers, content with their station. The name of these good people was Hoggins. Mr Hoggins was the Cranford doctor now; we disliked the name, and considered it coarse; but, as Miss Jenkyns said, if he changed it to Piggins it would not be much better. We had hoped to discover a relationship between him and that Marchioness of Exeter whose name was Molly Hoggins; but the man, careless of his own interests, utterly ignored and denied any such relationship; although, as dear Miss Jenkyns had said, he had a sister called Mary, and the same Christian names were very apt to run in families.

Soon after Miss Mary Hoggins married Mr Fitz-Adam, she disappeared from the neighbourhood for many years. She did not move in a sphere in Cranford society sufficiently high to make any of us care to know what Mr Fitz-Adam was. He died and was gathered to his fathers, without our ever having thought about him at all. And then Mrs Fitz-Adam reappeared in Cranford, 'as bold as a lion', Miss Pole said, a well-to-do widow, dressed in rustling black silk, so soon after her husband's death, that poor Miss Jenkyns was justified in the remark she made, that 'bombazine* would have shown a deeper sense of her loss'.

I remember the convocation of ladies, who assembled to decide whether or not Mrs Fitz-Adam should be called upon by the old blue-blooded inhabitants of Cranford. She had taken a large rambling house, which had been usually considered to confer a patent of gentility upon its tenant; because, once upon a time, seventy or eighty years before, the spinster daughter of an earl had resided in it. I am not sure if the inhabiting this house was not also believed to convey some unusual power of intellect; for the earl's daughter, Lady Jane, had a sister, Lady Anne, who had married a general officer, in the time of the American war;* and this general officer had written one or two comedies, which were still acted on the London boards; and which, when we saw them advertised, made us all draw up, and feel that Drury Lane* was paying a very pretty compliment to Cranford. Still, it was not at all a settled thing that Mrs Fitz-

Adam was to be visited, when dear Miss Jenkyns died; and, with her, something of the clear knowledge of the strict code of gentility went out too. As Miss Pole observed, 'As most of the ladies of good family in Cranford were elderly spinsters, or widows without children, if we did not relax a little, and become less exclusive, by-and-by we should have no society at all.'

Mrs Forrester continued on the same side.

'She had always understood that Fitz meant something aristocratic; there was Fitz-Roy – she thought that some of the King's children had been called Fitz-Roy: and there was Fitz-Clarence* now – they were the children of dear good King William the Fourth. Fitz-Adam! – it was a pretty name; and she thought it very probably meant "Child of Adam". No one, who had not some good blood in their veins, would dare to be called Fitz; there was a deal in a name – she had had a cousin who spelt his name with two little ffs – ffoulkes, – and he always looked down upon capital letters, and said they belonged to lately invented families. She had been afraid he would die a bachelor, he was so very choice. When he met with a Mrs ffaringdon, at a watering-place, he took to her immediately; and a very pretty genteel woman she was – a widow with a very good fortune; and "my cousin", Mr ffoulkes, married her; and it was all owing to her two little ffs.'

Mrs Fitz-Adam did not stand a chance of meeting with a Mr Fitz-anything in Cranford, so that could not have been her motive for settling there. Miss Matty thought it might have been the hope of being admitted in the society of the place, which would certainly be a very agreeable rise for *ci-devant** Miss Hoggins; and if this had been her hope, it would be cruel to disappoint her.

So everybody called upon Mrs Fitz-Adam – everybody but Mrs Jamieson, who used to show how honourable she was by never seeing Mrs Fitz-Adam, when they met at the Cranford parties. There would be only eight or ten ladies in the room, and Mrs Fitz-Adam was the largest of all, and she invariably used to stand up when Mrs Jamieson came in, and curtsey very low to her whenever she turned in her direction – so low, in fact, that I think Mrs Jamieson must have looked at the wall above her, for she never moved a muscle of her face, no more than if she had not seen her. Still Mrs Fitz-Adam persevered.

The spring evenings were getting bright and long, when three

or four ladies in calashes met at Miss Barker's door. Do you
know what a calash is? It is a covering worn over caps, not
unlike the heads fastened on old-fashioned gigs; but sometimes
it is not quite so large. This kind of head-gear always made an
awful impression on the children in Cranford; and now two or
three left off their play in the quiet sunny little street, and
gathered, in wondering silence, round Miss Pole, Miss Matty,
and myself. We were silent, too, so that we could hear loud,
suppressed whispers, inside Miss Barker's house: 'Wait, Peggy!
wait till I've run upstairs, and washed my hands. When I cough,
open the door; I'll not be a minute.'

And, true enough, it was not a minute before we heard a
noise, between a sneeze and a crow; on which the door flew
open. Behind it stood a round-eyed maiden, all aghast at the
honourable company of calashes, who marched in without a
word. She recovered presence of mind enough to usher us into a
small room, which had been the shop, but was now converted
into a temporary dressing-room. There we unpinned and shook
ourselves, and arranged our features before the glass into a
sweet and gracious company-face; and then, bowing backwards
with 'After you, ma'am', we allowed Mrs Forrester to take
precedence up the narrow staircase that led to Miss Barker's
drawing-room. There she sat, as stately and composed as though
we had never heard that odd-sounding cough, from which her
throat must have been even then sore and rough. Kind, gentle,
shabbily dressed Mrs Forrester was immediately conducted to
the second place of honour – a seat arranged something like
Prince Albert's near the Queen's* – good, but not so good. The
place of pre-eminence was, of course, reserved for the Honourable Mrs Jamieson, who presently came panting up the stairs –
Carlo rushing round her on her progress, as if he meant to trip
her up.

And now, Miss Betty Barker was a proud and happy woman!
She stirred the fire, and shut the door, and sat as near to it as
she could, quite on the edge of her chair. When Peggy came in,
tottering under the weight of the tea-tray, I noticed that Miss
Barker was sadly afraid lest Peggy should not keep her distance
sufficiently. She and her mistress were on very familiar terms in
their every-day intercourse, and Peggy wanted now to make
several little confidences to her, which Miss Barker was on
thorns to hear; but which she thought it her duty, as a lady, to

repress. So she turned away from all Peggy's asides and signs; but she made one or two very malapropos answers to what was said; and at last, seized with a bright idea, she exclaimed, 'Poor sweet Carlo! I'm forgetting him. Come downstairs with me, poor ittie doggie, and it shall have its tea, it shall!'

In a few minutes she returned, bland and benignant as before; but I thought she had forgotten to give the 'poor ittie doggie' anything to eat; judging by the avidity with which he swallowed down chance pieces of cake. The tea-tray was abundantly loaded. I was pleased to see it, I was so hungry; but I was afraid the ladies present might think it vulgarly heaped up. I know they would have done at their own houses; but somehow the heaps disappeared here. I saw Mrs Jamieson eating seed-cake, slowly and considerately, as she did everything; and I was rather surprised, for I knew she had told us, on the occasion of her last party, that she never had it in her house, it reminded her so much of scented soap. She always gave us Savoy biscuits.* However, Mrs Jamieson was kindly indulgent to Miss Barker's want of knowledge of the customs of high life; and, to spare her feelings, ate three large pieces of seed-cake, with a placid, ruminating expression of countenance, not unlike a cow's.

After tea there was some little demur and difficulty. We were six in number; four could play at Preference, and for the other two there was Cribbage.* But all, except myself – (I was rather afraid of the Cranford ladies at cards, for it was the most earnest and serious business they ever engaged in) – were anxious to be of the 'pool'. Even Miss Barker, while declaring she did not know Spadille from Manille,* was evidently hankering to take a hand. The dilemma was soon put an end to by a singular kind of noise. If a Baron's daughter-in-law could ever be supposed to snore, I should have said Mrs Jamieson did so then; for, overcome by the heat of the room, and inclined to doze by nature, the temptation of that very comfortable armchair had been too much for her, and Mrs Jamieson was nodding. Once or twice she opened her eyes with an effort, and calmly but unconsciously smiled upon us; but, by-and-by, even her benevolence was not equal to this exertion, and she was sound asleep.

'It is very gratifying to me,' whispered Miss Barker at the card-table to her three opponents, whom, notwithstanding her ignorance of the game, she was 'basting'* most unmercifully – 'very gratifying indeed, to see how completely Mrs Jamieson feels at home in my poor little dwelling; she could not have paid me a greater compliment.'

Miss Barker provided me with some literature, in the shape of three or four handsomely bound fashion-books ten or twelve years old, observing, as she put a little table and a candle for my especial benefit, that she knew young people liked to look at pictures. Carlo lay, and snorted, and started at his mistress's feet. He, too, was quite at home.

The card-table was an animated scene to watch; four ladies' heads, with niddle-noddling* caps, all nearly meeting over the middle of the table, in their eagerness to whisper quick enough and loud enough: and every now and then came Miss Barker's 'Hush, ladies! if you please, hush! Mrs Jamieson is asleep.'

It was very difficult to steer clear between Mrs Forrester's deafness and Mrs Jamieson's sleepiness. But Miss Barker managed her arduous task well. She repeated the whisper to Mrs Forrester, distorting her face considerably, in order to show, by the motions of her lips, what was said; and then she smiled kindly all round at us, and murmured to herself, 'Very gratifying, indeed; I wish my poor sister had been alive to see this day.'

Presently the door was thrown wide open; Carlo started to his feet, with a loud snapping bark, and Mrs Jamieson awoke: or, perhaps, she had not been asleep – as she said almost directly, the room had been so light she had been glad to keep her eyes shut, but had been listening with great interest to all our amusing and agreeable conversation. Peggy came in once more, red with importance. Another tray! 'Oh, gentility!' thought I, 'can you endure this last shock?' For Miss Barker had ordered (nay, I doubt not prepared, although she did say, 'Why! Peggy, what have you brought us?' and looking pleasantly surprised at the unexpected pleasure) all sorts of good things for supper – scalloped oysters, potted lobsters, jelly, a dish called 'little Cupids',* (which was in great favour with the Cranford ladies; although too expensive to be given, except on solemn and state occasions – macaroons sopped in brandy, I should have called it, if I had not known its more refined and classical name). In short, we were evidently to be feasted with all that was sweetest and best; and we thought it better to submit graciously, even at the cost of our gentility – which never ate suppers in general — but which, like most non-supper-eaters, was particularly hungry on all special occasions.

Miss Barker, in her former sphere, had, I dare say, been made acquainted with the beverage they call cherry-brandy. We none of us had ever seen such a thing, and rather shrank back when she proffered it us — 'just a little, leetle glass, ladies; after the oysters and lobsters, you know. Shellfish are sometimes thought not very wholesome.' We all shook our heads like female mandarins;* but, at last, Mrs Jamieson suffered herself to be persuaded, and we followed her lead. It was not exactly unpalatable, though so hot and so strong that we thought ourselves bound to give evidence that we were not accustomed to such things, by coughing terribly — almost as strangely as Miss Barker had done, before we were admitted by Peggy.

'It's very strong,' said Miss Pole, as she put down her empty glass; 'I do believe there's spirit in it.'

'Only a little drop — just necessary to make it keep!' said Miss Barker. 'You know we put brandy-paper over preserves to make them keep. I often feel tipsy myself from eating damson tart.'

I question whether damson tart would have opened Mrs Jamieson's heart as the cherry-brandy did; but she told us of a coming event, respecting which she had been quite silent till that moment.

'My sister-in-law, Lady Glenmire, is coming to stay with me.'

There was a chorus of 'Indeed!' and then a pause. Each one rapidly reviewed her wardrobe, as to its fitness to appear in the presence of a Baron's widow; for, of course, a series of small festivals were always held in Cranford on the arrival of a visitor at any of our friends' houses. We felt very pleasantly excited on the present occasion.

Not long after this, the maids and the lanterns were announced. Mrs Jamieson had the sedan chair, which had squeezed itself into Miss Barker's narrow lobby with some difficulty; and most literally, stopped the way. It required some skilful manœuvring on the part of the old chairmen (shoemakers by day; but, when summoned to carry the sedan, dressed up in a strange old livery — long great-coats, with small capes, coeval with the sedan, and similar to the dress of the class in Hogarth's pictures)* to edge, and back, and try at it again, and finally to succeed in carrying their burden out of Miss Barker's front-door. Then we heard their quick pit-a-pat along the quiet little street, as we put on our calashes, and pinned up our gowns; Miss Barker hovering about us with offers of help; which, if she had not remembered her former occupation, and wished us to forget it, would have been much more pressing.

Chapter 8
'YOUR LADYSHIP'

Early the next morning – directly after twelve – Miss Pole made her appearance at Miss Matty's. Some very trifling piece of business was alleged as a reason for the call; but there was evidently something behind. At last out it came.

'By the way, you'll think I'm strangely ignorant; but, do you really know, I am puzzled how we ought to address Lady Glenmire. Do you say, "Your Ladyship", where you would say "you" to a common person? I have been puzzling all morning; and are we to say "My lady", instead of "Ma'am"? Now, you knew Lady Arley – will you kindly tell me the most correct way of speaking to the Peerage?'

Poor Miss Matty! she took off her spectacles, and she put them on again – but how Lady Arley was addressed, she could not remember.

'It is so long ago!' she said. 'Dear! dear! how stupid I am! I don't think I ever saw her more than twice. I know we used to call Sir Peter, "Sir Peter", – but he came much oftener to see us than Lady Arley did. Deborah would have known in a minute. My lady – your ladyship. It sounds very strange, and as if it was not natural. I never thought of it before; but, now you have named it, I am all in a puzzle.'

It was very certain Miss Pole would obtain no wise decision from Miss Matty, who got more bewildered every moment, and more perplexed as to etiquettes of address.

'Well, I really think,' said Miss Pole, 'I had better just go and tell Mrs Forrester about our little difficulty. One sometimes grows nervous; and yet one would not have Lady Glenmire think we were quite ignorant of the etiquettes of high life in Cranford.'

'And will you just step in here, dear Miss Pole, as you come back, please; and tell me what you decide upon. Whatever you, and Mrs Forrester fix upon, will be quite right, I'm sure. "Lady Arley", "Sir Peter",' said Miss Matty, to herself, trying to recall the old forms of words.

'Who is Lady Glenmire?' asked I.

'Oh! she's the widow of Mr Jamieson – that's Mrs Jamieson's late husband, you know – widow of his eldest brother. Mrs Jamieson was a Miss Walker, daughter of Governor Walker. Your ladyship. My dear, if they fix on that way of speaking, you must just let me practise a little on you first, for I shall feel so foolish and hot, saying it the first time to Lady Glenmire.'

It was really a relief to Miss Matty when Mrs Jamieson came on a very unpolite errand. I notice that apathetic people have more quiet impertinence than any others; and Mrs Jamieson came now to insinuate pretty plainly, that she did not particularly wish that the Cranford ladies should call upon her sister-in-law. I can hardly say how she made this clear; for I grew very indignant and warm, while with slow deliberation she was explaining her wishes to Miss Matty, who, a true lady herself, could hardly understand the feeling which made Mrs Jamieson wish to appear to her noble sister-in-law as if she only visited 'county' families. Miss Matty remained puzzled and perplexed long after I had found out the object of Mrs Jamieson's visit.

When she did understand the drift of the honourable lady's call, it was pretty to see with what quiet dignity she received the intimation thus uncourteously given. She was not in the least hurt – she was of too gentle a spirit for that; nor was she exactly conscious of disapproving of Mrs Jamieson's conduct; but there was something of this feeling in her mind, I am sure, which made her pass from the subject to others, in a less flurried and more composed manner than usual. Mrs Jamieson was, indeed, the more flurried of the two, and I could see she was glad to take her leave.

A little while afterwards, Miss Pole returned, red and indignant. 'Well! to be sure! You've had Mrs Jamieson here, I find from Martha; and we are not to call on Lady Glenmire. Yes! I met Mrs Jamieson, half-way between here and Mrs Forrester's, and she told me; she took me so by surprise, I had nothing to say. I wish I had thought of something very sharp and sarcastic; I dare say I shall tonight. And Lady Glenmire is but the widow of a Scotch baron after all! I went on to look at Mrs Forrester's Peerage, to see who this lady was, that is to be kept under a glass case: widow of a Scotch peer – never sat in the House of Lords* – and as poor as Job* I dare say; and she – fifth daughter of some Mr Campbell or other. You are the daughter of a rector, at any rate, and related to the Arleys; and Sir Peter might have been Viscount Arley, everyone says.'

Miss Matty tried to soothe Miss Pole, but in vain. That lady, usually so kind and good-humoured, was now in a full flow of anger.

'And I went and ordered a cap this morning, to be quite ready,' said she, at last, – letting out the secret which gave sting to Mrs Jamieson's intimation. 'Mrs Jamieson shall see if it's so easy to get me to make fourth at a pool, when she has none of her fine Scotch relations with her!'

In coming out of church, the first Sunday on which Lady Glenmire appeared in Cranford, we sedulously talked together, and turned our backs on Mrs Jamieson and her guest. If we might not call on her, we would not even look at her, though we were dying with curiosity to know what she was like. We had the comfort of questioning Martha in the afternoon. Martha did not belong to a sphere of society whose observation could be an implied compliment to Lady Glenmire, and Martha had made good use of her eyes.

'Well, ma'am! is it the little lady with Mrs Jamieson, you mean? I thought you would like more to know how young Mrs Smith was dressed, her being a bride.' (Mrs Smith was the butcher's wife.)

Miss Pole said, 'Good gracious me! as if we cared about a Mrs Smith'; but was silent, as Martha resumed her speech.

'The little lady in Mrs Jamieson's pew had on, ma'am, rather an old black silk, and a shepherd's plaid cloak, ma'am, and very bright black eyes she had, ma'am, and a pleasant, sharp face; not over young, ma'am, but yet, I should guess, younger than Mrs Jamieson herself. She looked up and down the church, like a bird, and nipped up her petticoats, when she came out, as quick and sharp as ever I see. I'll tell you what, ma'am, she's more like Mrs Deacon, at the "Coach and Horses", nor any-one.'

'Hush, Martha!' said Miss Matty, 'that's not respectful!'

'Isn't it, ma'am? I beg pardon, I'm sure; but Jem Hearn said so as well. He said, she was just such a sharp, stirring sort of a body –'

'Lady,' said Miss Pole.

'Lady – as Mrs Deacon.'

Another Sunday passed away, and we still averted our eyes

from Mrs Jamieson and her guest, and made remarks to ourselves that we thought were very severe – almost too much so. Miss Matty was evidently uneasy at our sarcastic manner of speaking.

Perhaps by this time Lady Glenmire had found out that Mrs Jamieson's was not the gayest, liveliest house in the world; perhaps Mrs Jamieson had found out that most of the county families were in London, and that those who remained in the country were not so alive as they might have been to the circumstance of Lady Glenmire being in their neighbourhood. Great events spring out of small causes; so I will not pretend to say what induced Mrs Jamieson to alter her determination of excluding the Cranford ladies, and send notes of invitation all round for a small party, on the following Tuesday. Mr Mulliner himself brought them round. He *would* always ignore the fact of there being a back-door to any house, and gave a louder rat-tat than his mistress, Mrs Jamieson. He had three little notes, which he carried in a large basket, in order to impress his mistress with an idea of their great weight, though they might easily have gone into his waistcoat pocket.

Miss Matty and I quietly decided we would have a previous engagement at home: – it was the evening on which Miss Matty usually made candle-lighters of all the notes and letters of the week; for on Mondays her accounts were always made straight – not a penny owing from the week before; so, by a natural arrangement, making candle-lighters fell upon a Tuesday evening, and gave us a legitimate excuse for declining Mrs Jamieson's invitation. But before our answer was written, in came Miss Pole, with an open note in her hand.

'So!' she said. 'Ah! I see you have got your note, too. Better late than never. I could have told my Lady Glenmire she would be glad enough of our society before a fortnight was over.'

'Yes,' said Miss Matty, 'we're asked for Tuesday evening. And perhaps you would just kindly bring your work across and drink tea with us that night. It is my usual regular time for looking over the last week's bills, and notes, and letters, and making candle-lighters of them; but that does not seem quite reason enough for saying I have a previous engagement at home, though I meant to make it do. Now, if you would come, my conscience would be quite at ease, and luckily the note is not written yet.'

I saw Miss Pole's countenance change while Miss Matty was speaking.

'Don't you mean to go then?' asked she.

'Oh no!' said Miss Matty quietly. 'You don't either, I suppose?'

'I don't know,' replied Miss Pole. 'Yes, I think I do,' said she rather briskly; and on seeing Miss Matty look surprised, she added, 'You see one would not like Mrs Jamieson to think that anything she could do, or say, was of consequence enough to give offence; it would be a kind of letting down of ourselves, that I, for one, should not like. It would be too flattering to Mrs Jamieson, if we allowed her to suppose that what she had said affected us a week, nay ten days afterwards.'

'Well! I suppose it is wrong to be hurt and annoyed so long about anything; and, perhaps, after all, she did not mean to vex us. But I must say, I could not have brought myself to say the things Mrs Jamieson did about our not calling. I really don't think I shall go.'

'Oh, come! Miss Matty, you must go; you know our friend Mrs Jamieson is much more phlegmatic than most people, and does not enter into the little delicacies of feeling which you possess in so remarkable a degree.'

'I thought you possessed them, too, that day Mrs Jamieson called to tell us not to go,' said Miss Matty innocently.

But Miss Pole, in addition to her delicacies of feeling, possessed a very smart cap, which she was anxious to show to an admiring world; and so she seemed to forget all her angry words uttered not a fortnight before, and to be ready to act on what she called the great Christian principle of 'Forgive and forget'; and she lectured dear Miss Matty so long on this head, that she absolutely ended by assuring her it was her duty, as a deceased rector's daughter, to buy a new cap, and go to the party at Mrs Jamieson's. So 'we were most happy to accept', instead of 'regretting that we were obliged to decline'.

The expenditure in dress in Cranford was principally in that one article referred to. If the heads were buried in smart new caps, the ladies were like ostriches, and cared not what became of their bodies. Old gowns, white and venerable collars, any number of brooches, up and down and everywhere (some with dogs' eyes painted in them; some that were like small picture-frames with mausoleums and weeping-willows neatly executed in hair inside; some, again, with miniatures of ladies and gentlemen sweetly smiling out of a nest of stiff muslin) – old brooches for a permanent ornament, and new caps to suit the fashion of the day; the ladies of Cranford always dressed with chaste elegance and propriety, as Miss Barker once prettily expressed it.

And with three new caps, and a greater array of brooches than had ever been seen together at one time, since Cranford was a town, did Mrs Forrester, and Miss Matty, and Miss Pole appear on that memorable Tuesday evening. I counted seven brooches myself on Miss Pole's dress. Two were fixed negligently in her cap (one was a butterfly made of Scotch pebbles, which a vivid imagination might believe to be the real insect); one fastened her net neck-kerchief; one her collar; one ornamented the front of her gown, midway between her throat and waist; and another adorned the point of her stomacher.* Where the seventh was I have forgotten, but it was somewhere about her, I am sure.

But I am getting on too fast, in describing the dresses of the company. I should first relate the gathering, on the way to Mrs Jamieson's. That lady lived in a large house just outside the town. A road, which had known what it was to be a street, ran right before the house, which opened out upon it, without any intervening garden or court. Whatever the sun was about, he never shone on the front of that house. To be sure, the living-rooms were at the back, looking on to a pleasant garden; the front windows only belonged to kitchens and housekeepers' rooms, and pantries; and in one of them Mr Mulliner was reported to sit. Indeed, looking askance, we often saw the back of a head, covered with hair-powder,* which also extended itself over his coat-collar down to his very waist; and this imposing back was always engaged in reading the 'St James's Chronicle', opened wide, which, in some degree, accounted for the length of time the said newspaper was in reaching us – equal subscribers with Mrs Jamieson, though, in right of her honourableness, she always had the reading of it first. This very Tuesday, the delay in forwarding the last number had been particularly aggravating; just when both Miss Pole and Miss Matty, the former more especially, had been wanting to see it, in order to coach up the court-news, ready for the evening's interview with aristocracy. Miss Pole told us she had absolutely taken time by the fore-lock, and been dressed by five o'clock, in order to be ready, if the 'St James's Chronicle' should come in at the last moment – the very 'St James's Chronicle' which the powdered-head was tranquilly and composedly reading as we passed the accustomed window this evening.

'The impudence of the man!' said Miss Pole, in a low indignant whisper. 'I should like to ask him, whether his mistress pays her quarter-share for his exclusive use.'

We looked at her in admiration of the courage of her thought; for Mr Mulliner was an object of great awe to all of us. He seemed never to have forgotten his condescension in coming to live at Cranford. Miss Jenkyns, at times, had stood forth as the undaunted champion of her sex, and spoken to him on terms of equality; but even Miss Jenkyns could get no higher. In his pleasantest and most gracious moods, he looked like a sulky cockatoo. He did not speak except in gruff monosyllables. He would wait in the hall when we begged him not to wait, and then looked deeply offended because we had kept him there, while, with trembling, hasty hands, we prepared ourselves for appearing in company.

Miss Pole ventured on a small joke as we went upstairs, intended, though addressed to us, to afford Mr Mulliner some slight amusement. We all smiled, in order to seem as if we felt at our ease, and timidly looked for Mr Mulliner's sympathy. Not a muscle of that wooden face had relaxed; and we were grave in an instant.

Mrs Jamieson's drawing-room was cheerful; the evening sun came streaming into it, and the large square window was clustered round with flowers. The furniture was white and gold; not the later style, Louis Quatorze* I think they call it, all shells and twirls; no, Mrs Jamieson's chairs and tables had not a curve or bend about them. The chair and table legs diminished as they neared the ground, and were straight and square in all their corners. The chairs were all a-row against the walls, with the exception of four or five which stood in a circle round the fire. They were railed with white bars across the back, and knobbed with gold; neither the railings nor the knobs invited to ease. There was a japanned table devoted to literature, on which lay a Bible, a Peerage, and a Prayer-Book. There was another square Pembroke table* dedicated to the Fine Arts, on which there was a kaleidoscope, conversation-cards, puzzle-cards* (tied together to an interminable length with faded pink satin ribbon), and a box painted in fond imitation of the drawings which decorate tea-chests. Carlo lay on the worsted-worked rug, and ungraciously barked at us as we entered. Mrs Jamieson stood up, giving us each a torpid smile of welcome, and looking helplessly beyond us at Mr Mulliner, as if she hoped he would place us in chairs, for if he did not, she never could. I suppose he thought we could find our way to the circle round the fire, which reminded me of Stonehenge, I don't know why. Lady Glenmire came to the rescue of our hostess; and somehow or other we found ourselves for the first time placed agreeably, and not formally, in Mrs Jamieson's house. Lady Glenmire, now we had time to look at her, proved to be a bright little woman of middle age, who had been very pretty in the days of her youth, and who was even yet very pleasant-looking. I saw Miss Pole appraising her dress in the first five minutes; and I take her word, when she said the next day,

'My dear! ten pounds would have purchased every stitch she had on – lace and all.'

It was pleasant to suspect that a peeress could be poor, and partly reconciled us to the fact that her husband had never sat in the House of Lords; which, when we first heard of it, seemed a kind of swindling us out of our respect on false pretences; a sort of 'A Lord and No Lord' business.*

We were all very silent at first. We were thinking what we could talk about, that should be high enough to interest My Lady. There had been a rise in the price of sugar, which, as preserving-time was near, was a piece of intelligence to all our housekeeping hearts, and would have been the natural topic if Lady Glenmire had not been by. But we were not sure if the Peerage ate preserves – much less knew how they were made. At last, Miss Pole, who had always a great deal of courage and *savoir faire*,* spoke to Lady Glenmire, who on her part had seemed just as much puzzled to know how to break the silence as we were.

'Has your ladyship been to Court, lately?' asked she; and then gave a little glance round at us, half timid, and half triumphant, as much as to say, 'See how judiciously I have chosen a subject befitting the rank of the stranger!'

'I never was there in my life,' said Lady Glenmire, with a broad Scotch accent, but in a very sweet voice. And then, as if she had been too abrupt, she added, 'We very seldom went to London; only twice, in fact, during all my married life; and before I was married, my father had far too large a family' – (fifth daughter of Mr Campbell, was in all our minds, I am sure) – 'to take us often from our home, even to Edinburgh. Ye'll have been in Edinburgh, may be?' said she, suddenly brightening up with the hope of a common interest. We had none of us been there; but Miss Pole had an uncle who once had passed a night there, which was very pleasant.

Mrs Jamieson, meanwhile, was absorbed in wonder why Mr Mulliner did not bring the tea; and, at length, the wonder oozed out of her mouth.

'I had better ring the bell, my dear, had not I?' said Lady Glenmire, briskly.

'No – I think not – Mulliner does not like to be hurried.'

We should have liked our tea, for we dined at an earlier hour than Mrs Jamieson. I suspect Mr Mulliner had to finish the 'St James's Chronicle' before he chose to trouble himself about tea. His mistress fidgetted and fidgetted, and kept saying, 'I can't think why Mulliner does not bring tea. I can't think what he can be about.' And Lady Glenmire at last grew quite impatient, but it was a pretty kind of impatience after all; and she rung the bell sharply, on receiving a half permission from her sister-in-law to do so. Mr Mulliner appeared in dignified surprise. 'Oh!' said Mrs Jamieson, 'Lady Glenmire rang the bell; I believe it was for tea.'

In a few minutes tea was brought. Very delicate was the china, very old the plate, very thin the bread and butter, and very small the lumps of sugar. Sugar was evidently Mrs Jamieson's favourite economy. I question if the little filigree sugar-tongs, made something like scissors, could have opened themselves wide enough to take up an honest, vulgar, good-sized piece; and when I tried to take two little minnikin* pieces at once, so as not to be detected in too many returns to the sugar-basin, they absolutely dropped one, with a little sharp clatter, quite in a malicious and unnatural manner. But before this happened, we had had a slight disappointment. In the little silver jug was cream, in the larger one was milk. As soon as Mr Mulliner came in, Carlo began to beg, which was a thing our manners forbade us to do, though I am sure we were just as hungry; and Mrs Jamieson said she was certain we would excuse her if she gave

her poor dumb Carlo his tea first. She accordingly mixed a
saucer-full for him, and put it down for him to lap; and then
she told us how intelligent and sensible the dear little fellow
was; he knew cream quite well, and constantly refused tea with
only milk in it: so the milk was left for us, but we silently
thought we were quite as intelligent and sensible as Carlo, and
felt as if insult were added to injury, when we were called upon
to admire the gratitude evinced by his wagging his tail for the
cream, which should have been ours.

After tea we thawed down into common-life subjects. We
were thankful to Lady Glenmire for having proposed some more
bread and butter, and this mutual want made us better
acquainted with her than we should ever have been with talking
about the Court, though Miss Pole did say, she had hoped to
know how the dear Queen* was from someone who had seen
her.

The friendship, begun over bread and butter, extended on to
cards. Lady Glenmire played Preference to admiration, and was
a complete authority as to Ombre and Quadrille. Even Miss
Pole quite forgot to say 'my lady', and 'your ladyship', and said
'Basto!* ma'am'; 'you have Spadille,* I believe', just as quietly
as if we had never held the great Cranford parliament on the
subject of the proper mode of addressing a peeress.

As a proof of how thoroughly we had forgotten that we were
in the presence of one who might have sat down to tea with a
coronet, instead of a cap, on her head, Mrs Forrester related a
curious little fact to Lady Glenmire – an anecdote known to the
circle of her intimate friends, but of which even Mrs Jamieson
was not aware. It related to some fine old lace, the sole relic of
better days, which Lady Glenmire was admiring on Mrs Forrester's collar.

'Yes,' said that lady, 'such lace cannot be got now for either
love or money; made by the nuns abroad they tell me. They say
that they can't make it now, even there. But perhaps they can
now they've passed the Catholic Emancipation Bill.* I should
not wonder. But, in the meantime, I treasure up my lace very
much. I daren't even trust the washing of it to my maid' (the
little charity school-girl I have named before, but who sounded
well as 'my maid'). 'I always wash it myself. And once it had a
narrow escape. Of course, your ladyship knows that such lace
must never be starched or ironed. Some people wash it in sugar

and water; and some in coffee, to make it the right yellow
colour; but I myself have a very good receipt for washing it in
milk, which stiffens it enough, and gives it a very good creamy
colour. Well, ma'am, I had tacked it together (and the beauty of
this fine lace is, that when it is wet, it goes into a very little
space), and put it to soak in milk, when, unfortunately, I left the
room; on my return, I found pussy on the table, looking very
like a thief, but gulping very uncomfortably, as if she was half-
choked with something she wanted to swallow, and could not.
And, would you believe it? At first, I pitied her, and said, "Poor
pussy! poor pussy!" till, all at once, I looked and saw the cup of
milk empty – cleaned out! "You naughty cat!" said I; and I
believe I was provoked enough to give her a slap, which did no
good, but only helped the lace down – just as one slaps a
choking child on the back. I could have cried, I was so vexed;
but I determined I would not give the lace up without a struggle
for it. I hoped the lace might disagree with her, at any rate; but
it would have been too much for Job, if he had seen, as I did,
that cat come in, quite placid and purring, not a quarter of an
hour after, and almost expecting to be stroked. "No, pussy!"
said I; "if you have any conscience, you ought not to expect
that!" And then a thought struck me; and I rang the bell for my
maid, and sent her to Mr Hoggins, with my compliments, and
would he be kind enough to lend me one of his top-boots for an
hour? I did not think there was anything odd in the message;
but Jenny said, the young men in the surgery laughed as if they
would be ill, at my wanting a top-boot. When it came, Jenny
and I put pussy in, with her fore-feet straight down, so that they
were fastened, and could not scratch, and we gave her a tea-
spoonful of currant-jelly, in which (your ladyship must excuse
me) I had mixed some tartar emetic. I shall never forget how
anxious I was for the next half-hour. I took pussy to my own
room, and spread a clean towel on the floor. I could have kissed
her when she returned the lace to sight, very much as it had
gone down. Jenny had boiling water ready, and we soaked it
and soaked it, and spread it on a lavender-bush in the sun,
before I could touch it again, even to put it in milk. But now,
your ladyship would never guess that it had been in pussy's
inside.'

We found out, in the course of the evening, that Lady
Glenmire was going to pay Mrs Jamieson a long visit, as she

had given up her apartments in Edinburgh, and had no ties to take her back there in a hurry. On the whole, we were rather glad to hear this, for she had made a pleasant impression upon us; and it was also very comfortable to find, from things which dropped out in the course of conversation, that, in addition to many other genteel qualities, she was far removed from the vulgarity of wealth.

'Don't you find it very unpleasant, walking?' asked Mrs Jamieson, as our respective servants were announced. It was a pretty regular question from Mrs Jamieson, who had her own carriage in the coach-house, and always went out in a sedan-chair to the very shortest distances. The answers were nearly as much a matter of course.

'Oh dear, no! it is so pleasant and still at night!' 'Such a refreshment after the excitement of a party!' 'The stars are so beautiful!' This last was from Miss Matty.

'Are you fond of astronomy?' Lady Glenmire asked.

'Not very' – replied Miss Matty, rather confused at the moment to remember which was astronomy, and which was astrology – but the answer was true under either circumstance, for she read, and was slightly alarmed at, Francis Moore's astrological predictions;* and, as to astronomy, in a private and confidential conversation, she had told me, she never could believe that the earth was moving constantly, and that she would not believe it if she could, it made her feel so tired and dizzy whenever she thought about it.

In our pattens, we picked our way home with extra care that night; so refined and delicate were our perceptions after drinking tea with 'my lady'.

Chapter 9

SIGNOR BRUNONI

Soon after the events of which I gave an account in my last paper, I was summoned home by my father's illness; and for a time I forgot, in anxiety about him, to wonder how my dear friends at Cranford were getting on, or how Lady Glenmire could reconcile herself to the dulness of the long visit which she was still paying to her sister-in-law, Mrs Jamieson. When my father grew a little stronger I accompanied him to the sea-side, so that altogether I seemed banished from Cranford, and was deprived of the opportunity of hearing any chance intelligence of the dear little town for the greater part of that year.

Late in November – when we had returned home again, and my father was once more in good health – I received a letter from Miss Matty; and a very mysterious letter it was. She began many sentences without ending them, running them one into another, in much the same confused sort of way in which written words run together on blotting-paper. All I could make out was, that if my father was better (which she hoped he was), and would take warning and wear a great coat from Michaelmas to Lady-day, if turbans were in fashion,* could I tell her? such a piece of gaiety was going to happen as had not been seen or known of since Wombwell's lions* came, when one of them ate a little child's arm; and she was, perhaps, too old to care about dress, but a new cap she must have; and, having heard that turbans were worn, and some of the county families likely to come, she would like to look tidy, if I would bring her a cap from the milliner I employed; and oh, dear! how careless of her to forget that she wrote to beg I would come and pay her a visit next Tuesday; when she hoped to have something to offer me in the way of amusement, which she would not now more particularly describe, only sea-green was her favourite colour. So she ended her letter; but in a P.S. she added, she thought she might as well tell me what was the peculiar attraction to Cranford just now; Signor Brunoni was going to exhibit his wonderful magic in the Cranford Assembly Rooms, on Wednesday and Friday evening in the following week.

I was very glad to accept the invitation from my dear Miss Matty, independently of the conjuror; and most particularly anxious to prevent her from disfiguring her small gentle mousey face with a great Saracen's-head turban; and, accordingly I bought her a pretty, neat, middle-aged cap, which, however, was rather a disappointment to her when, on my arrival, she followed me into my bedroom, ostensibly to poke the fire, but in reality, I do believe, to see if the sea-green turban was not inside the cap-box with which I had travelled. It was in vain that I twirled the cap round on my hand to exhibit back and side fronts: her heart had been set upon a turban, and all she could do was to say, with resignation in her look and voice:

'I am sure you did your best, my dear. It is just like the caps all the ladies in Cranford are wearing, and they have had theirs for a year, I dare say. I should have liked something newer, I confess − something more like the turbans Miss Betty Barker tells me Queen Adelaide wears; but it is very pretty, my dear. And I dare say lavender will wear better than sea-green. Well, after all, what is dress that we should care about it! You'll tell me if you want anything, my dear. Here is the bell. I suppose turbans have not got down to Drumble yet?'

So saying, the dear old lady bemoaned herself out of the room, leaving me to dress for the evening, when, as she informed me, she expected Miss Pole and Mrs Forrester, and she hoped I should not feel myself too much tired to join the party. Of course I should not; and I made some haste to unpack and arrange my dress; but, with all my speed, I heard the arrivals and the buzz of conversation in the next room before I was ready. Just as I opened the door, I caught the words − 'I was foolish to expect anything very genteel out of the Drumble shops − poor girl! she did her best, I've no doubt.' But for all that, I had rather that she blamed Drumble and me than disfigured herself with a turban.

Miss Pole was always the person, in the trio of Cranford ladies now assembled, to have had adventures. She was in the habit of spending the morning in rambling from shop to shop; not to purchase anything (except an occasional reel of cotton, or a piece of tape), but to see the new articles and report upon them, and to collect all the stray pieces of intelligence in the town. She had a way, too, of demurely popping hither and thither into all sorts of places to gratify her curiosity on any point; a way which, if she had not looked so very genteel and prim, might have been considered impertinent. And now, by the expressive way in which she cleared her throat, and waited for all minor subjects (such as caps and turbans) to be cleared off the course, we knew she had something very particular to relate, when the due pause came – and I defy any people, possessed of common modesty, to keep up a conversation long, where one among them sits up aloft in silence, looking down upon all the things they chance to say as trivial and contemptible compared to what they could disclose, if properly entreated. Miss Pole began:

'As I was stepping out of Gordon's shop, today, I chanced to go into the George (my Betty has a second-cousin who is chamber-maid there, and I thought Betty would like to hear how she was), and, not seeing anyone about, I strolled up the staircase, and found myself in the passage leading to the Assembly Room (you and I remember the Assembly Room, I am sure, Miss Matty! and the *minuets de la cour*!)* so I went on, not thinking of what I was about, when, all at once, I perceived that I was in the middle of the preparations for tomorrow night – the room being divided with great clothes-maids,* over which Crosby's men were tacking red flannel; very dark and odd it seemed; it quite bewildered me, and I was going on behind the screens, in my absence of mind, when a gentleman (quite the gentleman, I can assure you), stepped forwards and asked if I had any business he could arrange for me. He spoke such pretty broken English, I could not help thinking of Thaddeus of Warsaw and the Hungarian Brothers, and Santo Sebastiani;* and while I was busy picturing his past life to myself, he had bowed me out of the room. But wait a minute! You have not heard half my story yet! I was going downstairs, when who should I meet but Betty's second cousin. So, of course, I stopped to speak to her for Betty's sake; and she told me that I had really seen the conjuror; the gentleman who spoke broken English was Signor Brunoni himself. Just at this moment he passed us on the stairs, making such a graceful bow, in reply to which I dropped a curtsey – all foreigners have such polite manners, one catches something of it. But when he had gone downstairs, I bethought me that I had dropped my glove in the Assembly Room (it was

safe in my muff all the time, but I never found it till afterwards);
so I went back, and, just as I was creeping up the passage left on
one side of the great screen that goes nearly across the room,
who should I see but the very same gentleman that had met me
before, and passed me on the stairs, coming now forwards from
the inner part of the room, to which there is no entrance – you
remember Miss Matty! – and just repeating in his pretty broken
English, the inquiry if I had any business there – I don't mean
that he put it quite so bluntly, but he seemed very determined
that I should not pass the screen – so, of course, I explained
about my glove, which, curiously enough, I found at that very
moment.'

Miss Pole then had seen the conjuror – the real live conjuror!
and numerous were the questions we all asked her: 'Had he a
beard?' 'Was he young or old?' 'Fair or dark?' 'Did he look –
'(unable to shape my question prudently, I put it in another
form) – 'How did he look?' In short, Miss Pole was the heroine
of the evening, owing to her morning's encounter. If she was not
the rose (that is to say the conjuror), she had been near it.

Conjuration, sleight of hand, magic, witchcraft were the
subjects of the evening. Miss Pole was slightly sceptical, and
inclined to think there might be a scientific solution found for
even the proceedings of the Witch of Endor.* Mrs Forrester
believed everything from ghosts to death-watches.* Miss Matty
ranged between the two – always convinced by the last speaker.
I think she was naturally more inclined to Mrs Forrester's side,
but a desire of proving herself a worthy sister to Miss Jenkyns
kept her equally balanced – Miss Jenkyns, who would never
allow a servant to call the little rolls of tallow that formed
themselves round candles, 'winding-sheets', but insisted on their
being spoken of as 'roly-poleys'! A sister of hers to be superstitious! It would never do.

After tea, I was dispatched downstairs into the dining-parlour
for that volume of the old encyclopædia which contained the
nouns beginning with C, in order that Miss Pole might prime
herself with scientific explanations for the tricks of the following
evening. It spoilt the pool at Preference which Miss Matty and
Mrs Forrester had been looking forward to, for Miss Pole
became so much absorbed in her subject, and the plates by
which it was illustrated, that we felt it would be cruel to disturb
her, otherwise than by one or two well-timed yawns, which I

threw in now and then, for I was really touched by the meek
way in which the two ladies were bearing their disappointment.
But Miss Pole only read the more zealously, imparting to us no
more interesting information than this:

'Ah! I see; I comprehend perfectly. A represents the ball. Put
A between B and D – no! between C and F, and turn the second
joint of the third finger of your left hand over the wrist of your
right H. Very clear indeed! My dear Mrs Forrester, conjuring
and witchcraft is a mere affair of the alphabet. Do let me read
you this one passage?'

Mrs Forrester implored Miss Pole to spare her, saying, from a
child upwards, she never could understand being read aloud to;
and I dropped the pack of cards, which I had been shuffling very
audibly; and by this discreet movement, I obliged Miss Pole to
perceive that Preference was to have been the order of the
evening, and to propose, rather unwillingly, that the pool should
commence. The pleasant brightness that stole over the other two
ladies' faces on this! Miss Matty had one or two twinges of self-
reproach for having interrupted Miss Pole in her studies: and
did not remember her cards well, or give her full attention to
the game, until she had soothed her conscience by offering to
lend the volume of the Encyclopædia to Miss Pole, who accepted
it thankfully, and said Betty should take it home when she came
with the lantern.

The next evening we were all in a little gentle flutter at the
idea of the gaiety before us. Miss Matty went up to dress
betimes, and hurried me until I was ready, when we found we
had an hour and a half to wait before the 'doors opened at seven
precisely'. And we had only twenty yards to go! However, as
Miss Matty said, it would not do to get too much absorbed in
anything, and forget the time; so, she thought we had better sit
quietly, without lighting the candles, till five minutes to seven.
So Miss Matty dozed, and I knitted.

At length we set off; and at the door, under the carriage-way
at the George, we met Mrs Forrester and Miss Pole: the latter
was discussing the subject of the evening with more vehemence
than ever, and throwing A's and B's at our heads like hail-
stones. She had even copied one or two of the 'receipts' – as she
called them – for the different tricks, on backs of letters, ready
to explain and to detect Signor Brunoni's arts.

We went into the cloak-room adjoining the Assembly Room;

Miss Matty gave a sigh or two to her departed youth, and the remembrance of the last time she had been there, as she adjusted her pretty new cap before the strange, quaint old mirror in the cloak-room. The Assembly Room had been added to the inn about a hundred years before, by the different county families, who met together there once a month during the winter, to dance and play at cards. Many a county beauty had first swam through the minuet that she afterwards danced before Queen Charlotte, in this very room. It was said that one of the Gunnings* had graced the apartment with her beauty; it was certain that a rich and beautiful widow, Lady Williams, had here been smitten with the noble figure of a young artist, who was staying with some family in the neighbourhood for professional purposes, and accompanied his patrons to the Cranford Assembly. And a pretty bargain poor Lady Williams had of her handsome husband, if all tales were true! Now, no beauty blushed and dimpled along the sides of the Cranford Assembly Room; no handsome artist won hearts by his bow, *chapeau bras* in hand: the old room was dingy; the salmon-coloured paint had faded into a drab; great pieces of plaster had chipped off from the white wreaths and festoons on its walls; but still a mouldy odour of aristocracy lingered about the place, and a dusty recollection of the days that were gone made Miss Matty and Mrs Forrester bridle up as they entered, and walk mincingly up the room, as if there were a number of genteel observers, instead of two little boys, with a stick of toffee between them with which to beguile the time.

We stopped short at the second front row; I could hardly understand why, until I heard Miss Pole ask a stray waiter if any of the County families were expected; and when he shook his head, and believed not, Mrs Forrester and Miss Matty moved forwards, and our party represented a conversational square. The front row was soon augmented and enriched by Lady Glenmire and Mrs Jamieson. We six occupied the two front rows, and our aristocratic seclusion was respected by the groups of shopkeepers who strayed in from time to time, and huddled together on the back benches. At least I conjectured so, from the noise they made, and the sonorous bumps they gave in sitting down; but when, in weariness of the obstinate green curtain, that would not draw up, but would stare at me with two odd eyes, seen through holes, as in the old tapestry story,*

I would fain have looked round at the merry chattering people behind me, Miss Pole clutched my arm, and begged me not to turn, for 'it was not the thing'. What 'the thing' was, I never could find out, but it must have been something eminently dull and tiresome. However, we all sat eyes right, square front, gazing at the tantalising curtain, and hardly speaking intelligibly, we were so afraid of being caught in the vulgarity of making any noise in a place of public amusement. Mrs Jamieson was the most fortunate, for she fell asleep.

At length the eyes disappeared – the curtain quivered – one side went up before the other, which stuck fast; it was dropped again, and, with a fresh effort, and a vigorous pull from some unseen hand, it flew up, revealing to our sight a magnificent gentleman in the Turkish costume, seated before a little table, gazing at us (I should have said with the same eyes that I had last seen through the hole in the curtain) with calm and condescending dignity, 'like a being of another sphere', as I heard a sentimental voice ejaculate behind me.

'That's not Signor Brunoni!' said Miss Pole decidedly, and so audibly that I am sure he heard, for he glanced down over his flowing beard at our party with an air of mute reproach. 'Signor Brunoni had no beard – but perhaps he'll come soon.' So she lulled herself into patience. Meanwhile, Miss Matty had reconnoitered through her eye-glass; wiped it, and looked again. Then she turned round, and said to me, in a kind, mild, sorrowful tone: –

'You see, my dear, turbans *are* worn.'

But we had no time for more conversation. The Grand Turk, as Miss Pole chose to call him, arose and announced himself as Signor Brunoni.

'I don't believe him!' exclaimed Miss Pole, in a defiant manner. He looked at her again, with the same dignified upbraiding in his countenance. 'I don't!' she repeated, more positively than ever. 'Signor Brunoni had not got that muffy sort of thing about his chin, but looked like a close-shaved Christian gentleman.'

Miss Pole's energetic speeches had the good effect of wakening up Mrs Jamieson, who opened her eyes wide, in sign of the deepest attention – a proceeding which silenced Miss Pole, and encouraged the Grand Turk to proceed, which he did in very broken English – so broken that there was no cohesion between the parts of his sentences; a fact which he himself perceived at last, and so left off speaking and proceeded to action.

Now we *were* astonished. How he did his tricks I could not imagine; no, not even when Miss Pole pulled out her pieces of paper and began reading aloud – or at least in a very audible whisper – the separate 'receipts' for the most common of his tricks. If ever I saw a man frown, and look enraged, I saw the Grand Turk frown at Miss Pole; but, as she said, what could be expected but unchristian looks from a Mussulman? If Miss Pole was sceptical, and more engrossed with her receipts and diagrams than with his tricks, Miss Matty and Mrs Forrester were mystified and perplexed to the highest degree. Mrs Jamieson kept taking her spectacles off and wiping them, as if she thought it was something defective in them which made the leger-demain;* and Lady Glenmire, who had seen many curious sights in Edinburgh, was very much struck with the tricks, and would not at all agree with Miss Pole, who declared that anybody could do them with a little practice – and that she would, herself, undertake to do all he did, with two hours given to study the Encyclopædia, and make her third finger flexible.

At last, Miss Matty and Mrs Forrester became perfectly awe-struck. They whispered together. I sat just behind them, so I could not help hearing what they were saying. Miss Matty asked Mrs Forrester, 'if she thought it was quite right to have come to see such things? She could not help fearing they were lending encouragement to something that was not quite—' a little shake of the head filled up the blank. Mrs Forrester replied, that the same thought had crossed her mind; she, too, was feeling very uncomfortable; it was so very strange. She was quite certain that it was her pocket-handkerchief which was in that loaf just now; and it had been in her own hand not five minutes before. She wondered who had furnished the bread? She was sure it could not be Dakin, because he was the churchwarden. Suddenly, Miss Matty half turned towards me: –

'Will you look, my dear – you are a stranger in the town, and it won't give rise to unpleasant reports – will you just look round and see if the rector is here? If he is, I think we may conclude that this wonderful man is sanctioned by the Church, and that will be a great relief to my mind.'

I looked, and I saw the tall, thin, dry, dusty rector, sitting surrounded by National School boys,* guarded by troops of his own sex from any approach of the many Cranford spinsters. His kind face was all agape with broad smiles, and the boys around him were in chinks* of laughing. I told Miss Matty that the Church was smiling approval, which set her mind at ease.

I have never named Mr Hayter, the rector, because I, as a well-to-do and happy young woman, never came in contact with him. He was an old bachelor, but as afraid of matrimonial reports getting abroad about him as any girl of eighteen: and he would rush into a shop, or dive down an entry, sooner than encounter any of the Cranford ladies in the street; and, as for the Preference parties, I did not wonder at his not accepting invitations to them. To tell the truth, I always suspected Miss Pole of having given very vigorous chase to Mr Hayter when he first came to Cranford; and not the less, because now she appeared to share so vividly in his dread lest her name should ever be coupled with his. He found all his interests among the poor and helpless; he had treated the National School boys this very night to the performance; and virtue was for once its own reward, for they guarded him right and left, and clung round him as if he had been the queen bee, and they the swarm. He felt so safe in their environment, that he could even afford to give our party a bow as we filed out. Miss Pole ignored his presence, and pretended to be absorbed in convincing us that we had been cheated, and had not seen Signor Brunoni after all.

Chapter 10

THE PANIC

I think a series of circumstances dated from Signor Brunoni's visit to Cranford, which seemed at the time connected in our minds with him, though I don't know that he had anything really to do with them. All at once all sorts of uncomfortable rumours got afloat in the town. There were one or two robberies – real *bonâ fide* robberies; men had up before the magistrates and committed for trial; and that seemed to make us all afraid of being robbed; and for a long time at Miss Matty's, I know, we used to make a regular expedition all round the kitchens and cellars every night, Miss Matty leading the way, armed with the poker, I following with the hearth-brush, and Martha carrying the shovel and fire-irons with which to sound the alarm; and by the accidental hitting together of them she often frightened us so much that we bolted ourselves up, all three together, in the back kitchen, or store-room, or wherever we happened to be, till, when our affright was over, we recollected ourselves, and set out afresh with double valiance. By day we heard strange stories from the shopkeepers and cottagers, of carts that went about in the dead of night, drawn by horses shod with felt, and guarded by men in dark clothes, going round the town, no doubt, in search of some unwatched house or some unfastened door.

Miss Pole, who affected great bravery herself, was the principal person to collect and arrange these reports, so as to make them assume their most fearful aspect. But we discovered that she had begged one of Mr Hoggins's worn-out hats to hang up in her lobby, and we (at least I) had my doubts as to whether she really would enjoy the little adventure of having her house broken into, as she protested she should. Miss Matty made no secret of being an arrant coward; but she went regularly through her housekeeper's duty of inspection – only the hour for this became earlier and earlier, till at last we went the rounds at half-past six, and Miss Matty adjourned to bed soon after seven, 'in order to get the night over the sooner'.

Cranford had so long piqued itself on being an honest and moral town, that it had grown to fancy itself too genteel and well-bred to be otherwise, and felt the stain upon its character at this time doubly. But we comforted ourselves with the assurance which we gave to each other, that the robberies could never have been committed by any Cranford person; it must have been a stranger or strangers, who brought this disgrace upon the town, and occasioned as many precautions as if we were living among the Red Indians or the French.

This last comparison of our nightly state of defence and fortification, was made by Mrs Forrester, whose father had served under General Burgoyne* in the American war, and whose husband had fought the French in Spain.* She indeed inclined to the idea that, in some way, the French were connected with the small thefts, which were ascertained facts, and the burglaries and highway robberies, which were rumours. She had been deeply impressed with the idea of French spies, at some time in her life; and the notion could never be fairly eradicated, but sprung up again from time to time. And now her theory was this: the Cranford people respected themselves too much, and were too grateful to the aristocracy who were so kind as to live near the town, ever to disgrace their bringing up by being dishonest or immoral; therefore, we must believe that the robbers were strangers – if strangers, why not foreigners? – if foreigners, who so likely as the French? Signor Brunoni spoke broken English like a Frenchman, and, though he wore a turban like a Turk, Mrs Forrester had seen a print of Madame de Staël with a turban on, and another of Mr Denon* in just such a dress as that in which the conjuror had made his appearance; showing clearly that the French, as well as the Turks, wore turbans: there could be no doubt Signor Brunoni was a Frenchman – a French spy, come to discover the weak and undefended places of England; and, doubtless, he had his accomplices; for her part, she, Mrs Forrester, had always had her own opinion of Miss Pole's adventure at the George Inn – seeing two men where only one was believed to be: French people had ways and means, which she was thankful to say the English knew nothing about; and she had never felt quite easy in her mind about going to see that conjuror; it was rather too much like a forbidden thing, though the Rector was there. In short, Mrs Forrester grew more excited than we had ever known her before; and, being an officer's daughter and widow, we looked up to her opinion, of course.

Really I do not know how much was true or false in the reports which flew about like wildfire just at this time; but it seemed to me then that there was every reason to believe that at Mardon (a small town about eight miles from Cranford) houses and shops were entered by holes made in the walls, the bricks being silently carried away in the dead of night, and all done so quietly that no sound was heard either in or out of the house. Miss Matty gave it up in despair when she heard of this. 'What was the use,' said she, 'of locks and bolts, and bells to the windows, and going round the house every night? That last trick was fit for a conjuror. Now she did believe that Signor Brunoni was at the bottom of it.'

One afternoon, about five o'clock, we were startled by a hasty knock at the door. Miss Matty bade me run and tell Martha on no account to open the door till she (Miss Matty) had reconnoitred through the window; and she armed herself with a footstool to drop down on the head of the visitor, in case he should show a face covered with black crape, as he looked up in answer to her inquiry of who was there. But it was nobody but Miss Pole and Betty. The former came upstairs, carrying a little hand-basket, and she was evidently in a state of great agitation.

'Take care of that!' said she to me, as I offered to relieve her of her basket. 'It's my plate. I am sure there is a plan to rob my house tonight. I am come to throw myself on your hospitality, Miss Matty. Betty is going to sleep with her cousin at the George. I can sit up here all night, if you will allow me; but my house is so far from any neighbours; and I don't believe we could be heard if we screamed ever so!'

'But,' said Miss Matty, 'what has alarmed you so much? Have you seen any men lurking about the house?'

'Oh yes!' answered Miss Pole. 'Two very bad-looking men have gone three times past the house, very slowly; and an Irish beggar-woman came not half an hour ago, and all but forced herself in past Betty, saying her children were starving, and she must speak to the mistress. You see, she said 'mistress', though there was a hat hanging up in the hall, and it would have been more natural to have said 'master'. But Betty shut the door in her face, and came up to me, and we got the spoons together, and sat in the parlour-window watching, till we saw Thomas

Jones going from his work, when we called to him and asked him to take care of us into the town.'

We might have triumphed over Miss Pole, who had professed such bravery until she was frightened; but we were too glad to perceive that she shared in the weaknesses of humanity to exult over her; and I gave up my room to her very willingly, and shared Miss Matty's bed for the night. But before we retired, the two ladies rummaged up, out of the recesses of their memory, such horrid stories of robbery and murder, that I quite quaked in my shoes. Miss Pole was evidently anxious to prove that such terrible events had occurred within her experience that she was justified in her sudden panic; and Miss Matty did not like to be outdone, and capped every story with one yet more horrible, till it reminded me, oddly enough, of an old story I had read somewhere, of a nightingale and a musician, who strove one against the other which could produce the most admirable music, till poor Philomel* dropped down dead.

One of the stories that haunted me for a long time afterwards, was of a girl, who was left in charge of a great house in Cumberland, on some particular fair-day, when the other servants all went off to the gaieties. The family were away in London, and a pedlar came by, and asked to leave his large and heavy pack in the kitchen, saying, he would call for it again at night; and the girl (a gamekeeper's daughter) roaming about in search of amusement, chanced to hit upon a gun hanging up in the hall, and took it down to look at the chasing;* and it went off through the open kitchen door, hit the pack, and a slow dark thread of blood came oozing out. (How Miss Pole enjoyed this part of the story, dwelling on each word as if she loved it!) She rather hurried over the further account of the girl's bravery, and I have but a confused idea that, somehow, she baffled the robbers with Italian irons,* heated red hot, and then restored to blackness by being dipped in grease.

We parted for the night with an awe-struck wonder as to what we should hear of in the morning – and, on my part, with a vehement desire for the night to be over and gone: I was so afraid lest the robbers should have seen, from some dark lurking-place, that Miss Pole had carried off her plate, and thus have a double motive for attacking our house.

But, until Lady Glenmire came to call next day, we heard of nothing unusual. The kitchen fire-irons were in exactly the same position against the back door, as when Martha and I had skilfully piled them up like spillikins,* ready to fall with an awful clatter, if only a cat had touched the outside panels. I had wondered what we should all do if thus awakened and alarmed, and had proposed to Miss Matty that we should cover up our faces under the bed-clothes, so that there should be no danger of the robbers thinking that we could identify them; but Miss Matty, who was trembling very much, scouted* this idea, and said we owed it to society to apprehend them, and that she should certainly do her best to lay hold of them, and lock them up in the garret till morning.

When Lady Glenmire came, we almost felt jealous of her. Mrs Jamieson's house had really been attacked; at least there were men's footsteps to be seen on the flower-borders, underneath the kitchen windows, 'where nae men should be'; and Carlo had barked all through the night as if strangers were abroad. Mrs Jamieson had been awakened by Lady Glenmire, and they had rung the bell which communicated with Mr Mulliner's room, in the third storey, and when his night-capped head had appeared over the bannisters, in answer to the summons, they had told him of their alarm, and the reasons for it; whereupon he retreated into his bedroom, and locked the door (for fear of draughts, as he informed them in the morning), and opened the window, and called out valiantly to say, if the supposed robbers would come to him he would fight them; but, as Lady Glenmire observed, that was but poor comfort, since they would have to pass by Mrs Jamieson's room and her own, before they could reach him, and must be of a very pugnacious disposition indeed, if they neglected the opportunities of robbery presented by the unguarded lower stories to go up to a garret, and there force a door in order to get at the champion of the house. Lady Glenmire, after waiting and listening for some time in the drawing-room, had proposed to Mrs Jamieson that they should go to bed; but that lady said she should not feel comfortable unless she sat up and watched; and, accordingly, she packed herself warmly up on the sofa, where she was found by the housemaid, when she came into the room at six o'clock, fast asleep; but Lady Glenmire went to bed, and kept awake all night.

When Miss Pole heard of this, she nodded her head in great satisfaction. She had been sure we should hear of something happening in Cranford that night; and we had heard. It was clear enough they had first proposed to attack her house; but when they saw that she and Betty were on their guard, and had carried off the plate, they had changed their tactics and gone to Mrs Jamieson's, and no one knew what might have happened if Carlo had not barked, like a good dog as he was!

Poor Carlo! his barking days were nearly over. Whether the gang who infested the neighbourhood were afraid of him; or whether they were revengeful enough for the way in which he had baffled them on the night in question to poison him; or whether, as some among the more uneducated people thought, he died of apoplexy, brought on by too much feeding and too little exercise; at any rate, it is certain that, two days after this eventful night, Carlo was found dead, with his poor little legs stretched out stiff in the attitude of running, as if by such unusual exertion he could escape the sure pursuer, Death.

We were all sorry for Carlo, the old familiar friend who had snapped at us for so many years; and the mysterious mode of his death made us very uncomfortable. Could Signor Brunoni be at the bottom of this? He had apparently killed a canary with only a word of command; his will seemed of deadly force; who knew but what he might yet be lingering in the neighbourhood willing all sorts of awful things!

We whispered these fancies among ourselves in the evenings; but in the mornings our courage came back with the daylight, and in a week's time we had got over the shock of Carlo's death; all but Mrs Jamieson. She, poor thing, felt it as she had felt no event since her husband's death; indeed Miss Pole said, that as the Honourable Mr Jamieson drank a good deal, and occasioned her much uneasiness, it was possible that Carlo's death might be the greater affliction. But there was always a tinge of cynicism in Miss Pole's remarks. However, one thing was clear and certain; it was necessary for Mrs Jamieson to have some change of scene; and Mr Mulliner was very impressive on this point, shaking his head whenever we inquired after his mistress, and speaking of her loss of appetite and bad nights very ominously; and with justice too, for if she had two characteristics in her natural state of health, they were a facility of eating and sleeping. If she could neither eat nor sleep, she must be indeed out of spirits and out of health.

Lady Glenmire (who had evidently taken very kindly to

Cranford), did not like the idea of Mrs Jamieson's going to Cheltenham, and more than once insinuated pretty plainly that it was Mr Mulliner's doing, who had been much alarmed on the occasion of the house being attacked, and since had said, more than once, that he felt it a very responsible charge to have to defend so many women. Be that as it might, Mrs Jamieson went to Cheltenham, escorted by Mr Mulliner; and Lady Glenmire remained in possession of the house, her ostensible office being to take care that the maid-servants did not pick up followers. She made a very pleasant-looking dragon: and, as soon as it was arranged for her stay in Cranford, she found out that Mrs Jamieson's visit to Cheltenham was just the best thing in the world. She had let her house in Edinburgh, and was for the time houseless, so the charge of her sister-in-law's comfortable abode was very convenient and acceptable.

Miss Pole was very much inclined to install herself as a heroine, because of the decided steps she had taken in flying from the two men and one woman, whom she entitled 'that murderous gang'. She described their appearance in glowing colours, and I noticed that every time she went over the story some fresh trait of villainy was added to their appearance. One was tall – he grew to be gigantic in height before we had done with him; he of course had black hair – and by and by, it hung in elf-locks over his forehead and down his back. The other was short and broad – and a hump sprouted out on his shoulder before we heard the last of him; he had red hair – which deepened into carrotty; and she was almost sure he had a cast in his eye – a decided squint. As for the woman, her eyes glared, and she was masculine-looking – a perfect virago; most probably a man dressed in woman's clothes: afterwards, we heard of a beard on her chin, and a manly voice and a stride.

If Miss Pole was delighted to recount the events of that afternoon to all inquirers, others were not so proud of their adventures in the robbery line. Mr Hoggins, the surgeon, had been attacked at his own door by two ruffians, who were concealed in the shadow of the porch, and so effectually silenced him, that he was robbed in the interval between ringing his bell and the servant's answering it. Miss Pole was sure it would turn out that this robbery had been committed by 'her men', and went the very day she heard of the report to have her teeth examined, and to question Mr Hoggins. She came to us afterwards; so we heard what she had heard, straight and direct from the source, while we were yet in the excitement and flutter of the agitation caused by the first intelligence; for the event had only occurred the night before.

'Well!' said Miss Pole, sitting down with the decision of a person who has made up her mind as to the nature of life and the world (and such people never tread lightly, or seat themselves without a bump) – 'Well, Miss Matty! men will be men. Every mother's son of them wishes to be considered Samson and Solomon rolled into one – too strong ever to be beaten or discomfited – too wise ever to be outwitted. If you will notice, they have always foreseen events, though they never tell one for one's warning before the events happen; my father was a man, and I know the sex pretty well.'

She had talked herself out of breath, and we should have been very glad to fill up the necessary pause as chorus, but we did not exactly know what to say, or which man had suggested this diatribe against the sex; so we only joined in generally, with a grave shake of the head, and a soft murmur of 'They are very incomprehensible, certainly!'

'Now only think,' said she. 'There I have undergone the risk of having one of my remaining teeth drawn (for one is terribly at the mercy of any surgeon-dentist; and I, for one, always speak them fair till I have got my mouth out of their clutches), and after all, Mr Hoggins is too much of a man to own that he was robbed last night.'

'Not robbed!' exclaimed the chorus.

'Don't tell me!' Miss Pole exclaimed, angry that we could be for a moment imposed upon. 'I believe he was robbed, just as Betty told me, and he is ashamed to own it: and, to be sure it was very silly of him to be robbed just at his own door; I dare say, he feels that such a thing won't raise him in the eyes of Cranford society, and is anxious to conceal it – but he need not have tried to impose upon me, by saying I must have heard an exaggerated account of some petty theft of a neck of mutton, which, it seems, was stolen out of the safe in his yard last week; he had the impertinence to add, he believed that that was taken by the cat. I have no doubt, if I could get at the bottom of it, it was that Irishman dressed up in woman's clothes, who came spying about my house, with the story about the starving children.'

After we had duly condemned the want of candour which Mr Hoggins had evinced, and abused men in general, taking him for the representative and type, we got round to the subject about which we had been talking when Miss Pole came in — namely, how far, in the present disturbed state of the country, we could venture to accept an invitation which Miss Matty had just received from Mrs Forrester, to come as usual and keep the anniversary of her wedding-day, by drinking tea with her at five o'clock, and playing a quiet pool afterwards. Mrs Forrester had said, that she asked us with some diffidence, because the roads were, she feared, very unsafe. But she suggested that perhaps one of us would not object to take the sedan; and that the others, by walking briskly, might keep up with the long trot of the chairmen, and so we might all arrive safely at Over Place, a suburb of the town. (No. That is too large an expression: a small cluster of houses separated from Cranford by about two hundred yards of a dark and lonely lane.) There was no doubt but that a similar note was awaiting Miss Pole at home; so her call was a very fortunate affair, as it enabled us to consult together. We would all much rather have declined this invitation; but we felt that it would not be quite kind to Mrs Forrester, who would otherwise be left to a solitary retrospect of her not very happy or fortunate life. Miss Matty and Miss Pole had been visitors on this occasion for many years; and now they gallantly determined to nail their colours to the mast, and to go through Darkness Lane rather than fail in loyalty to their friend.

But when the evening came, Miss Matty (for it was she who was voted into the chair, as she had a cold), before being shut down in the sedan, like jack-in-a-box, implored the chairmen, whatever might befall, not to run away and leave her fastened up there, to be murdered; and even after they had promised, I saw her tighten her features into the stern determination of a martyr, and she gave me a melancholy and ominous shake of the head through the glass. However, we got there safely, only rather out of breath, for it was who could trot hardest through Darkness Lane, and I am afraid poor Miss Matty was sadly jolted.

Mrs Forrester had made extra preparations in acknowledgement of our exertion in coming to see her through such dangers. The usual forms of genteel ignorance as to what her servants might send up were all gone through; and harmony and

Preference seemed likely to be the order of the evening, but for an interesting conversation that began I don't know how, but which had relation, of course, to the robbers who infested the neighbourhood of Cranford.

Having braved the dangers of Darkness Lane, and thus having a little stock of reputation for courage to fall back upon; and also, I dare say, desirous of proving ourselves superior to men (*videlicet** Mr Hoggins), in the article of candour, we began to relate our individual fears, and the private precautions we each of us took. I owned that my pet apprehension was eyes – eyes looking at me, and watching me, glittering out from some dull flat wooden surface; and that if I dared to go up to my looking-glass when I was panic-stricken, I should certainly turn it round, with its back towards me, for fear of seeing eyes behind me looking out of the darkness. I saw Miss Matty nerving herself up for a confession; and at last out it came. She owned that, ever since she had been a girl, she had dreaded being caught by her last leg, just as she was getting into bed, by someone concealed under the bed. She said, when she was younger and more active, she used to take a flying leap from a distance, and so bring both her legs up safely into bed at once; but that this had always annoyed Deborah, who piqued herself upon getting into bed gracefully, and she had given it up in consequence. But now the old terror would often come over her, especially since Miss Pole's house had been attacked (we had got quite to believe in the fact of the attack having taken place), and yet it was very unpleasant to think of looking under a bed, and seeing a man concealed, with a great fierce face staring out at you; so she had bethought herself of something – perhaps I had noticed that she had told Martha to buy her a penny ball, such as children play with – and now she rolled this ball under the bed every night; if it came out on the other side, well and good; if not, she always took care to have her hand on the bell-rope, and meant to call out John and Harry, just as if she expected men-servants to answer her ring.

We all applauded this ingenious contrivance, and Miss Matty sank back into satisfied silence, with a look at Mrs Forrester as if to ask for *her* private weakness.

Mrs Forrester looked askance at Miss Pole, and tried to change the subject a little, by telling us that she had borrowed a boy from one of the neighbouring cottages, and promised his parents a hundredweight of coals at Christmas, and his supper every evening, for the loan of him at nights. She had instructed him in his possible duties when he first came; and, finding him sensible, she had given him the major's sword (the major was her late husband), and desired him to put it very carefully behind his pillow at night, turning the edge towards the head of the pillow. He was a sharp lad, she was sure; for, spying out the major's cocked hat, he had said, if he might have that to wear he was sure he could frighten two Englishmen, or four Frenchmen, any day. But she had impressed upon him anew that he was to lose no time in putting on hats or anything else; but, if he heard any noise, he was to run at it with his drawn sword. On my suggesting that some accident might occur from such slaughterous and indiscriminate directions, and that he might rush on Jenny getting up to wash, and have spitted her before he had discovered that she was not a Frenchman, Mrs Forrester said she did not think that that was likely, for he was a very sound sleeper, and generally had to be well shaken, or cold-pigged* in a morning before they could rouse him. She sometimes thought such dead sleep must be owing to the hearty suppers the poor lad ate, for he was half-starved at home, and she told Jenny to see that he got a good meal at night.

Still this was no confession of Mrs Forrester's peculiar timidity, and we urged her to tell us what she thought would frighten her more than anything. She paused, and stirred the fire, and snuffed the candles, and then she said, in a sounding whisper, –

'Ghosts!'

She looked at Miss Pole, as much as to say she had declared it, and would stand by it. Such a look was a challenge in itself. Miss Pole came down upon her with indigestion, spectral illusions, optical delusions, and a great deal out of Dr Ferrier and Dr Hibbert* besides. Miss Matty had rather a leaning to ghosts, as I have said before, and what little she did say, was all on Mrs Forrester's side, who, emboldened by sympathy, protested that ghosts were a part of her religion; that surely she, the widow of a major in the army, knew what to be frightened at, and what not; in short, I never saw Mrs Forrester so warm either before or since, for she was a gentle, meek, enduring old lady in most things. Not all the elder-wine that ever was mulled, could this night wash out the remembrance of this difference between Miss Pole and her hostess. Indeed, when the elder-wine was brought in, it gave rise to the new burst of discussion: for Jenny, the little maiden who staggered under the tray, had to give evidence of having seen a ghost with her own eyes, not so many nights ago, in Darkness Lane – the very lane we were to go through on our way home.

In spite of the uncomfortable feeling which this last consideration gave me, I could not help being amused at Jenny's position, which was exceedingly like that of a witness being examined and cross-examined by two counsel who are not at all scrupulous about asking leading questions. The conclusion I arrived at was, that Jenny had certainly seen something beyond what a fit of indigestion would have caused. A lady all in white, and without her head, was what she deposed and adhered to, supported by a consciousness of the secret sympathy of her mistress under the withering scorn with which Miss Pole regarded her. And not only she, but many others, had seen this headless lady, who sat by the roadside wringing her hands as in deep grief. Mrs Forrester looked at us from time to time, with an air of conscious triumph; but then she had not to pass through Darkness Lane before she could bury herself beneath her own familiar bed-clothes.

We preserved a discreet silence as to the headless lady while we were putting on our things to go home, for there was no knowing how near the ghostly head and ears might be, or what spiritual connection they might be keeping up with the unhappy body in Darkness Lane; and therefore, even Miss Pole felt it was as well not to speak lightly on such subjects, for fear of vexing or insulting that woe-begone trunk. At least, so I conjecture; for, instead of the busy clatter usual in the operation, we tied on our cloaks as sadly as mutes at a funeral.* Miss Matty drew the curtains round the windows of the chair to shut out disagreeable sights; and the men (either because they were in spirits that their labours were so nearly ended, or because they were going down hill) set off at such a round and merry pace, that it was all Miss Pole and I could do to keep up with them. She had breath for nothing beyond an imploring 'Don't leave me!' uttered as she clutched my arm so tightly that I could not have quitted her, ghost or no ghost. What a relief it was when the men, weary of their burden and their quick trot, stopped just where Headingley-causeway branches off from Darkness Lane! Miss Pole unloosed me and caught at one of the men.

'Could not you – could not you take Miss Matty round by Headingley-causeway, – the pavement in Darkness Lane jolts so, and she is not very strong?'

A smothered voice was heard from the inside of the chair –

'Oh! pray go on! what is the matter? What is the matter? I will give you sixpence more to go on very fast; pray don't stop here.'

'And I'll give you a shilling,' said Miss Pole, with tremulous dignity, 'if you'll go by Headingley-causeway.'

The two men grunted acquiescence and took up the chair and went along the causeway, which certainly answered Miss Pole's kind purpose of saving Miss Matty's bones; for it was covered with soft thick mud, and even a fall there would have been easy, till the getting up came, when there might have been some difficulty in extrication.

Chapter 11

SAMUEL BROWN

The next morning I met Lady Glenmire and Miss Pole, setting out on a long walk to find some old woman who was famous in the neighbourhood for her skill in knitting woollen stockings. Miss Pole said to me, with a smile half kindly and half contemptuous upon her countenance, 'I have been just telling Lady Glenmire of our poor friend Mrs Forrester, and her terror of ghosts. It comes from living so much alone, and listening to the bug-a-boo stories of that Jenny of hers.' She was so calm and so much above superstitious fears herself, that I was almost ashamed to say how glad I had been of her Headingley-causeway proposition the night before, and turned off the conversation to something else.

In the afternoon Miss Pole called on Miss Matty to tell her of the adventure – the real adventure they had met with on their morning's walk. They had been perplexed about the exact path which they were to take across the fields, in order to find the knitting old woman, and had stopped to inquire at a little way-side public-house, standing on the high road to London, about three miles from Cranford. The good woman had asked them to sit down and rest themselves, while she fetched her husband, who could direct them better than she could; and, while they were sitting in the sanded parlour, a little girl came in. They thought that she belonged to the landlady, and began some trifling conversation with her; but, on Mrs Roberts's return, she told them that the little thing was the only child of a couple who were staying in the house. And then she began a long story, out of which Lady Glenmire and Miss Pole could only gather one or two decided facts; which were that, about six weeks ago, a light spring-cart had broken down just before their door, in which there were two men, one woman, and this child. One of the men was seriously hurt – no bones broken, only 'shaken', the landlady called it; but he had probably sustained some severe internal injury, for he had languished in their house ever since, attended by his wife, the mother of this little girl. Miss Pole had asked what he was, what he looked like. And Mrs Roberts had made answer that he was not like a gentleman, nor yet like a common person; if it had not been that he and his wife were such decent, quiet people, she could almost have thought he was a mountebank, or something of that kind, for they had a great box in the cart, full of she did not know what. She had helped to unpack it, and take out their linen and clothes, when the other man – his twin brother, she believed he was – had gone off with the horse and cart.

Miss Pole had begun to have her suspicions at this point, and expressed her idea that it was rather strange that the box and cart and horse and all should have disappeared; but good Mrs Roberts seemed to have become quite indignant at Miss Pole's implied suggestion; in fact, Miss Pole said, she was as angry as if Miss Pole had told her that she herself was a swindler. As the best way of convincing the ladies, she bethought her of begging them to see the wife; and, as Miss Pole said, there was no doubting the honest, worn, bronze face of the woman, who, at the first tender word from Lady Glenmire, burst into tears, which she was too weak to check, until some word from the landlady made her swallow down her sobs, in order that she might testify to the Christian kindness shown by Mr and Mrs Roberts. Miss Pole came round with a swing to as vehement a belief in the sorrowful tale as she had been sceptical before; and, as a proof of this, her energy in the poor sufferer's behalf was nothing daunted when she found out that he, and no other, was our Signor Brunoni, to whom all Cranford had been attributing all manner of evil this six weeks past! Yes! his wife said his proper name was Samuel Brown – 'Sam', she called him – but to the last we preferred calling him 'the Signor'; it sounded so much better.

The end of their conversation with the Signora Brunoni was, that it was agreed that he should be placed under medical advice, and for any expense incurred in procuring this Lady Glenmire promised to hold herself responsible; and had accordingly gone to Mr Hoggins to beg him to ride over to the Rising Sun that very afternoon, and examine into the Signor's real state; and as Miss Pole said, if it was desirable to remove him to Cranford to be more immediately under Mr Hoggins's eye, she would undertake to see for lodgings, and arrange about the rent. Mrs Roberts had been as kind as could be all throughout; but it was evident that their long residence there had been a slight inconvenience.

Before Miss Pole left us, Miss Matty and I were as full of the morning's adventure as she was. We talked about it all the evening, turning it in every possible light, and we went to bed anxious for the morning, when we should surely hear from someone what Mr Hoggins thought and recommended. For, as Miss Matty observed, though Mr Hoggins did say 'Jack's up', 'a fig for his heels',* and call Preference 'Pref', she believed he was a very worthy man, and a very clever surgeon. Indeed, we were rather proud of our doctor at Cranford, as a doctor. We often wished, when we heard of Queen Adelaide or the Duke of Wellington being ill,* that they would send for Mr Hoggins; but, on consideration, we were rather glad they did not, for if we were ailing, what should we do if Mr Hoggins had been appointed physician-in-ordinary to the Royal Family? As a surgeon we were proud of him; but as a man – or rather, I should say, as a gentleman – we could only shake our heads over his name and himself, and wished that he had read Lord Chesterfield's Letters* in the days when his manners were susceptible of improvement. Nevertheless, we all regarded his dictum* in the Signor's case as infallible; and when he said, that with care and attention he might rally, we had no more fear for him.

But although we had no more fear, everybody did as much as if there was great cause for anxiety – as indeed there was, until Mr Hoggins took charge of him. Miss Pole looked out clean and comfortable, if homely, lodgings; Miss Matty sent the sedan-chair for him; and Martha and I aired it well before it left Cranford, by holding a warming-pan full of red-hot coals in it, and then shutting it up close, smoke and all, until the time when he should get into it at the Rising Sun. Lady Glenmire undertook the medical department under Mr Hoggins's directions; and rummaged up all Mrs Jamieson's medicine glasses, and spoons, and bed-tables, in a free and easy way, that made Miss Matty feel a little anxious as to what that lady and Mr Mulliner might say, if they knew. Mrs Forrester made some of the bread-jelly,* for which she was so famous, to have ready as a refreshment in the lodgings when he should arrive. A present of this bread-jelly was the highest mark of favour dear Mrs Forrester could confer. Miss Pole had once asked her for the receipt, but she had met with a very decided rebuff; that lady told her that she could not part with it to anyone during her life, and that after her death it was bequeathed, as her executors would find, to Miss Matty. What Miss Matty – or, as Mrs Forrester called her (remembering the clause in her will, and the dignity of the occasion) Miss Matilda Jenkyns – might choose to do with the receipt when it came into her possession – whether to make it public, or to hand it down as an heir-loom – she did not know, nor would she dictate. And a mould of this admirable, digestible, unique bread-jelly was sent by Mrs Forrester to our poor sick conjuror. Who says that the aristocracy are proud? Here was a lady, by birth a Tyrrell, and descended from the great Sir Walter that shot King Rufus, and in whose veins ran the blood of him who murdered the little Princes in the Tower,* going every day to see what dainty dishes she could prepare for Samuel Brown, a mountebank! But, indeed, it was wonderful to see what kind feelings were called out by this poor man's coming amongst us. And also wonderful to see how the great Cranford panic, which had been occasioned by his first coming in his Turkish dress, melted away into thin air on his second coming – pale and feeble, and with his heavy filmy eyes, that only brightened a very little when they fell upon the countenance of his faithful wife, or their pale and sorrowful little girl.

Somehow, we all forgot to be afraid. I dare say it was, that finding out that he, who had first excited our love of the marvellous by his unprecedented arts, had not sufficient everyday gifts to manage a shying horse, made us feel as if we were ourselves again. Miss Pole came with her little basket at all hours of the evening, as if her lonely house, and the unfrequented road to it, had never been infested by that 'murderous gang'; Mrs Forrester said, she thought that neither Jenny nor she need mind the headless lady who wept and wailed in Darkness Lane, for surely the power was never given to such beings to harm those who went about to try to do what little good was in their power; to which Jenny, trembling, assented; but the mistress's theory had little effect on the maid's practice, until she had sewed two pieces of red flannel, in the shape of a cross, on her inner garment.

I found Miss Matty covering her penny ball – the ball that she used to roll under her bed – with gay-coloured worsted in rainbow stripes.

'My dear,' said she, 'my heart is sad for that little care-worn child. Although her father is a conjuror, she looks as if she had never had a good game of play in her life. I used to make very pretty balls in this way when I was a girl, and I thought I would try if I could not make this one smart and take it to Phœbe this afternoon. I think 'the gang' must have left the neighbourhood, for one does not hear any more of their violence and robbery now.'

We were all of us far too full of the Signor's precarious state to talk about either robbers or ghosts. Indeed, Lady Glenmire said, she never had heard of any actual robberies; except that two little boys had stolen some apples from Farmer Benson's orchard, and that some eggs had been missed on a market-day off Widow Hayward's stall. But that was expecting too much of us; we could not acknowledge that we had only had this small foundation for all our panic. Miss Pole drew herself up at this remark of Lady Glenmire's; and said 'that she wished she could agree with her as to the very small reason we had had for alarm; but, with the recollection of a man disguised as a woman, who had endeavoured to force herself into her house, while his confederates waited outside; with the knowledge gained from Lady Glenmire herself, of the foot-prints seen on Mrs Jamieson's flower-borders; with the fact before her of the audacious robbery committed on Mr Hoggins at his own door – ' But here Lady Glenmire broke in with a very strong expression of doubt as to whether this last story was not an entire fabrication, founded upon the theft of a cat; she grew so red while she was saying all this, that I was not surprised at Miss Pole's manner of bridling up, and I am certain if Lady Glenmire had not been 'her ladyship', we should have had a more emphatic contradiction than the 'Well, to be sure!' and similar fragmentary ejaculations, which were all that she ventured upon in my lady's presence. But when she was gone, Miss Pole began a long congratulation to Miss Matty that, so far they had escaped marriage, which she noticed always made people credulous to the last degree; indeed, she thought it argued great natural credulity in a woman if she could not keep herself from being married; and in what Lady Glenmire had said about Mr Hoggins's robbery, we had a specimen of what people came to, if they gave way to such a weakness; evidently, Lady Glenmire would swallow anything, if she could believe the poor vamped-up story about a neck of mutton and a pussy, with which he had tried to impose on Miss Pole, only she had always been on her guard against believing too much of what men said.

We were thankful, as Miss Pole desired us to be, that we had never been married; but I think, of the two, we were even more thankful that the robbers had left Cranford; at least I judge so from a speech of Miss Matty's that evening, as we sat over the fire, in which she evidently looked upon a husband as a great protector against thieves, burglars, and ghosts; and said, that she did not think that she should dare to be always warning young people of matrimony, as Miss Pole did continually; – to be sure, marriage was a risk, as she saw now she had had some experience; but she remembered the time when she had looked forward to being married as much as anyone.

'Not to any particular person, my dear,' said she, hastily checking herself up as if she were afraid of having admitted too much; 'only the old story, you know, of ladies always saying "*When* I marry", and gentlemen, "*If* I marry".' It was a joke spoken in rather a sad tone, and I doubt if either of us smiled; but I could not see Miss Matty's face by the flickering fire-light. In a little while she continued:

'But after all I have not told you the truth. It is so long ago, and no one ever knew how much I thought of it at the time, unless, indeed, my dear mother guessed; but I may say that there was a time when I did not think I should have been only Miss Matty Jenkyns all my life; for even if I did meet with anyone who wished to marry me now (and as Miss Pole says, one is never too safe), I could not take him – I hope he would not take it too much to heart, but I could *not* take him – or anyone but the person I once thought I should be married to, and he is dead and gone, and he never knew how it all came about that I said "no", when I had thought many and many a time – Well, it's no matter what I thought. God ordains it all, and I am very happy, my dear. No one has such kind friends as I,' continued she, taking my hand and holding it in hers.

If I had never known of Mr Holbrook, I could have said something in this pause, but as I had, I could not think of anything that would come in naturally, and so we both kept silence for a little time.

'My father once made us,' she began, 'keep a diary in two columns; on one side we were to put down in the morning what we thought would be the course and events of the coming day, and at night we were to put down on the other side what really had happened. It would be to some people rather a sad way of telling their lives' – (a tear dropped upon my hand at these words) – 'I don't mean that mine has been sad, only so very different to what I expected. I remember, one winter's evening, sitting over our bedroom fire with Deborah – I remember it as if it were yesterday – and we were planning our future lives – both of us were planning, though only she talked about it. She said she should like to marry an archdeacon, and write his charges;* and you know, my dear, she never was married, and, for aught I know, she never spoke to an unmarried archdeacon in her life. I never was ambitious, nor could I have written charges, but I thought I could manage a house (my mother used to call me her right hand), and I was always so fond of little children – the shyest babies would stretch out their little arms to come to me; when I was a girl, I was half my leisure time nursing in the neighbouring cottages – but I don't know how it was, when I grew sad and grave – which I did a year or two after this time – the little things drew back from me, and I am afraid I lost the knack, though I am just as fond of children as ever, and have a strange yearning at my heart whenever I see a mother with her baby in her arms. Nay, my dear,' – (and by a sudden blaze which sprang up from a fall of the unstirred coals, I saw that her eyes were full of tears – gazing intently on some vision of what might have been) – 'do you know, I dream sometimes that I have a little child – always the same – a little girl of about two years old; she never grows older, though I have dreamt about her for many years. I don't think I ever dream of any words or sound she makes; she is very noiseless and still, but she comes to me when she is very sorry or very glad, and I have wakened with the clasp of her dear little arms round my neck. Only last night – perhaps because I had gone to sleep thinking of this ball for Phœbe – my little darling came in my dream, and put up her mouth to be kissed, just as I have seen real babies do to real mothers before going to bed. But all this is nonsense, dear! only don't be frightened by Miss Pole from being married. I can fancy it may be a very happy state, and a little credulity helps one on through life very smoothly, – better than always doubting and doubting, and seeing difficulties and disagreeables in everything.'

If I had been inclined to be daunted from matrimony, it would not have been Miss Pole to do it; it would have been the lot of poor Signor Brunoni and his wife. And yet again, it was an encouragement to see how, through all their cares and sorrows, they thought of each other and not of themselves; and how keen were their joys, if they only passed through each other, or through the little Phœbe.

The Signora told me, one day, a good deal about their lives up to this period. It began by my asking her whether Miss Pole's story of the twin-brothers was true; it sounded so wonderful a likeness, that I should have had my doubts, if Miss Pole had not been unmarried. But the Signora, or (as we found out she preferred to be called) Mrs Brown, said it was quite true; that her brother-in-law was by many taken for her husband, which was of great assistance to them in their profession; 'though,' she continued, 'how people can mistake Thomas for the real Signor Brunoni, I can't conceive; but he says they do; so I suppose I must believe him. Not but what he is a very good man; I am sure I don't know how we should have paid our bill at the Rising Sun, but for the money he sends; but people must know very little about art, if they can take him for my husband. Why, Miss, in the ball trick, where my husband spreads his fingers wide, and throws out his little finger with quite an air and a grace, Thomas just clumps up his hand like a fist, and might have ever so many balls hidden in it. Besides, he has never been to India, and knows nothing of the proper sit of a turban.'

'Have you been in India?' said I, rather astonished.

'Oh yes! many a year, ma'am. Sam was a serjeant in the 31st; and when the regiment was ordered to India, I drew a lot to go,* and I was more thankful than I can tell; for it seemed as if it would only be a slow death to me to part from my husband. But, indeed, ma'am, if I had known all, I don't know whether I would not rather have died there and then, than gone through what I have done since. To be sure, I've been able to comfort Sam, and to be with him; but, ma'am, I've lost six children,' said she, looking up at me with those strange eyes, that I have never noticed but in mothers of dead children – with a kind of wild look in them, as if seeking for what they never more might find. 'Yes! Six children died off, like little buds nipped untimely, in that cruel India. I thought, as each died, I never could – I never would – love a child again; and when the next came, it had not only its own love, but the deeper love that came from the thoughts of its little dead brothers and sisters. And when Phœbe was coming, I said to my husband, "Sam, when the child is born, and I am strong, I shall leave you; it will cut my heart cruel; but if this baby dies too, I shall go mad; the madness is in me now; but if you let me go down to Calcutta, carrying my baby step by step, it will maybe work itself off; and I will save, and I will hoard, and I will beg, – and I will die, to get a passage home to England, where our baby may live!" God bless him! he said I might go; and he saved up his pay, and I saved every pice* I could get for washing or any way; and when Phœbe came, and I grew strong again, I set off. It was very lonely; through the thick forests, dark again with their heavy trees – along by the rivers' side – (but I had been brought up near the Avon in Warwickshire,* so that flowing noise sounded like home), from station to station,* from Indian village to village, I went along, carrying my child. I had seen one of the officer's ladies with a little picture, ma'am – done by a Catholic foreigner, ma'am – of the Virgin and the little Saviour, ma'am. She had him on her arm, and her form was softly curled round him, and their cheeks touched. Well, when I went to bid good-bye to this lady, for whom I had washed, she cried sadly; for she, too, had lost her children, but she had not another to save, like me; and I was bold enough to ask her, would she give me that print? And she cried the more, and said *her* children were with that little blessed Jesus; and gave it me, and told me she had heard it had been painted on the bottom of a cask, which made it have that round shape. And when my body was very weary, and my heart was sick – (for there were times when I misdoubted if I could ever reach my home, and there were times when I thought of my husband; and one time when I thought my baby was dying) – I took out that picture and looked at it, till I could have thought the mother spoke to me, and comforted me. And the natives were very kind. We could not understand one another; but they saw my baby on my breast, and they came out to me, and brought me rice and milk, and sometimes flowers – I have got some of the flowers dried. Then, the next morning, I was so tired! and they wanted me to stay with them – I could tell that – and tried to frighten me from going into the deep woods, which, indeed, looked very strange and dark; but it seemed to me as if Death was following me to take my baby away from me; and as if I must go on, and on – and I thought how God had cared for mothers ever since the world was made, and would care for me; so I bade them good-bye, and set off afresh. And once when my baby was ill, and both she and I needed rest, He led me to a place where I found a kind Englishman lived, right in the midst of the natives.'

'And you reached Calcutta safely at last?'

'Yes! safely. Oh! when I knew I had only two days' journey more before me, I could not help it, ma'am – it might be idolatry, I cannot tell – but I was near one of the native temples, and I went in it with my baby to thank God for his great mercy; for it seemed to me that where others had prayed before to their God, in their joy or in their agony, was of itself a sacred place. And I got as servant to an invalid lady, who grew quite fond of my baby aboard-ship; and, in two years' time, Sam earned his discharge, and came home to me, and to our child. Then he had to fix on a trade; but he knew of none; and, once, once upon a time, he had learnt some tricks from an Indian juggler; so he set up conjuring, and it answered so well that he took Thomas to help him – as his man, you know, not as another conjuror, though Thomas has set it up now on his own hook. But it has been a great help to us that likeness between the twins, and made a good many tricks go off well that they made up together. And Thomas is a good brother, only he has not the fine carriage of my husband, so that I can't think how he can be taken for Signor Brunoni himself, as he says he is.'

'Poor little Phœbe!' said I, my thoughts going back to the baby she carried all those hundred miles.

'Ah! you may say so! I never thought I should have reared her, though, when she fell ill in Chunderabaddad;* but that good, kind Aga* Jenkyns took us in, which I believe was the very saving of her.'

'Jenkyns!' said I.

'Yes! Jenkyns. I shall think all people of that name are kind; for here is that nice old lady who comes every day to take Phœbe a walk!'

But an idea had flashed through my head: could the Aga Jenkyns be the lost Peter? True, he was reported by many to be dead. But, equally true, some had said that he had arrived at the dignity of great Lama of Thibet.* Miss Matty thought he was alive. I would make further inquiry.

Chapter 12

ENGAGED TO BE MARRIED!

Was the 'poor Peter' of Cranford the Aga Jenkyns of Chunderabaddad, or was he not? As somebody says, that was the question.

In my own home, whenever people had nothing else to do, they blamed me for want of discretion. Indiscretion was my bugbear fault. Everybody has a bugbear fault; a sort of standing characteristic – a *pièce de résistance** for their friends to cut at; and in general they cut and come again. I was tired of being called indiscreet and incautious; and I determined for once to prove myself a model of prudence and wisdom. I would not even hint my suspicions respecting the Aga. I would collect evidence and carry it home to lay before my father, as the family friend of the two Miss Jenkynses.

In my search after facts, I was often reminded of a description my father had once given of a Ladies' Committee that he had had to preside over. He said he could not help thinking of a passage in Dickens, which spoke of a chorus in which every man took the tune he knew best,* and sang it to his own satisfaction. So, at this charitable committee, every lady took the subject uppermost in her mind, and talked about it to her own great contentment, but not much to the advancement of the subject they had met to discuss. But even that committee could have been nothing to the Cranford ladies when I attempted to gain some clear and definite information as to poor Peter's height, appearance, and when and where he was seen and heard of last. For instance, I remember asking Miss Pole (and I thought the question was very opportune, for I put it when I met her at a call at Mrs Forrester's, and both the ladies had known Peter, and I imagined that they might refresh each other's memories); I asked Miss Pole what was the very last thing they had ever heard about him; and then she named the absurd report to which I have alluded, about his having been elected great Lama of Thibet; and this was a signal for each lady to go off on her separate idea. Mrs Forrester's start was made on the Veiled

Prophet in *Lalla Rookh** – whether I thought he was meant for the Great Lama, though Peter was not so ugly, indeed rather handsome if he had not been freckled. I was thankful to see her double upon Peter; but, in a moment, the delusive lady was off upon Rowland's Kalydor,* and the merits of cosmetics and hair oils in general, and holding forth so fluently that I turned to listen to Miss Pole, who (through the llamas, the beasts of burden) had got to Peruvian bonds,* and the Share Market, and her poor opinion of joint-stock banks in general, and of that one in particular in which Miss Matty's money was invested. In vain I put in, 'When was it – in what year was it, that you heard that Mr Peter was the Great Lama?' They only joined issue to dispute whether llamas were carnivorous animals or not; in which dispute they were not quite on fair grounds, as Mrs Forrester (after they had grown warm and cool again) acknowledged that she always confused carnivorous and graminivorous together, just as she did horizontal and perpendicular; but then she apologised for it very prettily, by saying that in her day the only use people made of four-syllabled words was to teach how they should be spelt.

The only fact I gained from this conversation was that certainly Peter had last been heard of in India, 'or that neighbourhood'; and that this scanty intelligence of his whereabouts had reached Cranford in the year when Miss Pole had bought her India muslin gown, long since worn out (we washed it and mended it, and traced its decline and fall into a window-blind, before we could go on); and in a year when Wombwell came to Cranford,* because Miss Matty had wanted to see an elephant in order that she might the better imagine Peter riding on one; and had seen a boa-constrictor too, which was more than she wished to imagine in her fancy pictures of Peter's locality; – and in a year when Miss Jenkyns had learnt some piece of poetry off by heart, and used to say, at all the Cranford parties, how Peter was 'surveying mankind from China to Peru',* which everybody had thought very grand, and rather appropriate, because India was between China and Peru, if you took care to turn the globe to the left instead of the right.

I suppose all these inquiries of mine, and the consequent curiosity excited in the minds of my friends, made us blind and deaf to what was going on around us. It seemed to me as if the sun rose and shone, and as if the rain rained on Cranford just as usual, and I did not notice any sign of the times that could be considered as a prognostic of any uncommon event; and, to the best of my belief, not only Miss Matty and Mrs Forrester, but even Miss Pole herself, whom we looked upon as a kind of prophetess from the knack she had of foreseeing things before they came to pass – although she did not like to disturb her friends by telling them her fore-knowledge – even Miss Pole herself was breathless with astonishment, when she came to tell us of the astounding piece of news. But I must recover myself; the contemplation of it, even at this distance of time, has taken away my breath and my grammar, and unless I subdue my emotion, my spelling will go too.

We were sitting – Miss Matty and I much as usual; she in the blue chintz easy chair, with her back to the light, and her knitting in her hand – I reading aloud the St James's Chronicle. A few minutes more, and we should have gone to make the little alterations in dress usual before calling time (twelve o'clock) in Cranford. I remember the scene and the date well. We had been talking of the Signor's rapid recovery since the warmer weather had set in, and praising Mr Hoggins's skill, and lamenting his want of refinement and manner – (it seems a curious coincidence that this should have been our subject, but so it was) – when a knock was heard; a caller's knock – three distinct taps – and we were flying (that is to say, Miss Matty could not walk very fast, having had a touch of rheumatism) to our rooms, to change cap and collars, when Miss Pole arrested us by calling out as she came up the stairs, 'Don't go – I can't wait – it is not twelve, I know – but never mind your dress – I must speak to you.' We did our best to look as if it was not we who had made the hurried movement, the sound of which she had heard; for, of course, we did not like to have it supposed that we had any old clothes that it was convenient to wear out in the 'sanctuary of home', as Miss Jenkyns once prettily called the back parlour, where she was tying up preserves. So we threw our gentility with double force into our manners, and very genteel we were for two minutes while Miss Pole recovered breath, and excited our curiosity strongly by lifting up her hands in amazement, and bringing them down in silence, as if what she had to say was too big for words, and could only be expressed by pantomime.

'What do you think, Miss Matty? What *do* you think? Lady

Glenmire is to marry – is to be married, I mean – Lady Glenmire
– Mr Hoggins – Mr Hoggins is going to marry Lady Glenmire!'

'Marry!' said we. 'Marry! Madness!'

'Marry!' said Miss Pole, with the decision that belonged to
her character. 'I said Marry! as you do; and I also said, 'What a
fool my lady is going to make of herself!' I could have said
'Madness!' but I controlled myself, for it was in a public shop
that I heard of it. Where feminine delicacy is gone to, I don't
know! You and I, Miss Matty, would have been ashamed to
have known that our marriage was spoken of in a grocer's shop,
in the hearing of shopmen!'

'But,' said Miss Matty, sighing as one recovering from a blow,
'perhaps it is not true. Perhaps we are doing her injustice.'

'No!' said Miss Pole. 'I have taken care to ascertain that. I
went straight to Mrs Fitz-Adam, to borrow a cookery book
which I knew she had; and I introduced my congratulations
apropos of the difficulty gentlemen must have in house-keeping;
and Mrs Fitz-Adam bridled up, and said, that she believed it
was true, though how and where I could have heard it she did
not know. She said her brother and Lady Glenmire had come to
an understanding at last. 'Understanding!' such a coarse word!
But my lady will have to come down to many a want of
refinement. I have reason to believe Mr Hoggins sups on bread-
and-cheese and beer every night.'

'Marry!' said Miss Matty once again. 'Well! I never thought
of it. Two people that we know going to be married. It's coming
very near!'

'So near that my heart stopped beating, when I heard of it,
while you might have counted twelve,' said Miss Pole.

'One does not know whose turn may come next. Here, in
Cranford, poor Lady Glenmire might have thought herself safe,'
said Miss Matty, with a gentle pity in her tones.

'Bah!' said Miss Pole, with a toss of her head. 'Don't you
remember poor dear Captain Brown's song "Tibbie Fowler",*
and the line –

> Set her on the Tintock Tap,
> The wind will blaw a man 'till her.

'That was because "Tibbie Fowler" was rich I think.'

'Well! there is a kind of attraction about Lady Glenmire that
I, for one, should be ashamed to have.'

I put in my wonder. 'But how can she have fancied Mr Hoggins? I am not surprised that Mr Hoggins has liked her.'

'Oh! I don't know. Mr Hoggins is rich, and very pleasant-looking,' said Miss Matty, 'and very good-tempered and kind-hearted.'

'She has married for an establishment, that's it. I suppose she takes the surgery with it,' said Miss Pole, with a little dry laugh at her own joke. But, like many people who think they have made a severe and sarcastic speech, which yet is clever of its kind, she began to relax in her grimness from the moment when she made this allusion to the surgery; and we turned to speculate on the way in which Mrs Jamieson would receive the news. The person whom she had left in charge of her house to keep off followers from her maids, to set up a follower of her own! And that follower a man whom Mrs Jamieson had tabooed as vulgar, and inadmissible to Cranford society; not merely on account of his name, but because of his voice, his complexion, his boots, smelling of the stable, and himself, smelling of drugs. Had he ever been to see Lady Glenmire at Mrs Jamieson's? Chloride of lime would not purify the house in its owner's estimation if he had. Or had their interviews been confined to the occasional meetings in the chamber of the poor sick conjuror, to whom, with all our sense of the *mésalliance** we could not help allowing that they had both been exceedingly kind? And now it turned out that a servant of Mrs Jamieson's had been ill, and Mr Hoggins had been attending her for some weeks. So the wolf had got into the fold, and now he was carrying off the shepherdess. What would Mrs Jamieson say? We looked into the darkness of futurity as a child gazes after a rocket up in the cloudy sky, full of wondering expectation of the rattle, the discharge, and the brilliant shower of sparks and light. Then we brought ourselves down to earth and the present time, by questioning each other (being all equally ignorant, and all equally without the slightest data to build any conclusions upon) as to when IT would take place? Where? How much a year Mr Hoggins had? Whether she would drop her title? And how Martha and the other correct servants in Cranford would ever be brought to announce a married couple as Lady Glenmire and Mr Hoggins? But would they be visited? Would Mrs Jamieson let us? Or must we choose between the Honourable Mrs Jamieson and the degraded Lady Glenmire. We all liked Lady

Glenmire the best. She was bright, and kind, and sociable, and agreeable; and Mrs Jamieson was dull, and inert, and pompous, and tiresome. But we had acknowledged the sway of the latter so long, that it seemed like a kind of disloyalty now even to meditate disobedience to the prohibition we anticipated.

Mrs Forrester surprised us in our darned caps and patched collars; and we forgot all about them in our eagerness to see how she would bear the information, which we honourably left to Miss Pole to impart, although, if we had been inclined to take unfair advantage, we might have rushed in ourselves, for she had a most out-of-place fit of coughing for five minutes after Mrs Forrester entered the room. I shall never forget the imploring expression of her eyes, as she looked at us over her pocket-handkerchief. They said, as plain as words could speak, 'Don't let Nature deprive me of the treasure which is mine, although for a time I can make no use of it.' And we did not.

Mrs Forrester's surprise was equal to ours; and her sense of injury rather greater, because she had to feel for her Order,* and saw more fully than we could do how such conduct brought stains on the aristocracy.

When she and Miss Pole left us, we endeavoured to subside into calmness; but Miss Matty was really upset by the intelligence she had heard. She reckoned it up, and it was more than fifteen years since she had heard of any of her acquaintance going to be married, with the one exception of Miss Jessie Brown; and, as she said, it gave her quite a shock, and made her feel as if she could not think what would happen next.

I don't know if it is a fancy of mine, or a real fact, but I have noticed that, just after the announcement of an engagement in any set, the unmarried ladies in that set flutter out in an unusual gaiety and newness of dress, as much as to say, in a tacit and unconscious manner, 'We also are spinsters.' Miss Matty and Miss Pole talked and thought more about bonnets, gowns, caps, and shawls, during the fortnight that succeeded this call, than I had known them do for years before. But it might be the spring weather, for it was a warm and pleasant March; and merinoes and beavers,* and woollen materials of all sorts, were but ungracious receptacles of the bright sun's glancing rays. It had not been Lady Glenmire's dress that had won Mr Hoggins's heart, for she went about on her errands of kindness more shabby than ever. Although in the hurried glimpses I caught of her at church or elsewhere, she appeared rather to shun meeting any of her friends, her face seemed to have almost something of the flush of youth in it; her lips looked redder, and more trembling full than in their old compressed state, and her eyes dwelt on all things with a lingering light, as if she was learning to love Cranford and its belongings. Mr Hoggins looked broad and radiant, and creaked up the middle aisle at church in a bran-new pair of top-boots – an audible, as well as visible, sign of his purposed change of state; for the tradition went, that the boots he had worn till now were the identical pair in which he first set out on his rounds in Cranford twenty-five years ago; only they had been new-pieced, high and low, top and bottom, heel and sole, black leather and brown leather, more times than anyone could tell.

None of the ladies in Cranford chose to sanction the marriage by congratulating either of the parties. We wished to ignore the whole affair until our liege lady, Mrs Jamieson, returned. Till she came back to give us our cue, we felt that it would be better to consider the engagement in the same light as the Queen of Spain's legs* – facts which certainly existed, but the less said about the better. This restraint upon our tongues – for you see if we did not speak about it to any of the parties concerned, how could we get answers to the questions that we longed to ask? – was beginning to be irksome, and our idea of the dignity of silence was paling before our curiosity, when another direction was given to our thoughts, by an announcement on the part of the principal shopkeeper of Cranford, who ranged the trades from grocer and cheesemonger to man-milliner, as occasion required, that the Spring Fashions were arrived, and would be exhibited on the following Tuesday, at his rooms in High Street. Now Miss Matty had been only waiting for this before buying herself a new silk gown. I had offered, it is true, to send to Drumble for patterns, but she had rejected my proposal, gently implying that she had not forgotten her disappointment about the sea-green turban. I was thankful that I was on the spot now, to counteract the dazzling fascination of any yellow or scarlet silk.

I must say a word or two here about myself. I have spoken of my father's old friendship for the Jenkyns family; indeed, I am not sure if there was not some distant relationship. He had willingly allowed me to remain all the winter at Cranford, in consideration of a letter which Miss Matty had written to him, about the time of the panic, in which I suspect she had exaggerated my powers and my bravery as a defender of the house. But now that the days were longer and more cheerful, he was beginning to urge the necessity of my return; and I only delayed in a sort of odd forlorn hope that if I could obtain any clear information, I might make the account given by the Signora of the Aga Jenkyns tally with that of 'poor Peter', his appearance and disappearance, which I had winnowed out of the conversation of Miss Pole and Mrs Forrester.

Chapter 13

STOPPED PAYMENT

The very Tuesday morning on which Mr Johnson was going to show fashions, the post-woman brought two letters to the house. I say the post-woman, but I should say the postman's wife. He was a lame shoemaker, a very clean, honest man, much respected in the town; but he never brought the letters round except on unusual occasions, such as Christmas Day, or Good Friday; and on those days the letters, which should have been delivered at eight in the morning, did not make their appearance until two or three in the afternoon; for everyone liked poor Thomas, and gave him a welcome on these festive occasions. He used to say, 'he was welly stawed* wi' eating, for there were three or four houses where nowt would serve 'em but he must share in their breakfast'; and by the time he had done his last breakfast, he came to some other friend who was beginning dinner; but come what might in the day of temptation, Tom was always sober, civil, and smiling; and, as Miss Jenkyns used to say, it was a lesson in patience, that she doubted not would call out that precious quality in some minds, where, but for Thomas, it might have lain dormant and undiscovered. Patience was certainly very dormant in Miss Jenkyns's mind. She was always expecting letters, and always drumming on the table till the post-woman had called or gone past. On Christmas Day and Good Friday, she drummed from breakfast till church, from church-time till two o'clock – unless when the fire wanted stirring,* when she invariably knocked down the fire-irons, and scolded Miss Matty for it. But equally certain was the hearty welcome and the good dinner for Thomas; Miss Jenkyns standing over him like a bold dragoon, questioning him as to his children – what they were doing – what school they went to; upbraiding him if another was likely to make its appearance, but sending even the little babies the shilling and the mince-pie which was her gift to all the children, with half-a-crown in addition for both father and mother. The Post was not half of so much consequence to dear Miss Matty; but not for the world would she have diminished Thomas's welcome, and his dole, though I could see that she felt rather shy over the ceremony which had been regarded by Miss Jenkyns as glorious opportunity for giving advice and benefiting her fellow-creatures. Miss Matty would steal* the money all in a lump into his hand, as if she were ashamed of herself. Miss Jenkyns gave him each individual coin separate, with a 'There! that's for yourself; that's for Jenny', etc. Miss Matty would even beckon Martha out of the kitchen while he ate his food: and once, to my knowledge, winked at its rapid disappearance into a blue cotton pocket-handkerchief. Miss Jenkyns almost scolded him if he did not leave a clean plate, however heaped it might have been, and gave an injunction with every mouthful.

I have wandered a long way from the two letters that awaited us on the breakfast-table that Tuesday morning. Mine was from my father. Miss Matty's was printed. My father's was just a man's letter; I mean it was very dull, and gave no information beyond that he was well, that they had had a good deal of rain, that trade was very stagnant, and there were many disagreeable rumours afloat. He then asked me, if I knew whether Miss Matty still retained her shares in the Town and County Bank, as there were very unpleasant reports about it; though nothing more than he had always foreseen, and had prophesied to Miss Jenkyns years ago, when she would invest their little property in it – the only unwise step that clever woman had ever taken, to his knowledge – (the only time she ever acted against his advice, I knew). However, if anything had gone wrong, of course I was not to think of leaving Miss Matty while I could be of any use, etc.

'Who is your letter from, my dear? Mine is a very civil invitation, signed Edwin Wilson, asking me to attend an important meeting of the shareholders of the Town and County Bank, to be held in Drumble, on Thursday the twenty-first. I am sure, it is very attentive of them to remember me.'

I did not like to hear of this 'important meeting', for though I did not know much about business, I feared it confirmed what my father said: however, I thought, ill news always came fast enough, so I resolved to say nothing about my alarm, and merely told her that my father was well, and sent his kind regards to her. She kept turning over, and admiring her letter. At last she spoke: 'I remember their sending one to Deborah just like this;

but that I did not wonder at, for everybody knew she was so clear-headed. I am afraid I could not help them much; indeed, if they came to accounts, I should be quite in the way, for I never could do sums in my head. Deborah, I know, rather wished to go, and went so far as to order a new bonnet for the occasion; but when the time came, she had a bad cold; so they sent her a very polite account of what they had done. Chosen a Director, I think it was. Do you think they want me to help them to choose a Director? I am sure, I should choose your father at once.'

'My father has no shares in the Bank,' said I.

'Oh, no! I remember! He objected very much to Deborah's buying any, I believe. But she was quite the woman of business, and always judged for herself; and here, you see, they have paid eight per cent all these years.'

It was a very uncomfortable subject to me, with my half knowledge; so I thought I would change the conversation, and I asked at what time she thought we had better go and see the Fashions. 'Well, my dear,' she said, 'the thing is this; it is not etiquette to go till after twelve, but then, you see, all Cranford will be there, and one does not like to be too curious about dress and trimmings and caps, with all the world looking on. It is never genteel to be over-curious on these occasions. Deborah had the knack of always looking as if the latest fashion was nothing new to her; a manner she had caught from Lady Arley who did see all the new modes in London, you know. So I thought we would just slip down this morning, soon after breakfast; for I do want half a pound of tea; and then we could go up and examine the things at our leisure, and see exactly how my new silk gown must be made; and then, after twelve, we could go with our minds disengaged, and free from thoughts of dress.'

We began to talk of Miss Matty's new silk gown. I discovered that it would be really the first time in her life that she had had to choose anything of consequence for herself; for Miss Jenkyns had always been the more decided character, whatever her taste might have been; and it is astonishing how such people carry the world before them by the mere force of will. Miss Matty anticipated the sight of the glossy folds with as much delight as if the five sovereigns, set apart for the purchase, could buy all the silks in the shop; and (remembering my own loss of two hours in a toy-shop before I could tell on what wonder to spend a silver threepence) I was very glad that we were going early, that dear Miss Matty might have leisure for the delights of perplexity.

If a happy sea-green could be met with, the gown was to be sea-green: if not, she inclined to maize, and I to silver grey; and we discussed the requisite number of breadths until we arrived at the shop-door. We were to buy the tea, select the silk, and then clamber up the iron corkscrew stairs that led into what was once a loft, though now a Fashion show-room.

The young men at Mr Johnson's had on their best looks, and their best cravats, and pivotted* themselves over the counter with surprising activity. They wanted to show us upstairs at once; but on the principle of business first and pleasure afterwards, we stayed to purchase the tea. Here Miss Matty's absence of mind betrayed itself. If she was made aware that she had been drinking green tea* at any time, she always thought it her duty to lie awake half through the night afterward – (I have known her take it in ignorance many a time without such effects) – and consequently green tea was prohibited in the house; yet today she herself asked for the obnoxious article, under the impression that she was talking about the silk. However, the mistake was soon rectified; and then the silks were unrolled in good truth. By this time the shop was pretty well filled, for it was Cranford market-day, and many of the farmers and country people from the neighbourhood round came in, sleeking down their hair, and glancing shyly about from under their eyelids, as anxious to take back some notion of the unusual gaiety to the mistress or the lasses at home, and yet feeling that they were out of place among the smart shopmen and gay shawls, and summer prints. One honest-looking man, however, made his way up to the counter at which we stood, and boldly asked to look at a shawl or two. The other country folk confined themselves to the grocery side; but our neighbour was evidently too full of some kind intention towards mistress, wife, or daughter, to be shy; and it soon became a question with me, whether he or Miss Matty would keep their shopman the longest time. He thought each shawl more beautiful than the last; and, as for Miss Matty, she smiled and sighed over each fresh bale that was brought out; one colour set off another, and the heap together would, as she said, make even the rainbow look poor.

'I am afraid,' said she, hesitating, 'whichever I choose I shall wish I had taken another. Look at this lovely crimson! it would be so warm in winter. But spring is coming on, you know, I wish I could have a gown for every season,' said she, dropping her voice – as we all did in Cranford whenever we talked of anything we wished for but could not afford. 'However,' she continued in a louder and more cheerful tone, 'it would give me a great deal of trouble to take care of them if I had them; so, I think, I'll only take one. But which must it be, my dear?'

And now she hovered over a lilac with yellow spots, while I pulled out a quiet sage-green, that had faded into insignificance under the more brilliant colours, but which was nevertheless a good silk in its humble way. Our attention was called off to our neighbour. He had chosen a shawl of about thirty shillings' value; and his face looked broadly happy, under the antici-pation, no doubt, of the pleasant surprise he should give to some Molly or Jenny at home; he had tugged a leathern purse out of his breeches pocket, and had offered a five-pound note in payment for the shawl, and for some parcels which had been brought round to him from the grocery counter; and it was just at this point that he attracted our notice. The shopman was examining the note with a puzzled, doubtful air:

'Town and County Bank! I am not sure, sir, but I believe we have received a warning against notes issued by this bank only this morning. I will just step and ask Mr Johnson, sir; but I'm afraid, I must trouble you for payment in cash, or in a note of a different bank.'

I never saw a man's countenance fall so suddenly into dismay and bewilderment. It was almost piteous to see the rapid change.

'Dang it!'* said he, striking his fist down on the table, as if to try which was the harder; 'the chap talks as if notes and gold were to be had for the picking up.'

Miss Matty had forgotten her silk gown in her interest for the man. I don't think she had caught the name of the bank, and in my nervous cowardice, I was anxious that she should not; and so I began admiring the yellow-spotted lilac gown that I had been utterly condemning only a minute before. But it was of no use.

'What bank was it? I mean what bank did your note belong to?'

'Town and County Bank.'

'Let me see it,' said she quietly to the shopman, gently taking it out of his hand, as he brought it back to return it to the farmer.

Mr Johnson was very sorry, but, from information he had received, the notes issued by that bank were little better than waste paper.

'I don't understand it,' said Miss Matty to me in a low voice. 'That is our bank, is it not? – the Town and County Bank?'

'Yes,' said I. 'This lilac silk will just match the ribbons in your new cap, I believe,' I continued – holding up the folds so as to catch the light, and wishing that the man would make haste and be gone – and yet having a new wonder, that had only just sprung up, how far it was wise or right in me to allow Miss Matty to make this expensive purchase, if the affairs of the bank were really so bad as the refusal of the note implied.

But Miss Matty put on the soft dignified manner peculiar to her, rarely used, and yet which became her so well, and laying her hand gently on mine, she said,

'Never mind the silks for a few minutes, dear. I don't understand you, sir,' turning now to the shopman, who had been attending to the farmer. 'Is this a forged note?'

'Oh, no, ma'am. It is a true note of its kind; but you see, ma'am, it is a Joint Stock Bank, and there are reports out that it is likely to break. Mr Johnson is only doing his duty, ma'am, as I am sure Mr Dobson knows.'

But Mr Dobson could not respond to the appealing bow by any answering smile. He was turning the note absently over in his fingers, looking gloomily enough at the parcel containing the lately chosen shawl.

'It's hard upon a poor man,' said he, 'as earns every farthing with the sweat of his brow. However, there's no help for it. You must take back your shawl, my man; Lizzie must do on* with her cloak for a while. And yon figs for the little ones – I promised them to 'em – I'll take them; but the 'bacco, and the other things – '

'I will give you five sovereigns for your note, my good man,' said Miss Matty. 'I think there is some great mistake about it, for I am one of the shareholders, and I'm sure they would have told me if things had not been going on right.'

The shopman whispered a word or two across the table to Miss Matty. She looked at him with a dubious air.

'Perhaps so,' said she. 'But I don't pretend to understand

business; I only know, that if it is going to fail, and if honest people are to lose their money because they have taken our notes – I can't explain myself,' said she, suddenly becoming aware that she had got into a long sentence with four people for audience – 'only I would rather exchange my gold for the note, if you please,' turning to the farmer, 'and then you can take your wife the shawl. It is only going without my gown for a few days longer,' she continued, speaking to me. 'Then, I have no doubt, everything will be cleared up.'

'But if it is cleared up the wrong way?' said I.

'Why! then it will only have been common honesty in me, as a shareholder, to have given this good man the money. I am quite clear about it in my own mind; but, you know, I can never speak quite as comprehensively as others can; – only you must give me your note, Mr Dobson, if you please, and go on with your purchases with these sovereigns.'

The man looked at her with silent gratitude – too awkward to put his thanks into words; but he hung back for a minute or two, fumbling with his note.

'I'm loth to make another one lose instead of me, if it is a loss; but, you see, five pounds is a deal of money to a man with a family; and, as you say, ten to one in a day or two, the note will be as good as gold again.'

'No hope of that, my friend,' said the shopman.

'The more reason why I should take it,' said Miss Matty quietly. She pushed her sovereigns towards the man, who slowly laid his note down in exchange. 'Thank you. I will wait a day or two before I purchase any of these silks; perhaps you will then have a greater choice. My dear! will you come upstairs?'

We inspected the Fashions with as minute and curious an interest as if the gown to be made after them had been bought. I could not see that the little event in the shop below had in the least damped Miss Matty's curiosity as to the make of sleeves, or the sit of skirts. She once or twice exchanged congratulations with me on our private and leisurely view of the bonnets and shawls; but I was, all the time, not so sure that our examination was so utterly private, for I caught glimpses of a figure dodging behind the cloaks and mantles; and, by a dextrous move, I came face to face with Miss Pole, also in morning costume (the principal feature of which was her being without teeth, and wearing a veil to conceal the deficiency), come on the same errand as ourselves. But she quickly took her departure, because, as she said, she had a bad headache and did not feel herself up to conversation.

As we came down through the shop, the civil Mr Johnson was awaiting us; he had been informed of the exchange of the note for gold, and with much good feeling and real kindness, but with a little want of tact, he wished to condole with Miss Matty, and impress upon her the true state of the case. I could only hope that he had heard an exaggerated rumour, for he said that her shares were worse than nothing, and that the bank could not pay a shilling in the pound. I was glad that Miss Matty seemed still a little incredulous; but I could not tell how much of this was real or assumed, with that self-control which seemed habitual to ladies of Miss Matty's standing in Cranford, who would have thought their dignity compromised by the slightest expression of surprise, dismay, or any similar feeling to an inferior in station, or in a public shop. However, we walked home very silently. I am ashamed to say, I believe I was rather vexed and annoyed at Miss Matty's conduct, in taking the note to herself so decidedly. I had so set my heart upon her having a new silk gown, which she wanted sadly; in general she was so undecided anybody might turn her round; in this case I had felt that it was no use attempting it, but I was not the less put out at the result.

Somehow, after twelve o'clock, we both acknowledged to a sated curiosity about the Fashions; and to a certain fatigue of body (which was, in fact, depression of mind) that indisposed us to go out again. But still we never spoke of the note; till, all at once, something possessed me to ask Miss Matty, if she would think it her duty to offer sovereigns for all the notes of the Town and County Bank she met with? I could have bitten my tongue out the minute I had said it. She looked up rather sadly, and as if I had thrown a new perplexity into her already distressed mind; and for a minute or two, she did not speak. Then she said – my own dear Miss Matty – without a shade of reproach in her voice:

'My dear! I never feel as if my mind was what people call very strong; and it's often hard enough work for me to settle what I ought to do with the case right before me. I was very thankful to – I was very thankful, that I saw my duty this morning, with the poor man standing by me; but it's rather a strain upon me to keep thinking and thinking what I should do if such and such a thing happened; and, I believe, I had rather wait and see what really does come; and I don't doubt I shall be helped then, if I don't fidget myself, and get too anxious beforehand. You know, love, I'm not like Deborah. If Deborah had lived, I've no doubt she would have seen after them, before they had got themselves into this state.'

We had neither of us much appetite for dinner, though we tried to talk cheerfully about indifferent things. When we returned into the drawing-room, Miss Matty unlocked her desk and began to look over her account-books. I was so penitent for what I had said in the morning, that I did not choose to take upon myself the presumption to suppose that I could assist her; I rather left her alone, as, with puzzled brow, her eye followed her pen up and down the ruled page. By-and-by she shut the book, locked her desk, and came and drew a chair to mine, where I sat in moody sorrow over the fire. I stole my hand into hers; she clasped it, but did not speak a word. At last she said, with forced composure in her voice, 'If that bank goes wrong, I shall lose one hundred and forty-nine pounds thirteen shillings and four-pence a year; I shall only have thirteen pounds a year left.' I squeezed her hand hard and tight. I did not know what to say. Presently (it was too dark to see her face) I felt her fingers work convulsively in my grasp; and I knew she was going to speak again. I heard the sobs in her voice as she said, 'I hope it's not wrong – not wicked – but oh! I am so glad poor Deborah is spared this. She could not have borne to come down in the world, – she had such a noble, lofty spirit.'

This was all she said about the sister who had insisted upon investing their little property in that unlucky bank. We were later in lighting the candle than usual that night, and until that light shamed us into speaking, we sat together very silently and sadly.

However, we took to our work after tea with a kind of forced cheerfulness (which soon became real as far as it went), talking of that never-ending wonder, Lady Glenmire's engagement. Miss Matty was almost coming round to think it a good thing.

'I don't mean to deny that men are troublesome in a house. I don't judge from my own experience, for my father was neatness itself, and wiped his shoes on coming in as carefully as any woman; but still a man has a sort of knowledge of what should be done in difficulties, that it is very pleasant to have one at hand ready to lean upon. Now, Lady Glenmire, instead of being tossed about, and wondering where she is to settle, will be certain of a home among pleasant and kind people, such as our good Miss Pole and Mrs Forrester. And Mr Hoggins is really a very personable man; and as for his manners – why, if they are not very polished, I have known people with very good hearts and very clever minds too, who were not what some people reckoned refined, but who were both true and tender.'

She fell off into a soft reverie about Mr Holbrook, and I did not interrupt her, I was so busy maturing a plan I had had in my mind for some days, but which this threatened failure of the bank had brought to a crisis. That night, after Miss Matty went to bed, I treacherously lighted the candle again, and sat down in the drawing-room to compose a letter to the Aga Jenkyns – a letter which should affect him, if he were Peter, and yet seem a mere statement of dry facts if he were a stranger. The church clock pealed out two before I had done.

The next morning news came, both official and otherwise, that the Town and County Bank had stopped payment. Miss Matty was ruined.

She tried to speak quietly to me; but when she came to the actual fact, that she would have but about five shillings a week to live upon, she could not restrain a few tears.

'I am not crying for myself, dear,' said she, wiping them away; 'I believe I am crying for the very silly thought, of how my mother would grieve if she could know – she always cared for us so much more than for herself. But many a poor person has less; and I am not very extravagant, and, thank God, when the neck of mutton, and Martha's wages, and the rent, are paid, I have not a farthing owing. Poor Martha! I think she'll be sorry to leave me.'

Miss Matty smiled at me through her tears, and she would fain have had me see only the smile, not the tears.

Chapter 14

FRIENDS IN NEED

It was an example to me, and I fancy it might be to many others, to see how immediately Miss Matty set about the retrenchment which she knew to be right under her altered circumstances. While she went down to speak to Martha, and break the intelligence to her, I stole out with my letter to the Aga Jenkyns, and went to the Signor's lodgings to obtain the exact address. I bound the Signora to secrecy; and indeed, her military manners had a degree of shortness and reserve in them, which made her always say as little as possible, except when under the pressure of strong excitement. Moreover – (which made my secret doubly sure) – the Signor was now so far recovered as to be looking forward to travelling and conjuring again, in the space of a few days, when he, his wife, and little Phœbe, would leave Cranford. Indeed I found him looking over a great black and red placard, in which the Signor Brunoni's accomplishments were set forth, and to which only the name of the town where he would next display them was wanting. He and his wife were so much absorbed in deciding where the red letters would come in with most effect (it might have been the Rubric* for that matter), that it was some time before I could get my question asked privately, and not before I had given several decisions, the wisdom of which I questioned afterwards with equal sincerity as soon as the Signor threw in his doubts and reasons on the important subject. At last I got the address, spelt by sound; and very queer it looked! I dropped it in the post on my way home; and then for a minute I stood looking at the wooden pane, with a gaping slit, which divided me from the letter, but a moment ago in my hand. It was gone from me like life – never to be recalled. It would get tossed about on the sea, and stained with sea-waves perhaps; and be carried among palm-trees, and scented with all tropical fragrance; – the little piece of paper, but an hour ago so familiar and commonplace, had set out on its race to the strange wild countries beyond the Ganges!* But I could not afford to lose much time on this speculation. I hastened home, that Miss Matty might not miss me. Martha opened the door to me, her face swollen with crying. As soon as she saw me, she burst out afresh, and taking hold of my arm she pulled me in, and banged the door to, in order to ask me if indeed it was all true that Miss Matty had been saying.

'I'll never leave her! No! I won't. I told her so, and said I could not think how she could find in her heart to give me warning. I could not have had the face to do it, if I'd been her. I might ha' been just as good-for-nothing as Mrs Fitz-Adam's Rosy, who struck for wages after living seven years and a half in one place. I said I was not one to go and serve Mammon* at that rate; that I knew when I'd got a good Missus, if she didn't know when she'd got a good servant – '

'But Martha'; said I, cutting in while she wiped her eyes.

'Don't "but Martha" me,' she replied to my deprecatory tone.

'Listen to reason – '

'I'll not listen to reason,' she said – now in full possession of her voice, which had been rather choked with sobbing. 'Reason always means what someone else has got to say. Now I think what I've got to say is good enough reason. But, reason or not, I'll say it, and I'll stick to it. I've money in the Savings' Bank, and I've a good stock of clothes, and I'm not going to leave Miss Matty. No! not if she gives me warning every hour in the day!'

She put her arms akimbo, as much as to say she defied me; and, indeed, I could hardly tell how to begin to remonstrate with her, so much did I feel that Miss Matty in her increasing infirmity needed the attendance of this kind and faithful woman.

'Well!' said I at last –

'I'm thankful you begin with "well!" If you'd ha' begun with "but", as you did afore, I'd not ha' listened to you. Now you may go on.'

'I know you would be a great loss to Miss Matty, Martha – '

'I told her so. A loss she'd never cease to be sorry for,' broke in Martha, triumphantly.

'Still she will have so little – so very little – to live upon, that I don't see just now how she could find you food – she will even be pressed for her own. I tell you this, Martha, because I feel you are like a friend to dear Miss Matty – but you know she might not like to have it spoken about.'

Apparently this was even a blacker view of the subject than Miss Matty had presented to her; for Martha just sat down on the first chair that came to hand, and cried out loud – (we had been standing in the kitchen).

At last she put her apron down, and looking me earnestly in the face, asked, 'Was that the reason Miss Matty wouldn't order a pudding today? She said she had no great fancy for sweet things, and you and she would just have a mutton chop. But I'll be up to her. Never you tell, but I'll make her a pudding, and a pudding she'll like, too, and I'll pay for it myself; so mind you see she eats it. Many a one has been comforted in their sorrow by seeing a good dish come upon the table.'

I was rather glad that Martha's energy had taken the immediate and practical direction of pudding-making, for it staved off the quarrelsome discussion as to whether she should or should not leave Miss Matty's service. She began to tie on a clean apron, and otherwise prepare herself for going to the shop for the butter, eggs, and what else she might require; she would not use a scrap of the articles already in the house for her cookery, but went to an old tea-pot in which her private store of money was deposited, and took out what she wanted.

I found Miss Matty very quiet, and not a little sad; but by-and-by she tried to smile for my sake. It was settled that I was to write to my father, and ask him to come over and hold a consultation; and as soon as this letter was despatched, we began to talk over future plans. Miss Matty's idea was to take a single room, and retain as much of her furniture as would be necessary to fit up this, and sell the rest; and there to quietly exist upon what would remain after paying the rent. For my part, I was more ambitious and less contented. I thought of all the things by which a woman, past middle age, and with the education common to ladies fifty years ago, could earn or add to a living, without materially losing caste; but at length I put even this last clause on one side, and wondered what in the world Miss Matty could do.

Teaching was, of course, the first thing that suggested itself. If Miss Matty could teach children anything, it would throw her among the little elves in whom her soul delighted. I ran over her accomplishments. Once upon a time I had heard her say she could play, 'Ah! vous dirai-je, maman?'* on the piano; but that was long, long ago; that faint shadow of musical acquirement had died out years before. She had also once been able to trace out patterns very nicely for muslin embroidery, by dint of placing a piece of silver-paper over the design to be copied, and holding both against the window-pane, while she marked the scollop and eyelet-holes. But that was her nearest approach to the accomplishment of drawing, and I did not think it would go very far. Then again as to the branches of a solid English education – fancy-work and the use of the globes – such as the mistress of the Ladies' Seminary, to which all the tradespeople in Cranford sent their daughters, professed to teach; Miss Matty's eyes were failing her, and I doubted if she could discover the number of threads in a worsted-work pattern, or rightly appreciate the different shades required for Queen Adelaide's face, in the loyal wool-work* now fashionable in Cranford. As for the use of the globes, I had never been able to find it out myself, so perhaps I was not a good judge of Miss Matty's capability of instructing in this branch of education; but it struck me that equators and tropics, and such mystical circles, were very imaginary lines indeed to her, and that she looked upon the signs of the Zodiac as so many remnants of the Black Art.*

What she piqued herself upon, as arts, in which she excelled, was making candle-lighters, or 'spills' (as she preferred calling them), of coloured paper, cut so as to resemble feathers, and knitting garters in a variety of dainty stitches. I had once said, on receiving a present of an elaborate pair, that I should feel quite tempted to drop one of them in the street, in order to have it admired; but I found this little joke (and it was a very little one) was such a distress to her sense of propriety, and was taken with such anxious, earnest alarm, lest the temptation might some day prove too strong for me, that I quite regretted having ventured upon it. A present of these delicately-wrought garters, a bunch of gay 'spills', or a set of cards on which sewing-silk was wound in a mystical manner, were the well-known tokens of Miss Matty's favour. But would anyone pay to have their children taught these arts? or indeed would Miss Matty sell, for filthy lucre, the knack and the skill with which she made trifles of value to those who loved her?

I had to come down to reading, writing, and arithmetic; and, in reading the chapter every morning, she always coughed before coming to long words. I doubted her power of getting through a genealogical chapter, with any number of coughs. Writing she did well and delicately; but spelling! She seemed to think that the more out-of-the-way this was, and the more trouble it cost her, the greater the compliment she paid to her correspondent; and words that she would spell quite correctly in her letters to me, became perfect enigmas when she wrote to my father.

No! there was nothing she could teach to the rising generation of Cranford; unless they had been quick learners and ready imitators of her patience, her humility, her sweetness, her quiet contentment with all that she could not do. I pondered and pondered until dinner was announced by Martha, with a face all blubbered and swollen with crying.

Miss Matty had a few little peculiarities, which Martha was apt to regard as whims below her attention, and appeared to consider as childish fancies, of which an old lady of fifty-eight should try and cure herself. But today everything was attended to with the most careful regard. The bread was cut to the imaginary pattern of excellence that existed in Miss Matty's mind, as being the way which her mother had preferred; the curtain was drawn so as to exclude the dead-brick wall of a neighbour's stables, and yet left so as to show every tender leaf of the poplar which was bursting into spring beauty. Martha's tone to Miss Matty was just such as that good, rough-spoken servant usually kept sacred for little children, and which I had never heard her use to any grown-up person.

I had forgotten to tell Miss Matty about the pudding, and I was afraid she might not do justice to it; for she had evidently very little appetite this day; so I seized the opportunity of letting her into the secret while Martha took away the meat. Miss Matty's eyes filled with tears, and she could not speak, either to express surprise or delight, when Martha returned, bearing it aloft, made in the most wonderful representation of a lion *couchant** that ever was moulded. Martha's face gleamed with triumph, as she set it down before Miss Matty with an exultant 'There!' Miss Matty wanted to speak her thanks, but could not; so she took Martha's hand and shook it warmly, which set Martha off crying, and I myself could hardly keep up the necessary composure. Martha burst out of the room; and Miss Matty had to clear her voice once or twice before she could speak. At last she said, 'I should like to keep this pudding under a glass shade, my dear!' and the notion of the lion *couchant* with his currant eyes, being hoisted up to the place of honour on a mantel-piece, tickled my hysterical fancy, and I began to laugh, which rather surprised Miss Matty.

'I am sure, dear, I have seen uglier things under a glass shade before now,' said she.

So had I, many a time and oft; and I accordingly composed my countenance (and now I could hardly keep from crying), and we both fell to upon the pudding, which was indeed excellent – only every morsel seemed to choke us, our hearts were so full.

We had too much to think about to talk much that afternoon. It passed over very tranquilly. But when the tea-urn was brought in, a new thought came into my head. Why should not Miss Matty sell tea – be an agent to the East India Tea Company* which then existed? I could see no objections to this plan, while the advantages were many – always supposing that Miss Matty could get over the degradation of condescending to anything like trade. Tea was neither greasy, nor sticky – grease and stickiness being two of the qualities which Miss Matty could not endure. No shop-window would be required. A small genteel notification of her being licensed to sell tea, would, it is true, be necessary; but I hoped that it could be placed where no one could see it. Neither was tea a heavy article, so as to tax Miss Matty's fragile strength. The only thing against my plan was the buying and selling involved.

While I was giving but absent answers to the questions Miss Matty was putting – almost as absently – we heard a clumping sound on the stairs, and a whispering outside the door: which indeed once opened and shut as if by some invisible agency. After a little while, Martha came in, dragging after her a great tall young man, all crimson with shyness, and finding his only relief in perpetually sleeking down his hair.

'Please, ma'am, he's only Jem Hearn,' said Martha, by way of an introduction; and so out of breath was she, that I imagine she had had some bodily struggle before she could overcome his reluctance to be presented on the courtly scene of Miss Matilda Jenkyns's drawing-room.

'And please, ma'am, he wants to marry me off-hand. And please, ma'am, we want to take a lodger – just one quiet lodger, to make our two ends meet; and we'd take any house conformable; and, oh dear Miss Matty, if I may be so bold, would you have any objections to lodging with us? Jem wants it as much I do.' [To Jem:] – 'You great oaf! why can't you back me? – But he does want it, all the same, very bad – don't you, Jem? – only, you see, he's dazed at being called on to speak before quality.'

'It's not that,' broke in Jem. 'It's that you've taken me all on a sudden, and I didn't think for to get married so soon – and such quick work does flabbergast a man. It's not that I'm against it, ma'am,' (addressing Miss Matty), 'only Martha has such quick ways with her, when once she takes a thing into her head; and marriage, ma'am, – marriage nails a man, as one may say. I dare say I shan't mind it after it's once over.'

'Please, ma'am,' said Martha – who had plucked at his sleeve, and nudged him with her elbow, and otherwise tried to interrupt him all the time he had been speaking – 'don't mind him, he'll come to; 'twas only last night he was an-axing me, and an-axing me, and all the more because I said I could not think of it for years to come, and now he's only taken aback with the suddenness of the joy; but you know, Jem, you are just as full as me about wanting a lodger.' (Another great nudge.)

'Ay! if Miss Matty would lodge with us – otherwise I've no mind to be cumbered with strange folk in the house,' said Jem, with a want of tact which I could see enraged Martha, who was trying to represent a lodger as the great object they wished to obtain, and that, in fact, Miss Matty would be smoothing their path, and conferring a favour, if she would only come and live with them.

Miss Matty herself was bewildered by the pair: their, or rather Martha's sudden resolution in favour of matrimony staggered her, and stood between her and the contemplation of the plan which Martha had at heart. Miss Matty began, –

'Marriage is a very solemn thing, Martha.'

'It is indeed, ma'am,' quoth Jem. 'Not that I've no objections to Martha.'

'You've never let me a-be for asking me for to fix when I would be married,' said Martha – her face all a-fire, and ready to cry with vexation – 'and now you're shaming me before my missus and all.'

'Nay, now! Martha, don't ee! don't ee! only a man likes to have breathing-time,' said Jem, trying to possess himself of her hand, but in vain. Then seeing that she was more seriously hurt than he had imagined, he seemed to try to rally his scattered faculties, and with more straightforward dignity than, ten minutes before, I should have thought it possible for him to assume, he turned to Miss Matty, and said, 'I hope, ma'am, you know that I am bound to respect everyone who has been kind to Martha. I always looked on her as to be my wife – some time; and she has often and often spoken of you as the kindest lady that ever was; and though the plain truth is I would not like to be troubled with lodgers of the common run; yet if, ma'am, you'd honour us by living with us, I am sure Martha would do her best to make you comfortable; and I'd keep out of your way as much as I could, which I reckon would be the best kindness such an awkward chap as me could do.'

Miss Matty had been very busy with taking off her spectacles, wiping them, and replacing them; but all she could say was, 'Don't let any thought of me hurry you into marriage: pray don't! Marriage is such a very solemn thing!'

'But Miss Matilda will think of your plan, Martha,' said I – struck with the advantages that it offered, and unwilling to lose the opportunity of considering about it. 'And I'm sure neither she nor I can ever forget your kindness; nor yours either, Jem.'

'Why, yes, ma'am! I'm sure I mean kindly, though I'm a bit fluttered by being pushed straight ahead into matrimony, as it were, and mayn't express myself conformable.* But I'm sure I'm willing enough, and give me time to get accustomed; so, Martha, wench, what's the use of crying so, and slapping me if I come near?'

This last was *sotto voce*, and had the effect of making Martha bounce out of the room, to be followed and soothed by her lover. Whereupon Miss Matty sat down and cried very heartily, and accounted for it by saying that the thought of Martha being married so soon gave her quite a shock, and that she should never forgive herself if she thought she was hurrying the poor creature. I think my pity was more for Jem, of the two: but both Miss Matty and I appreciated to the full the kindness of the honest couple, although we said little about this, and a good deal about the chances and dangers of matrimony.

The next morning, very early, I received a note from Miss Pole, so mysteriously wrapped up, and with so many seals on it to secure secrecy, that I had to tear the paper before I could unfold it. And when I came to the writing I could hardly understand the meaning, it was so involved and oracular. I made out, however, that I was to go to Miss Pole's at eleven o'clock; the number *eleven* being written in full length as well as in numerals, and A.M. twice dashed under, as if I were very likely to come at eleven at night, when all Cranford was usually a-bed, and asleep by ten. There was no signature except Miss Pole's initials, reversed, P.E., but as Martha had given me the note, 'with Miss Pole's kind regards', it needed no wizard to find out who sent it; and if the writer's name was to be kept secret, it was very well that I was alone when Martha delivered it.

I went, as requested, to Miss Pole's. The door was opened to me by her little maid Lizzy, in Sunday trim, as if some grand event was impending over this work-day. And the drawing-room upstairs was arranged in accordance with this idea. The table was set out, with the best green card-cloth, and writing-materials upon it. On the little chiffonier* was a tray with a newly-decanted bottle of cowslip wine, and some ladies'-finger biscuits. Miss Pole herself was in solemn array, as if to receive visitors, although it was only eleven o'clock. Mrs Forrester was there, crying quietly and sadly, and my arrival seemed only to call forth fresh tears. Before we had finished our greetings, performed with lugubrious mystery of demeanour, there was another rat-tat-tat, and Mrs Fitz-Adam appeared, crimson with walking and excitement. It seemed as if this was all the company expected; for now Miss Pole made several demonstrations of being about to open the business of the meeting, by stirring the fire, opening and shutting the door, and coughing and blowing her nose. Then she arranged us all round the table, taking care to place me opposite to her; and last of all, she inquired of me, if the sad report was true, as she feared it was, that Miss Matty had lost all her fortune?

Of course, I had but one answer to make; and I never saw more unaffected sorrow depicted on any countenances, than I did there on the three before me.

'I wish Mrs Jamieson was here!' said Mrs Forrester at last; but to judge from Mrs Fitz-Adam's face, she could not second the wish.

'But without Mrs Jamieson,' said Miss Pole, with just a sound of offended merit in her voice, 'we, the ladies of Cranford, in my drawing-room assembled, can resolve upon something. I imagine we are none of us what may be called rich, though we all possess a genteel competency, sufficient for tastes that are elegant and refined, and would not, if they could, be vulgarly ostentatious.' (Here I observed Miss Pole refer to a small card concealed in her hand, on which I imagine she had put down a few notes.)

'Miss Smith,' she continued, addressing me (familiarly known as 'Mary' to all the company assembled, but this was a state occasion), 'I have conversed in private – I made it my business to do so yesterday afternoon – with these ladies on the misfortune which has happened to our friend, – and one and all of us have agreed that, while we have a superfluity, it is not only a duty but a pleasure, – a true pleasure, Mary!' – her voice was rather choked just here, and she had to wipe her spectacles before she could go on – 'to give what we can to assist her – Miss Matilda Jenkyns. Only, in consideration of the feelings of delicate independence existing in the mind of every refined female,' – I was sure she had got back to the card now – 'we wish to contribute our mites in a secret and concealed manner, so as not to hurt the feelings I have referred to. And our object in requesting you to meet us this morning, is, that believing you are the daughter – that your father is, in fact, her confidential adviser in all pecuniary matters, we imagined that, by consulting with him, you might devise some mode in which our contribution could be made to appear the legal due which Miss Matilda Jenkyns ought to receive from—. Probably, your father, knowing her investments, can fill up the blank.'

Miss Pole concluded her address, and looked round for approval and agreement.

'I have expressed your meaning, ladies, have I not? And while Miss Smith considers what reply to make, allow me to offer you some little refreshment.'

I had no great reply to make; I had more thankfulness at my heart for their kind thoughts than I cared to put into words; and so I only mumbled out something to the effect 'that I would name what Miss Pole had said to my father, and that if anything could be arranged for dear Miss Matty', – and here I broke down utterly, and had to be refreshed with a glass of cowslip wine before I could check the crying which had been repressed for the last two or three days. The worst was, all the ladies cried in concert. Even Miss Pole cried, who had said a hundred times that to betray emotion before anyone was a sign of weakness and want of self-control. She recovered herself into a slight degree of impatient anger, directed against me, as having set them all off; and, moreover, I think she was vexed that I could not make a speech back in return for hers; and if I had known beforehand what was to be said, and had had a card on which to express the probable feelings that would rise in my heart, I would have tried to gratify her. As it was, Mrs Forrester was the person to speak when we had recovered our composure.

'I don't mind, among friends, stating that I – no! I'm not poor exactly, but I don't think I'm what you may call rich; I wish I were, for dear Miss Matty's sake, – but, if you please, I'll write down, in a sealed paper, what I can give. I only wish it was more: my dear Mary, I do indeed.'

Now I saw why paper, pens, and ink, were provided. Every lady wrote down the sum she could give annually, signed the paper, and sealed it mysteriously. If their proposal was acceded to, my father was to be allowed to open the papers, under pledge of secrecy. If not, they were to be returned to their writers.

When this ceremony had been gone through, I rose to depart; but each lady seemed to wish to have a private conference with me. Miss Pole kept me in the drawing-room to explain why, in Mrs Jamieson's absence, she had taken the lead in this 'movement', as she was pleased to call it, and also to inform me that she had heard from good sources that Mrs Jamieson was coming home directly, in a state of high displeasure against her sister-in-law, who was forthwith to leave her house; and was, she believed, to return to Edinburgh that very afternoon. Of course this piece of intelligence could not be communicated before Mrs Fitz-Adam, more especially as Miss Pole was inclined to think that Lady Glenmire's engagement to Mr Hoggins could not possibly hold against the blaze of Mrs Jamieson's displeasure. A few hearty inquiries after Miss Matty's health concluded my interview with Miss Pole.

On coming downstairs, I found Mrs Forrester waiting for me at the entrance to the dining parlour; she drew me in, and when the door was shut, she tried two or three times to begin on some subject, which was so unapproachable apparently, that I began to despair of our ever getting to a clear understanding. At last out it came; the poor old lady trembling all the time as if it were a great crime which she was exposing to daylight, in telling me how very, very little she had to live upon; a confession which she was brought to make from a dread lest we should think that the small contribution named in her paper bore any proportion to her love and regard for Miss Matty. And yet that sum which she so eagerly relinquished was, in truth, more than a twentieth part of what she had to live upon, and keep house, and a little serving-maid, all as became one born a Tyrrell. And when the whole income does not nearly amount to a hundred pounds, to give up a twentieth of it will necessitate many careful economies, and many pieces of self-denial – small and insignificant in the world's account, but bearing a different value in another account-book that I have heard of. She did so wish she was rich, she said; and this wish she kept repeating, with no thought of herself in it, only with a longing, yearning desire to be able to heap up Miss Matty's measure of comforts.

It was some time before I could console her enough to leave her; and then, on quitting the house, I was waylaid by Mrs Fitz-Adam, who had also her confidence to make of pretty nearly the opposite description. She had not liked to put down all that she could afford, and was ready to give. She told me she thought she never could look Miss Matty in the face again if she presumed to be giving her so much as she should like to do. 'Miss Matty!' continued she, 'that I thought was such a fine young lady, when I was nothing but a country girl, coming to market with eggs and butter and such like things. For my father, though well to do, would always make me go on as my mother had done before me; and I had to come in to Cranford every Saturday and see after sales and prices, and what not. And one day, I remember, I met Miss Matty in the lane that leads to Combehurst; she was walking on the footpath which, you know, is raised a good way above the road, and a gentleman rode beside her, and was talking to her, and she was looking down at some primroses she had gathered, and pulling them all to pieces, and I do believe she was crying. But after she had passed, she turned round and ran after me to ask – oh so kindly – after my poor mother, who lay on her death-bed; and when I cried, she took hold of my hand to comfort me; and the gentleman waiting for her all the time; and her poor heart very full of something, I am sure; and I thought it such an honour to be spoken to in that pretty way by the rector's daughter, who visited at Arley Hall. I have loved her ever since, though perhaps I'd no right to do it; but if you can think of any way in which I might be allowed to give a little more without anyone knowing it, I should be so much obliged to you, my dear. And my brother would be delighted to doctor her for nothing – medicines, leeches, and all. I know that he and her ladyship – (my dear! I little thought in the days I was telling you of that I should ever come to be sister-in-law to a ladyship!) – would do anything for her. We all would.'

I told her I was quite sure of it, and promised all sorts of things, in my anxiety to get home to Miss Matty, who might well be wondering what had become of me, – absent from her two hours without being able to account for it. She had taken very little note of time, however, as she had been occupied in numberless little arrangements preparatory to the great step of giving up her house. It was evidently a relief to her to be doing something in the way of retrenchment; for, as she said, whenever she paused to think, the recollection of the poor fellow with his bad five-pound note came over her, and she felt quite dishonest; only if it made her so uncomfortable, what must it not be doing to the directors of the Bank, who must know so much more of the misery consequent upon this failure? She almost made me angry by dividing her sympathy between these directors (whom she imagined overwhelmed by self-reproach for the mismanagement of other people's affairs), and those who were suffering like her. Indeed, of the two, she seemed to think poverty a lighter burden than self-reproach; but I privately doubted if the directors would agree with her.

Old hoards were taken out and examined as to their money value, which luckily was small, or else I don't know how Miss Matty would have prevailed upon herself to part with such things as her mother's wedding-ring, the strange uncouth brooch with which her father had disfigured his shirt-frill, etc. However, we arranged things a little in order as to their pecuniary estimation, and were all ready for my father when he came the next morning.

I am not going to weary you with the details of all the business we went through; and one reason for not telling about them is, that I did not understand what we were doing at the time, and cannot recollect it now. Miss Matty and I sat assenting to accounts, and schemes, and reports, and documents, of which I do not believe we either of us understood a word; for my father was clear-headed and decisive, and a capital man of business, and if we made the slightest inquiry, or expressed the slightest want of comprehension, he had a sharp way of saying, 'Eh? eh?

it's as clear as daylight. What's your objection?' And as we had
not comprehended anything of what he had proposed, we found
it rather difficult to shape our objections; in fact, we never were
sure if we had any. So, presently Miss Matty got into a nervously
acquiescent state, and said 'Yes' and 'Certainly' at every pause,
whether required or not: but when I once joined in as chorus to
a 'Decidedly', pronounced by Miss Matty in a tremblingly
dubious tone, my father fired round at me and asked me 'What
there was to decide?' And I am sure, to this day, I have never
known. But, in justice to him, I must say, he had come over
from Drumble to help Miss Matty when he could ill spare the
time, and when his own affairs were in a very anxious state.

While Miss Matty was out of the room, giving orders for
luncheon – and sadly perplexed between her desire of honouring
my father by a delicate dainty meal, and her conviction that she
had no right now that all her money was gone, to indulge this
desire, – I told him of the meeting of Cranford ladies at Miss
Pole's the day before. He kept brushing his hand before his eyes
as I spoke; – and when I went back to Martha's offer the
evening before, of receiving Miss Matty as a lodger, he fairly
walked away from me to the window, and began drumming
with his fingers upon it. Then he turned abruptly round, and
said, 'See, Mary, how a good innocent life makes friends all
around. Confound it! I could make a good lesson out of it if I
were a parson; but as it is, I can't get a tail to my sentences –
only I'm sure you feel what I want to say. You and I will have a
walk after lunch, and talk a bit more about these plans.'

The lunch – a hot savoury mutton-chop, and a little of the
cold lion sliced and fried* – was now brought in. Every morsel
of this last dish was finished, to Martha's great gratification.
Then my father bluntly told Miss Matty he wanted to talk to
me alone, and that he would stroll out and see some of the old
places, and then I could tell her what plan we thought desirable.
Just before we went out, she called me back and said, 'Remember dear, I'm the only one left – I mean there's no one to be hurt
by what I do. I'm willing to do anything that's right and honest;
and I don't think, if Deborah knows where she is, she'll care so
very much if I'm not genteel; because, you see, she'll know all,
dear. Only let me see what I can, and pay the poor people as far
as I'm able.'

I gave her a hearty kiss, and ran after my father. The result of our conversation was this. If all parties were agreeable, Martha and Jem were to be married with as little delay as possible, and they were to live on in Miss Matty's present abode; the sum which the Cranford ladies had agreed to contribute annually, being sufficient to meet the greater part of the rent, and leaving Martha free to appropriate what Miss Matty should pay for her lodgings to any little extra comforts required. About the sale, my father was dubious at first. He said the old rectory furniture, however carefully used, and reverently treated, would fetch very little; and that little would be but as a drop in the sea of the debts of the Town and County Bank. But when I represented how Miss Matty's tender conscience would be soothed by feeling that she had done what she could, he gave way; especially after I had told him the five-pound-note adventure, and he had scolded me well for allowing it. I then alluded to my idea that she might add to her small income by selling tea; and, to my surprise (for I had nearly given up the plan), my father grasped at it with all the energy of a tradesman. I think he reckoned his chickens before they were hatched, for he immediately ran up the profits of the sales that she could effect in Cranford to more than twenty pounds a year. The small dining-parlour was to be converted into a shop, without any of its degrading character-istics; a table was to be the counter; one window was to be retained unaltered, and the other changed into a glass door. I evidently rose in his estimation, for having made this bright suggestion. I only hoped we should not both fall in Miss Matty's.

But she was patient and content with all our arrangements. She knew, she said, that we should do the best we could for her; and she only hoped, only stipulated, that she should pay every farthing that she could be said to owe for her father's sake, who had been so respected in Cranford. My father and I had agreed to say as little as possible about the Bank, indeed never to mention it again, if it could be helped. Some of the plans were evidently a little perplexing to her; but she had seen me sufficiently snubbed in the morning for want of comprehension to venture on too many inquiries now; and all passed over well, with a hope on her part that no one would be hurried into marriage on her account. When we came to the proposal that she should sell tea, I could see it was rather a shock to her; not on account of any personal loss of gentility involved, but only because she distrusted her own powers of action in a new line

of life, and would timidly have preferred a little more privation
to any exertion for which she feared she was unfitted. However,
when she saw my father was bent upon it, she sighed, and said
she would try; and if she did not do well, of course she might
give it up. One good thing about it was, she did not think men
ever bought tea; and it was of men particularly she was afraid.
They had such sharp loud ways with them; and did up accounts,
and counted their change so quickly! Now, if she might only sell
comfits* to children, she was sure she could please them!

Chapter 15

A HAPPY RETURN

Before I left Miss Matty at Cranford everything had been comfortably arranged for her. Even Mrs Jamieson's approval of her selling tea had been gained. That oracle had taken a few days to consider whether by so doing Miss Matty would forfeit her right to the privileges of society in Cranford. I think she had some little idea of mortifying Lady Glenmire by the decision she gave at last; which was to this effect: that whereas a married woman takes her husband's rank by the strict laws of precedence, an unmarried woman retains the station her father occupied. So Cranford was allowed to visit Miss Matty; and, whether allowed or not, it intended to visit Lady Glenmire.

But what was our surprise – our dismay – when we learnt that Mr and *Mrs Hoggins* were returning on the following Tuesday. Mrs Hoggins! Had she absolutely dropped her title, and so, in a spirit of bravado, cut the aristocracy to become a Hoggins! She, who might have been called Lady Glenmire to her dying day! Mrs Jamieson was pleased. She said it only convinced her of what she had known from the first, that the creature had a low taste. But 'the creature' looked very happy on Sunday at church; nor did we see it necessary to keep our veils down on that side of our bonnets on which Mr and Mrs Hoggins sat, as Mrs Jamieson did; thereby missing all the smiling glory of his face, and all the becoming blushes of hers. I am not sure if Martha and Jem looked more radiant in the afternoon, when they too made their first appearance. Mrs Jamieson soothed the turbulence of her soul, by having the blinds of her windows drawn down, as if for a funeral, on the day when Mr and Mrs Hoggins received callers; and it was with some difficulty that she was prevailed upon to continue the St James's Chronicle – so indignant was she with its having inserted the announcement of the marriage.

Miss Matty's sale went off famously. She retained the furniture of her sitting-room, and bedroom; the former of which she was to occupy till Martha could meet with a lodger who might wish to take it; and into this sitting-room and bedroom she had to cram all sorts of things, which were (the auctioneer assured her) bought in for her at the sale by an unknown friend. I always suspected Mrs Fitz-Adam of this; but she must have had an accessory, who knew what articles were particularly regarded by Miss Matty on account of their associations with her early days. The rest of the house looked rather bare, to be sure; all except one tiny bedroom, of which my father allowed me to purchase the furniture for my occasional use, in case of Miss Matty's illness.

I had expended my own small store in buying all manner of comfits and lozenges, in order to tempt the little people whom Miss Matty loved so much, to come about her. Tea in bright green canisters – and comfits in tumblers – Miss Matty and I felt quite proud as we looked round us on the evening before the shop was to be opened. Martha had scoured the boarded floor to a white cleanness, and it was adorned with a brilliant piece of oil-cloth on which customers were to stand before the table-counter. The wholesome smell of plaster and white-wash pervaded the apartment. A very small 'Matilda Jenkyns, licensed to sell tea' was hidden under the lintel of the new door, and two boxes of tea with cabalistic inscriptions all over them* stood ready to disgorge their contents into the canisters.

Miss Matty, as I ought to have mentioned before, had had some scruples of conscience at selling tea when there was already Mr Johnson in the town, who included it among his numerous commodities; and, before she could quite reconcile herself to the adoption of her new business, she had trotted down to his shop, unknown to me, to tell him of the project that was entertained, and to inquire if it was likely to injure his business. My father called this idea of hers 'great nonsense', and 'wondered how tradespeople were to get on if there was to be a continual consulting of each others' interests, which would put a stop to all competition directly'. And, perhaps, it would not have done in Drumble, but in Cranford it answered very well; for not only did Mr Johnson kindly put at rest all Miss Matty's scruples, and fear of injuring his business, but, I have reason to know, he repeatedly sent customers to her, saying that the teas he kept were of a common kind, but that Miss Jenkyns had all the choice sorts. And expensive tea is a very favourite luxury with well-to-do tradespeople, and rich farmers' wives, who turn up their noses at the Congou and Souchong prevalent at many tables of gentility, and will have nothing else than Gunpowder and Pekoe for themselves.

But to return to Miss Matty. It was really very pleasant to see how her unselfishness, and simple sense of justice, called out the same good qualities in others. She never seemed to think anyone would impose upon her, because she should be so grieved to do it to them. I have heard her put a stop to the asseverations of the man who brought her coals, by quietly saying, 'I am sure you would be sorry to bring me wrong weight'; and if the coals were short measure that time, I don't believe they ever were again. People would have felt as much ashamed of presuming on her good faith as they would have done on that of a child. But my father says, 'such simplicity might be very well in Cranford, but would never do in the world'. And I fancy the world must be very bad, for with all my father's suspicion of everyone with whom he has dealings, and in spite of all his many precautions, he lost upwards of a thousand pounds by roguery only last year.

I just stayed long enough to establish Miss Matty in her new mode of life, and to pack up the library, which the Rector had purchased. He had written a very kind letter to Miss Matty, saying, 'how glad he should be to take a library so well selected as he knew that the late Mr Jenkyns's must have been, at any valuation put upon them'. And when she agreed to this, with a touch of sorrowful gladness that they would go back to the Rectory, and be arranged on the accustomed walls once more, he sent word that he feared that he had not room for them all, and perhaps Miss Matty would kindly allow him to leave some volumes on her shelves. But Miss Matty said that she had her Bible, and Johnson's Dictionary, and should not have much time for reading, she was afraid. Still I retained a few books out of consideration for the Rector's kindness.

The money which he had paid, and that produced by the sale, was partly expended in the stock of tea, and part of it was invested against a rainy day; *i.e.* old age or illness. It was but a small sum, it is true; and it occasioned a few evasions of truth and white lies (all of which I think very wrong indeed – in theory – and would rather not put them in practice), for we knew Miss Matty would be perplexed as to her duty if she were aware of any little reserve-fund being made for her while the debts of the Bank remained unpaid. Moreover, she had never been told of the way in which her friends were contributing to pay the rent. I should have liked to tell her this; but the mystery of the affair gave a piquancy to their deed of kindness which the ladies were unwilling to give up; and at first Martha had to shirk many a perplexed question as to her ways and means of living in such a house; but by and by Miss Matty's prudent uneasiness sank down into acquiescence with the existing arrangement.

I left Miss Matty with a good heart. Her sales of tea during the first two days had surpassed my most sanguine expectations. The whole country round seemed to be all out of tea at once. The only alteration I could have desired in Miss Matty's way of doing business was, that she should not have so plaintively entreated some of her customers not to buy green tea – running it down as slow poison, sure to destroy the nerves, and produce all manner of evil. Their pertinacity in taking it, in spite of all her warnings, distressed her so much that I really thought she would relinquish the sale of it, and so lose half her custom; and I was driven to my wits' end for instances of longevity entirely attributable to a persevering use of green tea. But the final argument, which settled the question, was a happy reference of mine to the train oil* and tallow candles which the Esquimaux not only enjoy but digest. After that she acknowledged that 'one man's meat might be another man's poison', and contented herself thenceforward with an occasional remonstrance, when she thought the purchaser was too young and innocent to be acquainted with the evil effects green tea produced on some constitutions; and an habitual sigh when people old enough to choose more wisely would prefer it.

I went over from Drumble once a quarter at least, to settle the accounts, and see after the necessary business letters. And, speaking of letters, I began to be very much ashamed of remembering my letter to the Aga Jenkyns, and very glad I had never named my writing to anyone. I only hoped the letter was lost. No answer came. No sign was made.

About a year after Miss Matty set up shop, I received one of Martha's hieroglyphics, begging me to come to Cranford very soon. I was afraid that Miss Matty was ill, and went off that very afternoon, and took Martha by surprise when she saw me on opening the door. We went into the kitchen, as usual, to have our confidential conference; and then Martha told me she was expecting her confinement very soon – in a week or two; and she did not think Miss Matty was aware of it; and she wanted me to break the news to her, 'for indeed Miss!' continued Martha, crying hysterically, 'I'm afraid she won't approve of it; and I'm sure I don't know who is to take care of her as she should be taken care of, when I am laid up.'

I comforted Martha by telling her I would remain till she was about again; and only wished she had told me her reason for this sudden summons, as then I would have brought the requisite stock of clothes. But Martha was so tearful and tender-spirited, and unlike her usual self, that I said as little as possible about myself, and endeavoured rather to comfort Martha under all the probable and possible misfortunes which came crowding upon her imagination.

I then stole out of the house-door, and made my appearance, as if I were a customer, in the shop just to take Miss Matty by surprise, and gain an idea of how she looked in her new situation. It was warm May weather, so only the little half-door was closed; and Miss Matty sat behind her counter, knitting an elaborate pair of garters: elaborate they seemed to me, but the difficult stitch was no weight upon her mind, for she was singing in a low voice to herself as her needles went rapidly in and out. I call it singing, but I dare say a musician would not use that word to the tuneless yet sweet humming of the low worn voice. I found out from the words, far more than from the attempt at the tune, that it was the Old Hundredth* she was crooning to herself: but the quiet continuous sound told of content, and gave me a pleasant feeling, as I stood in the street just outside the door, quite in harmony with that soft May morning. I went in. At first she did not catch who it was, and stood up as if to serve me; but in another minute watchful pussy had clutched her knitting, which was dropped in her eager joy at seeing me. I found, after we had had a little conversation, that it was as Martha said, and that Miss Matty had no idea of the approaching household event. So I thought I would let things take their course, secure that when I went to her with the baby in my arms I should obtain that forgiveness for Martha which she was needlessly frightening herself into believing that Miss Matty would withhold, under some notion that the new claimant

would require attentions from its mother that it would be
faithless treason to Miss Matty to render.

But I was right. I think that must be an hereditary quality, for
my father says he is scarcely ever wrong. One morning, within a
week after I arrived, I went to call Miss Matty, with a little
bundle of flannel in my arms. She was very much awe-struck
when I showed her what it was, and asked for her spectacles off
the dressing-table, and looked at it curiously, with a sort of
tender wonder at its small perfection of parts. She could not
banish the thought of the surprise all day, but went about on
tip-toe, and was very silent. But she stole up to see Martha, and
they both cried with joy; and she got into a complimentary
speech to Jem, and did not know how to get out of it again, and
was only extricated from her dilemma by the sound of the shop-
bell, which was an equal relief to the shy, proud, honest Jem,
who shook my hand so vigorously when I congratulated him
that I think I feel the pain of it yet.

I had a busy life while Martha was laid up. I attended on Miss
Matty, and prepared her meals; I cast up her accounts, and
examined into the state of her canisters and tumblers. I helped
her too, occasionally, in the shop; and it gave me no small
amusement, and sometimes a little uneasiness, to watch her
ways there. If a little child came in to ask for an ounce of
almond-comfits (and four of the large kind which Miss Matty
sold weighed that much), she always added one more by 'way
of make-weight' as she called it, although the scale was handsomely turned before; and when I remonstrated against this, her
reply was, 'The little things like it so much!' There was no use
in telling her that the fifth comfit weighed a quarter of an ounce,
and made every sale into a loss to her pocket. So I remembered
the green tea, and winged my shaft with a feather out of her
own plumage.* I told her how unwholesome almond-comfits
were; and how ill excess in them might make the little children.
This argument produced some effect; for, henceforward, instead
of the fifth comfit, she always told them to hold out their tiny
palms, into which she shook either peppermint or ginger lozenges, as a preventive to the dangers that might arise from the
previous sale. Altogether the lozenge trade, conducted on these
principles, did not promise to be remunerative; but I was happy
to find she had made more than twenty pounds during the last
year by her sales of tea; and, moreover, that now she was

accustomed to it, she did not dislike the employment, which brought her into kindly intercourse with many of the people round about. If she gave them good weight they, in their turn, brought many a little country present to the 'old rector's daughter'; – a cream cheese, a few new-laid eggs, a little fresh ripe fruit, a bunch of flowers. The counter was quite loaded with these offerings sometimes, as she told me.

As for Cranford in general, it was going on much as usual. The Jamieson and Hoggins feud still raged, if a feud it could be called, when only one side cared much about it. Mr and Mrs Hoggins were very happy together; and, like most very happy people, quite ready to be friendly: indeed, Mrs Hoggins was really desirous to be restored to Mrs Jamieson's good graces, because of the former intimacy. But Mrs Jamieson considered their very happiness an insult to the Glenmire family, to which she had still the honour to belong; and she doggedly refused and rejected every advance. Mr Mulliner, like a faithful clansman, espoused his mistress's side with ardour. If he saw either Mr or Mrs Hoggins, he would cross the street, and appear absorbed in the contemplation of life in general, and his own path in particular, until he had passed them by. Miss Pole used to amuse herself with wondering what in the world Mrs Jamieson would do, if either she or Mr Mulliner, or any other member of her household, was taken ill; she could hardly have the face to call in Mr Hoggins after the way she had behaved to them. Miss Pole grew quite impatient for some indisposition or accident to befall Mrs Jamieson or her dependants, in order that Cranford might see how she would act under the perplexing circumstances.

Martha was beginning to go about again, and I had already fixed a limit, not very far distant, to my visit, when one afternoon, as I was sitting in the shop-parlour with Miss Matty – I remember the weather was colder now than it had been in May, three weeks before, and we had a fire, and kept the door fully closed – we saw a gentleman go slowly past the window, and then stand opposite to the door, as if looking out for the name which we had so carefully hidden. He took out a double eye-glass and peered about for some time before he could discover it. Then he came in. And, all on a sudden, it flashed across me that it was the Aga himself! For his clothes had an out-of-the-way foreign cut about them; and his face was deep brown as if tanned and re-tanned by the sun. His complexion contrasted oddly with his plentiful snow-white hair; his eyes were dark and piercing, and he had an odd way of contracting them, and puckering up his cheeks into innumerable wrinkles when he looked earnestly at objects. He did so to Miss Matty when he first came in. His glance had first caught and lingered a little upon me; but then turned, with the peculiar searching look I have described, to Miss Matty. She was a little fluttered and nervous, but no more so than she always was when any man came into her shop. She thought that he would probably have a note, or a sovereign at least, for which she would have to give change, which was an operation she very much disliked to perform. But the present customer stood opposite to her, without asking for anything, only looking fixedly at her as he drummed upon the table with his fingers, just for all the world as Miss Jenkyns used to do. Miss Matty was on the point of asking him what he wanted (as she told me afterwards), when he turned sharp to me: 'Is your name Mary Smith?'

'Yes!' said I.

All my doubts as to his identity were set at rest; and, I only wondered what he would say or do next, and how Miss Matty would stand the joyful shock of what he had to reveal. Apparently he was at a loss how to announce himself; for he looked round at last in search of something to buy, so as to gain time; and, as it happened, his eye caught on the almond-comfits, and he boldly asked for a pound of 'those things'. I doubt if Miss Matty had a whole pound in the shop; and besides the unusual magnitude of the order, she was distressed with the idea of the indigestion they would produce, taken in such unlimited quantities. She looked up to remonstrate. Something of tender relaxation in his face struck home to her heart. She said, 'It is – oh, sir! can you be Peter?' and trembled from head to foot. In a moment he was round the table, and had her in his arms, sobbing the tearless cries of old age. I brought her a glass of wine; for indeed her colour had changed so as to alarm me, and Mr Peter, too. He kept saying, 'I have been too sudden for you, Matty, – I have, my little girl.'

I proposed that she should go at once up into the drawing-room and lie down on the sofa there; she looked wistfully at her brother, whose hand she had held tight, even when nearly fainting; but on his assuring her that he would not leave her, she allowed him to carry her upstairs.

I thought that the best I could do, was to run and put the kettle on the fire for early tea, and then to attend to the shop, leaving the brother and sister to exchange some of the many thousand things they must have to say. I had also to break the news to Martha, who received it with a burst of tears, which nearly infected me. She kept recovering herself to ask if I was sure it was indeed Miss Matty's brother; for I had mentioned that he had gray hair and she had always heard that he was a very handsome young man. Something of the same kind perplexed Miss Matty at tea-time, when she was installed in the great easy chair opposite to Mr Jenkyns's, in order to gaze her fill. She could hardly drink for looking at him; and as for eating, that was out of the question.

'I suppose hot climates age people very quickly,' said she, almost to herself. 'When you left Cranford you had not a gray hair in your head.'

'But how many years ago is that?' said Mr Peter, smiling.

'Ah! true! yes! I suppose you and I are getting old. But still I did not think we were so very old! But white hair is very becoming to you, Peter,' she continued – a little afraid lest she had hurt him by revealing how his appearance had impressed her.

'I suppose I forgot dates too, Matty, for what do you think I have brought for you from India? I have an Indian muslin gown and a pearl necklace for you somewhere or other in my chest at Portsmouth.' He smiled as if amused at the idea of the incongruity of his presents with the appearance of his sister; but this did not strike her all at once, while the elegance of the articles did. I could see that for a moment her imagination dwelt complacently on the idea of herself thus attired; and instinctively she put her hand up to her throat – that little delicate throat which (as Miss Pole had told me) had been one of her youthful charms; but the hand met the touch of folds of soft muslin, in which she was always swathed up to her chin; and the sensation recalled a sense of the unsuitableness of a pearl necklace to her age. She said, 'I'm afraid I'm too old; but it was very kind of you to think of it. They are just what I should have liked years ago – when I was young!'

'So I thought, my little Matty. I remembered your tastes; they were so like my dear mother's.' At the mention of that name, the brother and sister clasped each other's hands yet more fondly; and although they were perfectly silent, I fancied they might have something to say if they were unchecked by my presence, and I got up to arrange my room for Mr Peter's occupation that night, intending myself to share Miss Matty's bed. But at my movement he started up. 'I must go and settle about a room at the George. My carpet-bag is there too.'

'No!' said Miss Matty in great distress – 'you must not go; please, dear Peter – pray, Mary – oh! you must not go!'

She was so much agitated that we both promised everything she wished. Peter sat down again, and gave her his hand, which for better security she held in both of hers, and I left the room to accomplish my arrangements.

Long, long into the night, far, far into the morning, did Miss Matty and I talk. She had much to tell me of her brother's life and adventures which he had communicated to her, as they had sat alone. She said that all was thoroughly clear to her; but I never quite understood the whole story; and when in after days I lost my awe of Mr Peter enough to question him myself, he laughed at my curiosity and told me stories that sounded so very much like Baron Munchausen's* that I was sure he was making fun of me. What I heard from Miss Matty was, that he had been a volunteer at the siege of Rangoon;* had been taken prisoner by the Burmese; had somehow obtained favour and eventual freedom from knowing how to bleed the chief of the small tribe in some case of dangerous illness; that on his release from years of captivity he had had his letters returned from England with the ominous word 'Dead' marked upon them; and believing himself to be the last of his race, he had settled down as an indigo planter; and had proposed to spend the remainder of his life in the country to whose inhabitants and modes of life he had become habituated; when my letter had reached him; and with the odd vehemence which characterised him in age as it had done in youth, he had sold his land and all his possessions to the first purchaser, and come home to the poor old sister, who was more glad and rich than any princess when she looked at him. She talked me to sleep at last, and then I was awakened by a slight sound at the door, for which she begged my pardon as she crept penitently into bed; but it seems that when I could no longer confirm her belief that the long-lost was really here –

under the same roof – she had begun to fear lest it was only a waking dream of hers; that there never had been a Peter sitting by her all that blessed evening – but that the real Peter lay dead far away beneath some wild sea-wave, or under some strange Eastern tree. And so strong had this nervous feeling of hers become that she was fain to get up and go and convince herself that he was really there by listening through the door to his even regular breathing – I don't like to call it snoring, but I heard it myself through two closed doors – and by-and-by it soothed Miss Matty to sleep.

I don't believe Mr Peter came home from India as rich as a Nabob;* he even considered himself poor, but neither he nor Miss Matty cared much about that. At any rate, he had enough to live upon 'very genteelly' at Cranford; he and Miss Matty together. And a day or two after his arrival, the shop was closed, while troops of little urchins gleefully awaited the showers of comfits and lozenges that came from time to time down upon their faces as they stood up-gazing at Miss Matty's drawing-room windows. Occasionally Miss Matty would say to them (half hidden behind the curtains), 'My dear children, don't make yourselves ill'; but a strong arm pulled her back, and a more rattling shower than ever succeeded. A part of the tea was sent in presents to the Cranford ladies; and some of it was distributed among the old people who remembered Mr Peter in the days of his frolicsome youth. The India muslin gown was reserved for darling Flora Gordon (Miss Jessie Brown's daughter). The Gordons had been on the Continent for the last few years, but were now expected to return very soon; and Miss Matty, in her sisterly pride, anticipated great delight in the joy of showing them Mr Peter. The pearl necklace disappeared; and about that time many handsome and useful presents made their appearance in the households of Miss Pole and Mrs Forrester; and some rare and delicate Indian ornaments graced the drawing-rooms of Mrs Jamieson and Mrs Fitz-Adam. I myself was not forgotten. Among other things, I had the handsomest bound and best edition of Dr Johnson's works that could be procured; and dear Miss Matty, with tears in her eyes, begged me to consider it as a present from her sister as well as herself. In short no one was forgotten; and what was more, everyone, however insignificant, who had shown kindness to Miss Matty at any time, was sure of Mr Peter's cordial regard.

Chapter 16

'PEACE TO CRANFORD'

It was not surprising that Mr Peter became such a favourite at Cranford. The ladies vied with each other who should admire him most; and no wonder; for their quiet lives were astonishingly stirred up by the arrival from India – especially as the person arrived told more wonderful stories than Sindbad the sailor;* and, as Miss Pole said, was quite as good as an Arabian night any evening. For my own part, I had vibrated all my life between Drumble and Cranford, and I thought it was quite possible that all Mr Peter's stories might be true although wonderful; but when I found, that if we swallowed an anecdote of tolerable magnitude one week, we had the dose considerably increased the next, I began to have my doubts; especially as I noticed that when his sister was present the accounts of Indian life were comparatively tame; not that she knew more than we did, perhaps less. I noticed also that when the Rector came to call, Mr Peter talked in a different way about the countries he had been in. But I don't think the ladies in Cranford would have considered him such a wonderful traveller if they had only heard him talk in the quiet way he did to him. They liked him the better, indeed, for being what they called 'so very Oriental'.

One day, at a select party in his honour, which Miss Pole gave, and from which, as Mrs Jamieson honoured it with her presence, and had even offered to send Mr Mulliner to wait, Mr and Mrs Hoggins and Mrs Fitz-Adam were necessarily excluded – one day at Miss Pole's Mr Peter said he was tired of sitting upright against the hard-backed uneasy chairs, and asked if he might not indulge himself in sitting cross-legged. Miss Pole's consent was eagerly given, and down he went with the utmost gravity. But when Miss Pole asked me, in an audible whisper, 'if he did not remind me of the Father of the Faithful?'* I could not help thinking of poor Simon Jones the lame tailor; and while Mrs Jamieson slowly commented on the elegance and convenience of the attitude, I remember how we had all followed that lady's lead in condemning Mr Hoggins for vulgarity because he simply crossed his legs as he sat still on his chair. Many of Mr Peter's ways of eating were a little strange amongst such ladies as Miss Pole, and Miss Matty, and Mrs Jamieson, especially when I recollected the untasted green peas and two-pronged forks at poor Mr Holbrook's dinner.

The mention of that gentleman's name recalls to my mind a conversation between Mr Peter and Miss Matty one evening in the summer after he returned to Cranford. The day had been very hot, and Miss Matty had been much oppressed by the weather; in the heat of which her brother revelled. I remember that she had been unable to nurse Martha's baby; which had become her favourite employment of late, and which was as much at home in her arms as in its mother's, as long as it remained a light weight – portable by one so fragile as Miss Matty. This day to which I refer, Miss Matty had seemed more than usually feeble and languid, and only revived when the sun went down, and her sofa was wheeled to the open window, through which, although it looked into the principal street of Cranford, the fragrant smell of the neighbouring hayfields came in every now and then, borne by the soft breezes that stirred the dull air of the summer twilight, and then died away. The silence of the sultry atmosphere was lost in the murmuring noises which came in from many an open window and door; even the children were abroad in the street, late as it was (between ten and eleven), enjoying the game of play for which they had not had spirits during the heat of the day. It was a source of satisfaction to Miss Matty to see how few candles were lighted even in the apartments of those houses from which issued the greatest signs of life. Mr Peter, Miss Matty and I, had all been quiet, each with a separate reverie, for some little time, when Mr Peter broke in –

'Do you know, little Matty, I could have sworn you were on the high road to matrimony when I left England that last time! If anybody had told me you would have lived and died an old maid then, I should have laughed in their faces.'

Miss Matty made no reply; and I tried in vain to think of some subject which should effectually turn the conversation; but I was very stupid; and before I spoke, he went on:

'It was Holbrook; that fine manly fellow who lived at Woodley, that I used to think would carry off my little Matty. You would not think it now, I dare say, Mary! but this sister of mine was once a very pretty girl – at least I thought so; and so I've a notion did poor Holbrook. What business had he to die before I came home to thank him for all his kindness to a good-for-nothing cub as I was? It was that that made me first think he cared for you; for in all our fishing expeditions it was Matty, Matty, we talked about. Poor Deborah! What a lecture she read me on having asked him home to lunch one day, when she had seen the Arley carriage in the town, and thought that my lady might call. Well, that's long years ago; more than half a lifetime! and yet it seems like yesterday! I don't know a fellow I should have liked better as a brother-in-law. You must have played your cards badly, my little Matty, somehow or another – wanted your brother to be a good go-between, eh! little one?' said he, putting out his hand to take hold of hers as she lay on the sofa – 'Why what's this? you're shivering and shaking, Matty, with that confounded open window. Shut it, Mary, this minute!'

I did so, and then stooped down to kiss Miss Matty, and see if she really were chilled. She caught at my hand, and gave it a hard squeeze – but unconsciously I think – for in a minute or two she spoke to us quite in her usual voice, and smiled our uneasiness away; although she patiently submitted to the pre-scriptions we enforced of a warmed bed, and a glass of weak negus.* I was to leave Cranford the next day, and before I went I saw that all the effects of the open window had quite vanished. I had superintended most of the alterations necessary in the house and household during the latter weeks of my stay. The shop was once more a parlour; the empty resounding rooms again furnished up to the very garrets.

There had been some talk of establishing Martha and Jem in another house; but Miss Matty would not hear of this. Indeed I never saw her so much roused as when Miss Pole had assumed it to be the most desirable arrangement. As long as Martha would remain with Miss Matty, Miss Matty was only too thankful to have her about her; yes, and Jem too, who was a very pleasant man to have in the house, for she never saw him from week's end to week's end. And as for the probable children, if they would all turn out such little darlings as her god-daughter Matilda, she should not mind the number, if Martha didn't. Besides the next was to be called Deborah; a point which Miss Matty had reluctantly yielded to Martha's stubborn determina-tion that her first-born was to be Matilda. So Miss Pole had to lower her colours, and even her voice, as she said to me that as Mr and Mrs Hearn were still to go on living in the same house with Miss Matty, we had certainly done a wise thing in hiring Martha's niece as an auxiliary.

I left Miss Matty and Mr Peter most comfortable and contented; the only subject for regret to the tender heart of the one and the social friendly nature of the other being the unfortunate quarrel between Mrs Jamieson and the plebeian Hogginses and their following. In joke I prophesied one day that this would only last until Mrs Jamieson or Mr Mulliner were ill, in which case they would only be too glad to be friends with Mr Hoggins; but Miss Matty did not like my looking forward to anything like illness in so light a manner; and, before the year was out, all had come round in a far more satisfactory way.

I received two Cranford letters on one auspicious October morning. Both Miss Pole and Miss Matty wrote to ask me to come over and meet the Gordons, who had returned to England alive and well, with their two children, now almost grown up. Dear Jessie Brown had kept her old kind nature, although she had changed her name and station; and she wrote to say that she and Major Gordon expected to be in Cranford on the fourteenth, and she hoped and begged to be remembered to Mrs Jamieson (named first, as became her honourable station), Miss Pole, and Miss Matty – could she ever forget their kindness to her poor father and sister? – Mrs Forrester, Mr Hoggins (and here again came in an allusion to kindness shown to the dead long ago), his new wife, who as such must allow Mrs Gordon to desire to make her acquaintance, and who was moreover an old Scotch friend of her husband's. In short, everyone was named, from the Rector – who had been appointed to Cranford in the interim between Captain Brown's death and Miss Jessie's marriage, and was now associated with the latter event – down to Miss Betty Barker; all were asked to the luncheon; all except Mrs Fitz-Adam, who had come to live in Cranford since Miss Jessie Brown's days, and whom I found rather moping on account of the omission. People wondered at Miss Betty Barker's being included in the honourable list; but then, as Miss Pole said, we must remember the disregard of the genteel proprieties of life in which the poor captain had educated his girls; and for his sake we swallowed our pride; indeed Mrs Jamieson rather took it as a compliment, as putting Miss Betty (formerly *her* maid) on a level with 'those Hogginses'.

But when I arrived in Cranford, nothing was as yet ascertained of Mrs Jamieson's own intentions; would the honourable lady go, or would she not? Mr Peter declared that she should and she would; Miss Pole shook her head and desponded. But Mr Peter was a man of resources. In the first place, he persuaded Miss Matty to write to Mrs Gordon, and to tell her of Mrs Fitz-Adam's existence, and to beg that one so kind, and cordial, and generous, might be included in the pleasant invitation. An answer came back by return of post, with a pretty little note for Mrs Fitz-Adam, and a request that Miss Matty would deliver it herself and explain the previous omission. Mrs Fitz-Adam was as pleased as could be, and thanked Miss Matty over and over again. Mr Peter had said, 'Leave Mrs Jamieson to me'; so we did; especially as we knew nothing that we could do to alter her determination if once formed.

I did not know, nor did Miss Matty, how things were going on, until Miss Pole asked me, just the day before Mrs Gordon came, if I thought there was anything between Mr Peter and Mrs Jamieson in the matrimonial line, for that Mrs Jamieson was really going to the lunch at the George. She had sent Mr Mulliner down to desire that there might be a foot-stool put to the warmest seat in the room, as she meant to come, and knew that their chairs were very high. Miss Pole had picked this piece of news up, and from it she conjectured all sorts of things, and bemoaned yet more. 'If Peter should marry, what would become of poor dear Miss Matty! And Mrs Jamieson, of all people!' Miss Pole seemed to think there were other ladies in Cranford who would have done more credit to his choice, and I think she must have had someone who was unmarried in her head, for she kept saying, 'It was so wanting in delicacy in a widow to think of such a thing.'

When I got back to Miss Matty's, I really did begin to think that Mr Peter might be thinking of Mrs Jamieson for a wife; and I was as unhappy as Miss Pole about it. He had the proof-sheet of a great placard in his hand. 'Signor Brunoni, Magician to the King of Delhi, the Rajah of Oude,* and the Great Lama of Thibet, etc. etc.', was going to 'perform in Cranford for one night only', – the very next night; and Miss Matty, exultant, showed me a letter from the Gordons, promising to remain over this gaiety, which Miss Matty said was entirely Peter's doing. He had written to ask the Signor to come, and was to be at all the expenses of the affair. Tickets were to be sent gratis to as many as the room would hold. In short, Miss Matty was charmed with the plan, and said that tomorrow Cranford would remind her of the Preston Guild,* to which she had been in her youth – a luncheon at the George, with the dear Gordons, and the Signor in the Assembly-room in the evening. But I – I looked only at the fatal words: –

Under the patronage of the HONOURABLE MRS JAMIESON

She, then, was chosen to preside over this entertainment of Mr Peter's; she was perhaps going to displace my dear Miss Matty in his heart, and make her life lonely once more! I could not look forward to the morrow with any pleasure; and every innocent anticipation of Miss Matty's only served to add to my annoyance.

So angry, and irritated, and exaggerating every little incident which could add to my irritation, I went on till we were all assembled in the great parlour at the George. Major and Mrs Gordon and pretty Flora and Mr Ludovic were all as bright and handsome and friendly as could be; but I could hardly attend to them for watching Mr Peter, and I saw that Miss Pole was equally busy. I had never seen Mrs Jamieson so roused and animated before; her face looked full of interest in what Mr Peter was saying. I drew near to listen. My relief was great when I caught that his words were not words of love, but that, for all his grave face, he was at his old tricks. He was telling her of his travels in India, and describing the wonderful height of the Himalaya mountains: one touch after another added to their size; and each exceeded the former in absurdity; but Mrs Jamieson really enjoyed all in perfect good faith. I suppose she required strong stimulants to excite her to come out of her apathy. Mr Peter wound up his account by saying that, of course, at that altitude there were none of the animals to be found that existed in the lower regions; the game – everything was different. Firing one day at some flying creature, he was very much dismayed, when it fell, to find that he had shot a cherubim! Mr Peter caught my eye at this moment, and gave me such a funny twinkle, that I felt sure he had no thoughts of Mrs

Jamieson as a wife, from that time. She looked uncomfortably amazed:

'But, Mr Peter – shooting a cherubim – don't you think – I am afraid that was sacrilege!'

Mr Peter composed his countenance in a moment, and appeared shocked at the idea! which, as he said truly enough, was now presented to him for the first time; but then Mrs Jamieson must remember that he had been living for a long time among savages – all of whom were heathens – some of them, he was afraid, were downright Dissenters. Then, seeing Miss Matty draw near, he hastily changed the conversation, and after a little while, turning to me, he said, 'Don't be shocked, prim little Mary, at all my wonderful stories; I consider Mrs Jamieson fair game, and besides, I am bent on propitiating her, and the first step towards it is keeping her well awake. I bribed her here by asking her to let me have her name as patroness for my poor conjuror this evening; and I don't want to give her time enough to get up her rancour against the Hogginses, who are just coming in. I want everybody to be friends, for it harasses Matty so much to hear of these quarrels. I shall go at it again by-and-by, so you need not look shocked. I intend to enter the Assembly-room tonight with Mrs Jamieson on one side, and my lady Mrs Hoggins on the other. You see if I don't.'

Somehow or another he did; and fairly got them into conversation together. Major and Mrs Gordon helped at the good work with their perfect ignorance of any existing coolness between any of the inhabitants of Cranford.

Ever since that day there has been the old friendly sociability in Cranford society; which I am thankful for, because of my dear Miss Matty's love of peace and kindliness. We all love Miss Matty, and I somehow think we are all of us better when she is near us.

THE END

THE CAGE
AT CRANFORD

THE CAGE AT CRANFORD

The Cage at Cranford appeared in Dickens's magazine All the
Year Round *on 28 November 1863, and J. G. Sharps has rightly
called it 'a kind of postscript' to* Cranford. *Miss Pole is central
to the 'action', and Mary Smith, now turned thirty, is back in
place: Miss Matty, Peter and Mr Hoggins appear, but are
somewhat reduced in the interests of the joke. And that joke,
about what the cage is for, just about comes off. Mrs Gaskell,
through her narrator, refers to the last mention of Cranford as
being in 1856, an inaccuracy for 1853, and the whole piece
lacks the vitality and warmth of* Cranford. *It was not included
in A. W. Ward's Knutsford edition of 1906, a sufficient indica-
tion that the Misses Gaskell did not give permission for this
slight sequel of their mother's to be reprinted.*

Have I told you anything about my friends at Cranford since
the year 1856? I think not.

You remember the Gordons, don't you? She that was Jessie
Brown, who married her old love, Major Gordon: and from
being poor became quite a rich lady: but for all that never forgot
any of her old friends in Cranford.

Well! the Gordons were travelling abroad, for they were very
fond of travelling; people who have had to spend part of their
lives in a regiment always are, I think. They were now in Paris,
in May, 1856, and were going to stop there, and in the
neighbourhood all summer, but Mr Ludovic was coming to
England soon; so Mrs Gordon wrote me word. I was glad she
told me, for just then I was waiting to make a little present to
Miss Pole, with whom I was staying; so I wrote to Mrs Gordon,
and asked her to choose me out something pretty and new and
fashionable, that would be acceptable to Miss Pole. Miss Pole
had just been talking a great deal about Mrs Fitz-Adam's caps
being so unfashionable, which I suppose made me put in that

word fashionable; but afterwards I wished I had sent to say my present was not to be too fashionable; for there *is* such a thing, I can assure you! The price of my present was not to be more than twenty shillings, but that is a very handsome sum if you put it in that way, though it may not sound so much if you only call it a sovereign.

Mrs Gordon wrote back to me, pleased, as she always was, with doing anything for her old friends. She told me she had been out for a day's shopping before going into the country, and had got a cage for herself of the newest and most elegant description, and had thought that she could not do better than get another like it as my present for Miss Pole, as cages were so much better made in Paris than anywhere else. I was rather dismayed when I read this letter, for, however pretty a cage might be, it was something for Miss Pole's own self, and not for her parrot, that I had intended to get. Here had I been finding ever so many reasons against her buying a new cap at Johnson's fashion-show, because I thought that the present which Mrs Gordon was to choose for me in Paris might turn out to be an elegant and fashionable head-dress; a kind of cross between a turban and a cap, as I see those from Paris mostly are; and now I had to veer round, and advise her to go as fast as she could, and secure Mr Johnson's cap before any other purchaser snatched it up. But Miss Pole was too sharp for me.

'Why, Mary,' said she, 'it was only yesterday you were running down that cap like anything. You said, you know, that lilac was too old a colour for me; and green too young; and that the mixture was very unbecoming.'

'Yes, I know,' said I; 'but I have thought better of it. I thought about it a great deal last night, and I think – I thought – they would neutralise each other; and the shadows of any colour are, you know – something I know – complementary colours.' I was not sure of my own meaning, but I had an idea in my head, though I could not express it. She took me up shortly.

'Child, you don't know what you are saying. And besides, I don't want compliments at my time of life. I lay awake, too, thinking of the cap. I only buy one ready-made once a year, and of course it's a matter for consideration; and I came to the conclusion that you were quite right.'

'Oh! dear Miss Pole! I was quite wrong; if you only knew – I did think it a very pretty cap – only – '

'Well! do just finish what you've got to say. You're almost as bad as Miss Matty in your way of talking, without being half as good as she is in other ways; though I'm very fond of you, Mary, I don't mean I am not; but you must see you're very off and on, and very muddle-headed. It's the truth, so you will not mind my saying so.'

It was just because it did seem like the truth at that time that I did mind her saying so; and, in despair, I thought I would tell her all.

'I did not mean what I said; I don't think lilac too old or green too young; and I think the mixture very becoming to you; and I think you will never get such a pretty cap again, at least in Cranford.' It was fully out, so far, at least.

'Then, Mary Smith, will you tell me what you did mean, by speaking as you did, and convincing me against my will, and giving me a bad night?'

'I meant – oh, Miss Pole, I meant to surprise you with a present from Paris; and I thought it would be a cap. Mrs Gordon was to choose it, and Mr Ludovic to bring it. I dare say it is in England now; only it's not a cap. And I did not want you to buy Johnson's cap, when I thought I was getting another for you.'

Miss Pole found this speech 'muddle-headed', I have no doubt, though she did not say so, only making an odd noise of perplexity. I went on: 'I wrote to Mrs Gordon, and asked her to get you a present – something new and pretty. I meant it to be a dress, but I suppose I did not say so; I thought it would be a cap, for Paris is so famous for caps, and it is – '

'You're a good girl, Mary' (I was past thirty, but did not object to being called a girl; and, indeed, I generally felt like a girl at Cranford, where everybody was so much older than I was), 'but when you want a thing, say what you want; it is the best way in general. And now I suppose Mrs Gordon has bought something quite different? – a pair of shoes, I dare say, for people talk a deal of Paris shoes. Anyhow, I'm just as much obliged to you, Mary, my dear. Only you should not go and spend your money on me.'

'It was not much money; and it was not a pair of shoes. You'll let me go and get the cap, won't you? It was so pretty – somebody will be sure to snatch it up.'

'I don't like getting a cap that's sure to be unbecoming.'

'But it is not; it was not. I never saw you look so well in anything,' said I.

'Mary, Mary, remember who is the father of lies!'

'But he's not my father,' exclaimed I, in a hurry, for I saw Mrs Fitz-Adam go down the street in the direction of Johnson's shop. 'I'll eat my words; they were all false: only just let me run down and buy you that cap – that pretty cap.'

'Well! run off, child. I liked it myself till you put me out of taste with it.'

I brought it back in triumph from under Mrs Fitz-Adam's very nose, as she was hanging in meditation over it; and the more we saw of it, the more we felt pleased with our purchase. We turned it on this side, and we turned it on that; and though we hurried it away into Miss Pole's bedroom at the sound of a double knock at the door, when we found it was only Miss Matty and Mr Peter, Miss Pole could not resist the opportunity of displaying it, and said in a solemn way to Miss Matty:

'Can I speak to you for a few minutes in private?' And I knew feminine delicacy too well to explain what this grave prelude was to lead to; aware how immediately Miss Matty's anxious tremor would be allayed by the sight of the cap. I had to go on talking to Mr Peter, however, when I would far rather have been in the bedroom, and heard the observations and comments.

We talked of the new cap all day; what gowns it would suit; whether a certain bow was not rather too coquettish for a woman of Miss Pole's age. 'No longer young', as she called herself, after a little struggle with the words, though at sixty-five she need not have blushed as if she were telling a falsehood. But at last the cap was put away, and with a wrench we turned our thoughts from the subject. We had been silent for a little while, each at our work with a candle between us, when Miss Pole began:

'It was very kind of you, Mary, to think of giving me a present from Paris.'

'Oh, I was only too glad to be able to get you something! I hope you will like it, though it is not what I expected.'

'I am sure I shall like it. And a surprise is always so pleasant.'

'Yes; but I think Mrs Gordon has made a very odd choice.'

'I wonder what it is. I don't like to ask, but there's a great deal in anticipation; I remember hearing dear Miss Jenkyns say that "anticipation was the soul of enjoyment", or something like that. Now there is no anticipation in a surprise; that's the worst of it.'

'Shall I tell you what it is?'

'Just as you like, my dear. If it is any pleasure to you, I am quite willing to hear.'

'Perhaps I had better not. It is something quite different to what I expected, and meant to have got; and I'm not sure if I like it as well.'

'Relieve your mind, if you like, Mary. In all disappointments sympathy is a great balm.'

'Well, then, it's something not for you; it's for Polly. It's a cage. Mrs Gordon says they make such pretty ones in Paris.'

I could see that Miss Pole's first emotion was disappointment. But she was very fond of her cockatoo, and the thought of his smartness in his new habitation made her be reconciled in a moment; besides that she was really grateful to me for having planned a present for her.

'Polly! Well, yes; his old cage is very shabby; he is so continually pecking at it with his sharp bill. I dare say Mrs Gordon noticed it when she called here last October. I shall always think of you, Mary, when I see him in it. Now we can have him in the drawing-room, for I dare say a French cage will be quite an ornament to the room.'

And so she talked on, till we worked ourselves up into high delight at the idea of Polly in his new abode, presentable in it even to the Honourable Mrs Jamieson. The next morning Miss Pole said she had been dreaming of Polly with her new cap on his head, while she herself sat on a perch in the new cage and admired him. Then, as if ashamed of having revealed the fact of imagining 'such arrant nonsense' in her sleep, she passed on rapidly to the philosophy of dreams, quoting some book she had lately been reading, which was either too deep in itself, or too confused in her repetition for me to understand it. After breakfast, we had the cap out again; and that in its different aspects occupied us for an hour or so; and then, as it was a fine day, we turned into the garden, where Polly was hung on a nail outside the kitchen window. He clamoured and screamed at the sight of his mistress, who went to look for an almond for him. I examined his cage meanwhile, old discoloured wicker-work, clumsily made by a Cranford basket-maker. I took out Mrs Gordon's letter; it was dated the fifteenth, and this was the twentieth, for I had kept it secret for two days in my pocket. Mr Ludovic was on the point of setting out for England when she wrote.

'Poor Polly!' said I, as Miss Pole, returning, fed him with the almond.

'Ah! Polly does not know what a pretty cage he is going to have,' said she, talking to him as she would have done to a child; and then turning to me, she asked when I thought it would come? We reckoned up dates, and made out that it might arrive that very day. So she called to her little stupid servant-maiden Fanny, and bade her go out and buy a great brass-headed nail, very strong, strong enough to bear Polly and the new cage, and we all three weighed the cage in our hands, and on her return she was to come up into the drawing-room with the nail and a hammer.

Fanny was a long time, as she always was, over her errands; but as soon as she came back, we knocked the nail, with solemn earnestness, into the house-wall, just outside the drawing-room window; for, as Miss Pole observed, when I was not there she had no one to talk to, and as in summer-time she generally sat with the window open, she could combine two purposes, the giving air and sun to Polly-Cockatoo, and the having his agreeable companionship in her solitary hours.

'When it rains, my dear, or even in a very hot sun, I shall take the cage in. I would not have your pretty present spoilt for the world. It was very kind of you to think of it; I am quite come round to liking it better than any present of mere dress; and dear Mrs Gordon has shown all her usual pretty observation in remembering my Polly-Cockatoo.'

'Polly-Cockatoo' was his grand name; I had only once or twice heard him spoken of by Miss Pole in this formal manner, except when she was speaking to the servants; then she always gave him his full designation, just as most people call their daughters Miss, in speaking of them to strangers or servants. But since Polly was to have a new cage, and all the way from Paris too, Miss Pole evidently thought it necessary to treat him with unusual respect.

We were obliged to go out to pay some calls; but we left strict orders with Fanny what to do if the cage arrived in our absence, as (we had calculated) it might. Miss Pole stood ready bonneted and shawled at the kitchen door, I behind her, and cook behind Fanny, each of us listening to the conversation of the other two.

'And Fanny, mind if it comes you coax Polly-Cockatoo nicely into it. He is very particular, and may be attached to his old cage, though it is so shabby. Remember, birds have their feelings as much as we have! Don't hurry him in making up his mind.'

'Please, ma'am, I think an almond would help him to get over his feelings,' said Fanny, dropping a curtsey at every speech, as she had been taught to do at her charity school.

'A very good idea, very. If I have my keys in my pocket I will give you an almond for him. I think he is sure to like the view up the street from the window; he likes seeing people, I think.'

'It's but a dull look-out into the garden; nowt but dumb flowers,' said cook, touched by this allusion to the cheerfulness of the street, as contrasted with the view from her own kitchen window.

'It's a very good look-out for busy peope,' said Miss Pole, severely. And then, feeling she was likely to get the worst of it in an encounter with her old servant, she withdrew with meek dignity, being deaf to some sharp reply; and of course I, being bound to keep order, was deaf too. It the truth must be told, we rather hastened our steps, until we had banged the street-door behind us.

We called on Miss Matty, of course; and then on Mrs Hoggins. It seemed as if ill-luck would have it that we went to the only two households of Cranford where there was the encumbrance of a man, and in both places the man was where he ought not to have been – namely, in his own house, and in the way. Miss Pole – out of civility to me, and because she really was full of the new cage for Polly, and because we all in Cranford relied on the sympathy of our neighbours in the veriest trifle that interested us – told Miss Matty, and Mr Peter, and Mr and Mrs Hoggins; he was standing in the drawing-room, booted and spurred, and eating his hunk of bread-and-cheese in the very presence of his aristocratic wife, my lady that was. As Miss Pole said afterwards, if refinement was not to be found in Cranford, blessed as it was with so many scions of county families, she did not know where to meet with it. Bread-and-cheese in a drawing-room! Onions next.

But for all Mr Hoggins's vulgarity, Miss Pole told him of the present she was about to receive.

'Only think! a new cage for Polly – Polly – Polly-Cockatoo, you know, Mr Hoggins. You remember him, and the bite he gave me once because he wanted to be put back in his cage, pretty bird?'

'I only hope the new cage will be strong as well as pretty, for I must say a – ' He caught a look from his wife, I think, for he stopped short. 'Well, we're old friends, Polly and I, and he put some practice in my way once. I shall be up the street this afternoon, and perhaps I shall step in and see this smart Parisian cage.'

'Do!' said Miss Pole, eagerly. 'Or, if you are in a hurry, look up at my drawing-room window; if the cage is come, it will be hanging out there, and Polly in it.'

We had passed the omnibus that met the train from London some time ago, so we were not surprised as we returned home to see Fanny half out of the window, and cook evidently either helping or hindering her. Then they both took their heads in; but there was no cage hanging up. We hastened up the steps.

Both Fanny and the cook met us in the passage.

'Please, ma'am,' said Fanny, 'there's no bottom to the cage, and Polly would fly away.'

'And there's no top,' exclaimed cook. 'He might get out at the top quite easy.'

'Let me see,' said Miss Pole, brushing past, thinking no doubt that her superior intelligence was all that was needed to set things to rights. On the ground lay a bundle, or a circle of hoops, neatly covered over with calico, no more like a cage for Polly-Cockatoo than I am like a cage. Cook took something up between her finger and thumb, and lifted the unsightly present from Paris. How I wish it had stayed there! – but foolish ambition has brought people to ruin before now; and my twenty shillings are gone, sure enough, and there must be some use or some ornament intended by the maker of the thing before us.

'Don't you think it's a mousetrap, ma'am?' asked Fanny, dropping her little curtsey.

For reply, the cook lifted up the machine, and showed how easily mice might run out; and Fanny shrank back abashed. Cook was evidently set against the new invention, and muttered about its being all of a piece with French things, French cooks, French plums (nasty dried-up things), French rolls (as had no substance in 'em).

Miss Pole's good manners, and desire of making the best of things in my presence, induced her to try and drown cook's mutterings.

'Indeed, I think it will make a very nice cage for Polly-Cockatoo. How pleased he will be to go from one hoop to another, just like a ladder, and with a board or two at the bottom, and nicely tied up at the top – '

Fanny was struck with a new idea.

'Please, ma'am, my sister-in-law has got an aunt as lives lady's-maid with Sir John's daughter – Miss Arley. And they did say as she wore iron petticoats all made of hoops – '

'Nonsense, Fanny!' we all cried; for such a thing had not been heard of in all Drumble, let alone Cranford, and I was rather looked upon in the light of a fast young woman by all the laundresses of Cranford, because I had two corded petticoats.

'Go mind thy business, wench,' said cook, with the utmost contempt. 'I'll warrant we'll manage th' cage without thy help.'

'It is near dinner-time, Fanny, and the cloth not laid,' said Miss Pole, hoping the remark might cut two ways; but cook had no notion of going. She stood on the bottom step of the stairs, holding the Paris perplexity aloft in the air.

'It might do for a meat-safe,' said she. 'Cover it o'er wi' canvas, to keep th' flies out. It is a good framework, I reckon, anyhow!' She held her head on one side, like a connoisseur in meat-safes, as she was.

Miss Pole said, 'Are you sure Mrs Gordon called it a cage, Mary? Because she is a woman of her word, and would not have called it so if it was not.'

'Look here; I have the letter in my pocket.'

' "I have wondered how I could best fulfil your commission for me to purchase something to the value of" – um, um, never mind – "fashionable and pretty for dear Miss Pole, and at length I have decided upon one of the new kind of 'cages' "(look here, Miss Pole; here is the word, C.A.G.E.), "which are made so much lighter and more elegant in Paris than in England. Indeed, I am not sure if they have ever reached you, for it is not a month since I saw the first of the kind in Paris." '

'Does she say anything about Polly-Cockatoo?' asked Miss Pole. 'That would settle the matter at once, as showing that she had him in her mind.'

'No – nothing.'

Just then Fanny came along the passage with the tray full of dinner-things in her hands. When she had put them down, she stood at the door of the dining-room taking a distant view of the article. 'Please, ma'am, it looks like a petticoat without any stuff in it; indeed it does, if I'm to be whipped for saying it.'

But she only drew down upon herself a fresh objurgation from the cook; and sorry and annoyed, I seized the opportunity of taking the thing out of cook's hand, and carrying it upstairs, for it was full time to get ready for dinner. But we had very little appetite for our meal, and kept constantly making suggestions, one to the other, as to the nature and purpose of this Paris 'cage', but as constantly snubbing poor little Fanny's reiteration of 'Please, ma'am, I do believe it's a kind of petticoat – indeed I do.' At length Miss Pole turned upon her with almost as much vehemence as cook had done, only in choicer language.

'Don't be so silly, Fanny. Do you think ladies are like children, and must be put in go-carts; or need wire guards like fires to surround them; or can get warmth out of bits of whalebone and steel; a likely thing indeed! Don't keep talking about what you don't understand.'

So our maiden was mute for the rest of the meal. After dinner we had Polly brought upstairs in her old cage, and I held out the new one, and we turned it about in every way. At length Miss Pole said:

'Put Polly-Cockatoo back, and shut him up in his cage. You hold this French thing up' (alas! that my present should be called a 'thing'), 'and I'll sew a bottom on to it. I'll lay a good deal, they've forgotten to sew in the bottom before sending it off.' So I held and she sewed; and then she held and I sewed, till it was all done. Just as we had put Polly-Cockatoo in, and were closing up the top with a pretty piece of old yellow ribbon – and, indeed, it was not a bad-looking cage after all our trouble – Mr Hoggins came upstairs, having been seen by Fanny before he had time to knock at the door.

'Hallo!' said he, almost tumbling over us, as we were sitting on the floor at our work. 'What's this?'

'It's this pretty present for Polly-Cockatoo,' said Miss Pole, raising herself up with as much dignity as she could, 'that Mary has had sent from Paris for me.' Miss Pole was in great spirits now we had got Polly in; I can't say that I was.

Mr Hoggins began to laugh in his boisterous vulgar way.

'For Polly – ha! ha! It's meant for you, Miss Pole – ha! ha! It's a new invention to hold your gowns out – ha! ha!'

'Mr Hoggins! you may be a surgeon, and a very clever one,

but nothing – not even your profession – gives you a right to be indecent.'

Miss Pole was thoroughly roused, and I trembled in my shoes. But Mr Hoggins only laughed the more. Polly screamed in concert, but Miss Pole stood in stiff rigid propriety, very red in the face.

'I beg your pardon, Miss Pole, I am sure. But I am pretty certain I am right. It's no indecency that I can see; my wife and Mrs Fitz-Adam take in a Paris fashion-book between 'em, and I can't help seeing the plates of fashions sometimes – ha! ha! ha! Look, Polly has got out of his queer prison – ha! ha! ha!'

Just then Mr Peter came in; Miss Matty was so curious to know if the expected present had arrived. Mr Hoggins took them by the arm, and pointed to the poor thing lying on the ground, but could not explain for laughing. Miss Pole said:

'Although I am not accustomed to give an explanation of my conduct to gentlemen, yet, being insulted in my own house by – by Mr Hoggins, I must appeal to the brother of my old friend – my very oldest friend. Is this article a lady's petticoat, or a bird's cage?'

She held it up as she made this solemn inquiry. Mr Hoggins seized the moment to leave the room, in shame, as I supposed, but, in reality, to fetch his wife's fashion-book; and, before I had completed the narration of the story of my unlucky commission, he returned, and, holding the fashion-plate open by the side of the extended article, demonstrated the identity of the two.

But Mr Peter had always a smooth way of turning off anger, by either his fun or a compliment. 'It is a cage,' said he, bowing to Miss Pole; 'but it is a cage for an angel, instead of a bird! Come along, Hoggins, I want to speak to you!'

And, with an apology, he took the offending and victorious surgeon out of Miss Pole's presence. For a good while we said nothing; and we were now rather shy of little Fanny's superior wisdom when she brought up tea. But towards night our spirits revived, and we were quite ourselves again, when Miss Pole proposed that we should cut up the pieces of steel or whalebone – which, to do them justice, were very elastic – and make ourselves two very comfortable English calashes out of them with the aid of a piece of dyed silk which Miss Pole had by her.

MR HARRISON'S
CONFESSIONS

Chapter 1

The fire was burning gaily. My wife had just gone upstairs to put baby to bed. Charles sat opposite to me, looking very brown and handsome. It was pleasant enough that we should feel sure of spending some weeks under the same roof, a thing which we had never done since we were mere boys. I felt too lazy to talk, so I ate walnuts and looked into the fire. But Charles grew restless.

'Now that your wife is gone upstairs, Will, you must tell me what I've wanted to ask you ever since I saw her this morning. Tell me all about the wooing and winning. I want to have the receipt for getting such a charming little wife of my own. Your letters only gave the barest details. So set to, man, and tell me every particular.'

'If I tell you all, it will be a long story.'

'Never fear. If I get tired, I can go to sleep, and dream that I am back again, a lonely bachelor, in Ceylon; and I can waken up when you have done, to know that I am under your roof. Dash away, man! "Once upon a time, a gallant young bachelor" – There's a beginning for you!'

'Well, then: "Once upon a time, a gallant young bachelor" was sorely puzzled where to settle, when he had completed his education as a surgeon – I must speak in the first person; I cannot go on as a gallant young bachelor. I had just finished walking the hospitals when you went to Ceylon, and, if you remember, I wanted to go abroad like you, and thought of offering myself as a ship-surgeon; but I found I should rather lose caste in my profession; so I hesitated, and, while I was hesitating, I received a letter from my father's cousin, Mr Morgan – that old gentleman who used to write such long letters of good advice to my mother, and who tipped me a five-pound note when I agreed to be bound apprentice to Mr Howard, instead of going to sea. Well, it seems the old gentleman had all along thought of taking me as his partner, if I turned out pretty well; and, as he heard a good account of me from an old friend of his, who was a surgeon at Guy's,* he wrote to propose this arrangement: I was to have a third of the profits for five years; after that, half; and eventually I was to succeed to the whole. It was no bad offer for a penniless man like me, as Mr Morgan had a capital country practice, and, though I did not know him personally, I had formed a pretty good idea of him, as an honourable, kind-hearted, fidgety, meddlesome old bachelor; and a very correct notion it was, as I found out in the very first half-hour of seeing him. I had had some idea that I was to live in his house, as he was a bachelor and a kind of family friend, and I think he was afraid that I should expect this arrangement; for, when I walked up to his door, with the porter carrying my portmanteau, he met me on the steps, and while he held my hand and shook it, he said to the porter, "Jerry, if you'll wait a moment, Mr Harrison will be ready to go with you, to his lodgings, at Jocelyn's, you know"; and then, turning to me, he addressed his first words of welcome. I was a little inclined to think him inhospitable, but I got to understand him better afterwards. "Jocelyn's," said he, "is the best place I have been able to hit upon in a hurry, and there is a good deal of fever about, which made me desirous that you should come this month – a low kind of typhoid, in the oldest part of the town. I think you'll be comfortable there for a week or two. I have taken the liberty of desiring my housekeeper to send down one or two things which give the place a little more of a home aspect – an easy-chair, a beautiful case of preparations, and one or two little matters in the way of eatables; but, if you'll take my advice, I've a plan in my head which we will talk about tomorrow morning. At present, I don't like to keep you standing out on the steps here; so I'll not detain you from your lodgings, where I rather think my housekeeper is gone to get tea ready for you."

'I thought I understood the old gentleman's anxiety for his own health, which he put upon care for mine; for he had on a kind of loose grey coat, and no hat on his head. But I wondered that he did not ask me indoors, instead of keeping me on the steps. I believe, after all, I made a mistake in supposing he was afraid of taking cold; he was only afraid of being seen in dishabille. And for his apparent inhospitality, I had not been long in Duncombe* before I understood the comfort of having one's house considered as a castle into which no one might intrude, and saw good reason for the practice Mr Morgan had established of coming to his door to speak to everyone. It was only the effect of habit that made him receive me so. Before long, I had the free run of his house.

'There was every sign of kind attention and forethought on the part of someone, whom I could not doubt to be Mr Morgan, in my lodgings. I was too lazy to do much that evening, and sat in the little bow-window which projected over Jocelyn's shop, looking up and down the street. Duncombe calls itself a town, but I should call it a village. Really, looking from Jocelyn's, it is a very picturesque place. The houses are anything but regular; they may be mean in their details; but altogether they look well; they have not that flat unrelieved front, which many towns of far more pretensions present. Here and there a bow-window – every now and then a gable, cutting up against the sky – occasionally a projecting upper storey – throws good effect of light and shadow along the street; and they have a queer fashion of their own of colouring the whitewash of some of the houses with a sort of pink blotting-paper tinge, more like the stone of which Mayence* is built than anything else. It may be very bad taste, but to my mind it gives a rich warmth to the colouring. Then, here and there a dwelling-house has a court in front, with a grass-plot on each side of the flagged walk, and a large tree or two – limes or horse-chestnuts – which send their great projecting upper branches over into the street, making round dry places of shelter on the pavement in the times of summer showers.

'While I was sitting in the bow-window, thinking of the contrast between this place and the lodgings in the heart of London, which I had left only twelve hours before – the window open here, and, although in the centre of the town, admitting only scents from the mignonette boxes on the sill, instead of the dust and smoke of— Street – the only sound heard in this, the principal street, being the voices of mothers calling their playing children home to bed, and the eight o'clock bell of the old parish church bimbomming* in remembrance of the curfew: while I was sitting thus idly, the door opened, and the little maid-servant, dropping a curtsey, said –

'"Please, sir, Mrs Munton's compliments, and she would be glad to know how you are after your journey."

'There! was not that hearty and kind? Would even the dearest chum I had at Guy's have thought of doing such a thing? while Mrs Munton, whose name I had never heard of before, was doubtless suffering anxiety till I could relieve her mind by sending back word that I was pretty well.

'"My compliments to Mrs Munton, and I am pretty well: much obliged to her." It was as well to say only 'pretty well', for 'very well' would have destroyed the interest Mrs Munton evidently felt in me. Good Mrs Munton! Kind Mrs Munton! Perhaps, also, young – handsome – rich – widowed Mrs Munton! I rubbed my hands with delight and amusement, and, resuming my post of observation, began to wonder at which house Mrs Munton lived.

'Again the little tap, and the little maid-servant –

'"Please, sir, the Miss Tomkinsons' compliments, and they would be glad to know how you feel yourself after your journey."

'I don't know why, but the Miss Tomkinsons' name had not such a halo about it as Mrs Munton's. Still it was very pretty in the Miss Tomkinsons to send and inquire. I only wished I did not feel so perfectly robust. I was almost ashamed that I could not send word I was quite exhausted by fatigue, and had fainted twice since my arrival. If I had but had a headache, at least! I heaved a deep breath: my chest was in perfect order; I had caught no cold; so I answered again –

'"Much obliged to the Miss Tomkinsons; I am not much fatigued; tolerably well: my compliments."

'Little Sally could hardly have got downstairs, before she returned, bright and breathless –

'"Mr and Mrs Bullock's compliments, sir, and they hope you are pretty well after your journey."

'Who would have expected such kindness from such an unpromising name? Mr and Mrs Bullock were less interesting, it is true, than their predecessors; but I graciously replied –

'"My compliments; a night's rest will perfectly recruit me."*

'The same message was presently brought up from one or two more unknown kind hearts. I really wished I were not so ruddy-looking. I was afraid I should disappoint the tender-hearted town when they saw what a hale young fellow I was. And I was almost ashamed of confessing to a great appetite for supper when Sally came up to inquire what I would have. Beefsteaks were so tempting; but perhaps I ought rather to have water-gruel, and go to bed. The beefsteak carried the day, however. I need not have felt such a gentle elation of spirits, as this mark of the town's attention is paid to everyone when they arrive after a journey. Many of the same people have sent to inquire after you – great, hulking, brown fellow as you are – only Sally spared you the infliction of devising interesting answers.

Chapter 2

'The next morning Mr Morgan came before I had finished breakfast. He was the most dapper little man I ever met. I see the affection with which people cling to the style of dress that was in vogue when they were beaux and belles, and received the most admiration. They are unwilling to believe that their youth and beauty are gone, and think that the prevailing mode is unbecoming. Mr Morgan will inveigh by the hour together against frock-coats, for instance, and whiskers. He keeps his chin close shaven, wears a black dress-coat, and dark-grey pantaloons; and in his morning round to his town patients, he invariably wears the brightest and blackest of Hessian boots,* with dangling silk tassels on each side. When he goes home, about ten o'clock, to prepare for his ride to see his country patients, he puts on the most dandy top-boots I ever saw, which he gets from some wonderful bootmaker a hundred miles off. His appearance is what one calls "jemmy";* there is no other word that will do for it. He was evidently a little discomfited when he saw me in my breakfast costume, with the habits which I brought with me from the fellows at Guy's; my feet against the fireplace, my chair balanced on its hind legs (a habit of sitting which I afterwards discovered he particularly abhorred); slippers on my feet (which, also, he considered a most ungentlemanly piece of untidiness 'out of a bedroom'); in short, from what I afterwards learned, every prejudice he had was outraged by my appearance on this first visit of his. I put my book down, and sprang up to receive him. He stood, hat and cane in hand.

'"I came to inquire if it would be convenient for you to accompany me on my morning's round, and to be introduced to a few of our friends." I quite detected the little tone of coldness, induced by his disappointment at my appearance, though he never imagined that it was in any way perceptible. 'I will be ready directly, sir,' said I; and bolted into my bedroom, only too happy to escape his scrutinising eye.

'When I returned, I was made aware, by sundry indescribable little coughs and hesitating noises, that my dress did not satisfy him. I stood ready, hat and gloves in hand; but still he did not offer to set off on our round. I grew very red and hot. At length he said –

' "Excuse me, my dear young friend, but may I ask if you have no other coat besides that – "cut away", I believe you call them? We are rather sticklers for propriety, I believe, in Duncombe; and much depends on a first impression. Let it be professional, my dear sir. Black is the garb of our profession. Forgive my speaking so plainly; but I consider myself *in loco parentis*."*

'He was so kind, so bland, and, in truth, so friendly, that I felt it would be most childish to take offence; but I had a little resentment in my heart at this way of being treated. However, I mumbled, "Oh, certainly, sir, if you wish it"; and returned once more to change my coat – my poor cut-away.

' "Those coats, sir, give a man rather too much of a sporting appearance, not quite befitting the learned professions; more as if you came down here to hunt than to be the Galen or Hippocrates* of the neighbourhood." He smiled graciously, so I smothered a sigh; for, to tell you the truth, I had rather anticipated – and, in fact, had boasted at Guy's of – the runs I hoped to have with the hounds; for Duncombe was in a famous hunting district. But all these ideas were quite dispersed when Mr Morgan led me to the inn-yard, where there was a horse-dealer on his way to a neighbouring fair, and "strongly advised me" – which in our relative circumstances was equivalent to an injunction – to purchase a little, useful, fast-trotting, brown cob, instead of a fine showy horse, "who would take any fence I put him to", as the horse-dealer assured me. Mr Morgan was evidently pleased when I bowed to his decision, and gave up all hopes of an occasional hunt.

'He opened out a great deal more after this purchase. He told me his plan of establishing me in a house of my own, which looked more respectable, not to say professional, than being in lodgings; and then he went on to say that he had lately lost a friend, a brother surgeon in a neighbouring town, who had left a widow with a small income, who would be very glad to live with me, and act as mistress to my establishment; thus lessening the expense.

' "She is a lady-like woman," said Mr Morgan, "to judge from the little I have seen of her; about forty-five or so; and may really be of some help to you in the little etiquettes of our profession – the slight delicate attentions which every man has to learn, if he wishes to get on in life. This is Mrs Munton's sir,' said he, stopping short at a very unromantic-looking green door, with a brass knocker,

'I had no time to say, "Who is Mrs Munton?" before we had heard Mrs Munton was at home, and were following the tidy elderly servant up the narrow carpeted stairs into the drawing-room. Mrs Munton was the widow of a former vicar, upwards of sixty, rather deaf; but like all the deaf people I have ever seen, very fond of talking; perhaps because she then knew the subject, which passed out of her grasp when another began to speak. She was ill of a chronic complaint, which often incapacitated her from going out; and the kind people of the town were in the habit of coming to see her and sit with her, and of bringing her the newest, freshest, tit-bits of news; so that her room was the centre of the gossip of Duncombe – not of scandal, mind; for I make a distinction between gossip and scandal. Now you can fancy the discrepancy between the ideal and the real Mrs Munton. Instead of any foolish notion of a beautiful blooming widow, tenderly anxious about the health of the stranger, I saw a homely, talkative, elderly person, with a keen observant eye, and marks of suffering on her face; plain in manner and dress, but still unmistakably a lady. She talked to Mr Morgan, but she looked at me; and I saw that nothing I did escaped her notice. Mr Morgan annoyed me by his anxiety to show me off; but he was kindly anxious to bring out every circumstance to my credit in Mrs Munton's hearing, knowing well that the town-crier had not more opportunities to publish all about me than she had.

' "What was that remark you repeated to me of Sir Astley Cooper's?"* asked he. It had been the most trivial speech in the world that I had named as we walked along, and I felt ashamed of having to repeat it: but it answered Mr Morgan's purpose, and before night all the town had heard that I was a favourite pupil of Sir Astley's (I had never seen him but twice in my life); and Mr Morgan was afraid that as soon as he knew my full value I should be retained by Sir Astley to assist him in his duties as surgeon to the Royal Family. Every little circumstance was pressed into the conversation which could add to my importance.

'"As I once heard Sir Robert Peel* remark to Mr Harrison, the father of our young friend here – The moons in August are remarkably full and bright." – If you remember, Charles, my father was always proud of having sold a pair of gloves to Sir Robert, when he was staying at the Grange, near Biddicombe, and I suppose good Mr Morgan had paid his only visit to my father at the time; but Mrs Munton evidently looked at me with double respect after this incidental remark, which I was amused to meet with, a few months afterwards, disguised in the statement that my father was an intimate friend of the Premier's, and had, in fact, been the adviser of most of the measures taken by him in public life. I sat by, half indignant and half amused. Mr Morgan looked so complacently pleased at the whole effect of the conversation, that I did not care to mar it by explanations; and, indeed, I had little idea at the time how small sayings were the seeds of great events in the town of Duncombe. When we left Mrs Munton's, he was in a blandly communicative mood.

'"You will find it a curious statistical fact, but five-sixths of our householders of a certain rank in Duncombe are women. We have widows and old maids in rich abundance. In fact, my dear sir, I believe that you and I are almost the only gentlemen in the place – Mr Bullock, of course, excepted. By gentlemen, I mean professional men. It behoves us to remember, sir, that so many of the female sex rely upon us for the kindness and protection which every man who is worthy of the name is always so happy to render."

'Miss Tomkinson, on whom we next called, did not strike me as remarkably requiring protection from any man. She was a tall, gaunt, masculine woman, with an air of defiance about her, naturally; this, however, she softened and mitigated, as far as she was able, in favour of Mr Morgan. He, it seemed to me, stood a little in awe of the lady, who was very *brusque* and plain-spoken, and evidently piqued herself on her decision of character and sincerity of speech.

'"So this is the Mr Harrison we have heard so much of from you, Mr Morgan? I must say, from what I had heard, that I had expected something a little more – hum – hum! But he's young yet; he's young. We have been all anticipating an Apollo,* Mr Harrison, from Mr Morgan's description, and an Æsculapius* combined in one; or, perhaps I might confine myself to saying Apollo, as he, I believe, was the god of medicine!"

'How could Mr Morgan have described me without seeing me? I asked myself.

'Miss Tomkinson put on her spectacles, and adjusted them on her Roman nose. Suddenly relaxing from her severity of inspection, she said to Mr Morgan – "But you must see Caroline. I had nearly forgotten it; she is busy with the girls, but I will send for her. She had a bad headache yesterday, and looked very pale; it made me very uncomfortable."

'She rang the bell, and desired the servant to fetch Miss Caroline.

'Miss Caroline was the younger sister – younger by twenty years; and so considered as a child by Miss Tomkinson, who was fifty-five, at the very least. If she was considered as a child, she was also petted and caressed, and cared for as a child; for she had been left as a baby to the charge of her elder sister; and when the father died, and they had to set up a school, Miss Tomkinson took upon herself every difficult arrangement, and denied herself every pleasure, and made every sacrifice in order that "Carry" might not feel the change in their circumstances. My wife tells me she once knew the sisters purchase a piece of silk, enough, with management, to have made two gowns; but Carry wished for flounces, or some such fal-lals;* and, without a word, Miss Tomkinson gave up her gown to have the whole made up as Carry wished, into one handsome one; and wore an old shabby affair herself as cheerfully as if it were Genoa velvet. That tells the sort of relationship between the sisters as well as anything, and I consider myself very good to name it thus early; for it was long before I found out Miss Tomkinson's real goodness, and we had a great quarrel first. Miss Caroline looked very delicate and die-away when she came in; she was as soft and sentimental as Miss Tomkinson was hard and masculine; and had a way of saying, "Oh, sister, how can you?" at Miss Tomkinson's startling speeches, which I never liked – especially as it was accompanied by a sort of protesting look at the company present, as if she wished to have it understood that she was shocked at her sister's *outré** manners. Now, that was not faithful between sisters. A remonstrance in private might have done good — though, for my own part, I have grown to like Miss Tomkinson's speeches and ways; but I don't like the way some people have of separating themselves from what may be unpopular in their relations. I know I spoke rather shortly to Miss Caroline when she asked me whether I could bear the change from "the great metropolis" to a little country village. In the first place, why could not she call it "London", or "town", and have done with it? And, in the next place, why should she not love the place that was her home well enough to fancy that everyone would like it when they came to know it as well as she did?

'I was conscious I was rather abrupt in my conversation with her, and I saw that Mr Morgan was watching me, though he pretended to be listening to Miss Tomkinson's whispered account of her sister's symptoms. But when we were once more in the street, he began, "My dear young friend" —

'I winced; for all the morning I had noticed that when he was going to give a little unpalatable advice, he always began with "My dear young friend". He had done so about the horse.

' "My dear young friend, there are one or two hints I should like to give you about your manner. The great Sir Everard Home* used to say, 'A general practitioner should either have a very good manner, or a very bad one.' Now, in the latter case, he must be possessed of talents and acquirements sufficient to ensure his being sought after, whatever his manner might be. But the rudeness will give notoriety to these qualifications. Abernethy* is a case in point. I rather, myself, question the taste of bad manners. I, therefore, have studied to acquire an attentive, anxious politeness, which combines ease and grace with a tender regard and interest. I am not aware whether I have succeeded (few men do) in coming up to my ideal; but I recommend you to strive after this manner, peculiarly befitting our profession. Identify yourself with your patients, my dear sir. You have sympathy in your good heart, I am sure, to really feel pain when listening to their account of their sufferings, and it soothes them to see the expression of this feeling in your manner. It is, in fact, sir, manners that make the man in our profession. I don't set myself up as an example — far from it; but — This is Mr Hutton's, our vicar; one of the servants is indisposed, and I shall be glad of the opportunity of introducing you. We can resume our conversation at another time."

'I had not been aware that we had been holding a conversation, in which, I believe, the assistance of two persons is required. Why had not Mr Hutton sent to ask after my health the evening before, according to the custom of the place? I felt rather offended.

Chapter 3

'The vicarage was on the north side of the street, at the end opening towards the hills. It was a long low house, receding behind its neighbours; a court was between the door and the street, with a flag-walk and an old stone cistern on the right-hand side of the door; Solomon's seal* growing under the windows. Someone was watching from behind the window-curtain; for the door opened, as if by magic, as soon as we reached it; and we entered a low room, which served as a hall, and was matted all over, with deep old-fashioned window-seats, and Dutch tiles in the fireplace; altogether it was very cool and refreshing, after the hot sun in the white and red street.

'"Bessie is not so well, Mr Morgan," said the sweet little girl of eleven or so, who had opened the door. "Sophy wanted to send for you; but papa said he was sure you would come soon this morning, and we were to remember that there were other sick people wanting you."

'"Here's Mr Morgan, Sophy," said she, opening the door into an inner room, to which we descended by a step, as I remember well; for I was nearly falling down it, I was so caught by the picture within. It was like a picture – at least, seen through the door-frame. A sort of mixture of crimson and sea-green in the room, and a sunny garden beyond; a very low casement window, open to the amber air; clusters of white roses peeping in; and Sophy sitting on a cushion on the ground, the light coming from above on her head, and a little sturdy round-eyed brother kneeling by her, to whom she was teaching the alphabet. It was a mighty relief to him when we came in, as I could see; and I am much mistaken if he was easily caught again to say his lesson, when he was once sent off to find papa. Sophy rose quietly; and of course we were just introduced, and that was all, before she took Mr Morgan upstairs to see her sick servant. I was left to myself in the room. It looked so like a home that it at once made me know the full charm of the word. There were books and work about, and tokens of employment; there was a child's plaything on the floor, and against the sea-green walls there hung a likeness or two, done in water-colours; one, I was sure, was that of Sophy's mother. The chairs and sofa were covered with chintz, the same as the curtains – a little pretty red rose on a white ground. I don't know where the crimson came from, but I am sure there was crimson somewhere; perhaps in the carpet. There was a glass door besides the window, and you went up a step into the garden. This was, first, a grass plot, just under the windows, and, beyond that, straight gravel walks, with box-borders and narrow flower-beds on each side, most brilliant and gay at the end of August, as it was then; and behind the flower-borders were fruit-trees trained over woodwork, so as to shut out the beds of kitchen-garden within.

'While I was looking round, a gentleman came in, who, I was sure, was the Vicar. It was rather awkward, for I had to account for my presence there.

'"I came with Mr Morgan; my name is Harrison," said I, bowing. I could see he was not much enlightened by this explanation, but we sat down and talked about the time of year, or some such matter, till Sophy and Mr Morgan came back. Then I saw Mr Morgan to advantage. With a man whom he respected, as he did the Vicar, he lost the prim, artificial manner he had in general, and was calm and dignified; but not so dignified as the Vicar. I never saw anyone like him. He was very quiet and reserved, almost absent at times; his personal appearance was not striking; but he was altogether a man you would talk to with your hat off whenever you met him. It was his character that produced this effect – character that he never thought about, but that appeared in every word, and look, and motion.

'"Sophy," said he, "Mr Morgan looks very warm; could you not gather a few jargonelle* pears off the south wall? I fancy there are some ripe there. Our jargonelle pears are remarkably early this year."

'Sophy went into the sunny garden, and I saw her take a rake and tilt at the pears, which were above her reach, apparently. The parlour had become chilly (I found out afterwards it had a

flag floor,* which accounts for its coldness), and I thought I
should like to go into the warm sun. I said I would go and help
the young lady; and, without waiting for an answer, I went into
the warm scented garden, where the bees were rifling the flowers,
and making a continual busy sound. I think Sophy had begun to
despair of getting the fruit, and was glad of my assistance. I
thought I was very senseless to have knocked them down so
soon, when I found we were to go in as soon as they were
gathered. I should have liked to have walked round the garden,
but Sophy walked straight off with the pears, and I could do
nothing but follow her. She took up her needlework while we
ate them: they were very soon finished, and, when the Vicar had
ended his conversation with Mr Morgan about some poor
people, we rose up to come away. I was thankful that Mr
Morgan had said so little about me. I could not have endured
that he should have introduced Sir Astley Cooper or Sir Robert
Peel at the vicarage; nor yet could I have brooked much mention
of my "great opportunities for acquiring a thorough knowledge
of my profession", which I had heard him describe to Miss
Tomkinson, while her sister was talking to me. Luckily, however, he spared me all this at the Vicar's. When we left, it was
time to mount our horses and go the country rounds, and I was
glad of it.

Chapter 4

'By-and-by the inhabitants of Duncombe began to have parties
in my honour. Mr Morgan told me it was on my account, or I
don't think I should have found it out. But he was pleased at
every fresh invitation, and rubbed his hands, and chuckled, as if
it was a compliment to himself, as in truth it was.

'Meanwhile, the arrangement with Mrs Rose had been
brought to a conclusion. She was to bring her furniture, and
place it in a house, of which I was to pay the rent. She was to be
the mistress, and, in return, she was not to pay anything for her
board. Mr Morgan took the house, and delighted in advising
and settling all my affairs. I was partly indolent, and partly
amused, and was altogether passive. The house he took for me

was near his own: it had two sitting-rooms downstairs, opening into each other by folding-doors, which were, however, kept shut in general. The back room was my consulting-room ("the library", he advised me to call it), and he gave me a skull to put on the top of my bookcase, in which the medical books were all ranged on the conspicuous shelves; while Miss Austen, Dickens, and Thackeray* were, by Mr Morgan himself, skilfully placed in a careless way, upside down or with their backs turned to the wall. The front parlour was to be the dining-room, and the room above was furnished with Mrs Rose's drawing-room chairs and table, though I found she preferred sitting downstairs in the dining-room close to the window, where, between every stitch, she could look up and see what was going on in the street. I felt rather queer to be the master of this house, filled with another person's furniture, before I had even seen the lady whose property it was.

Presently she arrived. Mr Morgan met her at the inn where the coach stopped, and accompanied her to my house. I could see them out of the drawing-room window, the little gentleman stepping daintily along, flourishing his cane, and evidently talking away. She was a little taller than he was, and in deep widow's mourning; such veils and falls, and capes and cloaks, that she looked like a black crape haycock.* When we were introduced, she put up her thick veil, and looked around and sighed.

'"Your appearance and circumstances, Mr Harrison, remind me forcibly of the time when I was married to my dear husband, now at rest. He was then, like you, commencing practice as a surgeon. For twenty years I sympathised with him, and assisted him by every means in my power, even to making up pills when the young man was out. May we live together in like harmony for an equal length of time! May the regard between us be equally sincere, although, instead of being conjugal, it is to be maternal and filial!"

'I am sure she had been concocting this speech in the coach, for she afterwards told me she was the only passenger. When she had ended, I felt as if I ought to have had a glass of wine in my hand to drink, after the manner of toasts. And yet I doubt if I should have done it heartily, for I did not hope to live with her for twenty years; it had rather a dreary sound. However, I only bowed and kept my thoughts to myself. I asked Mr Morgan, while Mrs Rose was upstairs taking off her things, to stay to tea; to which he agreed, and kept rubbing his hands with satisfaction, saying –

'"Very fine woman, sir; very fine woman! And what a manner! How she will receive patients, who may wish to leave a message during your absence. Such a flow of words to be sure!"

'Mr Morgan could not stay long after tea, as there were one or two cases to be seen. I would willingly have gone, and had my hat on, indeed, for the purpose, when he said it would not be respectful, "not the thing", to leave Mrs Rose the first evening of her arrival.

'"Tender deference to the sex – to a widow in the first months of her loneliness – requires a little consideration, my dear sir. I will leave that case at Miss Tomkinson's for you; you will perhaps call early tomorrow morning. Miss Tomkinson is rather particular, and is apt to speak plainly if she does not think herself properly attended to."

'I had often noticed that he shuffled off the visits to Miss Tomkinson's on me, and I suspect he was a little afraid of the lady.

'It was rather a long evening with Mrs Rose. She had nothing to do, thinking it civil, I suppose, to stop in the parlour, and not go upstairs and unpack. I begged I might be no restraint upon her if she wished to do so; but (rather to my disappointment) she smiled in a measured, subdued way, and said it would be a pleasure to her to become better acquainted with me. She went upstairs once, and my heart misgave me when I saw her come down with a clean folded pocket-handkerchief. Oh, my prophetic soul! – she was no sooner seated, than she began to give me an account of her late husband's illness, and symptoms, and death. It was a very common case, but she evidently seemed to think it had been peculiar. She had just a smattering of medical knowledge, and used the technical terms so very *mal-àpropos* that I could hardly keep from smiling; but I would not have done it for the world, she was evidently in such deep and sincere distress. At last she said –

'"I have the 'dognoses'* of my dear husband's complaint in my desk, Mr Harrison, if you would like to draw up the case for the *Lancet*.* I think he would have felt gratified, poor fellow, if he had been told such a compliment would be paid to his remains, and that his case should appear in those distinguished columns."

'It was rather awkward; for the case was of the very commonest, as I said before. However, I had not been even this short time in practice without having learnt a few of those noises which do not compromise one, and yet may bear a very significant construction if the listener chooses to exert a little imagination.

'Before the end of the evening, we were such friends that she brought me down the late Mr Rose's picture to look at. She told me she could not bear herself to gaze upon the beloved features; but that, if I would look upon the miniature, she would avert her face. I offered to take it into my own hands, but she seemed wounded at the proposal, and said she never, never could trust such a treasure out of her own possession; so she turned her head very much over her left shoulder, while I examined the likeness held by her extended right arm.

'The late Mr Rose must have been rather a good-looking jolly man; and the artist had given him such a broad smile, and such a twinkle about the eyes, that it really was hard to help smiling back at him. However, I restrained myself.

'At first Mrs Rose objected to accepting any of the invitations which were sent her to accompany me to the tea-parties in the town. She was so good and simple that I was sure she had no other reason than the one which she alleged – the short time that had elapsed since her husband's death; or else, now that I had had some experience of the entertainments which she declined so pertinaciously, I might have suspected that she was glad of the excuse. I used sometimes to wish that I was a widow. I came home tired from a hard day's riding, and, if I had but felt sure that Mr Morgan would not come in, I should certainly have put on my slippers and my loose morning coat, and have indulged in a cigar in the garden. It seemed a cruel sacrifice to society to dress myself in tight boots, and a stiff coat, and go to a five o'clock tea. But Mr Morgan read me such lectures upon the necessity of cultivating the goodwill of the people among whom I was settled, and seemed so sorry, and almost hurt, when I once complained of the dulness of these parties, that I felt I could not be so selfish as to decline more than one out of three. Mr Morgan, if he found that I had an invitation for the evening, would often take the longer round, and the more distant visits. I suspected him at first of the design, which I confess I often entertained, of shirking the parties; but I soon found out he was really making a sacrifice of his inclinations for what he considered to be my advantage.

Chapter 5

'There was one invitation which seemed to promise a good deal of pleasure. Mr Bullock (who is the attorney of Duncombe) was married a second time to a lady from a large provincial town; she wished to lead the fashion – a thing very easy to do, for everyone was willing to follow her. So, instead of giving a tea-party in my honour, she proposed a picnic to some old hall in the neighbourhood; and really the arrangements sounded tempting enough. Every patient we had seemed full of the subject – both those who were invited and those who were not. There was a moat round the house, with a boat on it; and there was a gallery in the hall, from which music sounded delightfully. The family to whom the place belonged were abroad, and lived at a newer and grander mansion when they were at home; there were only a farmer and his wife in the old hall, and they were to have the charge of the preparations. The little kind-hearted town was delighted when the sun shone bright on the October morning of our picnic; the shopkeepers and cottagers all looked pleased as they saw the cavalcade gathering at Mr Bullock's door. We were somewhere about twenty in number; a "silent few", she called us; but I thought we were quite enough. There were the Miss Tomkinsons, and two of their young ladies – one of them belonged to a "county family", Mrs Bullock told me in a whisper; then came Mr and Mrs and Miss Bullock, and a tribe of little children, the offspring of the present wife. Miss Bullock was only a step-daughter. Mrs Munton had accepted the invitation to join our party, which was rather unexpected by the host and hostess, I imagine, from little remarks that I overheard; but they made her very welcome. Miss Horsman (a maiden lady who had been on a visit from home till last week) was another. And last, there were the Vicar and his children. These, with Mr Morgan and myself, made up the party. I was very much pleased to see something more of the Vicar's family. He had come in occasionally to the evening parties, it is true; and spoken kindly to us all; but it was not his habit to stay very long at them. And his daughter was, he said, too young to visit. She had had the charge of her little sisters and brother since her mother's death, which took up a good deal of her time, and she was glad of the evenings to pursue her own studies. But today the case was different; and Sophy, and Helen, and Lizzie, and even little Walter, were all there, standing at Mrs Bullock's door; for we none of us could be patient enough to sit still in the parlour with Mrs Munton and the elder ones, quietly waiting for the two chaises and the spring-cart,* which were to have been there by two o'clock, and now it was nearly a quarter past. "Shameful! the brightness of the day would be gone." The sympathetic shopkeepers, standing at their respective doors with their hands in their pockets, had, one and all, their heads turned in the direction from which the carriages (as Mrs Bullock called them) were to come. There was a rumble along the paved street; and the shopkeepers turned and smiled, and bowed their heads congratulatingly to us; all the mothers and all the little children of the place stood clustering round the door to see us set off. I had my horse waiting; and, meanwhile, I assisted people into their vehicles. One sees a good deal of management on such occasions. Mrs Munton was handed first into one of the chaises; then there was a little hanging back, for most of the young people wished to go in the cart – I don't know why. Miss Horsman, however, came forward, and, as she was known to be the intimate friend of Mrs Munton, so far it was satisfactory. But who was to be third – bodkin* with two old ladies, who liked the windows shut? I saw Sophy speaking to Helen; and then she came forward and offered to be the third. The two old ladies looked pleased and glad (as everyone did near Sophy); so that chaise-full was arranged. Just as it was going off, however, the servant from the vicarage came running with a note for her master. When he had read it, he went to the chaise door, and I suppose told Sophy, what I afterwards heard him say to Mrs Bullock, that the clergyman of a neighbouring parish was ill, and unable to read the funeral service for one of his parishioners, who was to be buried that afternoon. The Vicar was, of course, obliged to go, and said he should not return home that night. It seemed a relief to some, I perceived, to be without the little restraint of his dignified presence. Mr Morgan came up just at the moment, having ridden hard all the morning to be in time to join our party; so we were resigned, on the whole, to the Vicar's absence. His own family regretted him the most, I noticed, and I liked them all the better for it. I believe that I came next in being sorry for his departure; but I respected and admired him, and felt always the better for having been in his company. Miss Tomkinson, Mrs Bullock, and the "county" young lady, were in the next chaise. I think the last would rather have been in the cart with the younger and merrier set, but I imagine that was considered *infra dig.** The remainder of the party were to ride and tie; and a most riotous laughing set they were. Mr Morgan and I were on horseback; at least I led my horse, with little Walter riding on him; his fat, sturdy legs standing stiff out on each side of my cob's broad back. He was a little darling, and chattered all the way, his sister Sophy being the heroine of all his stories. I found he owed this day's excursion entirely to her begging papa to let him come; nurse was strongly against it – "cross old nurse!" he called her once, and then said, "No, not cross; kind nurse; Sophy tells Walter not to say cross nurse." I never saw so young a child so brave. The horse shied at a log of wood. Walter looked very red, and grasped the mane, but sat upright like a little man, and never spoke all the time the horse was dancing. When it was over he looked at me, and smiled –

'"You would not let me be hurt, Mr Harrison, would you?" He was the most winning little fellow I ever saw.

'There were frequent cries to me from the cart, "Oh, Mr Harrison! do get us that branch of blackberries; you can reach it with your whip handle." "Oh, Mr Harrison! there were such splendid nuts on the other side of that hedge; would you just turn back for them?" Miss Caroline Tomkinson was once or twice rather faint with the motion of the cart, and asked me for my smelling-bottle, as she had forgotten hers. I was amused at the idea of my carrying such articles about with me. Then she thought she should like to walk, and got out, and came on my side of the road; but I found little Walter the pleasanter companion, and soon set the horse off into a trot, with which pace her tender constitution could not keep up.

'The road to the old hall was along a sandy lane, with high hedge-banks; the wych-elms almost met overhead. "Shocking farming!" Mr Bullock called out; and so it might be, but it was very pleasant and picturesque-looking. The trees were gorgeous, in their orange and crimson hues, varied by great dark green holly-bushes, glistening in the autumn sun. I should have thought the colours too vivid, if I had seen them in a picture, especially when we wound up the brow, after crossing the little bridge over the brook — (what laughing and screaming there was as the cart splashed through the sparkling water!) — and I caught the purple hills beyond. We could see the old hall, too, from that point, with its warm rich woods billowing up behind, and the blue waters of the moat lying still under the sunlight.

'Laughing and talking is very hungry work, and there was a universal petition for dinner when we arrived at the lawn before the hall, where it had been arranged that we were to dine. I saw Miss Carry take Miss Tomkinson aside, and whisper to her; and presently the elder sister came up to me, where I was busy, rather apart, making a seat of hay, which I had fetched from the farmer's loft for my little friend Walter, who, I had noticed, was rather hoarse, and for whom I was afraid of a seat on the grass, dry as it appeared to be.

'"Mr Harrison, Caroline tells me she has been feeling very faint, and she is afraid of a return of one of her attacks. She says she has more confidence in your medical powers than in Mr Morgan's. I should not be sincere if I did not say that I differ from her; but, as it is so, may I beg you to keep an eye upon her? I tell her she had better not have come if she did not feel well; but, poor girl, she had set her heart upon this day's pleasure. I have offered to go home with her; but she says, if she can only feel sure you are at hand, she would rather stay."

'Of course I bowed, and promised all due attendance on Miss Caroline; and in the meantime, until she did require my services, I thought I might as well go and help the Vicar's daughter, who looked so fresh and pretty in her white muslin dress, here, there, and everywhere, now in the sunshine, now in the green shade, helping everyone to be comfortable, and thinking of everyone but herself.

'Presently, Mr Morgan came up.

'"Miss Caroline does not feel quite well. I have promised your services to her sister."

'"So have I, sir. But Miss Sophy cannot carry this heavy basket."

'I did not mean her to have heard this excuse; but she caught it up and said –

'"Oh, yes, I can! I can take the things out one by one. Go to poor Miss Caroline, pray, Mr Harrison."

'I went; but very unwillingly, I must say. When I had once seated myself by her, I think she must have felt better. It was, probably, only a nervous fear, which was relieved when she knew she had assistance near at hand; for she made a capital dinner. I thought she would never end her modest requests for "just a little more pigeon-pie, or a merry-thought* of chicken". Such a hearty meal would, I hope, effectually revive her; and so it did; for she told me she thought she could manage to walk round the garden, and see the old peacock yews, if I would kindly give her my arm. It was very provoking; I had set my heart upon being with the Vicar's children. I advised Miss Caroline strongly to lie down a little, and rest before tea, on the sofa in the farmer's kitchen; you cannot think how persuasively I begged her to take care of herself. At last she consented, thanking me for my tender interest; she should never forget my kind attention to her. She little knew what was in my mind at the time. However, she was safely consigned to the farmer's wife, and I was rushing out in search of a white gown and a waving figure, when I encountered Mrs Bullock at the door of the hall. She was a fine, fierce-looking woman. I thought she had appeared a little displeased at my (unwilling) attentions to Miss Caroline at dinner-time; but now, seeing me alone, she was all smiles.

'"Oh, Mr Harrison, all alone! How is that? What are the young ladies about to allow such churlishness? And, by the way, I have left a young lady who will be very glad of your assistance, I am sure – my daughter, Jemima (her step-daughter, she meant). Mr Bullock is so particular, and so tender a father, that he would be frightened to death at the idea of her going into the boat on the moat unless she was with someone who could swim. He is gone to discuss the new wheel-plough with the farmer (you know agriculture is his hobby, although law, horrid law, is his business). But the poor girl is pining on the bank, longing for my permission to join the others, which I dare not give unless you will kindly accompany her, and promise, if any accident happens, to preserve her safe."

'Oh, Sophy, why was no one anxious about you?

Chapter 6

'Miss Bullock was standing by the water-side, looking wistfully, as I thought, at the water party; the sound of whose merry laughter came pleasantly enough from the boat, which lay off (for, indeed, no one knew how to row, and she was of a clumsy flat-bottomed build) about a hundred yards, "weather-bound", as they shouted out, among the long stalks of the water-lilies.

'Miss Bullock did not look up till I came close to her; and then, when I told her my errand, she lifted up her great, heavy, sad eyes, and looked at me for a moment. It struck me, at the time, that she expected to find some expression on my face which was not there, and that its absence was a relief to her. She was a very pale, unhappy-looking girl, but very quiet, and, if not agreeable in manner, at any rate not forward or offensive. I called to the party in the boat, and they came slowly enough through the large, cool, green lily-leaves towards us. When they got near, we saw there was no room for us, and Miss Bullock said she would rather stay in the meadow and saunter about, if I would go into the boat; and I am certain from the look on her countenance that she spoke the truth; but Miss Horsman called out, in a sharp voice, while she smiled in a very disagreeable knowing way –

'"Oh, mamma will be displeased if you don't come in, Miss Bullock, after all her trouble in making such a nice arrangement."

'At this speech the poor girl hesitated, and at last, in an undecided way, as if she was not sure whether she was doing right, she took Sophy's place in the boat. Helen and Lizzie landed with their sister, so that there was plenty of room for Miss Tomkinson, Miss Horsman, and all the little Bullocks; and the three vicarage girls went off strolling along the meadow side, and playing with Walter, who was in a high state of excitement. The sun was getting low, but the declining light was beautiful upon the water; and, to add to the charm of the time, Sophy and her sisters, standing on the green lawn in front of the hall, struck up the little German canon, which I had never heard before –

O wie wohl ist mir am Abend, etc.*

At last we were summoned to tug the boat to the landing-steps on the lawn, tea and a blazing wood fire being ready for us in the hall. I was offering my arm to Miss Horsman, as she was a little lame, when she said again, in her peculiar disagreeable way, "Had you not better take Miss Bullock, Mr Harrison? It will be more satisfactory."

'I helped Miss Horsman up the steps, however, and then she repeated her advice; so, remembering that Miss Bullock was in fact the daughter of my entertainers, I went to her; but, though she accepted my arm, I could perceive that she was sorry that I had offered it.

'The hall was lighted by the glorious wood fire in the wide old grate; the daylight was dying away in the west; and the large windows admitted but little of what was left, through their small leaded frames, with coats of arms emblazoned upon them. The farmer's wife had set out a great long table, which was piled with good things; and a huge black kettle sang on the glowing fire, which sent a cheerful warmth through the room as it crackled and blazed. Mr Morgan (who I found had been taking a little round in the neighbourhood among his patients) was there, smiling and rubbing his hands as usual. Mr Bullock was holding a conversation with the farmer at the garden-door on the nature of different manures, in which it struck me that, if Mr Bullock had the fine names and the theories on his side, the farmer had all the practical knowledge and the experience, and I know which I would have trusted. I think Mr Bullock rather liked to talk about Liebig* in my hearing; it sounded well, and was knowing. Mrs Bullock was not particularly placid in her mood. In the first place, I wanted to sit by the Vicar's daughter, and Miss Caroline as decidedly wanted to sit on my other side, being afraid of her fainting fits, I imagine. But Mrs Bullock called me to a place near her daughter. Now, I thought I had done enough civility to a girl who was evidently annoyed rather than pleased by my attentions, and I pretended to be busy stooping under the table for Miss Caroline's gloves, which were missing; but it was of no avail; Mrs Bullock's fine severe eyes were awaiting my reappearance, and she summoned me again.

'"I am keeping this place on my right hand for you, Mr Harrison. Jemima, sit still!"

'I went up to the post of honour and tried to busy myself with pouring out coffee to hide my chagrin; but, on my forgetting to empty the water put in ("to warm the cups", Mrs Bullock said), and omitting to add any sugar, the lady told me she would dispense with my services, and turn me over to my neighbour on the other side.

' "Talking to the younger lady was, no doubt, more Mr Harrison's vocation than assisting the elder one." I dare say it was only the manner that made the words seem offensive. Miss Horsman sat opposite to me, smiling away. Miss Bullock did not speak, but seemed more depressed than ever. At length, Miss Horsman and Mrs Bullock got to a war of inuendoes, which were completely unintelligible to me, and I was very much displeased with my situation; while, at the bottom of the table, Mr Morgan and Mr Bullock were making the young ones laugh most heartily. Part of the joke was Mr Morgan insisting upon making tea at the end; and Sophy and Helen were busy contriving every possible mistake for him. I thought honour was a very good thing, but merriment a better. Here was I in the place of distinction, hearing nothing but cross words. At last the time came for us to go home. As the evening was damp, the seats in the chaises were the best and most to be desired. And now Sophy offered to go in the cart; only she seemed anxious, and so was I, that Walter should be secured from the effects of the white wreaths of fog rolling up from the valley; but the little violent, affectionate fellow would not be separated from Sophy. She made a nest for him on her knee in one corner of the cart, and covered him with her own shawl; and I hoped that he would take no harm. Miss Tomkinson, Mr Bullock, and some of the young ones walked; but I seemed chained to the windows of the chaise, for Miss Caroline begged me not to leave her, as she was dreadfully afraid of robbers; and Mrs Bullock implored me to see that the man did not overturn them in the bad roads, as he had certainly had too much to drink.

'I became so irritable before I reached home, that I thought it was the most disagreeable day of pleasure I had ever had, and could hardly bear to answer Mrs Rose's never-ending questions. She told me, however, that from my account the day was so charming that she thought she should relax in the rigour of her seclusion, and mingle a little more in the society of which I gave so tempting a description. She really thought her dear Mr Rose would have wished it; and his will should be law to her after his death, as it had ever been during his life. In compliance, therefore, with his wishes, she would even do a little violence to her own feelings.

'She was very good and kind; not merely attentive to everything which she thought could conduce to my comfort, but willing to take any trouble in providing the broths and nourishing food which I often found it convenient to order, under the name of kitchen-physic, for my poorer patients; and I really did not see the use of her shutting herself up, in mere compliance with an etiquette, when she began to wish to mix in the little quiet society of Duncombe. Accordingly I urged her to begin to visit, and, even when applied to as to what I imagined the late Mr Rose's wishes on that subject would have been, answered for that worthy gentleman, and assured his widow that I was convinced he would have regretted deeply her giving way to immoderate grief, and would have been rather grateful than otherwise at seeing her endeavour to divert her thoughts by a few quiet visits. She cheered up, and said, "As I really thought so, she would sacrifice her own inclinations, and accept the very next invitation that came."

Chapter 7

'I was roused from my sleep in the middle of the night by a messenger from the vicarage. Little Walter had got the croup,* and Mr Morgan had been sent for into the country. I dressed myself hastily, and went through the quiet little street. There was a light burning upstairs at the vicarage. It was in the nursery. The servant, who opened the door the instant I knocked, was crying sadly, and could hardly answer my inquiries as I went upstairs, two steps at a time, to see my little favourite.

'The nursery was a great large room. At the farther end it was lighted by a common candle, which left the other end, where the door was, in shade; so I suppose the nurse did not see me come in, for she was speaking very crossly.

'"Miss Sophy!" said she, "I told you over and over again it was not fit for him to go, with the hoarseness that he had; and you would take him. It will break your papa's heart, I know; but it's none of my doing."

'Whatever Sophy felt, she did not speak in answer to this. She was on her knees by the warm bath, in which the little fellow was struggling to get his breath, with a look of terror on his face that I have often noticed in young children when smitten by a sudden and violent illness. It seems as if they recognised something infinite and invisible, at whose bidding the pain and the anguish come, from which no love can shield them. It is a very heart-rending look to observe, because it comes on the faces of those who are too young to receive comfort from the words of faith, or the promises of religion. Walter had his arms tight round Sophy's neck, as if she, hitherto his paradise-angel, could save him from the grave shadow of Death. Yes! of Death! I knelt down by him on the other side, and examined him. The very robustness of his little frame gave violence to the disease, which is always one of the most fearful by which children of his age can be attacked.

' "Don't tremble, Watty," said Sophy, in a soothing tone; "it's Mr Harrison, darling, who let you ride on his horse." I could detect the quivering in the voice, which she tried to make so calm and soft to quiet the little fellow's fears. We took him out of the bath, and I went for leeches. While I was away, Mr Morgan came. He loved the vicarage children as if he were their uncle; but he stood still and aghast at the sight of Walter – so lately bright and strong – and now hurrying along to the awful change – to the silent mysterious land, where, tended and cared for as he had been on earth, he must go – alone. The little fellow! the darling!

'We applied the leeches to his throat. He resisted at first; but Sophy, God bless her! put the agony of her grief on one side, and thought only of him, and began to sing the little songs he loved. We were all still. The gardener had gone to fetch the Vicar; but he was twelve miles off, and we doubted if he would come in time. I don't know if they had any hope; but, the first moment Mr Morgan's eyes met mine, I saw that he, like me, had none. The ticking of the house clock sounded through the dark leeches yet hanging to his fair, white throat. Still Sophy went on singing little lullabies, which she had sung under far different and happier circumstances. I remember one verse, because it struck me at the time as strangely applicable.

> Sleep, baby, sleep!
> Thy rest shall angels keep;
> While on the grass the lamb shall feed
> And never suffer want or need.
>   Sleep, baby, sleep.*

The tears were in Mr Morgan's eyes. I do not think either he or I could have spoken in our natural tones; but the brave girl went on clear though low. She stopped at last, and looked up.

' "He is better, is he not, Mr Morgan?"

' "No, my dear. He is – ahem" – he could not speak all at once. Then he said – "My dear! he will be better soon. Think of your mamma, my dear Miss Sophy. She will be very thankful to have one of her darlings safe with her, where she is."

'Still she did not cry. But she bent her head down on the little face, and kissed it long and tenderly.

' "I will go for Helen and Lizzie. They will be sorry not to see him again." She rose up and went for them. Poor girls, they came in, in their dressing-gowns, with eyes dilated with sudden emotion, pale with terror, stealing softly along, as if sound could disturb him. Sophy comforted them by gentle caresses. It was over soon.

'Mr Morgan was fairly crying like a child. But he thought it necessary to apologise to me, for what I honoured him for. "I am a little overdone by yesterday's work, sir. I have had one or two bad nights, and they rather upset me. When I was your age I was as strong and manly as anyone, and would have scorned to shed tears."

'Sophy came up to where we stood.

' "Mr Morgan! I am so sorry for papa. How shall I tell him?" She was struggling against her own grief for her father's sake. Mr Morgan offered to await his coming home; and she seemed thankful for the proposal. I, new friend, almost a stranger, might stay no longer. The street was as quiet as ever; not a shadow was changed; for it was not yet four o'clock. But during the night a soul had departed.

'From all I could see, and all I could learn, the Vicar and his daughter strove which should comfort the other the most. Each thought of the other's grief – each prayed for the other rather than for themselves. We saw them walking out, countrywards; and we heard of them in the cottages of the poor. But it was some time before I happened to meet either of them again. And then I felt, from something indescribable in their manner towards me, that I was one of the

> Peculiar people, whom Death had made dear.*

That one day at the old hall had done this. I was, perhaps, the last person who had given the poor little fellow any unusual pleasure. Poor Walter! I wish I could have done more to make his short life happy!

Chapter 8

'There was a little lull, out of respect to the Vicar's grief, in the visiting. It gave time to Mrs Rose to soften down the anguish of her weeds.

'At Christmas, Miss Tomkinson sent out invitations for a party. Miss Caroline had once or twice apologised to me because such an event had not taken place before; but, as she said, "the avocations of their daily life prevented their having such little *réunions* except in the vacations". And, sure enough, as soon as the holidays began, came the civil little note –

' "The Misses Tomkinson request the pleasure of Mrs Rose's and Mr Harrison's company at tea, on the evening of Monday, the 23rd inst. Tea at five o'clock."

'Mrs Rose's spirit roused, like a war-horse at the sound of the trumpet, at this. She was not of a repining disposition, but I do think she believed the party-giving population of Duncombe had given up inviting her, as soon as she had determined to relent, and accept the invitations, in compliance with the late Mr Rose's wishes.

'Such snippings of white love-ribbon as I found everywhere, making the carpet untidy! One day, too, unluckily, a small box was brought to me by mistake. I did not look at the direction, for I never doubted it was some hyoscyamus* which I was expecting from London; so I tore it open, and saw inside a piece of paper, with "No more grey hair", in large letters, upon it. I folded it up in a hurry, and sealed it afresh, and gave it to Mrs Rose; but I could not refrain from asking her, soon after, if she could recommend me anything to keep my hair from turning grey, adding that I thought prevention was better than cure. I think she made out the impression of my seal on the paper after that; for I learned that she had been crying, and that she talked about there being no sympathy left in the world for her since Mr Rose's death; and that she counted the days until she could rejoin him in the better world. I think she counted the days to Miss Tomkinson's party, too; she talked so much about it.

'The covers were taken off Miss Tomkinson's chairs, and curtains, and sofas; and a great jar full of artificial flowers was placed in the centre of the table, which, as Miss Caroline told me, was all her doing, as she doted on the beautiful and artistic in life. Miss Tomkinson stood, erect as a grenadier, close to the door, receiving her friends, and heartily shaking them by the hands as they entered; she said she was truly glad to see them. And so she really was.

'We had just finished tea, and Miss Caroline had brought out a little pack of conversation cards* – sheaves of slips of cardboard, with intellectual or sentimental questions on one set, and equally intellectual and sentimental answers on the other; and, as the answers were fit to any and all the questions, you may think they were a characterless and "wersh"* set of things. I had just been asked by Miss Caroline –

' "*Can you tell what those dearest to you think of you at this present time?*" and had answered –

' "*How can you expect me to reveal such a secret to the present company!*" when the servant announced that a gentleman, a friend of mine, wished to speak to me downstairs.

' "Oh, show him up, Martha; show him up!" said Miss Tomkinson, in her hospitality.

' "Any friend of our friend is welcome," said Miss Caroline, in an insinuating tone.

'I jumped up, however, thinking it might be someone on business; but I was so penned in by the spider-legged tables, stuck out on every side, that I could not make the haste I wished; and, before I could prevent it, Martha had shown up Jack Marshland, who was on his road home for a day or two at Christmas.

'He came up in a hearty way, bowing to Miss Tomkinson, and explaining that he had found himself in my neighbourhood, and had come over to pass a night with me, and that my servant had directed him where I was.

'His voice, loud at all times, sounded like Stentor's* in that little room, where we all spoke in a kind of purring way. He had no swell in his tones; they were *forte** from the beginning. At first it seemed like the days of my youth come back again, to hear full manly speaking; I felt proud of my friend, as he thanked Miss Tomkinson for her kindness in asking him to stay the evening. By-and-by he came up to me, and I dare say he thought he had lowered his voice, for he looked as if speaking confidentially, while in fact the whole room might have heard him.

'"Frank, my boy, when shall we have dinner at this good old lady's? I'm deuced hungry."

'"Dinner! Why, we had had tea an hour ago." While he yet spoke, Martha came in with a little tray, on which was a single cup of coffee and three slices of wafer bread-and-butter. His dismay, and his evident submission to the decrees of Fate, tickled me so much, that I thought he should have a further taste of the life I led from month's end to month's end, and I gave up my plan of taking him home at once, and enjoyed the anticipation of the hearty laugh we should have together at the end of the evening. I was famously punished for my determination.

'"Shall we continue our game?" asked Miss Caroline, who had never relinquished her sheaf of questions.

'We went on questioning and answering, with little gain of information to either party.

'"No such thing as heavy betting in this game, eh, Frank?" asked Jack, who had been watching us. "You don't lose ten pounds at a sitting, I guess, as you used to do at Short's. Playing for love, I suppose you call it."

'Miss Caroline simpered, and looked down. Jack was not thinking of her. He was thinking of the days we had had "at the Mermaid".* Suddenly he said, "Where were you this day last year, Frank?"

'"I don't remember!" said I.

'"Then I'll tell you. It's the 23rd – the day you were taken up* for knocking down the fellow in Long Acre, and that I had to bail you out ready for Christmas-day. You are in more agreeable quarters tonight."

'He did not intend this reminiscence to be heard, but was not in the least put out when Miss Tomkinson, with a face of dire surprise, asked –

' "Mr Harrison taken up, sir?"

' "Oh, yes, ma'am; and you see it was so common an affair with him to be locked up that he can't remember the dates of his different imprisonments."

'He laughed heartily; and so should I have done, but that I saw the impression it made. The thing was, in fact, simple enough, and capable of easy explanation. I had been made angry by seeing a great hulking fellow, out of mere wantonness, break the crutch from under a cripple; and I struck the man more violently than I intended, and down he went, yelling out for the police, and I had to go before the magistrate to be released. I disdained giving this explanation at the time. It was no business of theirs what I had been doing a year ago; but still Jack might have held his tongue. However, that unruly member of his was set a-going, and he told me afterwards he was resolved to let the old ladies into a little of life; and accordingly he remembered every practical joke we had ever had, and talked and laughed, and roared again. I tried to converse with Miss Caroline – Mrs Munton – anyone; but Jack was the hero of the evening, and everyone was listening to him.

' "Then he has never sent any hoaxing letters since he came here, has he? Good boy! He has turned over a new leaf. He was the deepest dog* at that I ever met with. Such anonymous letters as he used to send! Do you remember that to Mrs Walbrook, eh, Frank? That was too bad!" (the wretch was laughing all the time). "No; I won't tell about it – don't be afraid. Such a shameful hoax!" (laughing again).

' "Pray do tell," I called out; for he made it seem far worse than it was.

' "Oh no, no; you've established a better character – I would not for the world nip your budding efforts. We'll bury the past in oblivion."

'I tried to tell my neighbours the story to which he alluded; but they were attracted by the merriment of Jack's manner, and did not care to hear the plain matter of fact.

'Then came a pause; Jack was talking almost quietly to Miss Horsman. Suddenly he called across the room – "How many times have you been out with the hounds? The hedges were blind very late this year, but you must have had some good mild days since."

' "I have never been out," said I shortly.

' "Never! – whew! – Why, I thought that was the great attraction to Duncombe."

'Now was not he provoking! He would condole with me, and fix the subject in the minds of everyone present.

'The supper trays were brought in, and there was a shuffling of situations. He and I were close together again.

' "I say, Frank, what will you lay me that I don't clear that tray before people are ready for their second helping? I'm as hungry as a hound."

' "You shall have a round of beef and a raw leg of mutton when you get home. Only do behave yourself here."

' "Well, for your sake; but keep me away from those trays, or I'll not answer for myself. 'Hould me, or I'll fight,' as the Irishman said. I'll go and talk to that little old lady in blue, and sit with my back to those ghosts of eatables."

'He sat down by Miss Caroline, who would not have liked his description of her; and began an earnest, tolerably quiet conversation. I tried to be as agreeable as I could, to do away with the impression he had given of me; but I found that everyone drew up a little stiffly at my approach, and did not encourage me to make any remarks.

'In the middle of my attempts, I heard Miss Caroline beg Jack to take a glass of wine, and I saw him help himself to what appeared to be port; but in an instant he set it down from his lips, exclaiming, "Vinegar, by Jove!" He made the most horribly wry face: and Miss Tomkinson came up in a severe hurry to investigate the affair. It turned out it was some blackcurrant wine, on which she particularly piqued herself; I drank two glasses of it to ingratiate myself with her, and can testify to its sourness. I don't think she noticed my exertions, she was so much engrossed in listening to Jack's excuses for his *malàpropos** observation. He told her, with the gravest face, that he had been a teetotaller so long that he had but a confused recollection of the distinction between wine and vinegar, particularly eschewing the latter, because it had been twice fermented; and that he had imagined Miss Caroline had asked him to take toast-and-water, or he should never have touched the decanter.

Chapter 9

'As we were walking home, Jack said, "Lord, Frank! I've had such fun with the little lady in blue. I told her you wrote to me every Saturday, telling me the events of the week. She took it all in." He stopped to laugh; for he bubbled and chuckled so that he could not laugh and walk. "And I told her you were deeply in love" (another laugh); "and that I could not get you to tell me the name of the lady, but that she had light brown hair – in short, I drew from life, and gave her an exact description of herself; and that I was most anxious to see her, and implore her to be merciful to you, for that you were a most timid, faint-hearted fellow with women." He laughed till I thought he would have fallen down. "I begged her, if she could guess who it was from my description – I'll answer for it she did – I took care of that; for I said you described a mole on the left cheek, in the most poetical way, saying Venus* had pinched it out of envy at seeing anyone more lovely – oh, hold me up, or I shall fall – laughing and hunger make me so weak; – well, I say, I begged her, if she knew who your fair one could be, to implore her to save you. I said I knew one of your lungs had gone after a former unfortunate love-affair, and that I could not answer for the other if the lady here were cruel. She spoke of a respirator; but I told her that might do very well for the odd lung; but would it minister to a heart diseased?* I really did talk fine. I have found out the secret of eloquence – it's believing what you've got to say; and I worked myself well up with fancying you married to the little lady in blue."

'I got to laughing at last, angry as I had been; his impudence was irresistible. Mrs Rose had come home in the sedan,* and gone to bed; and he and I sat up over the round of beef and brandy-and-water till two o'clock in the morning.

'He told me I had got quite into the professional way of mousing* about a room, and mewing and purring according as my patients were ill or well. He mimicked me, and made me laugh at myself. He left early the next morning.

'Mr Morgan came at his usual hour; he and Marshland would never have agreed, and I should have been uncomfortable to see two friends of mine disliking and despising each other.

'Mr Morgan was ruffled; but with his deferential manner to women, he smoothed himself down before Mrs Rose – regretted that he had not been able to come to Miss Tomkinson's the evening before, and consequently had not seen her in the society she was so well calculated to adorn. But when we were by ourselves, he said –

'"I was sent for to Mrs Munton's this morning – the old spasms. May I ask what is this story she tells me about – about prison, in fact? I trust, sir, she has made some little mistake, and that you never were— that it is an unfounded report." He could not get it out – "that you were in Newgate* for three months!" I burst out laughing; the story had grown like a mushroom indeed. Mr Morgan looked grave. I told him the truth. Still he looked grave. "I've no doubt, sir, that you acted rightly; but it has an awkward sound. I imagined from your hilarity just now that there was no foundation whatever for the story. Unfortunately, there is."

'"I was only a night at the police-station. I would go there again for the same cause, sir."

'"Very fine spirit, sir – quite like Don Quixote;* but don't you see you might as well have been to the hulks at once?"

'"No, sir; I don't."

'"Take my word, before long, the story will have grown to that. However, we won't anticipate evil. *Mens conscia recti,** you remember, is the great thing. The part I regret is, that it may require some short time to overcome a little prejudice which the story may excite against you. However, we won't dwell on it. *Mens conscia recti*! Don't think about it, sir."

'It was clear he was thinking a good deal about it.

Chapter 10

'Two or three days before this time, I had had an invitation from the Bullocks to dine with them on Christmas-day. Mrs Rose was going to spend the week with friends in the town where she formerly lived; and I had been pleased at the notion of being received into a family, and of being a little with Mr Bullock, who struck me as a bluff, good-hearted fellow.

'But this Tuesday before Christmas-day, there came an invitation from the Vicar to dine there; there were to be only their own family and Mr Morgan. "Only their own family." It was getting to be all the world to me. I was in a passion with myself for having been so ready to accept Mr Bullock's invitation – coarse and ungentlemanly as he was; with this wife's airs of pretension and Miss Bullock's stupidity. I turned it over in my mind. No! I could not have a bad headache, which should prevent me going to the place I did not care for, and yet leave me at liberty to go where I wished. All I could do was to join the vicarage girls after church, and walk by their side in a long country ramble. They were quiet; not sad, exactly; but it was evident that the thought of Walter was in their minds on this day. We went through a copse where there were a good number of evergreens planted as covers for game. The snow was on the ground; but the sky was clear and bright, and the sun glittered on the smooth holly-leaves. Lizzie asked me to gather her some of the very bright red berries, and she was beginning a sentence with –

' "Do you remember" – when Helen said "*Hush*", and looked towards Sophy, who was walking a little apart, and crying softly to herself. There was evidently some connection between Walter and the holly-berries, for Lizzie threw them away at once when she saw Sophy's tears. Soon we came to a stile which led to an open breezy common, half-covered with gorse. I helped the little girls over it, and set them to run down the slope; but I took Sophy's arm in mine, and, though I could not speak, I think she knew how I was feeling for her. I could hardly bear to bid her good-bye at the vicarage gate; it seemed as if I ought to go in and spend the day with her.

'I vented my ill-humour in being late for the Bullocks' dinner. There were one or two clerks, towards whom Mr Bullock was patronising and pressing. Mrs Bullock was decked out in extraordinary finery. Miss Bullock looked plainer than ever; but she had on some old gown or other, I think, for I heard Mrs Bullock tell her she was always making a figure of herself. I began today to suspect that the mother would not be sorry if I took a fancy to the step-daughter. I was again placed near her at dinner, and, when the little ones came in to dessert, I was made to notice how fond of children she was – and, indeed, when one of them nestled to her, her face did brighten; but, the moment she caught this loud-whispered remark, the gloom came back again, with something even of anger in her look; and she was quite sullen and obstinate when urged to sing in the drawing-room. Mrs Bullock turned to me –

'"Some young ladies won't sing unless they are asked by gentlemen." She spoke very crossly. "If you ask Jemima, she will probably sing. To oblige me, it is evident she will not."

'I thought the singing, when we got it, would probably be a great bore; however, I did as I was bid, and went with my request to the young lady, who was sitting a little apart. She looked up at me with eyes full of tears, and said, in a decided tone (which, if I had not seen her eyes, I should have said was as cross as her mamma's), "No, sir, I will not." She got up, and left the room. I expected to hear Mrs Bullock abuse her for her obstinacy. Instead of that, she began to tell me of the money that had been spent on her education; of what each separate accomplishment had cost. "She was timid," she said, "but very musical. Wherever her future home might be, there would be no want of music." She went on praising her till I hated her. If they thought I was going to marry that great lubberly* girl, they were mistaken. Mr Bullock and the clerks came up. He brought out Liebig, and called me to him.

'"I can understand a good deal of this agricultural chemistry," said he, "and have put it in practice – without much success, hitherto, I confess. But these unconnected letters puzzle me a little. I suppose they have some meaning, or else I should say it was mere book-making to put them in."

'"I think they give the page a very ragged appearance," said Mrs Bullock, who had joined us. "I inherit a little of my late father's taste for books, and must say I like to see a good type, a broad margin, and an elegant binding. My father despised variety; how he would have held up his hands aghast at the cheap literature of these times! He did not require many books, but he would have twenty editions of those that he had; and he paid more for binding than he did for the books themselves. But elegance was everything with him. He would not have admitted your Liebig, Mr Bullock; neither the nature of the subject, nor the common type, nor the common way in which your book is got up, would have suited him."

'"Go and make tea, my dear, and leave Mr Harrison and me to talk over a few of these manures."

'We settled to it; I explained the meaning of the symbols, and the doctrine of chemical equivalents. At last he said, "Doctor! you're giving me too strong a dose of it at one time. Let's have a small quantity taken '*hodie*";* that's professional, as Mr Morgan would call it. Come in and call, when you have leisure, and give me a lesson in my alphabet. Of all you've been telling me I can only remember that C means carbon and O oxygen; and I see one must know the meaning of all these confounded letters before one can do much good with Liebig."

'"We dine at three," said Mrs Bullock. "There will always be a knife and fork for Mr Harrison. Bullock! don't confine your invitation to the evening!"

'"Why, you see, I've a nap always after dinner; so I could not be learning chemistry then."

'"Don't be so selfish, Mr B. Think of the pleasure Jemima and I shall have in Mr Harrison's society."

'I put a stop to the discussion by saying I would come in in the evenings occasionally, and give Mr Bullock a lesson, but that my professional duties occupied me invariably until that time.

'I liked Mr Bullock. He was simple, and shrewd; and to be with a man was a relief, after all the feminine society I went through every day.

Chapter 12

'The next morning I met Miss Horsman.

'"So you dined at Mr Bullock's yesterday, Mr Harrison? Quite a family party, I hear. They are quite charmed with you, and your knowledge of chemistry. Mr Bullock told me so, in Hodgson's shop, just now. Miss Bullock is a nice girl, eh, Mr Harrison?" She looked sharply at me. Of course, whatever I thought, I could do nothing but assent. "A nice little fortune, too – three thousands pounds, Consols,* from her own mother."

'What did I care? She might have three millions for me. I had begun to think a good deal about money, though, but not in connection with her. I had been doing up our books ready to send out our Christmas bills, and had been wondering how far the Vicar would consider three hundred a year, with a prospect of increase, would justify me in thinking of Sophy. Think of her I could not help; and, the more I thought of how good, and sweet, and pretty she was, the more I felt that she ought to have far more than I could offer. Besides, my father was a shopkeeper, and I saw the Vicar had a sort of respect for family. I determined to try and be very attentive to my profession. I was as civil as could be to everyone; and wore the nap off the brim of my hat by taking it off so often.

'I had my eyes open to every glimpse of Sophy. I am overstocked with gloves now that I bought at that time, by way of making errands into the shops where I saw her black gown. I bought pounds upon pounds of arrowroot, till I was tired of the eternal arrowroot puddings Mrs Rose gave me. I asked her if she could not make bread of it, but she seemed to think that would be expensive; so I took to soap as a safe purchase. I believe soap improves by keeping.

'The more I knew of Mrs Rose, the better I liked her. She was sweet, and kind, and motherly, and we never had any rubs. I hurt her once or twice, I think, by cutting her short in her long stories about Mr Rose. But I found out that when she had plenty to do she did not think of him quite so much; so I expressed a wish for Corazza shirts,* and, in the puzzle of devising how they were to be cut out, she forgot Mr Rose for some time. I was still more pleased by her way about some legacy her elder brother left her. I don't know the amount, but it was something handsome, and she might have set up housekeeping for herself; but, instead, she told Mr Morgan (who repeated it to me), that she should continue with me, as she had quite an elder sister's interest in me.

'The "county young lady", Miss Tyrrell, returned to Miss Tomkinson's after the holidays. She had an enlargement of the tonsils, which required to be frequently touched with caustic, so I often called to see her. Miss Caroline always received me, and kept me talking in her washed-out style, after I had seen my patient. One day she told me she thought she had a weakness about the heart, and would be glad if I would bring my stethoscope the next time, which I accordingly did! and, while I was on my knees listening to the pulsations, one of the young ladies came in. She said –

'"Oh dear! I never! I beg your pardon, ma'am", and scuttled out. There was not much the matter with Miss Caroline's heart: a little feeble in action or so, a mere matter of weakness and general languor. When I went down I saw two or three of the girls peeping out of the half-closed schoolroom door, but they shut it immediately, and I heard them laughing. The next time I called, Miss Tomkinson was sitting in state to receive me.

'"Miss Tyrrell's throat does not seem to make much progress. Do you understand the case, Mr Harrison, or should we have further advice. I think Mr Morgan would probably know more about it."

'I assured her it was the simplest thing in the world; that it always implied a little torpor in the constitution, and that we preferred working through the system, which of course was a slow process; and that the medicine the young lady was taking (iodide of iron) was sure to be successful, although the progress would not be rapid. She bent her head, and said, "It might be so; but she confessed she had more confidence in medicines which had some effect."

'She seemed to expect me to tell her something; but I had nothing to say, and accordingly I bade good-bye. Somehow, Miss Tomkinson always managed to make me feel very small, by a succession of snubbings; and, whenever I left her I had always to comfort myself under her contradictions by saying to myself, "Her saying it is so does not make it so." Or I invented good retorts which I might have made to her brusque speeches, if I had but thought of them at the right time. But it was provoking that I had not had the presence of mind to recollect them just when they were wanted.

Chapter 14

'On the whole, things went on smoothly. Mr Holden's legacy came in just about this time; and I felt quite rich. Five hundred pounds would furnish the house, I thought, when Mrs Rose left and Sophy came. I was delighted, too, to imagine that Sophy perceived the difference of my manner to her from what it was to anyone else, and that she was embarrassed and shy in consequence, but not displeased with me for it. All was so flourishing that I went about on wings instead of feet. We were very busy, without having anxious cares. My legacy was paid into Mr Bullock's hands, who united a little banking business to his profession of law. In return for his advice about investments (which I never meant to take, having a more charming, if less profitable, mode in my head), I went pretty frequently to teach him his agricultural chemistry. I was so happy in Sophy's blushes that I was universally benevolent, and desirous of giving pleasure to everyone. I went, at Mrs Bullock's general invitation, to dinner there one day unexpectedly: but there was such a fuss of ill-concealed preparation consequent upon my coming, that I never went again. Her little boy came in, with an audibly given message from the cook, to ask –

' "If this was the gentleman as she was to send in the best dinner-service and dessert for?"

'I looked deaf, but determined never to go again.

'Miss Bullock and I, meanwhile, became rather friendly. We found out that we mutually disliked each other, and were contented with the discovery. If people are worth anything, this sort of non-liking is a very good beginning of friendship. Every good quality is revealed naturally and slowly, and is a pleasant surprise. I found out that Miss Bullock was sensible, and even sweet-tempered, when not irritated by her step-mother's endeavours to show her off. But she would sulk for hours after Mrs Bullock's offensive praise of her good points. And I never saw such a black passion as she went into, when she suddenly came into the room when Mrs Bullock was telling me of all the offers she had had.

'My legacy made me feel up to extravagance. I scoured the country for a glorious nosegay of camellias, which I sent to Sophy on Valentine's-day. I durst not add a line; but I wished the flowers could speak, and tell her how I loved her.

'I called on Miss Tyrrell that day. Miss Caroline was more simpering and affected than ever, and full of allusions to the day.

' "Do you affix much sincerity of meaning to the little gallantries of this day, Mr Harrison?" asked she, in a languishing tone. I thought of my camellias, and how my heart had gone with them into Sophy's keeping; and I told her I thought one might often take advantage of such a time to hint at feelings one dared not fully express.

'I remembered afterwards the forced display she made, after Miss Tyrrell left the room, of a valentine. But I took no notice at the time; my head was full of Sophy.

'It was on that very day that John Brouncker, the gardener to all of us who had small gardens to keep in order, fell down and injured his wrist severely (I don't give you the details of the case, because they would not interest you, being too technical; if you've any curiosity, you will find them in the *Lancet* of August in that year). We all liked John, and this accident was felt like a town's misfortune. The gardens, too, just wanted doing up. Both Mr Morgan and I went directly to him. It was a very awkward case, and his wife and children were crying sadly. He himself was in great distress at being thrown out of work. He begged us to do something that would cure him speedily, as he could not afford to be laid up, with six children depending on him for bread. We did not say much before him; but we both thought the arm would have to come off, and it was his right arm. We talked it over when we came out of the cottage. Mr Morgan had no doubt of the necessity. I went back at dinner-time to see the poor fellow. He was feverish and anxious. He had caught up some expression of Mr Morgan's in the morning, and had guessed the measure we had in contemplation. He bade his wife leave the room, and spoke to me by myself.

' "If you please, sir, I'd rather be done for at once than have my arm taken off, and be a burden to my family. I'm not afraid of dying; but I could not stand being a cripple for life, eating bread, and not able to earn it."

'The tears were in his eyes with earnestness. I had all along been more doubtful about the necessity of the amputation than Mr Morgan. I knew the improved treatment in such cases. In his days there was much more of the rough and ready in surgical practice; so I gave the poor fellow some hope.

'In the afternoon I met Mr Bullock.

' "So you're to try your hand at an amputation, tomorrow, I hear. Poor John Brouncker! I used to tell him he was not careful enough about his ladders. Mr Morgan is quite excited about it. He asked me to be present, and see how well a man from Guy's could operate; he says he is sure you'll do it beautifully. Pah! no such sights for me, thank you."

'Ruddy Mr Bullock went a shade or two paler at the thought.

' "Curious, how professionally a man views these things! Here's Mr Morgan, who has been all along as proud of you as if you were his own son, absolutely rubbing his hands at the idea of this crowning glory, this feather in your cap! He told me just now he knew he had always been too nervous to be a good operator, and had therefore preferred sending for White from Chesterton. But now anyone might have a serious accident who liked, for you would be always at hand."

'I told Mr Bullock, I really thought we might avoid the amputation; but his mind was preoccupied with the idea of it, and he did not care to listen to me. The whole town was full of it. That is a charm in a little town, everybody is so sympathetically full of the same events. Even Miss Horsman stopped me to ask after John Brouncker with interest; but she threw cold water upon my intention of saving the arm.

'"As for the wife and family, we'll take care of them. Think what a fine opportunity you have of showing off, Mr Harrison!"

'That was just like her. Always ready with her suggestions of ill-natured or interested motives.

'Mr Morgan heard my proposal of a mode of treatment by which I thought it possible that the arm might be saved.

'"I differ from you, Mr Harrison," said he. "I regret it; but I differ *in toto** from you. Your kind heart deceives you in this instance. There is no doubt that amputation must take place — not later than tomorrow morning, I should say. I have made myself at liberty to attend upon you, sir; I shall be happy to officiate as your assistant. Time was when I should have been proud to be principal; but a little trembling in my arm incapacitates me."

'I urged my reasons upon him again; but he was obstinate. He had, in fact, boasted so much of my acquirements as an operator that he was unwilling I should lose this opportunity of displaying my skill. He could not see that there would be greater skill evinced in saving the arm; nor did I think of this at the time. I grew angry at his old-fashioned narrow-mindedness, as I thought it; and I became dogged in my resolution to adhere to my own course. We parted very coolly; and I went straight off to John Brouncker to tell him I believed that I could save the arm, if he would refuse to have it amputated. When I calmed myself a little, before going in and speaking to him, I could not help acknowledging that we should run some risk of lock-jaw;* but, on the whole, and after giving most earnest conscientious thought to the case, I was sure that my mode of treatment would be best.

'He was a sensible man. I told him the difference of opinion that existed between Mr Morgan and myself. I said that there might be some little risk attending the non-amputation, but that I should guard against it; and I trusted that I should be able to preserve the arm.

'"Under God's blessing," said he reverently. I bowed my head. I don't like to talk too frequently of the dependence which I always felt on that holy blessing, as to the result of my efforts; but I was glad to hear that speech of John's, because it showed a calm and faithful heart; and I had almost certain hopes of him from that time.

'We agreed that he should tell Mr Morgan the reason of his objections to the amputation, and his reliance on my opinion. I determined to recur to every book I had relating to such cases, and to convince Mr Morgan, if I could, of my wisdom. Unluckily, I found out afterwards that he had met Miss Horsman in the time that intervened before I saw him again at his own house that evening; and she had more than hinted that I shrunk from performing the operation, "for very good reasons no doubt. She had heard that the medical students in London were a bad set, and were not remarkable for regular attendance in the hospitals. She might be mistaken; but she thought it was, perhaps, quite as well poor John Brouncker had not his arm cut off by— Was there not such a thing as mortification coming on after a clumsy operation? It was, perhaps, only a choice of deaths!"

'Mr Morgan had been stung at all this. Perhaps I did not speak quite respectfully enough: I was a good deal excited. We only got more and more angry with each other; though he, to do him justice, was as civil as could be all the time, thinking that thereby he concealed his vexation and disappointment. He did not try to conceal his anxiety about poor John. I went home weary and dispirited. I made up and took the necessary applications to John; and, promising to return with the dawn of day (I would fain have stayed, but I did not wish him to be alarmed about himself), I went home, and resolved to sit up and study the treatment of similar cases.

'Mrs Rose knocked at the door.

'"Come in!" said I sharply.

'She said she had seen I had something on my mind all day, and she could not go to bed without asking if there was nothing she could do. She was good and kind; and I could not help telling her a little of the truth. She listened pleasantly; and I shook her warmly by the hand, thinking that though she might not be very wise, her good heart made her worth a dozen keen, sharp, hard people, like Miss Horsman.

'When I went at daybreak, I saw John's wife for a few minutes outside of the door. She seemed to wish her husband had been in Mr Morgan's hands rather than mine; but she gave me as good an account as I dared hope for of the manner in which her husband had passed the night. This was confirmed by my own examination.

'When Mr Morgan and I visited him together later on in the day, John said what we had agreed upon the day before; and I told Mr Morgan openly that it was by my advice that amputation was declined. He did not speak to me till we had left the house. Then he said – "Now, sir, from this time, I consider this case entirely in your hands. Only remember the poor fellow has a wife and six children. In case you come round to my opinion, remember that Mr White could come over, as he has done before, for the operation."

'So Mr Morgan believed I declined operating because I felt myself incapable! Very well! I was much mortified.*

'An hour after we parted, I received a note to this effect –

Dear Sir – I will take the long round today, to leave you at liberty to attend to Brouncker's case, which I feel to be a very responsible one.

J. Morgan

'This was kindly done. I went back, as soon as I could, to John's cottage. While I was in the inner room with him, I heard the Miss Tomkinsons' voices outside. They had called to inquire. Miss Tomkinson came in, and evidently was poking and snuffing about. (Mrs Brouncker told her that I was within; and within I resolved to be till they had gone.)

' "What is this close smell?" asked she. "I am afraid you are not cleanly.* Cheese! – cheese in this cupboard! No wonder there is an unpleasant smell. Don't you know how particular you should be about being clean when there is illness about?"

'Mrs Brouncker was exquisitely clean in general, and was piqued at these remarks.

' "If you please, ma'am, I could not leave John yesterday to do any house-work, and Jenny put the dinner things away. She is but eight years old."

'But this did not satisfy Miss Tomkinson, who was evidently pursuing the course of her observations.

' "Fresh butter, I declare! Well now, Mrs Brouncker, do you know I don't allow myself fresh butter at this time of the year? How can you save, indeed, with such extravagance!"

' "Please, ma'am," answered Mrs Brouncker, "you'd think it

strange, if I was to take such liberties in your house as you're taking here."

'I expected to hear a sharp answer. No! Miss Tomkinson liked true plain-speaking. The only person in whom she would tolerate round-about ways of talking was her sister.

'"Well, that's true," she said. "Still, you must not be above taking advice. Fresh butter is extravagant at this time of the year. However, you're a good kind of woman, and I've a great respect for John. Send Jenny for some broth as soon as he can take it. Come, Caroline, we have got to go on to Williams's."

'But Caroline said that she was tired, and would rest where she was till Miss Tomkinson came back. I was a prisoner for some time, I found. When she was alone with Mrs Brouncker, she said –

'"You must not be hurt by my sister's abrupt manner. She means well. She has not much imagination or sympathy, and cannot understand the distraction of mind produced by the illness of a worshipped husband." I could hear the loud sigh of commiseration which followed this speech. Mrs Brouncker said –

'"Please, ma'am, I don't worship my husband. I would not be so wicked."

'"Goodness! You don't think it wicked, do you? For my part, if . . . I should worship, I should adore him." I thought she need not imagine such improbable cases. But sturdy Mrs Brouncker said again –

'"I hope I know my duty better. I've not learned my Commandments for nothing. I know Whom I ought to worship."

'Just then the children came in, dirty and unwashed, I have no doubt. And now Miss Caroline's real nature peeped out. She spoke sharply to them, and asked them if they had no manners, little pigs as they were, to come brushing against her silk gown in that way? She sweetened herself again, and was as sugary as love when Miss Tomkinson returned for her, accompanied by one whose voice, "like winds in summer sighing",* I knew to be my dear Sophy's.

'She did not say much; but what she did say, and the manner in which she spoke, was tender and compassionate in the highest degree; and she came to take the four little ones back with her to the vicarage, in order that they might be out of their mother's way; the older two might help at home. She offered to wash their hands and faces; and when I emerged from my inner chamber, after the Miss Tomkinsons had left, I found her with a chubby child on her knees, bubbling and spluttering against her white wet hand, with a face bright, rosy, and merry under the operation. Just as I came in, she said to him, "There, Jemmy, now I can kiss you with this nice clean face."

'She coloured when she saw me. I liked her speaking, and I liked her silence. She was silent now, and I "lo'ed* her a' the better". I gave my directions to Mrs Brouncker, and hastened to overtake Sophy and the children; but they had gone round by the lane, I suppose, for I saw nothing of them.

'I was very anxious about the case. At night I went again. Miss Horsman had been there; I believe she was really kind among the poor, but she could not help leaving a sting behind her everywhere. She had been frightening Mrs Brouncker about her husband, and been, I have no doubt, expressing her doubts of my skill; for Mrs Brouncker began –

'"Oh, please, sir, if you'll only let Mr Morgan take off his arm, I will never think the worse of you for not being able to do it."

'I told her it was from no doubt of my own competency to perform the operation that I wished to save the arm; but that he himself was anxious to have it spared.

'"Ay, bless him! he frets about not earning enough to keep us, if he's crippled; but, sir, I don't care about that. I would work my fingers to the bone, and so would the children; I'm sure we'd be proud to do for him, and keep him; God bless him! it would be far better to have him only with one arm, than to have him in the churchyard, Miss Horsman says" –

'"Confound Miss Horsman!" said I.

'"Thank you, Mr Harrison," said her well-known voice behind me. She had come out, dark as it was, to bring some old linen to Mrs Brouncker; for, as I said before, she was very kind to all the poor people of Duncombe.

'"I beg your pardon"; for I really was sorry for my speech – or rather that she had heard it.

'"There is no occasion for any apology," she replied, drawing herself up, and pinching her lips into a very venomous shape.

'John was doing pretty well; but of course the danger of lock-jaw was not over. Before I left, his wife entreated me to take off the arm; she wrung her hands in her passionate entreaty. "Spare him to me, Mr Harrison," she implored. Miss Horsman stood by. It was mortifying enough; but I thought of the power which was in my hands, as I firmly believed, of saving the limb; and I was inflexible.

'You cannot think how pleasantly Mrs Rose's sympathy came in on my return. To be sure she did not understand one word of the case, which I detailed to her; but she listened with interest, and, as long as she held her tongue, I thought she was really taking it in; but her first remark was as *mal-àpropos* as could be.

'"You are anxious to save the tibia – I see completely how difficult that will be. My late husband had a case exactly similar, and I remember his anxiety; but you must not distress yourself too much, my dear Mr Harrison; I have no doubt it will end well."

'I knew she had no grounds for this assurance, and yet it comforted me.

'However, as it happened, John did fully as well as I could have hoped for; of course, he was long in rallying his strength; and, indeed, sea-air was evidently so necessary for his complete restoration, that I accepted with gratitude Mrs Rose's proposal of sending him to Highport for a fortnight or three weeks. Her kind generosity in this matter made me more desirous than ever of paying her every mark of respect and attention.

Chapter 15

'About this time there was a sale at Ashmeadow, a pretty house in the neighbourhood of Duncombe. It was likewise an easy walk, and the spring days tempted many people thither, who had no intention of buying anything, but who liked the idea of rambling through the woods, gay with early primroses and wild daffodils, and of seeing the gardens and house, which till now had been shut up from the ingress of the townspeople. Mrs Rose had planned to go, but an unlucky cold prevented her. She begged me to bring her a very particular account, saying she delighted in details, and always questioned Mr Rose as to the side-dishes of the dinners to which he went. The late Mr Rose's conduct was always held up as a model to me, by the way. I walked to Ashmeadow, pausing or loitering with different parties of townspeople, all bound in the same direction. At last I found the Vicar and Sophy, and with them I stayed. I sat by Sophy and talked and listened. A sale is a very pleasant gathering after all. The auctioneer, in a country place, is privileged to joke from his rostrum, and, having a personal knowledge of most of the people, can sometimes make a very keen hit at their circumstances, and turn the laugh against them. For instance, on the present occasion, there was a farmer present, with his wife, who was notoriously the grey mare. The auctioneer was selling some horse-cloths, and called out to recommend the article to her, telling her, with a knowing look at the company, that they would make her a dashing pair of trousers, if she was in want of such an article. She drew herself up with dignity, and said, "Come, John, we've had enough of this." Whereupon there was a burst of laughter, and in the midst of it John meekly followed his wife out of the place. The furniture in the sitting-rooms was, I believe, very beautiful, but I did not notice it much. Suddenly I heard the auctioneer speaking to me, "Mr Harrison, won't you give me a bid for this table?"

'It was a very pretty little table of walnut-wood. I thought it would go into my study well, so I gave him a bid. I saw Miss Horsman bidding against me, so I went off with full force, and at last it was knocked down to me. The auctioneer smiled, and congratulated me.

'"A most useful present for Mrs Harrison, when that lady comes."

'Everybody laughed. They like a joke about marriage; it is so easy of comprehension. But the table which I had thought was for writing, turned out to be a work-table, scissors and thimble complete. No wonder I looked foolish. Sophy was not looking at me, that was one comfort. She was busy arranging a nosegay of wood-anemone and wild sorrel.

'Miss Horsman came up, with her curious eyes.

'"I had no idea things were far enough advanced for you to be purchasing a work-table, Mr Harrison."

'I laughed off my awkwardness.

'"Did you not, Miss Horsman? You are very much behind-hand. You have not heard of my piano, then?"

'"No, indeed," she said, half uncertain whether I was serious or not. "Then it seems there is nothing wanting but the lady."

'"Perhaps she may not be wanting either," said I; for I wished to perplex her keen curiosity.

Chapter 16

'When I got home from my round, I found Mrs Rose in some sorrow.

'"Miss Horsman called after you left," said she. "Have you heard how John Brouncker is at Highport?"

'"Very well," replied I. "I called on his wife just now, and she had just got a letter from him. She had been anxious about him, for she had not heard for a week. However, all's right now; and she has pretty well enough of work, at Mrs Munton's, as her servant is ill. Oh, they'll do, never fear."

'"At Mrs Munton's? Oh, that accounts for it, then. She is so deaf, and makes such blunders."

'"Accounts for what?" asked I

'"Oh, perhaps I had better not tell you," hesitated Mrs Rose.

'"Yes, tell me at once. I beg your pardon, but I hate mysteries."

'"You are so like my poor dear Mr Rose. He used to speak to me just in that sharp, cross way. It is only that Miss Horsman called. She had been making a collection for John Brouncker's widow and" –

'"But the man's alive!" said I.

'"So it seems. But Mrs Munton had told her that he was dead. And she has got Mr Morgan's name down at the head of the list, and Mr Bullock's."

'Mr Morgan and I had got into a short, cool way of speaking to each other ever since we had differed so much about the treatment of Brouncker's arm; and I had heard once or twice of his shakes of the head over John's case. He would not have spoken against my method for the world, and fancied that he concealed his fears.

'"Miss Horsman is very ill-natured, I think," sighed forth Mrs Rose.

'I saw that something had been said of which I had not heard, for the mere fact of collecting money for the widow was good-natured, whoever did it; so I asked quietly, what she had said.

' "Oh, I don't know if I should tell you. I only know she made me cry; for I'm not well, and I can't bear to hear anyone that I live with abused."

'Come! this was pretty plain.

' "What did Miss Horsman say of me?" asked I, half laughing, for I knew there was no love lost between us.

' "Oh, she only said she wondered you could go to sales, and spend your money there, when your ignorance had made Jane Brouncker a widow, and her children fatherless."

' "Pooh! pooh! John's alive, and likely to live as long as you or I, thanks to you, Mrs Rose."

'When my work-table came home, Mrs Rose was so struck with its beauty and completeness, and I was so much obliged to her for her identification of my interests with hers, and the kindness of her whole conduct about John, that I begged her to accept of it. She seemed very much pleased; and, after a few apologies, she consented to take it, and placed it in the most conspicuous part of the front parlour, where she usually sat. There was a good deal of morning calling in Duncombe after the sale, and during this time the fact of John being alive was established to the conviction of all except Miss Horsman, who, I believe, still doubted. I myself told Mr Morgan, who immediately went to reclaim his money; saying to me, that he was thankful for the information; he was truly glad to hear it; and he shook me warmly by the hand for the first time for a month.

Chapter 17

'A few days after the sale, I was in the consulting-room. The servant must have left the folding-doors a little ajar, I think. Mrs Munton came to call on Mrs Rose; and the former being deaf, I heard all the speeches of the latter lady, as she was obliged to speak very loud in order to be heard. She began –

' "This is a great pleasure, Mrs Munton, so seldom as you are well enough to go out."

'Mumble, mumble, mumble, through the door.

'"Oh, very well, thank you. Take this seat, and then you can admire my new work-table, ma'am; a present from Mr Harrison."

'Mumble, mumble.

'"Who could have told you, ma'am? Miss Horsman? Oh, yes, I showed it Miss Horsman."

'Mumble, mumble.

'"I don't quite understand you, ma'am."

'Mumble, mumble.

'"I'm not blushing, I believe. I really am quite in the dark as to what you mean."

'Mumble, mumble.

'"Oh, yes, Mr Harrison and I are most comfortable together. He reminds me so of my dear Mr Rose – just as fidgety and anxious in his profession."

'Mumble, mumble.

'"I'm sure you are joking now, ma'am." Then I heard a pretty loud –

'"Oh, no;" mumble, mumble, mumble, for a long time.

'"Did he really? Well, I'm sure I don't know. I should be sorry to think he was doomed to be unfortunate in so serious an affair; but you know my undying regard for the late Mr Rose."

'Another long mumble.

'"You're very kind, I'm sure. Mr Rose always thought more of my happiness than his own" – a little crying – "but the turtle-dove has always been my ideal, ma'am."

'Mumble, mumble

'"No one could have been happier than I. As you say, it is a compliment to matrimony."

'Mumble.

'"Oh, but you must not repeat such a thing! Mr Harrison would not like it. He can't bear to have his affairs spoken about."

'Then there was a change of subject; and inquiry after some poor person, I imagine. I heard Mrs Rose say –

'"She has got a mucous membrane, I'm afraid, ma'am."

'A commiserating mumble.

'"Not always fatal. I believe Mr Rose knew some cases that lived for years after it was discovered that they had a mucous membrane." A pause. Then Mrs Rose spoke in a different tone.

'"Are you sure, ma'am, there is no mistake about what he said?"

'Mumble.

'"Pray don't be so observant, Mrs Munton; you find out too much. One can have no little secrets."

'The call broke up; and I heard Mrs Munton say in the passage, "I wish you joy, ma'am, with all my heart. There's no use denying it; for I've seen all along what would happen."

'When I went in to dinner, I said to Mrs Rose –

'"You've had Mrs Munton here, I think. Did she bring any news?" To my surprise, she bridled and simpered, and replied, 'Oh, you must not ask, Mr Harrison; such foolish reports!"'

'I did not ask, as she seemed to wish me not, and I knew there were silly reports always about. Then I think she was vexed that I did not ask. Altogether she went on so strangely that I could not help looking at her; and then she took up a hand-screen, * and held it between me and her. I really felt rather anxious.

'"Are you not feeling well." said I innocently.

'"Oh, thank you, I believe I'm quite well; only the room is rather warm, is it not?"

'"Let me put the blinds down for you? the sun begins to have a good deal of power." I drew down the blinds.

'"You are so attentive, Mr Harrison. Mr Rose himself never did more for my little wishes than you do."

'"I wish I could do more – I wish I could show you how much I feel" – her kindness to John Brouncker, I was going on to say; but I was just then called out to a patient. Before I went I turned back, and said –

'"Take care of yourself, my dear Mrs Rose; you had better rest a little."

'"For your sake, I will," said she tenderly.

'I did not care for whose sake she did it. Only I really thought she was not quite well, and required rest. I thought she was more affected than usual at tea-time; and could have been angry with her nonsensical ways once or twice, but that I knew the real goodness of her heart. She said she wished she had the power to sweeten my life as she could my tea. I told her what a comfort she had been during my late time of anxiety; and then I stole out to try if I could hear the evening singing at the vicarage, by standing close to the garden-wall.

Chapter 18

'The next morning I met Mr Bullock by appointment to talk a little about the legacy which was paid into his hands. As I was leaving his office, feeling full of my riches, I met Miss Horsman. She smiled rather grimly, and said –

' "Oh! Mr Harrison, I must congratulate you, I believe. I don't know whether I ought to have known, but as I do, I must wish you joy. A very nice little sum, too. I always said you would have money."

'So she had found out my legacy, had she? Well, it was no secret, and one likes the reputation of being a person of property. Accordingly I smiled, and said I was much obliged to her; and, if I could alter the figures to my liking, she might congratulate me still more.

'She said, "Oh, Mr Harrison, you can't have everything. It would be better the other way, certainly. Money is the great thing, as you've found out. The relation died most opportunely, I must say."

' "He was no relative," said I; 'only an intimate friend."

' "Dear-ah-me! I thought it had been a brother! Well, at any rate, the legacy is safe."

'I wished her good morning, and passed on. Before long I was sent for to Miss Tomkinson's.

'Miss Tomkinson sat in severe state to receive me. I went in with an air of ease, because I always felt so uncomfortable.

' "Is this true that I hear?" asked she, in an inquisitorial manner.

'I thought she alluded to my five hundred pounds; so I smiled, and said that I believed it was.

' "Can money be so great an object with you, Mr Harrison?" she asked again.

'I said I had never cared much for money, except as an assistance to any plan of settling in life; and then, as I did not like her severe way of treating the subject, I said that I hoped everyone was well; though of course I expected someone was ill, or I should not have been sent for.

'Miss Tomkinson looked very grave and sad. Then she

answered: "Caroline is very poorly – the old palpitations at the heart; but of course that is nothing to you."

'I said I was very sorry. She had a weakness there, I knew. Could I see her? I might be able to order something for her.

'I thought I heard Miss Tomkinson say something in a low voice about my being a heartless deceiver. Then she spoke up. "I was always distrustful of you, Mr Harrison. I never liked your looks. I begged Caroline again and again not to confide in you. I foresaw how it would end. And now I fear her precious life will be a sacrifice."

'I begged her not to distress herself, for in all probability there was very little the matter with her sister. Might I see her?

'"No!" she said shortly, standing up as if to dismiss me. "There has been too much of this seeing and calling. By my consent, you shall never see her again."

'I bowed. I was annoyed, of course. Such a dismissal might injure my practice just when I was most anxious to increase it.

'"Have you no apology, no excuse to offer?"

'I said I had done my best; I did not feel that there was any reason to offer an apology. I wished her good morning. Suddenly she came forwards.

'"Oh, Mr Harrison," said she, "if you have really loved Caroline, do not let a little paltry money make you desert her for another."

'I was struck dumb. Loved Miss Caroline! I loved Miss Tomkinson a great deal better, and yet I disliked her. She went on –

'"I have saved nearly three thousand pounds. If you think you are too poor to marry without money, I will give it all to Caroline. I am strong, and can go on working; but she is weak, and this disappointment will kill her." She sat down suddenly, and covered her face with her hands. Then she looked up.

'"You are unwilling, I see. Don't suppose I would have urged you if it had been for myself; but she has had so much sorrow." And now she fairly cried aloud. I tried to explain; but she would not listen, but kept saying, "Leave the house, sir! leave the house!" But I would be heard.

'"I have never had any feeling warmer than respect for Miss Caroline, and I have never shown any different feeling. I never for an instant thought of making her my wife, and she has had no cause in my behaviour to imagine I entertained any such intention."

' "This is adding insult to injury," said she. "Leave the house, sir, this instant!"

Chapter 19

'I went, and sadly enough. In a small town such an occurrence is sure to be talked about, and to make a great deal of mischief. When I went home to dinner I was so full of it, and foresaw so clearly that I should need some advocate soon to set the case in its right light, that I determined on making a confidante of good Mrs Rose. I could not eat. She watched me tenderly, and sighed when she saw my want of appetite.

' "I am sure you have something on your mind, Mr Harrison. Would it be – would it not be – a relief to impart it to some sympathising friend?"

'It was just what I wanted to do.

' "My dear kind Mrs Rose," said I, "I must tell you, if you will listen."

'She took up the fire-screen, and held it, as yesterday, between me and her.

' "The most unfortunate misunderstanding has taken place. Miss Tomkinson thinks that I have been paying attentions to Miss Caroline; when, in fact – may I tell you, Mrs Rose? – my affections are placed elsewhere. Perhaps you have found it out already?" for indeed I thought I had been too much in love to conceal my attachment to Sophy from anyone who knew my movements as well as Mrs Rose.

'She hung down her head, and said she believed she had found out my secret.

' "Then only think how miserably I am situated. If I have any hope – oh, Mrs Rose, do you think I have any hope" –

'She put the hand-screen still more before her face, and after some hesitation she said she thought "If I persevered – in time – I might have hope." And then suddenly got up, and left the room.

Chapter 20

'That afternoon I met Mr Bullock in the street. My mind was so full of the affair with Miss Tomkinson that I should have passed him without notice, if he had not stopped me short, and said that he must speak to me; about my wonderful five hundred pounds, I supposed. But I did not care for that now.

'"What is this I hear," said he severely, "about your engagement with Mrs Rose?"

'"With Mrs Rose!" said I, almost laughing, although my heart was heavy enough.

'"Yes! with Mrs Rose!" said he sternly.

'"I'm not engaged to Mrs Rose," I replied. "There is some mistake."

'"I'm glad to hear it, sir," he answered, "very glad. It requires some explanation, however. Mrs Rose has been congratulated, and has acknowledged the truth of the report. It is confirmed by many facts. The work-table you bought, confessing your intention of giving it to your future wife, is given to her. How do you account for these things, sir?"

'I said I did not pretend to account for them. At present a good deal was inexplicable; and, when I could give an explanation, I did not think that I should feel myself called upon to give it to him.

'"Very well, sir; very well," replied he, growing very red. "I shall take care and let Mr Morgan know the opinion I entertain of you. What do you think that man deserves to be called who enters a family under the plea of friendship, and takes advantage of his intimacy to win the affections of the daughter, and then engages himself to another woman?"

'I thought he referred to Miss Caroline. I simply said I could only say that I was not engaged; and that Miss Tomkinson had been quite mistaken in supposing I had been paying any attentions to her sister beyond those dictated by mere civility.

'"Miss Tomkinson! Miss Caroline! I don't understand to what you refer. Is there another victim to your perfidy? What I allude to are the attentions you have paid to my daughter, Miss Bullock."

'Another! I could but disclaim, as I had done in the case of

Miss Caroline; but I began to be in despair. Would Miss Horsman, too, come forward as a victim to my tender affections? It was all Mr Morgan's doing, who had lectured me into this tenderly deferential manner. But, on the score of Miss Bullock, I was brave in my innocence. I had positively disliked her; and so I told her father, though in more civil and measured terms, adding that I was sure the feeling was reciprocal.

'He looked as if he would like to horsewhip me. I longed to call him out.

'"I hope my daughter has had sense enough to despise you; I hope she has, that's all. I trust my wife may be mistaken as to her feelings."

'So, he had heard all through the medium of his wife. That explained something, and rather calmed me. I begged he would ask Miss Bullock if she had ever thought I had any ulterior object in my intercourse with her, beyond mere friendliness (and not so much of that, I might have added). I would refer it to her.

'"Girls," said Mr Bullock, a little more quietly, "do not like to acknowledge that they have been deceived and disappointed. I consider my wife's testimony as likely to be nearer the truth than my daughter's, for that reason. And she tells me she never doubted but that, if not absolutely engaged, you understood each other perfectly. She is sure Jemima is deeply wounded by your engagement to Mrs Rose."

'"Once for all, I am not engaged to anybody. Till you have seen your daughter, and learnt the truth from her, I will wish you farewell."

'I bowed in a stiff, haughty manner, and walked off homewards. But when I got to my own door, I remembered Mrs Rose, and all that Mr Bullock had said about her acknowledging the truth of the report of my engagement to her. Where could I go to be safe? Mrs Rose, Miss Bullock, Miss Caroline – they lived as it were at the three points of an equilateral triangle; here was I in the centre. I would go to Mr Morgan's, and drink tea with him. There, at any rate, I was secure from anyone wanting to marry me; and I might be as professionally bland as I liked, without being misunderstood. But there, too, a *contretemps**
awaited me.

Chapter 21

'Mr Morgan was looking grave. After a minute or two of humming and hawing, he said –

'"I have been sent for to Miss Caroline Tomkinson, Mr Harrison. I am sorry to hear of this. I am grieved to find that there seems to have been some trifling with the affections of a very worthy lady. Miss Tomkinson, who is in sad distress, tells me that they had every reason to believe that you were attached to her sister. May I ask if you do not intend to marry her?"

'I said, nothing was farther from my thoughts.

'"My dear sir," said Mr Morgan, rather agitated, "do not express yourself so strongly and vehemently. It is derogatory to the sex to speak so. It is more respectful to say, in these cases, that you do not venture to entertain a hope; such a manner is generally understood, and does not sound like such positive objection."

'"I cannot help it, sir; I must talk in my own natural manner. I would not speak disrespectfully of any woman; but nothing should induce me to marry Miss Caroline Tomkinson; not if she were Venus herself, and Queen of England into the bargain. I cannot understand what has given rise to the idea."

'"Indeed, sir; I think that is very plain. You have a trifling case to attend to in the house, and you invariably make it a pretext for seeing and conversing with the lady."

'"That was her doing, not mine!" said I vehemently.

'"Allow me to go on. You are discovered on your knees before her – a positive injury to the establishment, as Miss Tomkinson observes; a most passionate valentine is sent; and, when questioned, you acknowledge the sincerity of meaning which you affix to such things." He stopped; for in his earnestness he had been talking more quickly than usual, and was out of breath. I burst in with my explanations –

'"The valentine I know nothing about."

'"It is in your handwriting," said he coldly. "I should be most deeply grieved to – in fact, I will not think it possible of your father's son. But I must say, it is in your handwriting."

'I tried again, and at last succeeded in convincing him that I had been only unfortunate, not intentionally guilty of winning

Miss Caroline's affections. I said that I had been endeavouring, it was true, to practise the manner he had recommended, of universal sympathy, and recalled to his mind some of the advice he had given me. He was a good deal hurried.

' "But, my dear sir, I had no idea that you would carry it out to such consequences. 'Philandering', Miss Tomkinson called it. That is a hard word, sir. My manner had been always tender and sympathetic; but I am not aware that I ever excited any hopes; there never was any report about me. I believe no lady was ever attached to me. You must strive after this happy medium, sir."

'I was still distressed. Mr Morgan had only heard of one, but there were three ladies (including Miss Bullock) hoping to marry me. He saw my annoyance.

' "Don't be too much distressed about it, my dear sir; I was sure you were too honourable a man, from the first. With a conscience like yours, I would defy the world."

'He became anxious to console me, and I was hesitating whether I would not tell him all my three dilemmas, when a note was brought in to him. It was from Mrs Munton. He threw it to me, with a face of dismay.

> Mr dear Mr Morgan, – I most sincerely congratulate you on the happy matrimonial engagement I hear you have formed with Miss Tomkinson. All previous circumstances, as I have just been remarking to Miss Horsman, combine to promise you felicity. And I wish that every blessing may attend your married life. – Most sincerely yours,
>
> *Jane Munton*

'I could not help laughing, he had been so lately congratulating himself that no report of the kind had ever been circulated about himself. He said –

' "Sir! this is no laughing matter; I assure you it is not."

'I could not resist asking, if I was to conclude that there was no truth in the report.

' "Truth, sir! it's a lie from beginning to end. I don't like to speak too decidedly about any lady; and I've a great respect for Miss Tomkinson; but I do assure you, sir, I'd as soon marry one of Her Majesty's Life Guards. I would rather; it would be more suitable. Miss Tomkinson is a very worthy lady; but she's a perfect grenadier."

'He grew very nervous. He was evidently insecure. He thought it not impossible that Miss Tomkinson might come and marry him, *vi et armis.** I am sure he had some dim idea of abduction in his mind. Still, he was better off than I was; for he was in his own house, and report had only engaged him to one lady; while I stood, like Paris, among three contending beauties. Truly, an apple of discord* had been thrown into our little town. I suspected at the time, what I know now, that it was Miss Horsman's doing; not intentionally, I will do her the justice to say. But she had shouted out the story of my behaviour to Miss Caroline up Mrs Munton's trumpet; and that lady, possessed with the idea that I was engaged to Mrs Rose, had imagined the masculine pronoun to relate to Mr Morgan, whom she had seen only that afternoon *tête-à-tête* with Miss Tomkinson, condoling with her in some tender deferential manner, I'll be bound.

Chapter 22

'I was very cowardly. I positively dared not go home; but at length I was obliged to. I had done all I could to console Mr Morgan, but he refused to be comforted. I went at last. I rang at the bell. I don't know who opened the door, but I think it was Mrs Rose. I kept a handkerchief to my face, and, muttering something about having a dreadful toothache, I flew up to my room and bolted the door. I had no candle; but what did that signify. I was safe. I could not sleep; and when I did fall into a sort of doze, it was ten times worse wakening up. I could not remember whether I was engaged or not. If I was engaged, who was the lady? I had always considered myself as rather plain than otherwise; but surely I had made a mistake. Fascinating I certainly must be; but perhaps I was handsome. As soon as day dawned, I got up to ascertain the fact at the looking-glass. Even with the best disposition to be convinced, I could not see any striking beauty in my round face, with an unshaven beard and a nightcap like a fool's cap* at the top. No! I must be content to be plain, but agreeable. All this I tell you in confidence. I would not have my little bit of vanity known for the world. I fell asleep towards morning. I was awakened by a tap at my door. It was Peggy: she put in a hand with a note. I took it.

'"It is not from Miss Horsman?" said I, half in joke, half in very earnest fright.

'"No, sir; Mr Morgan's man brought it."

'I opened it. It ran thus —

My Dear Sir, — It is now nearly twenty years since I have had a little relaxation, and I find that my health requires it. I have also the utmost confidence in you, and I am sure this feeling is shared by our patients. I have, therefore, no scruple in putting in execution a hastily-formed plan, and going to Chesterton to catch the early train on my way to Paris. If your accounts are good, I shall remain away probably a fortnight. Direct to Meurice's. — Yours most truly,

J. Morgan

P.S. — Perhaps it may be as well not to name where I am gone, especially to Miss Tomkinson.

'He had deserted me. He — with only one report — had left me to stand my ground with three.

'"Mrs Rose's kind regards, sir, and it's nearly nine o'clock. Breakfast has been ready this hour, sir."

'"Tell Mrs Rose I don't want any breakfast. Or stay" (for I was very hungry), "I will take a cup of tea and some toast up here."

'Peggy brought the tray to the door.

'"I hope you're not ill, sir?" said she kindly.

'"Not very. I shall be better when I get into the air."

'"Mrs Rose seems sadly put about,"* said she; "she seems so grieved like."

'I watched my opportunity, and went out by the side-door in the garden.

Chapter 23

'I had intended to ask Mr Morgan to call at the vicarage, and give his parting explanation before they could hear the report. Now I thought that, if I could see Sophy, I would speak to her myself; but I did not wish to encounter the Vicar. I went along the lane at the back of the vicarage, and came suddenly upon Miss Bullock. She coloured, and asked me if I would allow her to speak to me. I could only be resigned; but I thought I could probably set one report at rest by this conversation.

'She was almost crying.

'"I must tell you, Mr Harrison, I have watched you here in order to speak to you. I heard with the greatest regret of papa's conversation with you yesterday." She was fairly crying. "I believe Mrs Bullock finds me in her way, and wants to have me married. It is the only way in which I can account for such a complete misrepresentation as she had told papa. I don't care for you, in the least, sir. You never paid me any attentions. You've been almost rude to me; and I have liked you the better. That's to say, I never have liked you."

'"I am truly glad to hear what you say," answered I. "Don't distress youself. I was sure there was some mistake."

'But she cried bitterly.

'"It is so hard to feel that my marriage – my absence – is desired so earnestly at home. I dread every new acquaintance we form with any gentleman. It is sure to be the beginning of a series of attacks on him, of which everybody must be aware, and to which they may think I am a willing party. But I should not much mind if it were not for the conviction that she wishes me so earnestly away. Oh, my own dear mamma, you would never—"

'She cried more than ever. I was truly sorry for her, and had just taken her hand, and began – "My dear Miss Bullock"— when the door in the wall of the vicarage garden opened. It was the Vicar letting out Miss Tomkinson, whose face was all swelled with crying. He saw me; but he did not bow, or make any sign. On the contrary, he looked down as from a severe eminence, and shut the door hastily. I turned to Miss Bullock.

'"I am afraid the Vicar has been hearing something to my

disadvantage from Miss Tomkinson, and it is very awkward" –
She finished my sentence – "To have found us here together.
Yes; but, as long as we understand that we do not care for each
other, it does not signify what people say."

'"Oh, but to me it does," said I. "I may, perhaps, tell you –
but do not mention it to a creature – I am attached to Miss
Hutton."

'"To Sophy! Oh, Mr Harrison, I am so glad; she is such a
sweet creature. Oh, I wish you joy."

'"Not yet; I have never spoken about it."

'"Oh, but it is certain to happen." She jumped with a
woman's rapidity to a conclusion. And then she began to praise
Sophy. Never was a man yet who did not like to hear the praises
of his mistress. I walked by her side; we came past the front of
the vicarage together. I looked up, and saw Sophy there, and she
saw me.

'That afternoon she was sent away – sent to visit her aunt
ostensibly; in reality, because of the reports of my conduct,
which were showered down upon the Vicar, and one of which
he saw confirmed by his own eyes.

Chapter 24

'I heard of Sophy's departure as one heard of everything, soon
after it had taken place. I did not care for the awkwardness of
my situation, which had so perplexed and amused me in the
morning. I felt that something was wrong; that Sophy was taken
away from me. I sank into despair. If anybody liked to marry
me, they might. I was willing to be sacrificed. I did not speak to
Mrs Rose. She wondered at me, and grieved over my coldness, I
saw; but I had left off feeling anything. Miss Tomkinson cut me
in the street; and it did not break my heart. Sophy was gone
away; that was all I cared for. Where had they sent her to? Who
was her aunt that she should go and visit her? One day I met
Lizzie, who looked as though she had been told not to speak to
me; but I could not help doing so.

'"Have you heard from your sister?" said I.

'"Yes."

'"Where is she? I hope she is well."

'"She is at the Leoms" – I was not much wiser. "Oh yes, she is very well. Fanny says she was at the Assembly last Wednesday, and danced all night with the officers."

'I thought I would enter myself a member of the Peace Society* at once. She was a little flirt, and a hard-hearted creature. I don't think I wished Lizzie good-bye.

Chapter 25

'What most people would have considered a more serious evil than Sophy's absence, befell me. I found that my practice was falling off. The prejudice of the town ran strongly against me. Mrs Munton told me all that was said. She heard it through Miss Horsman. It was said – cruel little town – that my negligence or ignorance had been the cause of Walter's death; that Miss Tyrrell had become worse under my treatment; and that John Brouncker was all but dead, if he was not quite, from my mismanagement. All Jack Marshland's jokes and revelations, which had, I thought, gone to oblivion, were raked up to my discredit. He himself, formerly, to my astonishment, rather a favourite with the good people of Duncombe, was spoken of as one of my disreputable friends.

'In short, so prejudiced were the good people of Duncombe that I believe a very little would have made them suspect me of a brutal highway robbery, which took place in the neighbourhood about this time. Mrs Munton told me, à propos* of the robbery, that she had never yet understood the cause of my year's imprisonment in Newgate; she had no doubt, from what Mr Morgan had told her, there was some good reason for it; but if I would tell her the particulars, she would like to know them.

'Miss Tomkinson sent for Mr White, from Chesterton, to see Miss Caroline; and, as he was coming over, all our old patients seemed to take advantage of it, and send for him too.

'But the worst of all was the Vicar's manner to me. If he had cut me, I could have asked him why he did so. But the freezing change in his behaviour was indescribably, though bitterly felt.

I heard of Sophy's gaiety from Lizzie. I thought of writing to her. Just then Mr Morgan's fortnight of absence expired. I was wearied out by Mrs Rose's tender vagaries, and took no comfort from her sympathy, which indeed I rather avoided. Her tears irritated, instead of grieving, me. I wished I could tell her at once that I had no intention of marrying her.

Chapter 26

'Mr Morgan had not been at home above two hours before he was sent for to the vicarage. Sophy had come back, and I had never heard of it. She had come home ill and weary, and longing for rest; and the *rest* seemed approaching with awful strides. Mr Morgan forgot all his Parisian adventures, and all his terror of Miss Tomkinson, when he was sent for to see her. She was ill of a fever, which made fearful progress. When he told me, I wished to force the vicarage door, if I might but see her. But I controlled myself; and only cursed my weak indecision, which had prevented my writing to her. It was well I had no patients: they would have had but a poor chance of attention. I hung about Mr Morgan, who might see her, and did see her. But, from what he told me, I perceived that the measures he was adopting were powerless to check so sudden and violent an illness. Oh! if they would but let me see her! But that was out of the question. It was not merely that the Vicar had heard of my character as a gay Lothario,* but that doubts had been thrown out of my medical skill. The accounts grew worse. Suddenly my resolution was taken. Mr Morgan's very regard for Sophy made him more than usually timid in his practice. I had my horse saddled, and galloped to Chesterton. I took the express train to town. I went to Dr——. I told him every particular of the case. He listened; but shook his head. He wrote down a prescription, and recommended a new preparation, not yet in full use – a preparation of a poison, in fact.

'"It may save her," said he. "It is a chance, in such a state of things as you describe. It must be given on the fifth day, if the pulse will bear it. Crabbe* makes up the preparation most skilfully. Let me hear from you, I beg."

'I went to Crabbe's; I begged to make it up myself; but my hands trembled, so that I could not weigh the quantities. I asked the young man to do it for me. I went, without touching food, to the station, with my medicine and my prescription in my pocket. Back we flew through the country. I sprang on Bay Maldon, which my groom had in waiting, and galloped across the country to Duncombe.

'But I drew bridle when I came to the top of the hill – the hill above the old hall, from which we catch the first glimpse of the town, for I thought within myself that she might be dead; and I dreaded to come near certainty. The hawthorns were out in the woods, the young lambs were in the meadows, the song of the thrushes filled the air; but it only made the thought the more terrible.

'"What if, in this world of hope and life, she lies dead!"* I heard the church bells soft and clear. I sickened to listen. Was it the passing bell?* No! it was ringing eight o'clock. I put spurs to my horse, down hill as it was. We dashed into the town. I turned him, saddle and bridle, into the stable-yard, and went off to Mr Morgan's.

'"Is she"— said I. "How is she?"

'"Very ill. My poor fellow, I see how it is with you. She may live – but I fear. My dear sir, I am very much afraid."

'I told him of my journey and consultation with Dr——, and showed him the prescription. His hands trembled as he put on his spectacles to read it.

'"This is a very dangerous medicine, sir," said he, with his finger under the name of the poison.

'"It is a new preparation," said I. "Dr—— relies much upon it."

'"I dare not administer it," he replied. "I have never tried it. It must be very powerful. I dare not play tricks in this case."

'I believe I stamped with impatience; but it was all of no use. My journey had been in vain. The more I urged the imminent danger of the case requiring some powerful remedy, the more nervous he became.

'I told him I would throw up the partnership. I threatened him with that, though, in fact, it was only what I felt I ought to do, and had resolved upon before Sophy's illness, as I had lost the confidence of his patients. He only said –

'"I cannot help it, sir. I shall regret it for your father's sake;

but I must do my duty. I dare not run the risk of giving Miss Sophy this violent medicine – a preparation of a deadly poison."

'I left him without a word. He was quite right in adhering to his own views, as I can see now; but at the time I thought him brutal and obstinate.

Chapter 27

'I went home. I spoke rudely to Mrs Rose, who awaited my return at the door. I rushed past, and locked myself in my room. I could not go to bed.

'The morning sun came pouring in, and enraged me, as everything did since Mr Morgan refused. I pulled the blind down so violently that the string broke. What did it signify? The light might come in. What was the sun to me? And then I remembered that that sun might be shining on her – dead.

'I sat down and covered my face. Mrs Rose knocked at the door. I opened it. She had never been in bed, and had been crying too.

'"Mr Morgan wants to speak to you, sir."

'I rushed back for my medicine, and went to him. He stood at the door, pale and anxious.

'"She's alive, sir," said he, "but that's all. We have sent for Dr Hamilton. I'm afraid he will not come in time. Do you know, sir, I think we should venture – with Dr——'s sanction – to give her that medicine. It is but a chance; but it is the only one, I'm afraid." He fairly cried before he had ended.

'"I've got it here," said I, setting off to walk; but he could not go so fast.

'"I beg your pardon, sir," said he, "for my abrupt refusal last night."

'"Indeed, sir," said I; "I ought much rather to beg your pardon. I was very violent."

'"Oh! never mind! never mind! Will you repeat what Dr—— said?"

'I did so; and then I asked, with a meekness that astonished myself, if I might not go in and administer it.

'"No, sir," said he, "I'm afraid not. I am sure your good heart would not wish to give pain. Besides, it might agitate her, if she has any consciousness before death. In her delirium she has often mentioned your name; and, sir, I'm sure you won't name it again, as it may, in fact, be considered a professional secret; but I did hear our good Vicar speak a little strongly about you; in fact, sir, I did hear him curse you. You see the mischief it might make in the parish, I'm sure, if this were known."

'I gave him the medicine, and watched him in, and saw the door shut. I hung about the place all day. Poor and rich all came to inquire. The county people drove up in their carriages – the halt* and the lame came on their crutches. Their anxiety did my heart good. Mr Morgan told me that she slept, and I watched Dr Hamilton into the house. The night came on. She slept. I watched round the house. I saw the light high up, burning still and steady. Then I saw it moved. It was the crisis, in one way or other.

Chapter 28

'Mr Morgan came out. Good old man! The tears were running down his cheeks: he could not speak; but kept shaking my hands. I did not want words. I understood that she was better.

'"Dr Hamilton says, it was the only medicine that could have saved her. I was an old fool, sir. I beg your pardon. The Vicar shall know all. I beg your pardon, sir, if I was abrupt."

'Everything went on brilliantly from this time.

'Mr Bullock called to apologise for his mistake, and consequent upbraiding. John Brouncker came home, brave and well.

'There was still Miss Tomkinson in the ranks of the enemy; and Mrs Rose too much, I feared, in the ranks of the friends.

Chapter 29

'One night she had gone to bed, and I was thinking of going. I had been studying in the back room, where I went for refuge from her in the present position of affairs – (I read a good number of surgical books about this time, and also "Vanity Fair")* – when I heard a loud, long-continued knocking at the door, enough to waken the whole street. Before I could get to open it, I heard that well-known bass of Jack Marshland's – once heard, never to be forgotten – pipe up the negro song –

Who's dat knocking at de door?

'Though it was raining hard at the time, and I stood waiting to let him in, he would finish his melody in the open air; loud and clear along the street it sounded. I saw Miss Tomkinson's night-capped head emerge from a window. She called out "Police! police!"

'Now there were no police, only a rheumatic constable, in the town; but it was the custom of the ladies, when alarmed at night, to call an imaginary police, which had, they thought, an intimidating effect; but, as everyone knew the real state of the unwatched town, we did not much mind it in general. Just now, however, I wanted to regain my character. So I pulled Jack in, quavering as he entered.

'"You've spoilt a good shake," said he, "that's what you have. I'm nearly up to Jenny Lind; and you see I'm a nightin-gale,* like her."

'We sat up late; and I don't know how it was, but I told him all my matrimonial misadventures.

'"I thought I could imitate your hand pretty well," said he. "My word! it was a flaming valentine! No wonder she thought you loved her!"

'"So that was your doing, was it? Now I'll tell you what you shall do to make up for it. You shall write me a letter confessing your hoax – a letter that I can show."

'"Give me a pen and paper, my boy! you shall dictate. 'With a deeply penitent heart' – Will that do for a beginning?"

'I told him what to write; a simple, straightforward confession of his practical joke. I enclosed it in a few lines of regret that, unknown to me, any of my friends should have so acted.

Chapter 30

'All this time I knew that Sophy was slowly recovering. One day I met Miss Bullock, who had seen her.

' "We have been talking about you," said she, with a bright smile; for, since she knew I disliked her, she felt quite at her ease, and could smile very pleasantly. I understood that she had been explaining the misunderstanding about herself to Sophy; so that, when Jack Marshland's note had been sent to Miss Tomkinson's, I thought myself in a fair way to have my character established in two quarters. But the third was my dilemma. Mrs Rose had really so much of my true regard for her good qualities, that I disliked the idea of a formal explanation, in which a good deal must be said on my side to wound her. We had become very much estranged ever since I had heard of this report of my engagement to her. I saw that she grieved over it. While Jack Marshland stayed with us, I felt at my ease in the presence of a third person. But he told me confidentially he durst not stay long, for fear some of the ladies should snap him up, and marry him. Indeed I myself did not think it unlikely that he would snap one of them up if he could. For when we met Miss Bullock one day, and heard her hopeful, joyous account of Sophy's progress (to whom she was a daily visitor), he asked me who that bright-looking girl was? And when I told him she was the Miss Bullock of whom I had spoken to him, he was pleased to observe that he thought I had been a great fool, and asked me if Sophy had anything like such splendid eyes. He made me repeat about Miss Bullock's unhappy circumstances at home, and then became very thoughtful – a most unusual and morbid symptom in his case.

'Soon after he went, by Mr Morgan's kind offices and explanations, I was permitted to see Sophy. I might not speak much; it was prohibited, for fear of agitating her. We talked of the weather and the flowers and we were silent. But her little white thin hand lay in mine; and we understood each other without words. I had a long interview with the Vicar afterwards, and came away glad and satisfied.

'Mr Morgan called in the afternoon, evidently anxious, though he made no direct inquiries (he was too polite for that), to hear the result of my visit at the vicarage. I told him to give me joy. He shook me warmly by the hand, and then rubbed his own together. I thought I would consult him about my dilemma with Mrs Rose, who, I was afraid, would be deeply affected by my engagement.

'"There is only one awkward circumstance," said I – "about Mrs Rose." I hesitated how to word the fact of her having received congratulations on her supposed engagement with me, and her manifest attachment; but, before I could speak, he broke in –

'"My dear sir, you need not trouble yourself about that; she will have a home. In fact, sir," said he, reddening a little, "I thought it would, perhaps, put a stop to those reports connecting my name with Miss Tomkinson's, if I married someone else. I hoped it might prove an efficacious contradiction. And I was struck with admiration for Mrs Rose's undying memory of her late husband. Not to be prolix, I have this morning obtained Mrs Rose's consent to – to marry her, in fact, sir!" said he, jerking out the climax.

'Here was an event! Then Mr Morgan had never heard the report about Mrs Rose and me. (To this day, I think she would have taken me, if I had proposed.) So much the better.

'Marriages were in the fashion that year. Mr Bullock met me one morning, as I was going to ride with Sophy. He and I had quite got over our misunderstanding, thanks to Jemima, and were as friendly as ever. This morning he was chuckling aloud as he walked.

'"Stop, Mr Harrison!" he said, as I went quickly past. "Have you heard the news? Miss Horsman has just told me Miss Caroline has eloped with young Hoggins!* She is ten years older than he is! How can her gentility like being married to a tallow-chandler? It is a very good thing for her, though," he added, in a more serious manner; "old Hoggins is very rich; and, though he's angry just now, he will soon be reconciled."

'Any vanity I might have entertained on the score of the three ladies who were, at one time, said to be captivated by my charms, was being rapidly dispersed. Soon after Mr Hoggins's marriage, I met Miss Tomkinson face to face, for the first time since our memorable conversation. She stopped me, and said –

' "Don't refuse to receive my congratulations, Mr Harrison, on your most happy engagement to Miss Hutton. I owe you an apology, too, for my behaviour when I last saw you at our house. I really did think Caroline was attached to you then; and it irritated me, I confess, in a very wrong and unjustifiable way. But I heard her telling Mr Hoggins only yesterday that she had been attached to him for years; ever since he was in pinafores, she dated it from; and when I asked her afterwards how she could say so, after her distress on hearing the false report about you and Mrs Rose, she cried, and said I never had understood her; and that the hysterics which alarmed me so much were simply caused by eating pickled cucumber. I am very sorry for my stupidity and improper way of speaking; but I hope we are friends now, Mr Harrison, for I should wish to be liked by Sophy's husband."

'Good Miss Tomkinson, to believe the substitution of indigestion for disappointed affection! I shook her warmly by the hand; and we have been all right ever since. I think I told you she is baby's godmother.

Chapter 31

'I had some difficulty in persuading Jack Marshland to be groomsman; but, when he heard all the arrangements, he came. Miss Bullock was bridesmaid. He liked us all so well, that he came again at Christmas, and was far better behaved than he had been the year before. He won golden opinions* indeed. Miss Tomkinson said he was a reformed young man. We dined all together at Mr Morgan's (the Vicar wanted us to go there; but, from what Sophy told me, Helen was not confident of the mincemeat, and rather dreaded so large a party). We had a jolly day of it. Mrs Morgan was as kind and motherly as ever. Miss Horsman certainly did set out a story that the Vicar was thinking of Miss Tomkinson for his second; or else, I think, we had no other report circulated in consequence of our happy, merry

Christmas-day; and it is a wonder, considering how Jack
Marshland went on with Jemima.'

Here Sophy came back from putting baby to bed; and Charles
wakened up.

NOTES

Where any notes have been derived from another edition, an acknowledgement to the Editor of that edition is given. I have learned much from studying two modern editions. These are the World's Classics *Cranford*, edited by Elizabeth Porges Watson (Oxford, 1980) and the Penguin English Library text edited by Peter Keating (Penguin, 1976).

Cranford

p. 3 the Amazons: in Greek mythology, a nation of warrior-women. They were on the side of the Trojans during the Greek siege of Troy: their leader, Penthesilea, was killed by Achilles, who was smitten with the beauty of the corpse.

p. 3 Drumble: Mrs Gaskell's name for Manchester, in the north of England.

p. 3 to speck them: i.e., stain them.

p. 3 the even tenor of their lives ... : cf Thomas Gray (1716–71), 'Elegy Written in a Country Churchyard' (1751), l. 76: 'They kept the noiseless tenor of their way', where 'even' was sometimes printed for 'noiseless'.

p. 4 Miss Tyler, of cleanly memory: this is identified by Elizabeth Porges Watson (hereafter Watson) as being from Robert Southey's *Life and Correspondence* (1849), in which he refers to the exacting standards of cleanliness insisted upon by his aunt, Miss Tyler.

p. 7 Miss Betty Barker: she is called Betsy in editions up to and including the one used here (1853) in this first chapter, but afterwards she is referred to as 'Betty'. I have therefore followed Watson and Keating in altering it to 'Betty' here.

p. 9 'Preference': popular card-game of the period, similar to whist.

p. 10 Jock of Hazeldean: by Sir Walter Scott (1771–1832). It is a ballad having four verses, the first of which is ancient, the other three being written by Scott (1816).

p. 10 'The Pickwick Papers' ... (They were then publishing in parts):

The Posthumous Papers of the Pickwick Club ... , Dickens's first novel, was issued in monthly shilling numbers from April 1836 to November 1837. There was no number for June 1837, since Dickens was prostrated with grief at the death (on 7 May) of his beloved sister-in-law, Mary Hogarth.

p. 10 Dr Johnson: (1709–84), Miss Jenkyns's favourite author, poet, essayist, novelist, the maker of the first great *Dictionary of the English Language* (1755), he talked great literature as well and inspired the first major biography, Boswell's *Life of Johnson* (1789).

p. 11 the 'swarry' which Sam Weller gave at Bath: 'swarry' is the French 'soirée', meaning an evening party. Sam is invited by a 'select company' of Bath footmen to this gathering (*The Pickwick Papers*, Chapter 38) and has a fine time ridiculing their pomposity and pretentiousness, though they are largely unaware of his satire.

p. 11 'Rasselas': Dr Johnson's novel was published in 1759, and subtitled 'Prince of Abyssinia'. Its theme is the impossibility of gaining true happiness. Margaret Drabble refers to its 'wise and humane melancholy'.

p. 11 Mr Boz: Dickens used this pseudonym for his sketches and also for the monthly issues of *The Pickwick Papers*. It derives from the nickname of his younger brother (real name Augustus), dubbed Moses then nasally shortened by Dickens to 'Boz'.

p. 11 Rasselas and Imlac: the Prince of Abyssinia and the old philosopher respectively in Dr Johnson's novel.

p. 11 the 'Rambler': Dr Johnson's periodical, issued twice weekly between 20 March 1750 and 14 March 1752.

p. 11 *forte*: strong point.

p. 12 *sotto voce*: beneath the breath.

p. 13 bakehouse: strictly, a place with ovens for baking bread but, in this context, communal baking for the poor is obviously meant.

p. 14 fain: willingly (now archaic, very rarely used).

p. 14 Brutus wig: i.e., rough-cropped, after the style of the Roman Brutus, who was much admired by the French during the Revolutionary period.

p. 14 *au fait*: i.e., up to date with.

p. 15 Flint's: celebrated haberdashers in London. (Watson supplies additional information which suggests that the phrasing here recognisably echoes a popular song).

p. 15 the Hebrew prophetess: Deborah, the twelfth century BC judge and prophetess. See Judges 4 and 5 for her triumph against the Canaanites.

p. 15 quondam: one time, former.

p. 15 'plumed wars': both Watson and Keating pick up the *Othello* reference here – 'Farewell the plumed troops and the big wars' (III, iii, 353).

p. 16 'the feast of reason and the flow of soul': Alexander Pope (1688–1744), 'Imitations of Horace', The First Satire of the Second Book, l. 128.

p. 16 'the pure wells of English undefiled': from *The Faerie Queene*, IV, ii, the penultimate line of stanza 32. Spenser (1552–99), is here praising Chaucer – 'Dan Chaucer, well of English undefyled.'

p. 18 a rolling three-piled sentence: long, clause upon clause, in the manner of Dr Johnson.

p. 19 cotched it up: i.e., lifted it, caught it up.

p. 20 dissuasives: unusual usage, here meaning 'persuasions against it'.

p. 22 'Though He slay me, yet will I trust in Him': see Job 13:15.

p. 24 Galignani: the newspaper was called *Galignani's Messenger*. It was founded by Giovanni Galignani (1757–1821) in 1814 in Paris, and had a large circulation among English readers in Europe.

p. 25 Lucy in 'Old Poz': Watson identifies 'Old Poz' as being by Maria Edgeworth (1761–1849) in *The Parent's Assistant*, 1795, and says that it is Lucy 'who unravels the plot'.

p. 25 the 'Christmas Carol': Charles Dickens's popular Christmas story was published in December 1843.

p. 26 'Hortus Siccus': a dry garden (Latin), i.e., plants dried and formed into a book.

p. 27 'followers': i.e., young men who came courting the servants.

p. 28 'settle her': see her comfortable.

p. 29 a screen: a hand-screen, its employment here conveying the humour of the situation.

p. 30 'Army List': i.e., the list of commissioned officers in the British Army.

p. 31 Blue Beard: from the story by Charles Perrault (1628–1703) of the merciless wife-killer Bluebeard, who has murdered his wives in turn, but the last one, who discovers the bodies, survives. The story was translated into English in 1729.

p. 31 '**Leave me, leave me to repose**': from Thomas Gray's 'The Descent of Odin' (1768), 'l. 50, spoken by 'the Scandinavian prophetess'.

p. 31 the '**pride which apes humility**': identified by Keating and Watson as being from 'The Devil's Thoughts' by Coleridge and Southey, first published in the *Morning Post* in September 1799.

p. 32 **blowing up my castle**: i.e., destroying my day-dream.

p. 33 **mousseline-de-laine**: fine woollen or woollen and cotton material (Watson).

p. 33 **Don Quixote-looking**: i.e., resembling the eccentric, comic hero of Cervantes' (1547–1616) *Don Quixote* (1605, 1616), the greatest of all Spanish novels.

p. 33 **sarsenet**: soft material used for lining garments.

p. 34 **a fly**: a one-horse carriage, light and hence capable of speed.

p. 34 **Woodley**: Watson points out that this may be drawn from Sandlebridge in Cheshire.

p. 35 **Shakespeare and George Herbert**: the quotations from Shakespeare (1564–1616) would come largely from the plays. George Herbert (1593–1633), who was ordained in 1624, was a major metaphysical poet who wrote among other things the exquisite 'Virtue', which begins 'Sweet day, so cool, so calm, so bright'.

p. 35 **Byron**: Lord Byron (1788–1824), author of *Don Juan*, was a leading Romantic poet.

p. 35 **Goethe ... 'Ye ever-verdant palaces'**: Goethe (1749–1832) was one of the greatest German writers, in poetry, prose, philosophy, for example. He exerted a tremendous influence on his contemporaries, and was a major force in European literature. For a note on the quotation see *The Gaskell Society Journal*, 1994, pp. 111–12.

p. 35 **flag-floor**: i.e., made of flags – flat, generally rectangular stone slabs.

p. 36 **as Aminé ate her grains of rice after her previous feast with the Ghoul**: in the *Arabian Nights* she was the wife of Sadi Nouman who had previously fed on human flesh.

p. 37 **I saw, I imitated, I survived**: Mary Smith's parody of Julius Caesar's 'I came, I saw, I conquered.'

p. 37 calashes: hooped silk hoods which had been introduced in the eighteenth century.

p. 38 'The cedar spreads his dark-green layers of shade': from Alfred Lord Tennyson's (1809–92) poem 'The Gardener's Daughter' (1842), l. 115 ('A cedar spread his dark-green layers of shade').

p. 38 'Blackwood': A monthly magazine founded by William Blackwood in 1817, it was known as *Maga*, and first published Mrs Gaskell's great contemporary, George Eliot.

p. 38 Black as ash-buds in March: 'The Gardener's Daughter', l. 28 ('More black than ashbuds in the front of March').

p. 38 'Locksley Hall': by Tennyson, and published in 1842. See Introduction p. xxiii–iv.

p. 38 that beautiful poem of Dr Johnson's: as we might expect, Miss Matty is imprecise. No poem of Dr Johnson's fits.

p. 40 without noticing Martha's intelligence to her: i.e., without revealing what Martha had said about her.

p. 41 a capable kitchen: Martha probably means large, with a great deal of room.

p. 42 Arley Hall: Watson draws attention to the fact that there is actually a mansion called this 'in the parish of great Budworth, near Northwich'.

p. 42 'that wicked Paris, where they are always having Revolutions': typical of Miss Pole's flair for exaggeration, though she has in mind the events of 1789 which precipitated the French Revolution and the events of July 1830 which established Louis Phillippe as King. Mrs Gaskell is writing a couple of years after the Revolution of 1848 which saw the triumph of Louis Napoleon.

p. 45 'keep blind-man's holiday': proverbial, equated with darkness or twilight.

p. 46 Tonquin beans: the fragrant seed of the South American tonka tree used in scents and perfumes.

p. 46 a huge full-bottomed wig: note the date 1774, when the Rector was 27 years old: the picture referred to would be when he was much older.

p. 47 'Paduasoy': i.e., of thick silk.

p. 48 J. and J. Rivingtons: the name of a famous publishing firm founded in 1711, their speciality being works of a theological nature.

p. 49 *dum memor ipse mei . . . artus*: from Virgil's *Aeneid*, Book IV, l. 336 (Mrs Gaskell omits *hos* after *spiritus*): 'While memory lasts, while the spirit still animates my frame' (Keating).

p. 49 **figured away**: i.e., was represented as.

p. 49 *carmen*: poem (but it can also mean 'song').

p. 49 **'Gentleman's Magazine'**: founded in 1731, it lasted until 1914. The founder, Cave, was a friend of Dr Johnson, who was a regular contributor.

p. 49 **M. T. Ciceronis Epistolæ**: Cicero (106–43BC), the celebrated Roman writer, politician and orator.

p. 49 **'forrard'**: i.e. forward, precocious.

p. 50 **'a vale of tears'**: thus James Montgomery (1771–1854) – 'Beyond this vale of tears/There is a life above/Unmeasured by the flight of years/And all that life is love'.

p. 50 **Mrs Chapone**: (1727–1801), the English essayist and blue-stocking, she was a friend of Johnson's, contributed to the *Rambler*, and is best remembered for her *Letters on the Improvement of the Mind* (1772).

p. 50 **Mrs Carter . . . Epictetus**: Mrs Carter (1717–1806), scholar and poet, another friend of Johnson's, was celebrated for her translation of Epictetus, the Stoic philosopher of the first century.

p. 50 **'I canna be fashed'**: 'I can't be bothered'.

p. 50 **the old original Post**: i.e., before the Penny Post of 1840.

p. 51 **Miss Edgeworth's 'Patronage' . . . wafers**: Maria Edgeworth published *Patronage* in 1813: a wafer was the small piece of red paper which sealed the letter.

p. 51 **sesquipedalian**: i.e., (employing) a number of syllables.

p. 51 **Herod, Tetrarch of Idumea**: Miss Matty is certainly confused. Herod the Great ruled Judea, one of his sons, also called Herod, ruled Idumea while another ruled Ituria. Tetrarch – ruler of the fourth part of an area.

p. 51 **to repel the invasion of Buonaparte**: Napoleon Buonaparte (1769–1821), French general and Emperor in the post-Revolutionary period. In the early years of the nineteenth century the threat of a French invasion hung over England. Napoleon was finally defeated by the Allies at Waterloo (1815).

p. 51 **the fable of the Boy and the Wolf**: the allusion is to the shepherd boy who used to cry 'wolf' merely to mock his neighbours: when a wolf eventually did turn up, and proceeded to slaughter his flock, no one would come to help him.

p. 52 the salt-mines: these are identified by Watson as being at Northwich, some 7 miles away.

p. 52 David and Goliath: see 1 Samuel:17 for the account. Goliath the Philistine is slain in verses 50–1.

p. 52 Apollyon and Abaddon: see Revelation 9:11 'They had for their king the angel of the abyss, whose name in Hebrew is Abaddon, and in Greek, Apollyon, or the Destroyer.'

p. 52 Shrewsbury: famous public school founded by King Edward VI (1547–53).

p. 52 *Bonus Bernardus non videt omnia*: proverbial – 'The good Bernard does not see all.'

p. 55 St James's Chronicle: the court paper which was founded in 1760. It reflected the views of the Establishment in Church and State.

p. 56 shovel-hat: a broad-brimmed hat. It was hard but turned up at the sides and was fairly standard wear among the clergy.

p. 58 Queen Esther and King Ahasuerus: see the Book of Esther, particularly 1–6, for the full story of how she became Queen.

p. 60 Dor: this has been corrected from 'Don' to 'Dor' correctly, I think, by Watson, assuming that this is a familiar form of 'Deborah'.

p. 63 some great war in India: although India is mentioned in Mrs Brown's account, Peter himself says that he took part in 'the siege of Rangoon'. The British captured Rangoon, then the capital of Lower Burma, in 1826.

p. 65 John Bullish ... Mounseers: John Bull, a humorous symbol of strength and Britishness, derives from John Arbuthnot's satire 'The History of John Bull' (1712) in which the Church of England is represented as his mother. 'Mounseers' is an anglicised, sneering version of 'Monsieurs'.

p. 66 Queen Adelaide ... King William: the first (1762–1849), wife of the second, William IV (1765–1837). He ruled from 1830–7.

p. 66 mess: i.e., liquid, pulpy food.

p. 66 *passée*: out of date, hence, unfashionable.

p. 67 her pool at Preference: see note on 'Preference' p. 9.

p. 68 bombazine: thick dress material used for mourning clothes.

p. 68 in the time of the American War: i.e., of Independence (1776–83).

p. 68 Drury Lane: a reference to the celebrated London theatre, founded in 1663, twice burned down and restored.

p. 69 Fitz-Clarence: 'Fitz' is often the prefix which indicates illegitimacy. The Fitz-Clarences were William IV's children by a mistress before he become King.

p. 69 *ci-devant*: one-time, previously.

p. 70 a seat arranged something like Prince Albert's near the Queen's: Queen Victoria (1819–1901) married Prince Albert of Saxe-Coburg (1819–61). As her Consort, he officially occupied an inferior position to the Queen.

p.oo Savoy biscuits: thin sponge biscuits, often joined as 'fingers'.

p. 71 Cribbage: a card game which involves the use of the complete pack. The cribbage board has pegs with which to mark the points scored by each player.

p. 71 Spadille from Manille: i.e., the Ace of Spades and the second best trump or honour in the card games of Ombre and Quadrille (see note p. 84).

p. 71 'basting': in Ombre, failing to win the game or incurring a forfeit.

p. 72 niddle-noddling: i.e., nodding repeatedly.

p. 72 'little Cupids': Watson calls this 'a kind of macaroon syllabub'.

p. 73 like female mandarins: i.e., all together, representing uniformity and agreement.

p. 73 Hogarth's pictures: William Hogarth (1697–1764), famous English painter who depicted the vices and follies of his age, his work evincing a deep moral purpose. He reached a wide public through the popularity of his prints.

p. 76 never sat in the House of Lords: the number of Scottish peers allowed to take their seats in the House of Lords was limited by the Act of Union of 1707, which dissolved the Scottish Parliament.

p. 76 as poor as Job: proverbial from the beginning of the fourteenth century. See Job 1.22 for the account of his misfortunes.

p. 80 stomacher: the pointed front of a dress covering the breast and reaching down to the waist. It was sometimes embroidered or jewelled.

p. 80 hair-powder: used by male servants, though it would probably be out of date at this time, and is therefore an ironic comment on Mr Mulliner.

p. 81 Louis Quatorze: Louis the Fourteenth (1638–1715). Keating points out that the ornate style here mentioned enjoyed a new vogue after Waterloo (1815).

p. 81 square Pembroke table: i.e., with two folding leaves.

p. 81 conversation-cards, puzzle-cards: (i) Mrs Gaskell describes these in Chapter 8 of *Mr Harrison's Confessions* as having questions on one side and answers on the other, but the answers fit any of the questions and are thus nonsensical. (ii) Watson's suggestion that George Eliot describes these in Chapter 60 of *Middlemarch* (1871–2) is a reasonable one. She cites the first description here, but the auctioneer Borthrop Trumbull also refers to 'No less than five hundred printed in a beautiful red' and asks, 'What can promote innocent mirth, and I may say virtue, more than a good riddle?' He then provides an example, almost like those still found in Christmas crackers today.

p. 82 'A Lord and No Lord' business: both Watson and Keating indicate that this may be a reference to the title of an anonymous ballad written in 1726.

p. 82 *savoir faire*: i.e., knowing how to act correctly in any given situation.

p. 83 minnikin: very small indeed, diminutive.

p. 84 the dear Queen: i.e., Victoria, who came to the throne in 1837.

p. 84 Basto: the Ace of Clubs in the card games Ombre and Quadrille, played with a pack of forty cards.

p. 84 Spadille: see third note p. 71.

p. 84 the Catholic Emancipation Bill: the Bill was passed in 1829. It removed the various civil disabilities imposed upon Catholics by earlier legislation.

p. 86 Francis Moore's astrological predictions: Francis Moore (1657–1715) was the English astrologer who, in 1700, published 'Old Moore's' astrological almanac.

p. 87 if turbans were in fashion: with increased Eastern travel from the eighteenth century onwards, and the influence of this on fashion, turbans were periodically popular well into the nineteenth century.

p. 87 Wombwell's lions: part of the travelling menagerie which was very popular throughout England in the nineteenth century, its founder being George Wombwell (1778–1850).

p. 89 *minuets de la cour*: i.e., minuets (slow, stately dances) of the court.

p. 89 **clothes-maids**: clothes-horses.

p. 89 **Thaddeus of Warsaw and the Hungarian Brothers, and Santo Sebastiani**: the first is by Jane Porter (1776–1850), her romantic novel achieving great success when it came out in 1803. The second is by her younger sister Anna Maria (1780–1832): this novel, about the French Revolution, came out in 1807 and ran to many editions. The third is difficult to identify, but Watson suggests that it is either Anna Maria's *Don Sebastian* (1809) or Catherine Cuthbertson's *Santo Sebastiano* (1806).

p. 90 **the Witch of Endor**: a reference to I Samuel 28:7–25, in which Saul seeks out the woman in fear of the Philistine power.

p. 90 **death-watches**: i.e., the death-watch beetle seen as a portent of death.

p. 92 **the Gunnings**: Maria and Elizabeth, two 'beauties' of the period who married into nobility.

p. 92 *chapeau bras*: fashionable hat having three corners, easily folded and carried.

p. 92 **the old tapestry story**: not identified.

p. 94 **legerdemain**: trickery.

p. 94 **National School boys**: in 1811 the National Society was founded to promote the education of the poor, and this is a reference to one of the schools which was established as a result.

p. 95 **in chinks**: Mrs Gaskell uses the term 'chinked' in *Ruth* (1853). The phrase here means 'gasping, choking spasmodically'. Obviously the boys are enjoying the show.

p. 97 **General Burgoyne**: (1722–92). In the American War of Independence (1776–83) he fought at Bunker Hill in 1775, captured Ticonderoga, but was forced to surrender to General Gates at Saratoga Springs (1777).

p. 97 **fought the French in Spain**: i.e., in the Peninsular War (1808–14). Here the British, Spanish and Portuguese (under Wellington) were resisting in another area of Napoleonic conquest.

p. 97 **Madame de Staël ... Mr Denon**: the first, the famous French writer (1766–1817) who established a literary salon and wielded great political influence. The second, Baron Dominique-Vivant Denon

(1747–1825), who accompanied Napoleon on his Egyptian campaign and was also his Keeper of Museums. (Watson and Keating)

p. 99 a nightingale and a musician . . . Philomel: according to Keating the story is quoted in Miss Mitford's *Our Village* (1824), a book thought to have influenced Mrs Gaskell in her writing of *Cranford*. In classical mythology Philomela, raped by Tereus, was later changed into a nightingale: hence Philomel has become the name for the bird.

p. 99 chasing: figures or designs embossed on metal.

p. 99 Italian irons: used for delicate textures like frills.

p. 100 spillikins: splinters of wood which have to be removed from a pile one at a time without disturbing the others: this is in the nature of a game.

p. 100 scouted: rejected scornfully.

p. 105 *videlicet*: namely.

p. 106 cold-pigged: i.e., have cold water thrown over him. A pig is a piece of earthenware.

p. 106 Dr Ferrier and Dr Hibbert: identified by Watson and Keating as writers on illusions and apparitions.

p. 107 as mutes at a funeral: hired mourners.

p. 111 'Jack's up' 'a fig for his heels': Mr Hoggins is commenting on cribbage while he is playing, and this would be thought common. The turning up of the jack wins an extra point.

p. 111 the Duke of Wellington being ill: the victor of Waterloo and later Prime Minister, he organised the military against the Chartists in 1848. Mrs Gaskell is subtly documenting the concerns of the period of her action here, the wider gossip complementing the local.

p. 111 Lord Chesterfield's Letters: Chesterfield (1694–1773) was the statesman and orator who is primarily remembered for his *Letters to his Son*, which were published in the year following his death.

p. 111 dictum: pronouncement, word.

p. 111 bread-jelly: a recipe of bread-crumbs, cream, gelatine, eggs and cinnamon, which is set in a mould.

p. 112 the great Sir Walter that shot King Rufus . . . the little Princes in the Tower. William II, known as Rufus, was killed by an arrow in 1100, the marksman supposedly being Walter Tyrrell. Sir James Tyrrell was executed in 1502: he confessed to the murder of the Princes in the Tower (these were Edward and Richard) in 1483.

p. 115 write his charges: i.e., his directions, his orders to his subordinates.

p. 116 I drew a lot to go: presumably this means that some wives could accompany their husbands if they were fortunate enough to choose correctly in some chance test, i.e. drawing the longest (or shortest) of a number of pieces of string.

p. 117 pice: the smallest of Indian coins, hence the emphasis here.

p. 117 near the Avon in Warwickshire: Mrs Gaskell had spent part of her schooldays at the Misses Byerleys' school at Stratford-on-Avon.

p. 117 station to station: these were the military outposts.

p. 118 Chunderabaddad: Indian-sounding name of Mrs Gaskell's own invention.

p. 118 Aga: Turkish for 'Lord', and used by Indians of English civilians as a mark of respect.

p. 118 Lama of Thibet: reference to the high-ranking leader of the Buddhist religion in Tibet.

p. 119 *pièce de résistance*: most important or remarkable characteristic.

p. 119 Dickens ... every man took the tune he knew best: another reference to *The Pickwick Papers*, here Chapter 32. Jack Hopkins sings ' "The King, God bless him", which he sang as loud as he could, to a novel air, compounded of "The Bay of Biscay" and "A Frog he would". The chorus was of the essence of the song; and, as each gentleman sang it to the tune he knew best, the effect was very striking indeed.'

p. 120 the Veiled Prophet in *Lalla Rookh*: the first part of *Lalla Rookh* (1817) by the Irish writer Thomas Moore (1779–1852) is headed 'The Veiled Prophet of Khorassan': he is revealed as 'the Prophet-Chief/The Great Mokanna' (ll.8–9).

p. 120 Rowland's Kalydor: popular cosmetic of the time, used on the face.

p. 120 Peruvian bonds: i.e., bonds or vouchers issued in exchange for money which had been loaned to the Peruvian Government: presumably a form of security.

p. 120 Wombwell came to Cranford: see note on Wombwell p. 87.

p. 120 'surveying mankind from China to Peru': much quoted line from Dr Johnson's 'The Vanity of Human Wishes' – 'Let Observation with extensive view/Survey mankind from China to Peru'.

p. 122 'Tibbie Fowler': identified by Watson as a traditional Scots song, published in 1796.

p. 123 *mésalliance*: a marriage with someone thought to be of a lower social position.

p. 124 her Order: i.e., rank, status in society.

p. 124 and merinoes and beavers: Spanish fine wool and a heavy woollen cloth like beaver fur.

p. 125 the Queen of Spain's legs: both Watson and Keating give the source as Madame d'Aulnoy's *Memoires de la Cour d'Espagne* (1692). The implication is the observance of current etiquette – not mentioning something until it is permitted to do so.

p. 127 welly stawed: nearly finished. The implication is that he is offered so much that he can't take it.

p. 127 wanted stirring: needed rousing up.

p. 128 steal: place covertly.

p. 130 pivotted: unusual usage, presumably meaning that they turned this way and that in trying to be helpful.

p. 130 green tea: tea made from leaves dried by steam and not fermented.

p. 131 Dang it: an expression of disgust or despair.

p. 132 do on: i.e., make do.

p. 137 the Rubric: Mrs Gaskell is undoubtedly referring to the direction for the conduct of divine service in the liturgy: generally it means a 'heading'.

p. 137 the Ganges: the great sacred river of India whose waters have the power to cleanse all sin.

p. 138 serve Mammon: see particularly Matthew 6:24 – 'No servant can be the slave of two masters . . . You cannot serve God and Money.'

p. 139 *'Ah! vous dirai-je, maman?'*: a French song current in England by the end of the eighteenth century – 'Ah, what shall I say to you, mama?'

p. 140 the loyal wool-work: Watson identifies this as being the form of worsted work popular until the late 1820s, but out of date by the 1840s.

p. 140 the Black Art: black magic, emanating from the Devil.

p. 141 *couchant*: at rest, lying.

p. 142 East India Tea Company: founded in 1600. Its long lease of power came to an end in 1858: its monopoly had already been greatly reduced in 1834.

p. 144 conformable: Jem probably means here 'in an agreeable or proper way'.

p. 145 chiffonier: small cupboard with a sideboard top.

p. 150 the cold lion sliced and fried: the remains of the specially made pudding served again.

p. 152 comfits: sugar-coated sweets.

p. 154 cabalistic inscriptions all over them: reference to the writing, presumably in Chinese, on the tea-chests which are described in Chapter 8. 'Cabalistic' derives from the mystical Jewish tradition. This is Mrs Gaskell once more maintaining her ironic tone.

p. 156 train oil: oil from the whale, so named from the Dutch word 'traen'.

p. 157 the Old Hundredth: the hymn tune which is based on the 100th Psalm, hence its name.

p. 158 winged my shaft ... her own plumage: i.e., used her own arguments against her.

p. 162 stories that sounded so very much like Baron Munchausen's: Baron Munchausen (1720–97) was a German soldier who published a number of richly embroidered and marvellous stories. They were first published in English as *Baron Munchausen's Narrative of his Marvellous Travels and Campaigns in Russia* (1785).

p. 162 the siege of Rangoon: Rangoon was captured during the first Burmese War in 1826.

p. 163 a Nabob: at the time, one returning from India or the East, having made a fortune.

p. 164 Sindbad the sailor: whose stories comprise seven voyages in the *Arabian Nights*.

p. 164 the Father of the Faithful: Watson makes a case for this being Abraham, citing Galatians 3:6–9 and Romans 4:11.

p. 166 negus: hot wine and water, with sugar, lemon and spice, named after its inventor Colonel Negus, who died in 1732.

p. 168 the King of Delhi, the Rajah of Oude: large claims, using the capital of India and one of its provinces as (false) advertising. But remember that Peter is orchestrating this, and that it is his joke.

p. 169 **the Preston Guild**: a guild of merchants whose charter dates back to the early fourteenth century. Miss Matty obviously went to one of their festivals, which were held once in five years.

Mr Harrison's Confessions

Where a note is derived from Edgar Wright's edition of *My Lady Ludlow and Other Stories* (World's Classics, 1989) an acknowledgement is given.

p. 187 **Guy's**: the celebrated teaching hospital in London named after its founder Thomas Guy (1644–1724) in 1722.

p. 188 **Duncombe**: the Knutsford of Mrs Gaskell's childhood, the basis for Cranford.

p. 189 **Mayence**: i.e., Mainz, on the Rhine, one of the oldest cities in Germany.

p. 189 **bimbomming**: note the superb onomatopoeic effect of this word.

p. 190 **recruit me**: i.e., set me up again, give me back my strength.

p. 191 **Hessian boots**: as described here, high boots worn by Hessian (German) soldiers of the period.

p. 191 **jemmy**: dandified, smart, neat (the word 'dandy' is used in the previous sentence).

p. 192 *in loco parentis*: (standing) in the place of a parent (to).

p. 192 **Galen or Hippocrates**: the first the Greek physician, one of the founders of medicine (131–201), the second the father of medicine, born 460BC.

p. 193 **Sir Astley Cooper**: the latter (1768–1841) is the English surgeon, born in Norfolk, who had a specialized knowledge of anatomy.

p. 194 **Sir Robert Peel**: (1788–1850), Tory statesman who changed his views and supported Catholic Emancipation in 1829 and the repeal of the Corn Laws in 1846.

p. 195 **Apollo**: one of the principal Greek gods, son of Zeus and Leto, identified with the sun, and inspirational in art, poetry and, appropriately here, medicine.

p. 195 **Æsculapius**: son of Apollo, famed for his healing qualities.

p. 195 **fal-lals**: i.e., ostentatious decoration.

p. 195 *outré*: indecorous, beyond what is acceptable or conventional.

p. 196 Sir Everard Home: (1756–1832), eminent surgeon (Wright).

p. 196 Abernethy: John Abernethy (1764–1831), surgeon and professor at St Bartholomew's Hospital (Wright).

p. 197 Solomon's seal: plants having arching stems and drooping green/white flowers.

p. 198 jargonelle: early ripening variety.

p. 199 flag-floor: i.e. made of rectangular stone blocks.

p. 200 Miss Austen, Dickens, and Thackeray: major novelists. Jane Austen (1775–1817), whose ironic narrative mode in some ways anticipates Mrs Gaskell's. Dickens (1812–1870), her great contemporary to whose journal she contributed *Cranford* and *North and South* among others: and W. M. Thackeray (1811–63), who had recently achieved his major triumph with *Vanity Fair* (1848).

p. 200 black crape haycock: a somewhat grotesque emphasis, a haycock being a heap of hay arranged like a cone.

p. 201 dognoses: diagnoses.

p. 201 the *Lancet*: the medical journal which acts as a commentary on the achievements and discoveries of the medical profession, founded in 1823.

p. 204 two chaises and the spring-cart: varieties of light, horse-drawn vehicles.

p. 204 bodkin: here, the third person crammed in on a seat for two, compared to the thinness of a needle.

p. 205 *infra dig*: beneath one's dignity.

p. 207 merry-thought: wishbone.

p. 208 German canon ... 'O wie wohl ist mir am Abend': part-song, 'Oh, how well I am in the evening'.

p. 209 Liebig: celebrated German chemist (1803–73).

p. 211 croup: inflammation of the larynx in children, producing a hard cough and attendant breathing difficulties; a major killer in the nineteenth century and earlier.

p. 213 Sleep, baby, sleep!: Wright says that the translation is by the American Elizabeth Payson Prentiss (1818–78).

p. 214 Peculiar people ... made dear: I have been unable to trace this.

p. 214 hyoscyamus: poisonous herbaceous plant from which a narcotic drug is obtained.

p. 215 conversation cards: see note on *Cranford* p. 81.

p. 215 'wersh': having insufficient salt, tasteless.

p. 216 like Stentor's: Stentor was the Greek herald with the loud voice described by Homer in the *Iliad*, hence the adjective 'stentorian'.

p. 216 *forte*: here, strong, powerful. See, for different usage, final note to *Cranford*, p. 11.

p. 216 the Mermaid: the celebrated tavern where poets gathered to talk and drink from the time of Shakespeare onwards.

p. 216 taken up: arrested.

p. 217 deepest dog: most cunning person.

p. 218 *mal-àpropos*: inappropriate, unsuitable.

p. 219 Venus: the Roman goddess of wedded love.

p. 219 would it minister to a heart diseased?: As Wright points out, this is an echo of *Macbeth* V.iii.40 – 'Canst thou not minister to a mind diseased?'

p. 219 sedan: chair slung on horizontal poles and carried by two men, in which the person was carried.

p. 219 mousing: moving stealthily, quickly.

p. 220 Newgate: degrading London prison dating back to 1218. It was destroyed by the Great Fire of 1666, rebuilt in 1770, destroyed in 1904, the Central Criminal Court being built on its site.

p. 220 Don Quixote: see second note on *Cranford* p. 33.

p. 220 *Mens conscia recti*: a mind aware of the right (Virgil, *Aeneid* I, 604).

p. 222 lubberly: clumsy.

p. 223 'hodie': daily (i.e., to be taken every day according to the prescription).

p. 224 Consols: loans to the Government at different times and at different rates which are consolidated into one common loan.

p. 225 Corazza shirts: Wright points out that 'corazza' is the Italian for 'cuirass', and that this type of shirt reflects the interest in England in things Italian as the struggle for Italian independence gained pace.

p. 229 *in toto*: completely.

p. 229 lock-jaw: tetanus, the variety causing the jaw to remain closed or clamped.

p. 231 mortification ... mortified: there is much play on the word, a punning sequence which reflects Mrs Gaskell's natural humour (and Harrison's as well).

p. 231 cleanly: unusual word, here meaning (not) habitually clean.

p. 232 'like winds in summer sighing': untraced.

p. 233 lo'ed: loved.

p. 239 hand-screen: see note on *Cranford* p. 29.

p. 244 *contretemps*: awkward occurrence.

p. 247 *vi et armis*: by force and arms.

p. 247 Paris ... apple of discord: Paris was the son of Priam and Hecuba who was called upon to judge between Athena, Hera and Aphrodite over the disputed golden apple. He was in favour of Aphrodite. Later Paris ran off with Helen, the wife of Menelaus, and thus started the Trojan War.

p. 247 a fool's cap: i.e., as worn by a clown or jester.

p. 248 put about: i.e., upset.

p. 251 the Peace Society: mounted a campaign for peace through large meetings and demonstrations in Manchester and Birmingham, as well as London, from 1843 onwards.

p. 251 *à propos*: with relation or reference to.

p. 252 a gay Lothario: a loose-living character in Nicholas Rowe's play *The Fair Penitent* (1703), now proverbial for a lover ('gay' is not meant in its modern connotation, but merely suggests light-heartedness, lack of moral responsibility.)

p. 252 Crabbe: the name is perhaps significantly chosen, for Mrs Gaskell's first writings in verse, 'Sketches Among the Poor', were after the manner of George Crabbe (1754–1832), called by Byron 'though nature's sternest painter, yet the best'.

p. 253 'What if, in this world ... lies dead: untraced.

p. 253 the passing bell: i.e., which is tolled at a funeral.

p. 255 the halt: the crippled.

p. 256 'Vanity Fair': see note p. 200.

p. 256 Jenny Lind ... I'm a nightingale: Jenny Lind (1820–87), the internationally famous soprano who was known as the 'Swedish nightingale'.

p. 258 young Hoggins: note the name, also used in *Cranford*.

p. 259 He won golden opinions: another echo of *Macbeth*: 'I have bought/Golden opinions from all sorts of people . . .' (I.vii.32–3).

ELIZABETH GASKELL AND HER CRITICS

The following extracts are from letters written by Charlotte Brontë to Mrs Gaskell. Charlotte fascinated the author of *Cranford* who, later, at the instigation of Charlotte's father, the Revd. Patrick Brontë, was to write her life (1857). The third extract below relates to the volume edition, the others to the serial publication. Charlotte's striking independence of tone and attitude is at once apparent.

(i) 22 January 1851:

I told you that book opened like a daisy; I now tell you it finished like a herb – a balsamic herb with healing in its leaves. That small volume has beauty for commencement, gathers power in progress, and closes in pathos; no thought can be truer than that of Mrs Brown's persistent, irrational but more touching partiality for her son. The little story is fresh, natural, religious; no more need be said.

(ii) 22 May 1852:

I read 'Visiting at Cranford' with that sort of pleasure which seems always too brief in its duration: I wished the paper had been twice as long. Mr Thackeray ought to take a series of articles such as these – retire with them to his chamber, put himself to bed, and lie there – till he had learnt by diligent study how to be satirical without being exquisitely bitter. Satirical you are – however; I believe a little more so than you think.

(iii) 9 July 1853:

I have read it over twice; once to myself, and once aloud to my Father. I find it pleasurable reading – graphic, pithy, penetrating, shrewd, yet kind and indulgent.

A thought occurs to me. Do you – who have so many friends, so large a circle of acquaintance – find it easy, when you sit down to write – to isolate yourself from all those ties and their sweet associations – as to be quite *your own woman* – uninfluenced, unswayed by the consciousness of how your work may affect other minds – what blame, what sympathy it may call forth? Does no luminous cloud ever come between you and the severe Truth – as you know it in your own secret and clear-seeing Soul? In a word, are you never tempted to make your characters more amiable than the life – by the inclination to assimilate your thoughts to the thoughts of those who always *feel* kindly, but sometimes fail to *see* justly? Don't answer this question. It is not intended to be answered.

(From *Elizabeth Gaskell: The Critical Heritage*, ed., Angus Easson, Routledge, 1991, p. 193)

This is an unsigned review of *Cranford* by Henry Fothergill Chorley which appeared in the *Athenaeum*, 25 June 1853. Note the perception of the classic status later achieved by the 'collection of sketches'.

This collection of sketches – making up a little book which should prove a permanent addition to English fiction – originally appeared in *Household Words*. Possibly, it was commenced by accident, rather than on any settled plan; but if this was the case, the author early became alive to the happy thought pervading it; – since she has wrought it out just enough and not too much – so as to produce a picture of manners, motives and feelings which is perfect. Her theme, it is true, has not an iota of romance, or poetry, or heroism in it such as will attract lovers of excitement. There are no wicked and hardened rich people – no eloquent and virtuous paupers – in *Cranford*. The scene is a small drowsy country town, such as will hardly have an existence a quarter of a century hence: the persons are a few foolish and faded gentle-women of limited incomes, moving round the younger daughter of a deceased rector, as central figure – and their gentilities, their sociabilities, their topics, and their panics fill many pages. But the beauty of the book lies in this, – that our author has vindicated the 'soul of goodness' living and breathing and working in an orbit so limited and among beings so inane and so frivolous as those whom she has displayed. Touches of love and kindness, of simple self-sacrifice and of true womanly tenderness, are scattered throughout the record; and with no appeal, and for no applause, but naturally and truthfully just as they are found in the current of real life. Then, there is rare humour in the airs and graces of would-be finery which the half-dozen heroines display, – in their total ignorance of the world, in their complacent credulity, in their irritable curiosity about all that touches matrimony. The main figure, Miss Matilda, is finished with an artist's hand. Her gentleness of heart and depth of affection, her conscientious and dignified sense of right, her perpetual shelter under the precepts and counsels of beloved ones that have gone home before her, – invest the character with an interest which is unique, when her weakness of intellect and narrowness of training are also considered. There is not a single blemish or inconsistency to be pointed out, in short, from first to last; – there is hardly a solitary incident which is not of every-day occurrence – unless it be, the opportune return of Peter in reply to the Cranford Chronicler's letter, – and if this be not permitted, what becomes of the last chapters of 'The Vicar of Wakefield'? – After its kind, this tale cannot be commended too cordially.

(From *Elizabeth Gaskell: The Critical Heritage*, ed., Angus Easson, Routledge, 1991, pp. 194–5)

Here is another contemporary appraisal, a combination of summary and criticism (and praise) from an unsigned review in the *Examiner*, 23 July 1853.

This is not a book to be described or criticised other than by a couple of words of advice – *Read it*. It is a book you should judge for yourself. If we told you it contained a story, that would be hardly true – yet read only a dozen pages, and you are among real people, getting interested about them, affected by what affects them, and as curious to know what will come of it all as if it were an affair of your own. We should mislead you if we said that here is a book remarkable for the finish of its descriptions, the accuracy with which its characters are drawn, the charm which it gives to a variety of natural pictures of life – in short the etc., etc. which mark the good humour and high satisfaction of the critic, quite as much as the particular merits of the writer. The real truth is that *Cranford* contains hardly a bit of formal description from first to last, that not a single person in it is thought worth a page of the regular drawing and colouring which is the novelist's stock in trade, and that of variety it has only as much as a dull little country town might at any time present you, with a parcel of not very wise old maids for its heroines, and, for its catastrophe, the failure of a county bank. But watch the people introduced from chapter to chapter – see them unconsciously describe *themselves* as they reveal their own foibles and vanities – observe, as you get to know them better, what unselfish and solid kindnesses underlie their silly trivial ways – and confess that the writer of this unpretending little volume, with hardly the help of any artifice the novelist most relies upon, and showing you but a group of the most ordinary people surrounded by the commonest occurrences of human life, has yet had the art to interest you as by something of your own experience, a reality you have actually met with, and felt yourself the better for having known. *Cranford* is the most perfect little book of its kind that has been published for many a day.

It is a collection of papers that appeared in Dickens's *Household Words*. Cranford is the name of a small dull sleepy provincial town, all the smaller, duller, and sleepier for the greatness, vivacity, and vigilance of its enterprising neighbour, the busy commercial Drumble, distant only twenty miles on a railroad. Everybody that has got any business in the world of course is off to Drumble, and Cranford is left to a batch of faded old maids and widows, very poor but remarkably genteel, having a thorough distaste for that sour grapes Man, and tolerant only of Mr Hoggins the surgeon and Mr Hayter the rector as corporeal and spiritual necessities. For a chapter or so, indeed, one man does succeed in planting himself at Cranford – and a thoroughly good man he is; but his voice is too large for the rooms, and his ways too broad and hearty for the place, and, though one finds it difficult to read what befalls him with unmoistened eyes, yet it is felt on the whole to be better that he should disappear, no matter by what means . . .

Miss Matilda, or Miss Matty as she is more frequently called, is quite the heroine of the book. Before it ends, we somehow have taken her entirely into our hearts – her and the whole of her little history. She is the younger daughter of the late Rector of Cranford; and what kind of old-world clergyman the late rector was, and how he wooed and married his wife, and of what kind were the joys and sorrows of their quiet English home, and how the two daughters were left lone women at last, at the head of the spinster aristocracy of Cranford, we read over Miss Matty's shoulders one night as she burns her old family letters. It is all a piece of genuine truth – the reflection of a thousand such kind and blameless histories. Miss Matty is living by herself now, for even her sister Deborah is dead; and she has many old-fashioned prejudices, and silly little weaknesses and ways: – but there is such a righteous nature underneath them, such a true and tender heart, such a noble regard for what is just to others at even the cost of injustice to herself – that the impression of all that human goodness making itself felt in such simple, quiet, unromantic guise, has a thoroughly delightful effect. We shall always be pleased to think of Miss Matty Jenkyns . . .

Her adversity is but of brief duration, we are happy to inform the reader. She is still at Cranford, and we hope still visited by that sly and sagacious young lady, 'Mary Smith', whose occasional railway trips from Drumble have led to the pleasant though unauthorised disclosures now made to the world at large. For Miss Mary Smith cannot help revealing not a little of her own character in making so free with the characters of her friends – and a young woman more shrewd or penetrating, sharper in the midst of her indulgence, more critical behind her kindliness, or more knowing under that meek look of unconsciousness she is perpetually putting on, we have not encountered for a very long time. Just take her description of a little party which the aspiring Miss Betsy Barker (retired milliner) was permitted to give to what we may call the Upper House, or House of Ladies, of Cranford . . .

(From *Elizabeth Gaskell: The Critical Heritage*, ed., Angus Easson, Routledge, 1991, pp. 195–7)

A. Stanton Whitfield was a Gaskell enthusiast, but was quick to point out limitations in her work: these might be tested against late twentieth-century appraisals which credit her with a much greater sophistication and literary awareness:

> Someone has said that *Cranford* is without plot, purpose, or melodrama. The papers garnered together under the cherished village-name are not essays. Together they do not make a story. They have no literary derivation in the true sense of that misunderstood term. In them there is the refinement of Addison, with something of the vigour of Swift.
>
> There is a feeling that *Cranford* is a legacy of Miss Austen's sensibility. The Miss Jenkyns are like two of Jane's heroines grown old, and they seem a bit strange in their native surroundings. The sketches also invite comparison with Miss Austen's work because there is the same dramatic tendency in the construction of her writings as in those of Mrs Gaskell, because, in other words, both writers re-create in our minds the incidents they present; to us their pages are not so much descriptions as facts themselves. There the comparison must end, for, in *Cranford*, Mrs Gaskell was a portrayer – not a plotter, and in this respect, with her delicate outlines of personalities, her book seems more akin to the *De Coverley* papers. Somehow the spirit of the eighteenth century haunts *Cranford*; something of 'the elegant shrubbery and the fragrant parterre', but lacking the close atmosphere and the artificial lights. The serenity of Dr Primrose is not unlike that of Miss Matty, and they are both symbols of potential humanity.
>
> Critics have compared *Cranford* to the scenic work of *Our Village*. The present writer has searched Miss Mitford's tedious

pages in vain for a similarity either apparent or real. Miss Mitford was no lover of moonlight; she did not like that 'cold, pale, trembling ray'. Hers was the mirth of content. She was, in Mrs Browning's happy phrase, 'a sort of prose Crabbe in the sun'.

Cranford conjures up other names. Charles Lamb, of course, and the same species of healthful humour, genuine and delightful, is sustained in the *Alhambra* and other writings of Washington Irving. There is a passage in Chapter 11 which calls to mind *The Dream Children* of Elia. It was prompted by the same *human* touch. This same outlook drew Sir Walter Raleigh's attention to the lovable faults of Addison's *Sir Roger*, whose 'virtues may be smiled at as well as praised', a phrase which it would not be inappropriate to steal for either of the Miss Jenkyns.

It is this human element that calls forth our admiration, respect, and love. The utter pettinesses of the provincial life described in *Cranford* are drowned in its wide-embracing humanity. An old-time fragrance emanates from the memory of it; an old-world flavour of lavender, rosemary, and sweet basil mingled with kind and gentle personalities. Just as we solace ourselves with it, so we feel that Mrs Gaskell solaced herself. *Cranford* alone amongst her writings did she re-read, because she was nurtured in the environment of *Cranford*. She captured the spirits of Miss Matty, Miss Pole, and the Hon. Mrs Jamieson as they passed before her. She made her escape into her own true world.

The lack of form in *Cranford*, imposed by the conditions under which it was written as 'papers', is atoned for by its spontaneity; indeed this lack of constraint forges a union of spirit that makes the book one harmonious gesture.

There is a grace of movement and a pleasant flow which is difficult to define. Her delivery is generally so equable that it flows through our ears as the fragrance of lavender passes the nostrils, or the Iris sky-blue meets the eye. Occasionally she jars upon the ear. From Chapter 3 we cite a passage wherein the ambiguous use of a pronoun is decidedly unpleasant.

> I had once or twice tried, on such occasions, to prevail on Miss Matty to stay, and had succeeded in her sister's lifetime. I held up a screen, and did not look, and, as she said, she tried not to make the noise very offensive; but now that she was left alone, she seemed quite horrified when I begged her to remain with me in the warm dining-parlour, and enjoy her orange as she liked best. And so it was in everything. Miss Jenkyns's rules were made more stringent than ever, because the framer of them was gone where there could be no appeal. In all things else Miss Matilda was meek and undecided to a fault. I have heard Fanny turn her round twenty times in a morning about dinner, just as the little hussy chose; and I sometimes fancy

she worked on Miss Matilda's weakness in order to bewilder her, and to make her feel more in the power of her clever servant. I determined that I would not leave her until I had seen what sort of a person Martha was; and, if I found her trustworthy, I would tell her not to trouble her mistress with every little decision.

(From A. Stanton Whitfield: *Mrs Gaskell: Her Life and Work*, Routledge, 1929, pp. 135–9)

Annette B. Hopkins did much in the mid-twentieth century to build Mrs Gaskell's reputation through a detailed attention to her life and the influences which made her. *Cranford* rightfully received special treatment:

John Forster, who wrote Mrs Gaskell enthusiastically on the appearance of nearly every number of *Cranford*, told her some time in 1853: 'They positively grow better and better. I never saw so nice, so exquisite a touch. The little book which collects them will be a "hit" if there be any taste left for that kind of social painting.' He proved himself a true prophet.

The contemporary admirer of *Cranford* who was responsible for starting the book on its way to fame was Dickens. Whether he was familiar with its modest beginnings in *Sartain's Magazine* in 1849 is doubtful. What Mrs Gaskell must have sent in as a new story he accepted in good faith and published in the number of *Household Words* for December 13th, 1851; this became the first two chapters of the novel in book form: 'Our Society' and 'The Captain'. This fact implies no censure of Mrs Gaskell. These chapters show that her old essay, 'The Last Generation in England', was completely made over, with omissions and additions, some of the incidents in the essay being removed to later chapters of the book. It was practically a new story. Indeed, she seems to have forgotten the little sketch altogether, when she wrote Ruskin: 'The beginning of Cranford was one paper in "Household Words", and I never meant to write more . . .'

Much of value in 'The Last Generation in England' the author did not use again. Happily, she retained the incident of the unfortunate cow that fell into a lime pit and lost most of her hair and was compensated by her devoted mistress with grey flannel drawers and waistcoat. When this episode reappears, in *Cranford*, it has gained in dramatic interest from being attached to a definite personality. Miss Betsy Barker and her Alderney are both respected citizens in Cranford society. Another incident fortunately preserved is the strange mishap of what became a famous bit of lace. In the book it belongs to Mrs Forrester, one of the 'poorer ladies', but she still managed to keep up appearances with 'my maid' (actually a little charity-school girl). As an example of the elegant economy practised in Cranford, Mrs Forrester once soaked her piece of fine old lace in a saucer of milk to restore its creamy colour. But leaving the room for an unguarded moment, she returned to find that lace and milk had both disappeared down 'pussy's inside'. Mrs Forrester was a lady of resources, and soon found a way to recover her heirloom. This precious lace whose progress through feline interior was so miraculously stayed, was real lace in more senses than one. Retired forever after from active duty, it became a treasured possession in the Gaskell family, and handed down to the third generation, it has been inspected with awe by the present writer. The tale of the Alderney cow, also, as more than one contemporary testified, was based on an actual incident. Thus did the author glide almost imperceptibly from fact into fiction.

That Mrs Gaskell dipped into her own past for many other details: characters, customs, happenings – the two Jenkyns sisters and their brother Peter who disappeared from home as a boy, to be gone for many years; the eccentric bachelor, Mr Holbrook, the Royal George hotel (described in Chapter 1), with its oak panelled assembly room where Signor Brunoni performed his incredible tricks – the identifying of these details and others – has become the stock-in-trade of many a writer on *Cranford*. It is tempting to trace originals, but more important to realize that whatever the source of her characters the author has here transmuted them with unerring psychological perceptiveness into creatures of the imagination which yet are drawn with a fidelity to truth that raises them to the plane of universal significance.

Dickens received the *Cranford* 'paper', as he called it, with characteristic enthusiasm. One can almost hear his hearty chuckle as his practised eye moved swiftly down the sheets of foolscap covered with Mrs Gaskell's clear, flowing hand. 'I was so delighted with it,' he wrote the author on December 4th, 'that I put it first in the number.' And his subsequent letters referring to *Cranford* during the two years that it ran very irregularly, as a serial, continue in the same complimentary vein. On December 21st he writes her, playfully, of the portion for the second number.

> If you were not the most suspicious of women, always looking for soft sawder in the purest metal of praise, I should call your paper delightful, and touched in the tenderest and most delicate manner. Being what you are, I confine myself to the observation that I have called it A Love Affair at Cranford, and sent it off to the printer.

(From Annette B. Hopkins: *Elizabeth Gaskell: Her Life and Work*, John Lehmann, 1952, pp. 104–5)

The centenary of Mrs Gaskell's death in 1965 saw a reawakening of biographical and critical interest. Arthur Pollard sets out the range of *Cranford* concerns:

> Mrs Forrester, by contrast, is quiet and retiring. It is perhaps of some importance that she lives farthest away, and her housekeeping represents elegant economy on the veriest shoestring in a 'baby-house of a dwelling' and 'one little charity-school maiden' as her domestic staff. In her house, however, there is hospitality and friendship; reference is made to 'extra preparation', and the conversation is lively, even if rather gruesome (the visit takes place during the great robbery panic). This contrasts with Mrs Jamieson's tea-party which is formal and dependent on the whims of the insolent man-servant Mulliner. Mrs Gaskell goes into detail about the perfections of that occasion, the china, the plate, even the thin bread and butter – but there is cream for the dog and milk for the guests; and not until after tea, and then only under the influence of Lady Glenmire, does the occasion 'thaw down'. I have noted Mrs Jamieson's absence from the meeting to assist Miss Matty. On that same occasion Mrs Forrester waited for Mary Smith,

> > The poor old lady trembling all the time as if it were a great crime which she was exposing to daylight, in telling me how very, very little she had to live upon; a confession which she was brought to make from a dread lest we should think that the small contribution named in her paper bore any proportion to her love and regard for Miss Matty.

Not even the humour of *Cranford* is free from pathos, and even the apparently inconsequential story of the cat that swallowed the lace is touched with it, for it is a story told at the grand Mrs Jamieson's by the poor Mrs Forrester, and it relates to the lace she is wearing, 'the sole relic of better days'.

Humour and pathos are subtly intermingled in Mrs Gaskell's treatment of sex in *Cranford*. Both are present, for instance, in Miss Matty's account of her special fear of finding a man under her bed and the ridiculous means – rolling a ball from one side to the other – which she adopted to reassure herself. Sex is an important theme in the book. There is much in the lives of the Cranford spinsters which suggests sexual unfulfilment. They display a mixture of curiosity and fear about men. Captain Brown, and perhaps in some of the implications Surgeon Hoggins, make their world look very trivial. Out of this comes humour, perhaps best of all in Miss Pole's weighty remark: 'My father was a man, and I know the sex pretty well'. There are places in the book's treatment of this theme where pointed contrast is made between the fact that is and the fantasy that might have been, with resultant pathos. Such, for example, is Miss Matty's revelation of her frustrated motherhood-desire. Sometimes, the humour mixes wryly with the pathos, as when she takes to wearing widows' caps after the death of Holbrook. There are contrasts also between Holbrook's and Miss Matty's uncompleted lives and the natural emotional development of the servant Martha and her lover Jem Hearn. It is easy, however, to exaggerate, and even with these latter characters it seems better to indicate their importance in terms of general human kindness rather than in those of a more specialized sexual interpretation. Miss Matty's kindness allows Martha to have her 'follower'; in due time that kindness receives its reward in their provision for her at the time of the catastrophe. To claim more than this is to risk the danger of distortion.

Sex is but one theme; others are class, money, taste, the cramping effects of a small provincial, outdated society. The question of rank and class is centred critically upon Mrs Jamieson. All the behaviour of this self-conscious aristocrat is boorish. Not only does she ignore Mrs Fitz-Adam, but in lesser details also Mrs Gaskell takes care to expose her bad manners – in her late arrival at Betsy Barker's tea-party, her supercilious comments (for example, on seed cake reminding her of scented soap) and her greater concern for her pet-dog Carlo than for her social acquaintances. Mrs Jamieson exploits her rank, and it is therefore appropriate that her relative and social equal, Lady Glenmire, should explode her pretensions. By contrast with Mrs Jamieson, Martha and Jem Hearn show that humanity matters more than class. They show, too, that it matters more than money. Money does matter, even though the Cranford ladies try to ignore this fact. This is one important point in the chapter on Miss Matty's financial ruin. By changing the bad note she both shows that money does matter and yet ignores the fact that it does. Humanity matters more than money. Yet we are never allowed to ignore elegant economy. Financially life is a struggle, but a small income may yet be a happy sufficiency. Miss Matty's candle, reluctantly lighted and early extinguished, is a recurring image to remind us. Even her ultimate happiness is secured on a competency rather than a fortune. 'I don't believe Mr Peter came home from India as rich as a nabob; he even considered himself poor, . . . he had enough to live on "very genteelly" at Cranford; he and Miss Matty together'.

'Genteel' reminds us of standards at Cranford, of matters of taste and etiquette. Everything must be done in the proper way. Appearances must be kept up. Here also Mrs Jamieson's vulgarity is exposed, and never more tellingly than through the insolence of the servant Mulliner who always calls at the front door instead of at the servants' entrance. Mrs Gaskell, however, is for the most part more gentle in her satire on etiquette, as, for instance, in Miss Matty's visit to see the new fashions:

> It is not etiquette to go till after twelve; but then, you see, all Cranford will be there . . . So I thought we would just slip down this morning, soon after breakfast – for I do want half-a-pound of tea.

(From Arthur Pollard: *Mrs Gaskell: Novelist and Biographer*, Manchester University Press, 1965, pp. 80–3)

One of the leading contemporary Gaskell scholars and critics is Angus Easson. In the following extract he reveals some of the particularities of *Cranford*:

> With the second story, Gaskell had needed to reintroduce Mary Smith into Cranford society, a narrator important for the sense of the larger life of Drumble, the pattern of the advancing world, behind which Cranford falls further and further. Even Mary develops, marginally, in her contacts between the two worlds, and she mediates for the reader between his opinions, which she now holds, and Cranford's opinions, which she has shed but does not despise. Mary's observation chronicles the 'history of English domestic life'. Mary had feared her connection with Cranford would cease after Miss Jenkyns's death:

> > at least, that it would have to be kept up by correspondence, which bears much the same relation to personal intercourse that the books of dried plants I sometimes see ('Hortus Siccus', I think they call the thing) do to the living and fresh flowers in the lanes and meadows.

> So Mary may believe, yet Gaskell is able in 'Old Letters' to show a past age brought to light through its correspondence. Old letters may be like dried plants to those that have no key; still, read with memory and feeling they expand out like Japanese flowers into new life. Miss Matty brings out the family letters soon after Holbrook's death, as though reminded of her own mortality and the need for preparation. In her acceptance of her father's, of Deborah's, judgment on Holbrook we may see little more than the burden of the past, of convention. The reading of the letters animates that intermingling, like wheat and tares, of the love and custom which are Miss Matty's life. The ritual springs typically for Gaskell out of physical circumstances: the economy on candles,

the detail of contrivance necessary 'to keep our two candles of the same length, ready to be lighted, and to look as if we burnt two always'. The customs of Cranford are not quaint eccentricities divorced from human nature, but habits linked by past experience to present need. Gaskell uses these quirks to tell the story:

> One night, I remember that this candle economy particularly annoyed me . . . especially as Miss Matty had fallen asleep, and I did not like to stir the fire and run the risk of awakening her; so I could not even sit on the rug, and scorch myself with sewing by firelight, according to my usual custom. I fancied Miss Matty must be dreaming of her early life; for she spoke one or two words in her uneasy sleep bearing reference to persons who were dead long before. When Martha brought in the lighted candle and tea, Miss Matty started into wakefulness, with a strange, bewildered look around, as if we were not the people she expected to see about her. There was a little sad expression that shadowed her face as she recognized me; but immediately afterwards she tried to give me her usual smile. All through tea-time, her talk ran upon the days of her childhood and youth. Perhaps this reminded her of the desirableness of looking over all the old family letters, and destroying such as ought not to be allowed to fall into the hands of strangers; for she had often spoken of the necessity of this task, but had always shrunk from it, with a timid dread of something painful.

The first impression of the letters is sensuous, the smell of Tonquin beans that Mary 'had always noticed . . . about any of the things which had belonged' to Miss Matty's mother. The letters, yellow now with age, have in them 'a vivid and intense sense of the present time', so that Miss Matty's father, the Rector, whom Mary has only known 'from a picture in the dining-parlour, stiff and stately, in a huge full-bottomed wig, with gown, cassock, and bands, and his hand upon a copy of the only sermon he ever published', becomes a lover, wooing his wife with 'short homely sentences, right fresh from the heart', while his bride-to-be is full of clothes, particularly the white 'Paduasoy', which in time is material for a christening robe as marriage directs her from self to a new object of affection in the child. Gaskell never mocks, though she delights in the delicate human comedy; when, for instance, the Rector discovered that dress did mean something to his bride 'and then he sent her a letter, which had evidently accompanied a whole box full of finery . . . This was the first letter, ticketed in a frail delicate hand, "From my dearest John"'. It is human because it is two people coming together in a union where there is an intellectual incompatibility, even an emotional one, and yet which can develop as a working, loving relationship, from the ideal ardour of the Rector, who dominates the early part of the correspondence, to the domestic practicality of his wife, who had workaday qualities that stand the wear of years:

> But this was nothing to a fit of writing classical poetry which soon seized him, in which his Molly figured as 'Maria'. The letter containing the *carmen* was endorsed by her, 'Hebrew verses sent me by my honoured husband. I thowt to have had a letter about killing the pig, but must wait . . .'

Other letters follow – including Miss Jenkyns's own compositions – and Peter begins to emerge. After the strange joke on Deborah, all those years ago, it is Mary who first reads one of the letters returned unopened to his mother, 'and I, a stranger, not born at the time when this occurrence took place, was the one to open it'. So past and present mell together: Mrs Jenkyns speaks to Mary Smith and Gaskell achieves what Southey wished to write, a history of English domestic manners, conveying the strangeness, the otherness of early times and the way such manners were articulated in the frame of human behaviour, in Miss Matty's parents and her lover and the world of candle economy.

The seriousness of *Cranford* lies above all in the episode of Miss Matty's greatest heroism, her insistence that as a shareholder she is responsible for the Town and Country Bank's integrity. She is put to the test partly through that model sister Miss Jenkyns, the investment made at Deborah's insistence against Mary's father's advice. The heroism (the quiet heroism of the sufferer, unperceived as something even required of her; only the observer fully understands the nature of the action) is made more poignant by the pleasure it frustrates, one significantly related back again to Deborah:

> We began to talk of Miss Matty's new silk gown. I discovered that it would be really the first time in her life that she had had to choose anything of consequence for herself: for Miss Jenkyns had always been the more decided character, whatever her taste had been . . .

The choice proves to be one of more consequence than Mary imagined. Miss Matty's qualities are pity and integrity, the heart against the head: 'My dear, I never feel as if my mind was what people call very strong . . . I was very thankful, that I saw my duty this morning, with the poor man standing by me'. So Miss Matty rises to the challenge and sells tea, while Martha precipitates Jem into marriage to help (well that Matty allowed her a follower) and the ladies of Cranford show their kind offices in response to real need (significantly Mrs Jamieson, the most positively dislikeable, is away in Cheltenham). Peter's return, then, after this dismissal of Deborah, is a kind of reward, but not a melodramatic release from misery by a *deus ex machina*. Not only has the possibility of his arrival been rumoured far off, his return does not artificially rescue Miss Matty from the consequences of her action; she has already rescued herself (indeed, she enjoys selling tea) and Peter's return is an emotional rather than material completion – though his sister's financial circumstances certainly improve immensely.

Cranford seems to have passed into folk consciousness. On my first reading, many years ago, I was intrigued to find in the tale of the pedlar's pack a variant of a horror story well known from my grandmother's telling: her version was of a coffin and suspicion was roused by the servant insisting 'I see a grey eye'. Whether they have a common source, I don't know, but the power of both suggests how Gaskell could call on the art of the folk narrator. The book has been reprinted many times and it was Gaskell's own favourite amongst her works.

A curious pendant to Cranford is the short satire, *The Cage at Cranford*, published in *All the Year Round*, 28 November 1863, and set in 1856, by which time Miss Matty on a strict chronology would be in her early seventies. The focus shifts though to Miss Pole and to the 'cage' that Mary Smith has sent from France, in reality the support for the excessive crinoline dresses of the late 1850s and 1860s, but taken literally by Cranford to be a bird cage. Satire on fashion is the main point, and presumably Cranford was a convenient, established milieu (certainly backward in fashions) for the ridicule, where only Fanny the maid, a charity child, recognizes what the object is and she is snubbed for her offered information. The vast crinolines were much mocked (as *Punch* cartoons show), yet despite being the 'ugliest fashion that ever caricatured the human form divine' and symptomatic, as Mme Mohl's biographer saw them, of the general corruption of French society under the Second Empire, and despite Jane Welsh Carlyle's glum reaction to the photograph of a friend, that the 'crinoline quite changes her character and makes her a stranger for me. I want the one that is, as I have always seen her, a sensible girl with no crinoline', no mockery was to remove it and Gaskell's assault remains a good-humoured and ineffective joke.

(From Angus Easson: *Elizabeth Gaskell*, Routledge & Kegan Paul, 1979, pp. 105-8)

So detailed was J. G. Sharps's study of Mrs Gaskell that it failed to meet the centenary in 1965: it appeared in 1970, and is an invaluable full-scale companion to Mrs Gaskell's works:

Possibly Mrs Gaskell was a sort of artistic alchemist: sometimes she produced the pure gold, by fusing into a composite fictional personage traits taken from several different people whom she actually knew, or had known; on other occasions, no doubt, nothing was transmuted. The characters here [*Mr Harrison's Confessions*], however, are not fully developed, and so warrant but a passing glance. Mr Hutton, the vicar, is rather a shadowy figure; nor are most of his family portrayed at length. His son, Walter, does indeed come alive, yet the unfortunate sentimental death-bed scene mars the force of his presentation; Sophy, the vicar's eldest daughter, seen through the infatuated eyes of Mr Harrison, is sufficient for her part. The Bullock family have considerable vitality, especially their head, a solicitor with leanings like Mrs Gaskell's father towards scientific, though not very successful, agriculture. All the medical men are, in their different ways, convincing, as are the ladies of Duncombe.

Since, in *Mr Harrison's Confessions*, Mrs Gaskell's comic gifts bulk large for the first time, although to be sure they were not absent in earlier work, we may consider them in a little detail. 'The tale is', in the opinion of Miss Hopkins, 'pure farce'; but this opinion needs qualification. Certainly one finds many farcical situations: there is the episode where Jack Marshland drinks blackcurrant wine believing it port, his consequential face-pulling being excused on the grounds of a professed teetotalism; there is the scene in which Mr Harrison kneels before Caroline Tomkinson to test a weakness of the heart which proved emotional rather than physical. Nevertheless the story contains more than farce; Miss Hopkins herself goes on, in apparent contradiction, to mention Mrs Gaskell's 'light, satirically humorous tone'. However some of Mrs Gaskell's humour is undeniably a little heavy-handed – the position of Mr Harrison, allegedly engaged to three ladies, none of whom he loved, may have its funny side; but when Mr Morgan is by rumour reputed to be on the point of marriage the reader feels this is too much of a good thing. Yet there is another side. Mrs Gaskell's treatment of Mrs Rose is, for instance, in her best humorous manner. With a smile one recalls that lady looking over her shoulder as she shows her late husband's miniature to Mr Harrison; mixing her medical terms when discussing Brouncker's injuries; holding up a hand-screen in preparation for Mr Harrison's expected proposal.

In her opening chapter Mrs Gaskell skilfully evokes the kindness of Duncombe in a way which also brings out its amusing aspect. As soon as he arrived, enquiries were made concerning Mr Harrison's health, the first to ask being a certain Mrs Munton. Thereupon he beguiled himself by guessing the lady's characteristics from so suggestive a surname; soon after came the Miss Tomkinsons.

> I don't know why, but the Miss Tomkinsons' name had not such a halo about it as Mrs Munton's. Still it was very pretty in the Miss Tomkinsons to send and inquire. I only wished I did not feel so perfectly robust. I was almost ashamed that I could not send word I was quite exhausted by fatigue, and had fainted twice since my arrival. If I had but had a headache, at least! I heaved a deep breath: my chest was in perfect order; I had caught no cold; so I answered again—
> 'Much obliged to the Miss Tomkinsons: I am not much fatigued; tolerably well: my compliments.'

The tone and manner of the above passage are not omnipresent. In the character of Miss Horsman, for example, Mrs Gaskell shows a less genial aspect of Duncombe. Miss Horsman delighted to cast aspersions upon the moral and professional qualities of Mr Harrison. On the other hand ' "she was really kind among the poor" ', although even here ' "she could not help leaving a sting behind her" '. To illustrate further, Mrs Gaskell's treatment of the superficially sweet and sugary Miss Caroline Tomkinson indicates clearly her real disposition: this is done by a typically feminine method, by observing Miss Caroline's behaviour with children (those of the invalid Brouncker).

> Just then the children came in, dirty and unwashed, I have no doubt. And now Miss Caroline's real nature peeped out. She spoke sharply to them, and asked them if they had no manners, little pigs as they were, to come brushing against her silk gown in that way? She sweetened herself again, and was as sugary as love when Miss Tomkinson returned for her . . .

One of the memorable events in *Mr Harrison's Confessions* is the picnic to the nearby old hall. Mrs Chadwick aptly remarks upon the 'choice descriptions of country scenery, showing that Mrs Gaskell must have been a keen observer of nature'; she identifies the hall with Tabley – an identification confirmed by Mrs Gaskell's own account of visits made there. Observation of a different sort is found in Mrs Gaskell's sketch of the townspeople as they waited for the pleasure-seekers to depart; the sense of a 'social occasion' is excellently rendered.

> . . . the sympathetic shopkeepers, standing at their respective doors with their hands in their pockets, had, one and all, their heads turned in the direction from which the carriages (as Mrs Bullock called them) were to come. There was a rumble along the paved street; and the shopkeepers turned and smiled, and bowed their heads congratulatingly to us; all the mothers and all the little children of the place stood clustering round the door to see us set off.

(From J. G. Sharps: *Mrs Gaskell's Observation and Invention: A Study of Her Non-Biographic Works*, Linden Press, 1970, pp. 116–18)

One of the major feminist investigations is by Patsy Stoneman. Note her detailed and fresh focus on Miss Matty:

> Genteel as the code appears, moreover, it is belligerently maintained. The Rev. Jenkyns gives his son a public flogging for insubordination. Miss Jenkyns sees Captain Brown's denigration of Johnson as 'a challenge' and gives a 'finishing blow or two' to her defence. Mrs Jamieson conducts a one-sided 'feud' with Lady Glenmire, supported by 'Mr Mulliner, like a faithful clansman' – the Scottish clans are an extreme example of adversarial government in which disputes are settled by warfare. This belligerence is adopted by Cranford's Amazons as the 'language' of dominance, but they use it to defend a code which defines them as 'relative creatures'.
>
> Dodsworth is thus wrong to take Miss Jenkyns as the feminist focus of the novel. Feminist critics emphasise Cranford's supportive female relationships, and especially Miss Matty, who in many ways epitomises what Noddings calls a feminine ethic. She opposes the competitive commercialism of Drumble, for instance. When the bank fails, her response is not self-interest but 'common honesty' towards the holders of bank-notes and 'sympathy' for the bank directors, to whom, in accordance with Noddings's ethic, she attributes the best of motives (Noddings, 1984: p. 123). She will not start her tea business without making sure that it will not injure the general grocer. The businessman, Mr Smith, ' "wondered how tradespeople were to get on if there was to be a continual consulting of each other's interest, which would put a stop to all competition directly" '. The answer, as Noddings would hope, is that 'her unselfishness and simple sense of justice called out the same good qualities in others'.
>
> Matty is also opposed to 'the strict code of gentility' wherever it threatens personal relationships. She is Peter's confidante in his practical jokes and likens her angry father to King Ahasuerus. She finds a humane reason to visit Mrs Fitz-Adam and disassociates herself from Mrs Jamieson's exclusiveness. Although she is timid at the thought of a burglar, she faces her bankruptcy with quiet courage. Above all, she is loving – a characteristic demonstrated, as so often in Elizabeth Gaskell's stories, by a fondness for nursing babies. When she loses her money, her example calls out the best in all her friends, and in the meeting of ladies which creates a trust fund for her support, we see the idea of a female community in a

very positive light. For these reasons Patricia Wolfe makes Miss Matty her heroine, and Nina Auerbach claims that 'in the verbal and commercial battle of nineteenth-century England, the cooperative female community defeats the warrior world that proclaims itself the real one' (Auerbach, 1978: p. 87).

I would argue, however, that although the 'cooperative female community' is admirable, it is not triumphant. All it can do is to make the best of the little space allowed it. We do no service to women by ignoring the extent to which Miss Matty and the others have been diminished as human beings by the constraints of femininity. Matty herself is feeble and inactive, preferring darkness and often falling asleep. Though barely fifty, she has the senile fragility born of an eventless life. Even in the crisis of her bankruptcy, she 'would timidly have preferred a little more privation to any exertion'. This stasis also characterises Mrs Jamieson, who exhibits 'the wearied manner of the Scandinavian prophetess, – "Leave me, leave me to repose"'. Mrs Jamieson is 'fat and inert' and frequently falls asleep. Miss Matty falls asleep while Mr Holbrook reads a poem, just as the 'infants' Mary Barton and Sylvia Robson do, and is startled by the decisive actions of men – by Peter's flight and Holbrook's journey to Paris. The mere turning of the earth makes her feel 'so tired and dizzy whenever she thought about it'. She is intimidated by male control of language, so that 'words that she would spell quite correctly in her letters to me, became perfect enigmas when she wrote to my father'. As 'we did not read much, or walk much' in Cranford, much ingenuity is needed to find topics of conversation. The proliferation of specialised names of fabrics – 'mousseline-de-laine', 'sarsenet', 'Paduasoy', 'bombazine' – reflects that narrowing preoccupation with dress deplored by Mary Wollstonecraft.

The ignorance of all the Cranford ladies, which appears merely comic in Chapter 1, becomes baffling when Mary Smith tries to get information about Peter's whereabouts through a maze of loosely associated ideas involving the Great Lama of Thibet, the veiled prophet in Lalla Rookh, Rowlands' Kalydor, through llamas to Peruvian bonds and joint-stock banks:

> In vain I put in 'When was it – in what year was it that you heard that Mr Peter was the Great Lama?' They only joined issue to dispute whether llamas were carnivorous animals or not; in which dispute they were not quite on fair grounds, as Mrs Forrester . . . acknowledged that she always confused carnivorous and graminivorous together, just as she did horizontal and perpendicular; but then she apologized for it very prettily, by saying that in her day the only use people made of four-syllabled words was to teach how they should be spelt.

When Miss Matty is faced with penury, her ignorance becomes poignant:

> I thought of all the things by which a woman, past middle age, and with the education common to ladies fifty years ago, could earn or add to a living, without materially losing caste; but at length I put even this last chance to one side, and wondered what in the world Miss Matty could do.

In spite of her dignity and courage and her loving nature, Miss Matty is not a heroine in the sense of being a model for admiration. She is rather a victim of the nineteenth century's systematic infantilisation of women.

(From Patsy Stoneman: *Elizabeth Gaskell*, Key Women Writers series, Harvester Press, 1987, pp. 90–3)

In her recent definitive biographical and critical study Jenny Uglow indicates the important and enduring qualities of *Cranford*. Here is a full consciousness of what I can best describe as Mrs Gaskell's own intense range of awareness in this novel:

> Paternal authority, taken to excess, blights rather than fosters life. Gaskell asks us to look elsewhere for male strength and finds it first in the combination of skill and courage with an underrated 'feminine' capacity to care, a quality which saves lives – as the doctor, Mr Hoggins, despite his vulgar bread and cheese suppers and creaking boots, saves Signor Brunoni, as Captain Brown saves Lord Mauleverer in the wars, nurses his daughter and saves the child at Cranford station, as Peter Jenkyns cures the chief of a Burmese tribe and little Phoebe Brunoni in India. And men have other strengths which the women of Cranford, with their meagre education and sheltered lives, sadly lack. They have a wider knowledge of the globe (about which the ladies are woefully muddled) and a familiarity with learning and literature (the Rector's classics, Mr Holbrook's love of poetry). They bring into the women's enclosed lives a hint of transgressive magic (in Signor Brunoni's tricks, in Peter Jenkyns's traveller's tales). The wider sphere in which they move may embrace war, empire and cut-throat trade, but the men who actually enter Cranford's life – from Captain Brown onwards – have a beneficial effect in prompting the women to modify those rules which have bound as well as supported them.
>
> *Cranford* is not a separatist Utopia, but an appeal *against* separate spheres, an argument for preserving the independence and the precious qualities of this female community, while opening

the gates to the boys who gaze at the flowers through the railings. The model of society which it asks us to consider is one where men and women live together side by side and benefit from both 'masculine' and 'feminine' virtues. It is a model of partnership based not on marriage but on a bond where the balance of power is less unequal, that of brother and sister, reunited – like Matty and Peter Jenkyns – after too long apart. *Cranford* is a rich and rewarding book. Yet its richness is very subtle and its comedy so delicate that it can seem to repudiate analysis as too heavy, a violation of its mood. We are not asked, as we are with Gaskell's serious novels, to think as we read. Instead we are cajoled into acceptance of underlying arguments by our surrender to the absurdity of inconsequential detail and apparently casual or odd conjunctions. The surface of the text lulls, surprises and distracts; it works by sleight of hand, like Signor Brunoni's conjuring. 'Don't you think Mrs Gaskell charming?' Dickens asked Forster in 1852. 'Charm' is a dread word in Gaskell criticism, often used to belittle her achievement, but in this case it is right. The spell the stories cast comes from the telling, the minutely particular creation of a self-contained world.

Cranford constantly undercuts solemnity, its humour resting on an upside-down sense of priorities which endow 'realism' with the unreality, crazy logic, leaping connections and total divorce between language and meaning later found in Lewis Carroll. Miss Matty, who can never remember the difference between astrology and astronomy, *does* believe astrological predictions but tells Mary confidentially that she can *not* believe 'that the earth was moving constantly, and that she would not believe it if she could, it made her feel so tired and dizzy when she thought about it'. Later, desperately trying to pin down a rumour that Peter Jenkyns had somehow become the 'Great Lama' of Tibet, Mary finds herself listening to a dispute as to whether llamas are carnivores . . .

The women have no suspicion that they might be deemed comic or absurd. They cannot see anything wrong, or even at all odd, in their ignorance and in their preoccupation with the concrete and immediate as opposed to the intellectual. The priorities of the everyday can be just as serious – one of the old Rector's high-flown epistles, enclosing a tender Latin lyric, is endorsed in the margin: 'Hebrew verses sent me by my honoured husband. I had thowt to have had a letter about killing the pig, but must wait.'

The technique of juxtaposing the profound to the everyday is brilliantly employed in *Cranford*, both to puncture pretension and to reconcile comic surface with emotional depth. The shock when Peter runs away is felt in the heap of wilting petals, intended for the cowslip wine that his mother will now never make. Martha's sympathy and love for the ruined Miss Matty is expressed not in tearful consolations but in a pudding, and no ordinary pudding at that, but a 'lion *couchant*' with currant eyes, a creation worthy, Matty says in all seriousness, of being kept under a glass shade. She cannot understand why Mary laughs:

> 'I am sure, dear, I have seen uglier things under a glass shade before now,' said she.
> So had I, many a time and oft, and I accordingly composed my countenance (and now I could hardly keep from crying), and we both fell to upon the pudding, which was indeed excellent – only every morsel seemed to choke us, our hearts were so full. (Ch. 14)

The whole story of Matty and Mr Holbrook is cast in this vein. Matty does not meet her old lover after thirty years in a romantic setting but in the shop, where she is choosing silk 'to match a grey and black *mousseline de laine*' and he is asking for woollen gloves. The impact of the encounter is shown simply by the way the silks are forgotten and the gloves unpurchased. When Matty visits his house, Woodley, the site of her youthful hopes, Holbrook tries to express his feelings indirectly through poetry, particularly Tennyson's 'Locksley Hall' (1842), a poem which Gaskell does not quote, but which her readers would associate with lost love and youth, with the rejection of modernity, commerce, war and class violence, and also with a bitter taunt against women's inconstancy:

> I am shamed thro' all my nature to have loved so slight a thing
>
> Weakness to be wroth with weakness! woman's pleasure, woman's pain—
> Nature made them blinder motions bounded in a shallower brain;
>
> Woman is the lesser man, and all thy passions, matched with mine,
> Are as moonlight unto sunlight, and as water unto wine—.

Matty and Miss Pole, however, are unlikely to hear this message:

> nothing would serve him but he must read us the poems he had been speaking of; and Miss Pole encouraged him in his proposal, I thought, because she wished me to hear his beautiful reading, of which she had boasted; but she afterwards said it was because she had got to a difficult part of her crochet, and wanted to count her stitches without having to talk. Whatever he had proposed would have been right to Miss Matty; although she did fall sound asleep within five minutes after he had begun a long poem called 'Locksley Hall', and had a comfortable nap, unobserved, till he ended; when the cessation of his voice wakened her up, and she said, feeling that something was expected, and that Miss Pole was counting—
> 'What a pretty book!' (Ch. 4)

A few days later, fired by youthful vigour, Mr Holbrook sets off to Paris. Before leaving he gives Matty the book she had admired; its contents, its author, are still a blank to her.

> And he was gone. But he had given her a book, and he had called her Matty, just as he used to do thirty years ago.
> 'I wish he would not go to Paris,' said Miss Matilda anxiously. 'I don't believe frogs will agree with him; he used to have to be very careful of what he ate, which was curious in so strong-looking a young man.' (Ch. 4)

It is the last time they meet. When Mr Holbrook dies on his return from France, Matty's unspoken grief is expressed only by that most Cranfordian object, a new bonnet. But as she silently reviews that lost opportunity of love, she decides to overturn one of her deepest ingrained codes, inherited from Deborah, and suggests that she *might* allow her maid Martha a follower. The all too real present springs up to replace the past: 'Please, Ma'am, here's Jem Hearn, and he's a joiner, making three-and-sixpence a day, and six foot one in his stocking feet.' 'Though Miss Matty was startled,' the story concludes, 'she submitted to Fate and Love.'

From Jenny Uglow: *Elizabeth Gaskell: A Habit of Stories*, Faber & Faber, 1993, pp. 288–91)

SUGGESTIONS FOR FURTHER READING

Biography and Criticism

There has been considerable treatment of Mrs Gaskell in depth over the last twenty years or so. The following is a selection merely, with brief evaluative comment, with one or two early studies which have some biographical or critical significance.

George F. Payne, *Mrs Gaskell and Knutsford* (Manchester, Clarkson and Griffiths, 1905). Source book of locations, history and other identifications. Interesting photographs.

A. Stanton Whitfield, *Mrs Gaskell: Her Life and Work* (Routledge, 1929). Rambling, but with some insights.

A. B. Hopkins, *Elizabeth Gaskell: Her Life and Work* (John Lehmann, 1952). Intelligent appraisal before the real interest started, well-researched and documented, with positive insights.

J. G. Sharps, *Mrs Gaskell's Observation and Invention: A Study of Her Non-Biographic Works* (Linden Press, 1970). A must for the Gaskell enthusiast. Introductions to each of the works, with biographical and critical information, superbly researched: a mass of detail which makes it the complete companion to Gaskell studies.

Winifred Gérin, *Elizabeth Gaskell: a Biography* (Oxford University Press, 1976). A good, well-written life.

Arthur Pollard, *Mrs Gaskell: Novelist and Biographer* (Manchester University Press, 1965). Excellent chapter on *Cranford*, pp. 62-85).

Angus Easson, *Elizabeth Gaskell* (Routledge & Kegan Paul, 1979). Wide-ranging critical investigation, particularly good on the shorter works.

Patsy Stoneman, *Eizabeth Gaskell* (Harvester Press, Key Women Writers series, 1987). Mrs Gaskell seen in the light of feminist theory, provocative and stimulating.

Angus Easson ed., *Elizabeth Gaskell: The Critical Heritage* (Routledge, 1991). A selection of contemporary reviews and judgments, but also a very useful extension of these in the form of comments and opinions up to 1910.

Letters

J. A. V. Chapple and A. Pollard eds, *The Letters of Mrs Gaskell* (Manchester University Press, 1966). The best possible introduction to Mrs Gaskell, showing her primarily in her domestic situation with her family worries and concerns, and her emergence as a writer.

J. A. V. Chapple with J. G. Sharps, *Elizabeth Gaskell: A Portrait in Letters* (Manchester University Press, 1980). As above, stimulating, delightful.

The Gaskell Society (founded 1985) produces a *Newsletter* and *The Gaskell Society Journal*, both of which are invaluable for students and enthusiasts of Mrs Gaskell.

TEXT SUMMARIES

Cranford

Chapter 1: Our Society
Cranford – predominance of women – 'Elegant economy' – impact of Captain Brown – his family – Cranford parties – literary disagreement.

Chapter 2: The Captain
Miss Brown's illness – the Captain and Miss Jenkyns – later return of narrator – death of the Captain – death of Miss Brown – arrival of Major Gordon – look into future with Miss Jessie happily married.

Chapter 3: A Love Affair of Long Ago
Miss Jenkyns's death – Miss Matty afterwards – servants and followers – Major Jenkyns's visit – Miss Matty's past romance – meeting with Mr Holbrook.

Chapter 4: A Visit to an Old Bachelor
Mr Holbrook's invitation – the visit described – his literary tastes – his reading – his intention to visit Paris – Miss Pole brings news of his death – Miss Matty and 'widowhood' – her allowing Martha a follower.

Chapter 5: Old Letters
The economy over candles – bundles of old letters examined – Miss Matty's parents – Miss Jenkyns's letters – past scare of French invasion.

Chapter 6: Poor Peter
Parental ambitions for Peter – his range of jokes – his dressing up – flogged by the Rector – runs away – sad aftermath – the Rector's repentance – Peter leaves country – mother dies – Deborah looks after Rector – Peter's one return – switch to Martha's follower.

Chapter 7: Visiting
Cranford society lines defined – the visit to Miss Barker – tea, cards, cherry brandy – Mrs Jamieson gives the news of Lady Glenmire's forthcoming visit.

Chapter 8: 'Your Ladyship'
Modes of address – Mrs Jamieson's snobbery – reactions – Lady Glenmire described – the meeting – the indolence of Mr Mulliner – the down-to-earth nature of Lady Glenmire – the tea itself.

Chapter 9: Signor Brunoni
Miss Smith returns after visit home – Miss Pole encounters 'Signor Brunoni' – the evening entertainment – Signor Brunoni's tricks – Miss Pole's discomfort – Mr Hayter and the boys.

Chapter 10: The Panic
Rumours of robberies – Miss Pole and her exaggerations – Mrs Jamieson's house 'attacked' – different reactions of Mulliner and Lady Glenmire – the death of Carlo – Miss Pole's adventure – 'ghosts'.

Chapter 11: Samuel Brown
Another adventure for Miss Pole – Hoggins attends Signor Brunoni – his reduced state – reminiscences of Miss Matty – her dream child – Mrs Brown's recollections of India – kindness of the Aga Jenkyns – speculation re 'poor Peter'.

Chapter 12: Engaged to be Married!
Breathless arrival of Miss Pole – rumours that Mr Hoggins is to marry Lady Glenmire – various reactions – Miss Matty rather upset – local judgment in abeyance.

Chapter 13: Stopped Payment
Miss Matty's letter from Town and County Bank – visit to Johnson's shop – Miss Matty's generous action – her revelations of what she stands to lose – Mary Smith writes to the Aga Jenkyns – Miss Matty ruined – her concern for Martha.

Chapter 14: Friends in Need
Martha and the pudding – plans for economies – Miss Matty to sell tea – Jem and Martha to marry – Miss Matty to lodge with them – Miss Pole organises ladies' committee to help – individual sacrifices and financial straits – the tea idea adopted.

Chapter 15: A Happy Return
Miss Matty's sale – return of the Hogginses – Miss Matty's way of life – Martha's baby – Miss Matty's reaction – return of poor Peter – his being reunited with Miss Matty – their long talks – Peter's tall traveller's tales.

Chapter 16: Peace to Cranford
Peter a Cranford favourite – his jokes, party in his honour – his reminiscences about Holbrook – the Jamieson-Hoggins quarrel – the fear that Peter will marry Mrs Jamieson – unfounded? – the return of the Gordons – Peter's jokes continue – social nature of the town stressed.

Mr Harrison's Confessions

Chapter 1
Narrator tells of his first medical appointment – Mr Morgan's partner in Duncombe – his finding lodgings – contrast with London – Harrison's vanity.

Chapter 2
A round of visits – Harrison shown off socially – the number of women patients – name-dropping – Morgan's advice on behaviour.

Chapter 3
Harrison meets Sophy, the Vicar's daughter – he is much taken with her.

Chapter 4
Parties in his honour – takes house – Mrs Rose housekeeper – offers to help him – he is embarrassed.

Chapter 5
The Bullocks' picnic – Sophy and little Walter – detail on the visit to the old hall – Harrison frustrated because he longs to be with Sophy.

Chapter 6
Takes care of Miss Horsman and Miss Bullock – Sophy protects Walter against the fog – Mrs Rose says she will go into society.

Chapter 7
Walter has croup – dies despite treatment – Sophy brave in this adversity.

Chapter 8
Vicar's grief – arrival of Jack Marshland – his joke about Harrison's arrest – Jack causes him further embarrassment – Jack drinks blackcurrant vinegar in error.

Chapter 9
Jack tells how he has misrepresented Frank (Harrison) – mocks his 'doctorly' behaviour – Mr Morgan put out by rumours that Frank has been in Newgate.

Chapter 10
Harrison's sympathy for Sophy.

Chapter 11
The Bullocks' dinner – the attempts to bring Harrison and Miss Bullock together – discussions with Mr Bullock on scientific matters.

Chapter 12
Meeting with Miss Horsman – he is probed about the Bullock dinner –
Harrison absorbed with thinking of Sophy.

Chapter 13
Respect for Mrs Rose – Miss Caroline Tomkinson's heart – Miss
Tyrrell's throat gives cause for concern.

Chapter 14
Harrison's own legacy – sends camellias to Sophy – John Brouncker's
accident – fears re amputation – Harrison saves Brouncker's arm.

Chapter 15
The sale at Ashmeadow – the auctioneer's cunning – Harrison buys
table for the future.

Chapter 16
Rumours about the death of Brouncker – they are not true.

Chapter 17
Mrs Munton's visit – more rumours – Harrison kind to Mrs Rose –
she seems to be regarding him tenderly.

Chapter 18
Harrison 'congratulated' by Miss Horsman – Miss Tomkinson says he
has been remiss about Miss Caroline – has let Caroline down –
Harrison a little bewildered.

Chapter 19
Mrs Rose affects to believe that Harrison loves her.

Chapter 20
Mr Bullock asks him about his affair with Mrs Rose – says he has
misled Miss Bullock – Harrison insists that he is engaged to no one.

Chapter 21
Mr Morgan accuses him of trifling with Miss Caroline's affections –
Harrison nearly confides in him – Morgan himself seems frightened by
rumours which concern him too.

Chapter 22
Harrison gets note from Morgan to say he has gone to Paris.

Chapter 23
Harrison meets Miss Bullock – the latter says her mother wants to
marry her off – Harrison tells her of his attachment to Sophy.

Chapter 24
Harrison learns that Sophy has been dancing with officers.

Chapter 25
Harrison's practice falling off because of rumours – Sophy's father distant to him.

Chapter 26
Sophy comes home ill – Morgan attends her – Harrison obtains supposedly dangerous prescription for her.

Chapter 27
Vicar still distant – prescription to be tried.

Chapter 28
Sophy saved by the medicine.

Chapter 29
Jack returns – further disturbance.

Chapter 30
Harrison sees Sophy – Morgan arranges to marry Mrs Rose – Caroline elopes with young Hoggins – Miss Tomkinson apologises.

Chapter 31
The marriage of Harrison and Sophy – Jack is best man.

ACKNOWLEDGEMENTS

The editor and publishers wish to thank the following for permission to use copyright material:

Centaur Press for material from J. G. Sharps's, *Mrs Gaskell's Observation and Invention: A Study of Her Non-Biographic Works*, 1970, pp. 116–18;

Faber & Faber Ltd. for material from Jenny Uglow, *Elizabeth Gaskell: A Habit of Stories*, 1993;

Harvester Wheatsheaf and Indiana University Press for material from Patsy Stoneman, *Elizabeth Gaskell*, Key Women Writers series, 1987, pp. 90–3;

Routledge for material from Angus Easson, *Elizabeth Gaskell*, Routledge & Kegan Paul, 1979, pp. 105–8;

Every effort has been made to trace all the copyright holders but if any have been inadvertently overlooked the publishers will be pleased to make the necessary arrangement at the first opportunity.

CLASSIC FICTION
IN EVERYMAN

A SELECTION

Frankenstein
MARY SHELLEY
A masterpiece of Gothic terror in its original 1818 version **£3.99**

Dracula
BRAM STOKER
One of the best known horror stories in the world **£3.99**

The Diary of A Nobody
GEORGE AND WEEDON GROSSMITH
A hilarious account of suburban life in Edwardian London **£4.99**

Some Experiences and Further Experiences of an Irish R. M.
SOMERVILLE AND ROSS
Gems of comic exuberance and improvisation **£4.50**

Three Men in a Boat
JEROME K. JEROME
English humour at its best **£2.99**

Twenty Thousand Leagues under the Sea
JULES VERNE
Scientific fact combines with fantasy in this prophetic tale of underwater adventure **£4.99**

The Best of Father Brown
G. K. CHESTERTON
An irresistible selection of crime stories – unique to Everyman **£4.99**

The Collected Raffles
E. W. HORNUNG
Dashing exploits from the most glamorous figure in crime fiction **£4.99**

£5.99

CLASSIC NOVELS
IN EVERYMAN

A SELECTION

The Way of All Flesh
SAMUEL BUTLER
A savagely funny odyssey from joy-
less duty to unbridled liberalism **£4.99**

Born in Exile
GEORGE GISSING
A rationalist's progress towards love
and compromise in class-ridden
Victorian England **£4.99**

David Copperfield
CHARLES DICKENS
One of Dickens's best-loved novels,
brimming with humour **£3.99**

The Last Chronicle of Barset
ANTHONY TROLLOPE
Trollope's magnificent conclusion
to his Barsetshire novels **£4.99**

He Knew He Was Right
ANTHONY TROLLOPE
Sexual jealousy, money and
women's rights within marriage –
a novel ahead of its time **£6.99**

Tess of the D'Urbervilles
THOMAS HARDY
The powerful, poetic classic of
wronged innocence **£3.99**

Tom Jones
HENRY FIELDING
The wayward adventures of one of
literatures most likeable heroes
£5.99

Wuthering Heights
and Poems
EMILY BRONTË
A powerful work of genius – one of
the great masterpieces of literature
£3.50

The Master of Ballantrae
and Weir of Hermiston
R. L. STEVENSON
Together in one volume, two great
novels of high adventure and family
conflict **£4.99**

£5.99

DRAMA
IN EVERYMAN

A SELECTION

Everyman and Medieval Miracle Plays
EDITED BY A. C. CAWLEY
A selection of the most popular medieval plays **£3.99**

Complete Plays and Poems
CHRISTOPHER MARLOWE
The complete works of this fascinating Elizabethan in one volume **£5.99**

Complete Poems and Plays
ROCHESTER
The most sexually explicit – and strikingly modern – writing of the seventeenth century **£6.99**

Restoration Plays
Five comedies and two tragedies representing the best of the Restoration stage **£7.99**

Female Playwrights of the Restoration: Five Comedies
Rediscovered literary treasures in a unique selection **£5.99**

Poems and Plays
OLIVER GOLDSMITH
The most complete edition of Goldsmith available **£4.99**

Plays, Poems and Prose
J. M. SYNGE
The most complete edition of Synge available **£6.99**

Plays, Prose Writings and Poems
OSCAR WILDE
The full force of Wilde's wit in one volume **£4.99**

A Doll's House/The Lady from the Sea/The Wild Duck
HENRIK IBSEN
A popular selection of Ibsen's major plays **£4.99**

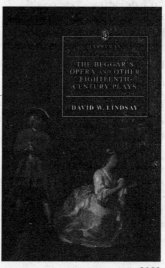

£6.99

AVAILABILITY

All books are available from your local bookshop or direct from
**Littlehampton Book Services Cash Sales, 14 Eldon Way, Lineside Estate,
Littlehampton, West Sussex BN17 7HE.** PRICES ARE SUBJECT TO CHANGE.

To order any of the books, please enclose a cheque (in £ sterling) made payable to
Littlehampton Book Services, or phone your order through with credit card details (Access,
Visa or Mastercard) on 0903 721596 (24 hour answering service) stating card number and
expiry date. Please add £1.25 for package and postage to the total value of your order.

In the USA, for further information and a complete catalogue call 1-800-526-2778.

POETRY
IN EVERYMAN

A SELECTION

Silver Poets of the Sixteenth Century

EDITED BY

DOUGLAS BROOKS-DAVIES
A new edition of this famous
Everyman collection **£6.99**

Complete Poems

JOHN DONNE
The father of metaphysical verse in
this highly-acclaimed edition **£6.99**

Complete English Poems, Of Education, Areopagitica

JOHN MILTON
An excellent introduction to
Milton's poetry and prose **£6.99**

Selected Poems

JOHN DRYDEN
A poet's portrait of Restoration
England **£4.99**

Selected Poems and Prose

PERCY BYSSHE SHELLEY
'The essential Shelley' in one
volume **£3.50**

Women Romantic Poets 1780-1830: An Anthology

Hidden talent from the Romantic era
rediscovered **£5.99**

Poems in Scots and English

ROBERT BURNS
The best of Scotland's greatest lyric
poet **£4.99**

Selected Poems

D. H. LAWRENCE
A new, authoritative selection
spanning the whole of Lawrence's
literary career **£4.99**

The Poems

W. B. YEATS
Ireland's greatest lyric poet
surveyed in this ground-breaking
edition **£7.99**

EVERYMAN'S
BOOK OF
EVERGREEN
VERSE

EDITED BY
DAVID HERBERT

£5.99

THE EVERYMAN SHAKESPEARE
EDITED BY JOHN F. ANDREWS

The Everyman Shakespeare is the most comprehensive, up-to-date paperback edition of the plays and poems, featuring:

• face-to-face text and notes

• a chronology of Shakespeare's life and times

• a rich selection of critical and theatrical responses to the play over the centuries

• foreword by an actor or director describing the play in performance

• up-to-date commentary on the play

ALREADY PUBLISHED
The Merchant of Venice	£2.99
Romeo and Juliet	£2.99
Macbeth	£2.99
A Midsummer Night's Dream	£2.99

MARCH
Antony and Cleopatra	£3.99
Hamlet	£2.99

JUNE
Measure for Measure	£2.99
The Tempest	£2.99

AUGUST
Othello	£2.99
Twelfth Night	£2.99

PRICES ARE SUBJECT TO CHANGE.

£2.99

AVAILABILITY

All books are available from your local bookshop or direct from
Littlehampton Book Services Cash Sales, 14 Eldon Way, Lineside Estate, Littlehampton, West Sussex BN17 7HE. PRICES ARE SUBJECT TO CHANGE.

To order any of the books, please enclose a cheque (in £ sterling) made payable to Littlehampton Book Services, or phone your order through with credit card details (Access, Visa or Mastercard) on 0903 721596 (24 hour answering service) stating card number and expiry date. Please add £1.25 for package and postage to the total value of your order.

In the USA, for further information and a complete catalogue call 1-800-526-2778.

WOMEN'S WRITING IN EVERYMAN

A SELECTION

Female Playwrights of the Restoration
FIVE COMEDIES
Rediscovered literary treasures in a unique selection **£5.99**

The Secret Self
SHORT STORIES BY WOMEN
'A superb collection' *Guardian* **£4.99**

Short Stories
KATHERINE MANSFIELD
An excellent selection displaying the remarkable range of Mansfield's talent **£3.99**

Women Romantic Poets 1780-1830: An Anthology
Hidden talent from the Romantic era rediscovered **£5.99**

Selected Poems
ELIZABETH BARRETT BROWNING
A major contribution to our appreciation of this inspiring and innovative poet **£5.99**

Frankenstein
MARY SHELLEY
A masterpiece of Gothic terror in its original 1818 version **£3.99**

The Life of Charlotte Brontë
ELIZABETH GASKELL
A moving and perceptive tribute by one writer to another **£4.99**

Vindication of the Rights of Woman and The Subjection of Women
MARY WOLLSTONECRAFT
AND J. S. MILL
Two pioneering works of early feminist thought **£4.99**

The Pastor's Wife
ELIZABETH VON ARNIM
A funny and accomplished novel by the author of *Elizabeth and Her German Garden* **£5.99**

£6.99

ESSAYS, CRITICISM AND HISTORY IN EVERYMAN

A SELECTION

The Embassy to Constantinople and Other Writings
LIUDPRAND OF CREMONA
An insider's view of political machinations in medieval Europe **£5.99**

Speeches and Letters
ABRAHAM LINCOLN
A key document of the American Civil War **£4.99**

Essays
FRANCIS BACON
An excellent introduction to Bacon's incisive wit and moral outlook **£3.99**

Puritanism and Liberty: Being the Army Debates (1647-49) from the Clarke Manuscripts
A fascinating revelation of Puritan minds in action **£7.99**

Biographia Literaria
SAMUEL TAYLOR COLERIDGE
A masterpiece of criticism, marrying the study of literature with philosophy **£4.99**

Essays on Literature and Art
WALTER PATER
Insights on culture and literature from a major voice of the 1890s **£3.99**

Chesterton on Dickens: Criticisms and Appreciations
A landmark in Dickens criticism, rarely surpassed **£4.99**

Essays and Poems
R. L. STEVENSON
Stevenson's hidden treasures in a new selection **£4.99**

THE NATURAL HISTORY OF SELBORNE
GILBERT WHITE

£3.99

SHORT STORY COLLECTIONS IN EVERYMAN

A SELECTION

The Secret Self 1: Short Stories by Women
'A superb collection' *Guardian* **£4.99**

Selected Short Stories and Poems
THOMAS HARDY
The best of Hardy's Wessex in a unique selection **£4.99**

The Best of Sherlock Holmes
ARTHUR CONAN DOYLE
All the favourite adventures in one volume **£4.99**

Great Tales of Detection Nineteen Stories
Chosen by Dorothy L. Sayers **£3.99**

Short Stories
KATHERINE MANSFIELD
A selection displaying the remarkable range of Mansfield's writing
£3.99

Selected Stories
RUDYARD KIPLING
Includes stories chosen to reveal the 'other' Kipling **£4.50**

The Strange Case of Dr Jekyll and Mr Hyde and Other Stories
R. L. STEVENSON
An exciting selection of gripping tales from a master of suspense **£3.99**

The Day of Silence and Other Stories
GEORGE GISSING
Gissing's finest stories, available for the first time in one volume **£4.99**

Selected Tales
HENRY JAMES
Stories portraying the tensions between private life and the outside world **£5.99**

£4.99

AVAILABILITY
All books are available from your local bookshop or direct from
Littlehampton Book Services Cash Sales, 14 Eldon Way, Lineside Estate, Littlehampton, West Sussex BN17 7HE. PRICES ARE SUBJECT TO CHANGE.

To order any of the books, please enclose a cheque (in £ sterling) made payable to Littlehampton Book Services, or phone your order through with credit card details (Access, Visa or Mastercard) on 0903 721596 (24 hour answering service) stating card number and expiry date. Please add £1.25 for package and postage to the total value of your order.

In the USA, for further information and a complete catalogue call 1-800-526-2778.

PHILOSOPHY AND RELIGIOUS WRITING IN EVERYMAN

A SELECTION

Ethics
SPINOZA
Spinoza's famous discourse on the power of understanding **£4.99**

Critique of Pure Reason
IMMANUEL KANT
The capacity of the human intellect examined **£6.99**

A Discourse on Method, Meditations, and Principles
RENÉ DESCARTES
Takes the theory of mind over matter into a new dimension **£4.99**

Philosophical Works including the Works on Vision
GEORGE BERKELEY
An eloquent defence of the power of the spirit in the physical world **£4.99**

Utilitarianism, On Liberty, Considerations on Representative Government
J. S. MILL
Three radical works which transformed political science **£5.99**

Utopia
THOMAS MORE
A critique of contemporary ills allied with a visionary ideal for society **£3.99**

An Essay Concerning Human Understanding
JOHN LOCKE
A central work in the development of modern philosophy **£5.99**

Hindu Scriptures
The most important ancient Hindu writings in one volume **£6.99**

Apologia Pro Vita Sua
JOHN HENRY NEWMAN
A moving and inspiring account of a Christian's spiritual journey **£5.99**

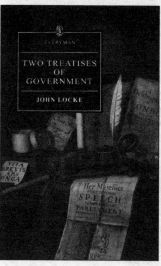

£3.99

AVAILABILITY

All books are available from your local bookshop or direct from
Littlehampton Book Services Cash Sales, 14 Eldon Way, Lineside Estate, Littlehampton, West Sussex BN17 7HE. PRICES ARE SUBJECT TO CHANGE.

To order any of the books, please enclose a cheque (in £ sterling) made payable to Littlehampton Book Services, or phone your order through with credit card details (Access, Visa or Mastercard) on 0903 721596 (24 hour answering service) stating card number and expiry date. Please add £1.25 for package and postage to the total value of your order.

In the USA, for further information and a complete catalogue call 1-800-526-2778.

DYLAN THOMAS
IN EVERYMAN

The only paperback editions of Dylan Thomas's poetry and prose

Collected Poems 1934-1953
Definitive edition of Thomas's own
selection of his work **£3.99**

Collected Stories
First and only collected edition of
Dylan Thomas's stories **£4.99**

The Colour of Saying
Anthology of verse spoken by
Thomas, reflecting his taste in poetry
£3.95

A Dylan Thomas Treasury
Appealing anthology of poems,
stories and broadcasts **£4.99**

The Loud Hill of Wales
Selection of poems and prose full of
Thomas's love of Wales **£3.99**

**The Notebook Poems
1930-1934**
Definitive edition of Thomas's
'preparatory poems' **£4.99**

Poems
Collection of nearly 200 poems by
Dylan Thomas **£3.50**

**Portrait of the Artist as a
Young Dog**
Dylan Thomas's classic evocation
of his youth in suburban Swansea
£2.99

Selected Poems
Representative new selection of
Thomas's work **£2.99**

Under Milk Wood
One of the most enchanting works
for broadcasting ever written **£2.99**

EVERYMAN

COLLECTED POEMS
1934 – 1953

DYLAN THOMAS

£3.99